ORDER OF THE RAVEN

Book One of Raven's Call

S.L. Bishopstone

ISBN-13: 9798673366424
ISBN-10: 1477123456

Cover design by: MM Rainey
Library of Congress Control Number: 2018675309
Printed in the United States of America

To H&A, my personal super duo.
No time spent with you is ever wasted.

1

'Of course, maybe I'm already there.' Connie rocked forward, her palms planted firmly on either side of the laptop screen. Her inbox was empty, and it was getting harder to clamp down on her frustration. She was dimly aware of the streaming National Geographic documentary droning on in the background. She huffed at the empty inbox and grinned, tight-lipped, at the photograph of Katherine Johnson – the renowned NASA mathematician – that was stuck to the wall above her desk. She needed something else to focus on.

She grabbed her boots from the box and slumped cross-legged to the floor, her oversized grey NASA sweater cocooning her. She began brushing one of the long boots methodically, concentrating on working the polish into the walnut leather while the documentary rambled on. It was about black holes, but it was disappointingly pedestrian. She was tempted to switch it off.

Around the walls were various star charts, cluttered with notes Connie had made from her own telescope, which was pointing out of the large window. She worked on a mark on the upper calf of the boot, pushing the tassels and buckle out of the way so she could polish the leather beneath. They were a glorious second-hand buy, a brilliant birthday present from her mum and she was determined to look after them. She kept working until the boots gleamed. Finally satisfied, Connie returned them to their box. Her eyes wandered back to the laptop sitting amongst piles of paper on her bedroom desk. She got up and tapped the mousepad, closing the irritating documentary, her fingers drumming on the table. It would have pinged if there was anything to see. Her finger hovered. She clicked her email again, both inbox and junk folder remained stubbornly empty.

Connie sighed. *Why was it taking so long?* She walked over to the wardrobe where her costume was hanging. Connie wrinkled her nose at the flouncy steampunk miniskirt. It was really too young for her now, a bit too Alice in Wonderland. She sighed and plucked some hairs from it before turning back to the computer where a circle with a dot and lower case "e" inside it, making the appearance of a man in the moon, bounced around the sleeping screen. She'd put the logo there as a talisman when she'd made her application at the beginning of the school year. It was now nearly May.

Annoyed, she pulled up the European Space Agency's website. The little man in the moon logo sat quietly in the upper right-hand side of the screen next to a lower case "esa." As logos went, it looked decidedly friendly, especially alongside the caption "United Space in Europe." She clicked through to DSEP, the agency's new Deep Space Exploration Programme, hoping to see an update on the progress of applications to their inaugural intake, but there was nothing.

'What's taking them so long?' she asked the empty room, letting out a frustrated growl. Katherine Johnson stared placidly back at her. Beneath that photograph was a row of four post-cards. Black and white prints of Gertrude Bell, Captain James Cook, Frank Wild and Katherine Routledge, all notable explorers who'd grown up within twenty miles of Connie's home, and Wild one of only two men to get the Polar Medal crossed with four bars, meaning he'd made five polar expeditions in his lifetime. She smiled at the handwritten quote scrawled at the bottom of his picture, "Once you've been to the white unknown, you can never escape the call of the little voices."

Below the line of explorers, Connie had placed a picture of herself, standing proudly at the top of a high ropes course having successfully com-pleted the air rounds; large cuts of wood, about a foot in diameter, suspended on a thin set of wires that you had to bounce across like step-ping stones to get to a platform on the far side. The rounds flexed on the wires, making it hard to get a steady purchase on them. They were also suspended thirty feet in the air. That day Connie had bounced across the air rounds easily and asked the instructor at the end why anyone thought it was hard. He'd laughed and pointed to Connie's harness and rope. 'Try it without that and then tell me it's easy,' he'd said. Connie crinkled her nose at the picture. She was still the only one of the group who had managed it.

She pushed a thick strand of wiry brown-black curls from her face, pursed her lips and looked back at Wild's quote. The comment was about the call of the Antarctic, but Connie felt the same way about the cosmos, the night sky drew her gaze every single night. It was why she'd applied to the ESA and the quote had formed the basis for her entry essay. She huffed grumpily, 'Well, I might get to boldly go, if they'll just tell me I got in,' she said to the portraits, her nose wrinkling. Dad jokes. Someone had to make them. She grinned at the images and flicked on the screen again. Her inbox remained empty.

'Connie, post,' came her mother's voice from downstairs. 'There's one with a man in the moon on it addressed to you.'

Connie flew across the room and slammed the door open, careering down the stairs.

'Where is it?' she asked, tearing into the light, airy kitchen diner.

'Good morning,' said Mum, looking up from her computer, her jet black braids immaculately twisted into a complex weave atop her head. 'Is that your Dad's jumper?'

Mum was perched on a stool at the breakfast bar that divided the two halves of the room. The post was sitting on the bar between Mum's laptop and two cups of coffee, a rack of steaming toast, two plates and a butter dish. Connie ignored the toast and coffee, instead rifling through the post.

'Morning. Where is it?' Connie asked again, distracted. Her mother held a letter up, smiling. A beam of sunlight glanced off the crisp, white envelope and burnished her mother's deep mahogany skin. Connie shrieked, unconcerned with the loud, ugly sound and grabbed the envelope from her mum, turning it over to see the moon motif and "esa" in the right hand corner. This. Was. It.

She tore the envelope open and unfolded the letter inside, her hands shaking as she skimmed over the contents, dimly aware of her mother watching in anticipation. Pleasantries, pleasantries. Here – there it was. She read it and stopped. She blinked and read it again, her shoulders slumping and her energy fizzing away. From the corner of her eye she saw her mum crease manicured eyebrows in concern. Connie pursed her lips and took a breath before reading out loud. 'Dear Ms Rees, thank you for your application to the inaugural Deep Space Exploration intake of the European Space Agency's Youth Development Programme. This is a hallmark endeavour for the Agency and we were delighted with the extraordinary quality of applicants, all of whom we are sure would be wonderful additions to the ambitious programme of exploration to which the ESA has committed over the next three decades.

'Your application has been considered in detail and we very much liked the premise of your motivation for joining the ESA, especially with regard to your juxtaposition of the pivotal work of pioneers like Katherine Johnson and the grand history of exploration and explorers in your home region. However, we felt that you focussed too much on their accomplishments and your admiration for them, rather than your own ambitions and skills in relation to the deep space exploration upon which the development track to which you applied is centred.

'The panel also wondered why, when you showed such great admiration for the achievements of women in the fields of mathematics and bold endeavour, you did not include the UK's first astronaut, Helen Sharman. It is the opinion of the panel that your attention is too heavily oriented toward your local area and the terrestrial. It is therefore with regret that we must inform you that you have not been selected for the programme.' Connie trailed off and stared blankly at the letter. Somehow it sounded worse when she said it out loud. Final.

She could sense, rather than see, her mother watching her. Connie gulped back tears. She didn't look up.

'I'm sorry, love,' said Mum softly. 'Is that all it says?'

'Doesn't it say enough?' asked Connie, sliding onto the other stool and pushing the letter across the breakfast bar. She pulled a slice of toast from the rack and spread butter on it, more for something to do than because she felt hungry. She pulled one of the coffees toward her and took a sip before staring into it. Mum picked up the letter and scanned it, her lips moving as she read. 'You've been wait-listed,' she said, looking at Connie.

'What?' Connie almost jumped off the stool.

'Didn't you read it all?'

'I didn't see that bit.' Connie grabbed for the letter and Mum handed it back to her, amused. She scanned it again, excitement starting to bubble, before deflating. 'Mum, this is, like, a one-in-a-million shot. It relies on someone not taking a place. Who's going to pass up on this? And even if, by some miracle they do, I'll still have to compete against the others they've put on the wait-list.' She sat back down with a huff, knocking her cup over.

'Careful,' Mum said, grabbing her laptop off the counter as brown liquid spread across the surface and stained a stack of notes, causing ink to blotch and run.

'Sorry,' said Connie, grabbing a tea towel and dabbing at the coffee, frowning as she tried to make out the calculations on the paper. They looked complex. 'What are you working on, anyway?'

'Just some new proofs for the lab, we're running some new simulations. I'm hoping they'll yield some insight into the way dark matter alters anticipated motion.'

'Can I come and see it?'

'It's not a tourist facility, Connie,' Mum said, putting her laptop down on the counter and lifting her sodden notebook of calculations over to the draining board to dry. Connie mopped up the remaining coffee.

'Seriously, Mum? It's not like I'm going to damage the equipment. And Boulby is pretty much unique, some of the instruments they don't even have at the ESA. It might give me an edge for the wait-listing.' She leaned on the counter, swinging on tiptoes and grinning.

Mum looked over her shoulder. Connie was taller than her mum now, so Mum had to lift her chin to meet Connie's eyes. 'This would be the opportunity that would have to have a miracle to come about?' she asked, her tongue pushed into a corner of her mouth, eyebrows raised.

Connie grinned wider.

'Go on, Cheshire Cat.' Mum shooed her away. 'You need to get ready. We don't want to miss the start of the festival.'

Connie headed to the door. She was almost through it before she realised. Hanging on the edge of the door she swung her head back into the room and looked at her mum, who was pulling on a steampunk shearling aviator jacket that was decorated with odd devices.

'You're not wearing the explorer,' Connie said.

Mum looked around, adjusting the collar of the jacket and zipping it up. 'No, today felt more like an aviator sort of day, but the goggles are still in my room. Bring them back down with you. And hurry.'

'Will do,' said Connie, heading up the stairs, grinning again. No need for her kiddie costume if Mum was going as an aviator.

Connie threw open her mum's wardrobe, rifling through the rack. She pulled a suit carrier out and opened it, her eyes lighting up at the sight of her mum's beautiful steampunk explorer outfit. This was so much better than hers. She folded it over her arm and ran to her room, grabbing a flying cap with telescopic goggles as she left.

Back in her own room, Connie hung the suit carrier on her mirror and pulled out some forest green leggings from a drawer, disregarding her mother's breeches; they'd be too short for her anyway. It made Connie think that her dad must be tall. She'd never met him and her mum didn't keep any pictures. Whenever Connie asked, Mum said only that despite the fact she loved him dearly, time and tide had conspired to keep them apart. Connie had no idea what that meant and today wasn't a day she felt like thinking about it. She pulled her boots on, lying back on her bed and flexing her toes to the ceiling so she could draw the tasselled zip, which was on the outside of her leg, up. It took a couple of heaves, but once they were on, the boots felt like slippers. She turned to the suit carrier and pulled out a rich, discreetly tapestried red dress, pulling it on and smoothing it down over her hips so the elongated, triangular-tipped sides of the skirt fell in neat waves. The rich forest green trim shone in the light and set off the earthy tones in the red. Although the sides reached below Connie's knees, the front and back of the dress only came to mid-thigh and on the whole it was a bit loose. Connie was more svelte than Mum, but it was ok, the outfit's multi-banded cross belt and hip holster would smooth it all out. Connie pulled the leather cross belt over her head and buckled it into place before shrugging into a brace of long knives, buckling the clasp over her chest. She glanced at herself in the mirror, the bright undertones in her tawny skin, which was much lighter than her mum's, set off by the dress. This was so cool. She felt like she could take on the world.

She cocked her head, spiral curls falling over her face. She pinned her hair half-back with a beak clip and frowned at her reflection. Something was missing. She grabbed her mum's accessories, attaching an overworked torch and a multi-geared, dialled ratchet to the cross belt before sliding a series of darts and pins into slots on the leather. She pulled a set of burnished goggle-binoculars on top of her head and teased a few strands of riotous curls loose to complete her look. She turned out the accessories bag, looking for the last piece. The Henge Time-keeper, a little brass pocket watch that instead of having a face and hands, had a series of tiny obelisks and markings that indicated the movement of the planets ranged about its face, was missing. The idea was that you could gauge time not just in hours like a normal pocket watch, but in respect of infinity. Complete nonsense of course, but it was a fantastic gimmick. She'd have to ask Mum where it was, she couldn't go without it, it was so ludicrous it was the best part of the costume.

She slid her phone into the coin purse on the cross belt and headed for the stairs.

'Mum, got your flying cap,' Connie shouted from the hall. She glanced in the mirror and adjusted her own set of goggles to a jauntier angle, nodding in approval at the effect.

'Apparently, that's not all you've gotten,' said Mum closing the kitchen door behind her. 'Why're you wearing my outfit?'

Connie turned, a soppy expression fixed on her

face. 'I really needed a boost after the letter,' she said, pushing out her bottom lip and opening her eyes comically wide. 'And it goes great with my brilliant birthday botas.' She did a little twirl and knocked into the hall console table. 'Ow,' she said, rubbing at her thigh.

'Knock it off,' said Mum, smirking at her.

'Ok,' Connie shrugged and rolled her eyes, 'I like it better than mine and you weren't wearing it. Couldn't find your Henge Timekeeper though, do you know where it is?'

Mum raised her eyebrows, 'I don't know where you got your brass neck from, young lady.'

'Dad?'

'Mmm.' Mum frowned briefly. 'Should be in the pocket of my breeches, didn't you check? Oh, you aren't wearing them.'

'Too short for me,' Connie said, darting back up the stairs.

'I like the green leggings, anyway,' Mum shouted after her. 'Maybe I'll steal them from you next time.'

'They'll be too long for you,' Connie called over her shoulder, rifling through the pockets of the breeches until she found the Henge Timekeeper. She clattered back down the stairs, jumped the bottom two and grinned up at her mum from under her spiral curls. 'Found it,' she said, then frowned. 'Why're you looking at me like that?'

'Like what?'

'Like you've just done some dark matter calculations and made a breakthrough that's going to change our understanding of the universe.'

'Am I?' Mum smiled and pulled the flying cap over her weave. She turned to check her reflection in the hall mirror, a faint smile still playing across her face.

'Yeah, stop it, it's weird.' Connie pushed the end of a chain into a slit on the cross belt and placed the Timekeeper into a small messenger pouch hanging alongside it, buttoning up the flap. She looked up. Mum was staring at her again, her head cocked to one side. 'I said stop it,' said Connie.

Mum flashed her a grin and picked up the car keys, twirling them on her finger. 'Shall we?'

Connie nodded and Mum headed out of the door, leaving Connie to lock up.

As she turned the key, Connie shivered despite the warm morning. She looked up to see a bright blue sky with a white sliver hanging just above the house. A sickle moon.

'Earthshine,' she murmured, feeling a wave of sadness. She looked down. She wasn't going to Tirol, where the new training academy for the ESA had been built, in the autumn. She wasn't on the programme. This was a scenario that had never occurred to her. She looked at her toes, chewing on the inside of her lip until she heard a beep.

She looked around to see Mum leaning across

the passenger seat, waving at her from the Nissan Leaf. She hadn't even heard the car start, it ran so quietly.

Connie slouched over to the car and climbed in, buckling up her seatbelt and forcing her face into a relaxed expression.

'Try again,' said Mum, pulling forward to the end of the drive.

'What?'

'Try not looking dispirited again. That was a rubbish attempt,' Mum said, scanning the traffic, waiting for a gap.

Connie pushed out a wan smile and shrugged. 'The earthshine just caught me off guard, that's all,' she said, flicking a finger up at the windscreen to where the sickle moon hung above them. 'Won't get to see the moon first hand now. It's sad.' She shrugged.

Mum flicked on an indicator and turned right onto the main road. 'You got wait-listed, so what? You've still got a shot, it's just not the straight-forward road you planned on.'

'Mum, I worked my backside off with that application. I put everything I knew about physics, survival, exploration and astronomy into it, and I still wasn't good enough. If there is a wait-list contest, how will I compete?'

'Connie, stop feeling sorry for yourself,' Mum said, pulling up at a set of traffic lights. A family group ambled across the road in front of them. 'If you do eventually get onto the programme, there'll be all sorts of setbacks. Being able to deal with the situation in front of you is paramount if you really want to be an astronaut.' She glanced over at Connie, 'So, have your five minutes, then snap out of it. Deal?'

'Deal,' Connie said, slouching down in the passenger seat. She knew better than to argue with her mum.

The light turned green and Mum pulled the car away. They drifted on amongst the Saturday morning traffic and turned into Preston Park where a huge, eccentrically handprinted sign proclaimed the May Day Steampunk and Victoriana Festival. Connie sat up as they entered the grounds and her mum drew the car to a stop at the insistence of a hi-vis jacketed parking steward.

'You'll need to use the overflow car park, please, ladies,' he said, checking their parking pass.

'Of course,' said Mum, handing him a pair of tickets before winding behind the butterfly house to the overflow car park.

Connie stared out of the window at the crowds of people. The field in front of the hall was covered in tents and marquees, and dotted with the odd overwrought penny farthing wobbling about. There were people dressed in an array of steampunk attire, as well as others, in a weekend uniform of jeans and t-shirts, who'd evidently come to enjoy the spectacle rather than participate. They all mingled and there was a vibrant hum about the grounds.

'It's huge this year,' Connie said, craning her neck to look up at an ornate, fringed hot air balloon tethered twenty feet above the ground in the centre of the field.

'At least that's improved your mood,' Mum said as she pulled into a parking spot indicated by another steward. 'You think you can keep that up now?' She leaned her head on the head rest and looked at Connie.

Connie shrugged and felt a weight lift from her shoulders, the hum of the festival already calling her. 'Five minutes is up,' she said, opening the car door.

'Indeed it is,' Mum replied, climbing out and locking the car. 'Let's go have some fun.'

2

1738, North Yorkshire

The warmth of the day seeped through the thick brick walls, radiating into the upper schoolroom. The sunlight outside was beckoning, the waft of fresh grass blowing in through the windows, tantalising the class of boys. None were more than fourteen and all were stupefied by the wilting heat. Despite this, the boys sat upright, facing to the front while the school master droned through the lesson. One by one their eyes glazed over, long blinks turning into nodding heads in the stifling room. In the back row, one boy, who was not more than eleven, began to lean forward, his head drooping dangerously.

A cane thudded down on his desk, jolting him upright and he looked wide-eyed at the master, who was glowering at him from inside his billowing black school robes. 'You, boy. You dare to sleep in my classroom?'

'N-n-n-no, sir,' the boy stammered, terrified, not of the master, but of what might happen if he lost his place at the school. His father was so proud of him and the boy did not want to disappoint his father.

'You were sleeping. Do not lie to me, boy,' the

master said. 'I do not think Mr Skottowe will be pleased if I tell him you are both lazy and a liar.'

'I wasn't sleeping, master, in truth I was not,' the boy said. He had no memory of dozing off. He loved learning, even in this stifling heat.

'Then you will tell me –' The master cut off at the sound of a snicker behind him. He spun, robes flapping. The boy breathed a sigh of relief at the diversion.

'Something funny, Pace?'

'No, master. I believe I have a touch of the hay fever,' said the boy who had laughed.

'Mmm.' The master was unconvinced.

A bell rang, sounding a slow clang, clang, clang as it swung in a steady arc. All of the boys sat a little straighter, the sound rousing them. The school master closed his book with a thud. 'You may all go,' he said.

As one the boys rose, chairs clattering as they were tucked under the rows of narrow desks. They streamed for the door and the boy went with them, relieved to have escaped punishment. His mind wasn't firing well today.

'Except you,' the master barked, his hand pointing at the boy though his back was still turned.

The boy stopped, blinking hard, his hands gripping the back of a chair as Pace slid past him, smirking. The boy tensed, his eyes fixed on his whitening knuckles. From the corner of his eye he saw the master turn around, the cane lightly tapping against his thigh.

'Tell me, boy, how one might calculate the saleable wheat produced on a seven acre in a good year?'

The boy looked down, gulping. He really had been trying to pay attention.

'Well?' the master asked.

The boy eyed the cane switch that was now dangling limply from the Master's hand and took a deep breath, forcing his sluggish brain into action. The answer wouldn't come. He tried stalling. 'An average acre produces sixteen and a half bushels of wheat in a good year, master, but you, you, need about two and a half bushels from the yield for planting, which leaves fourteen bushels per acre. So, seven acres would produce, err.' He paused, his mind refused the calculation. He was normally so quick. His eyes bulged.

'Hand, boy.'

'Ninety-eight bushels, master. It's, it's ninety-eight bushels.' The boy clenched his hands, locking his arms ramrod straight by his side. He breathed hard, not daring to look up. The answer had come, but it had been terrifyingly hard. The master was silent for what seemed an eternity.

'Acceptable.' The master sighed. 'You may go, but do not sleep in my class again, boy.'

'No, master, thank you,' the boy said.

The master turned in a cloud of robes and strode away between the rows of desks to the front of the room.

The boy ran down the stairs on the outside of the schoolhouse, skipping past a cart and horse on the dirt track that ran alongside the school building. He crossed the road and headed north across the village. The other boys, he knew, would have headed for the stream that ran on the southern side. He didn't care, he didn't want to see them right now. His mind wasn't working the way he was used to and he craved solitude. He still felt panicked by the master's threat.

He raced across the green, darting between a slew of cottages that seemed to be falling into one another, disturbing several chickens as he did, their angry clucks following behind him. The boy paid them no attention, skipping over muddy puddles as he wound his way across the high street and out from between the houses. His eyes were fixed on the sugarloaf hill on the edge of the moor. It presided over the village, its summit some eight hundred feet above him. Sweat began to bead on his brow and back as the boy left the village behind, but nevertheless he smiled, relaxing in the peace of the country lane. He knew he should be going straight back to the farm, his father was a labourer and needed him, but with such clear skies and this glorious sunlight the view from Roseberry's top was sure to be fine. He would be able to see far out over the sea to the east and might even be able to see all the way to the central ridge of the Pennines in the west.

He reached a wood line at the base of the hill. Roseberry was blanketed with woodland all around its bottom half and at this time of year, the earth between the trees was carpeted purple with harebells. The boy walked into the trees and the air filled with the gentle rustle of leaves, the buzzing of bumble bees and the warble of birdsong. His shoulders slackened, the weight of his anxiety receding as he walked through the carpet of flowers and began to climb.

3

Connie and her mum set off across the grounds towards the tent village at the centre of the festival. They wove through a crowd that was variously decked out in a range of Victorian, Colonial and Old West US styled clothing with distinctive technological flamboyancies. There was also a sea of plague masks, top hats, bonnets and terminator style arm pieces everywhere Connie looked, along with musical boxes and fairground organs that blended into a cacophony of joyous noise as the two threaded their way toward the centre of the makeshift steampunk village. Away to her right, on the edge of the slope down to the river, was the old aviary, the grey steel frame of the giant bird cage twisted with streamers. Connie realised there must be some sort of art display fluttering inside the battered interior. The aviary had never been stocked during her lifetime but Mum had told Connie about the birds that had been kept there when she was a child. Connie made a note to go and look at the aviary art installation later, but right now, the energy of the festival was drawing her on, away from the big structure.

She moved along with the river of people and

felt her steps liven as she slid in between two women – twins by the look of them – who were styled as buccaneers, mixing heavy Victorian skirts with bright red, brocaded cavalry jackets and long pistols decorated with cogs and dials. Connie carried on, dimly aware that Mum was no longer beside her. She glanced back and saw her mum looking at one of the stalls, flicking through a rack of aeronautical paraphernalia next to a man wearing a pith helmet. Connie frowned; there was something that was almost familiar about the man. He turned, glanced at her and winked. It was Paul, one of the technicians from the Boulby lab. He looked radically different in steampunk. Connie jerked her thumb behind her, pointing to the centre of the fair and mouthed, *Tell Mum for me.*

Paul gave her a thumbs up and Connie grinned, wheeling around. She jerked back, leaping out of the way of man, also wearing a pith helmet and royal blue jacket, riding solo on a tandem bicycle. He rang his bell and carried on up the pathway toward the hall, oblivious to the fact he'd almost knocked Connie over. She sighed and shook her head, watching him disappear, ringing his bell. Some people had no manners, whatever their get up.

She walked toward the bandstand on the far side of the field, scanning the sea of people ambling around the striped and floral patterned tents. She thought back to her quick reflexes in missing Pith Helmet and suddenly felt unstoppable amidst the crowd. She began to walk more confidently, feeling more relaxed in the explorer outfit than she ever had as the Alice in Wonderland figure. Off to one side, the balloon hung in the sky, thick ropes tethering it twenty feet in the air. Beside it she could see a high scaffold, strung with two ropes. Two men in jeans and t-shirts were hauling themselves up it. It looked like they were racing. She cocked her head and set off toward them, sliding through the crowds, imagining herself striding through some unknown jungle, exploring it anew.

'That's quite a swagger you've got going on there.'

Connie spun to her left and saw a tanned man leaning on carved pole. He had a heavy, battered overcoat worn over a black, military style uniform, with a burnished sword at his side. It was an oddly elegant thing, somewhere between a katana and a sabre. His headdress, blackened goggles with a shiny, beaked nose piece, like a strange pointed gas mask – the beak was too short and straight for a plague mask – pushed back a thick set of tawny dreadlocks that came almost to his waist. The whole ensemble was set off by twinkling grey eyes and a cavalier smile.

'Nice costume,' he said, a light American twang more audible now. He pushed himself upright. 'Are the knives just for show or can you really use them?'

Connie stepped back, her eyes narrowing. 'I've had some practise,' she said, flexing her fingers by her sides, drawing her feet into a ready stance.

The man cocked an eyebrow at her feet and burst out laughing. It was a warm, throaty sound that was quite disarming, 'Calm down, Explorer Girl. It's possible to get too wrapped up in the fantasy of all of this.' He raised an eyebrow. 'John Bartitsu,' he said, offering her a hand. Connie didn't take it and he dropped it, shrugging. 'I'm doing the weapons display in the Victorian Street.' He motioned to the Hall's Victorian Quarter, part of the permanent museum exhibit in the grounds. 'One of my staff hasn't made it. Was just wondering if you might be able to help out, that's all.' He shrugged again and pulled a card from his pocket, offering it to her. Connie took it uncertainly, spinning it in her fingers. It was decidedly cool, a holographic style transparent card that appeared to have a sabre brandished by a crow-like bird embedded in the middle. Across it, in plain script, were the words John Bartitsu, Master at Arms, Ancient, Medieval and Victorian Weaponry.

Connie looked at it, biting her lip. 'Sorry, I'm not great.' She shrugged and smiled apologetically at Bartitsu, who gave her an upside down smile.

'Shame,' he said, 'You looked like you had something about you the way you strode about.' He clapped her on the shoulder and stepped into the crowd. 'Looks can be deceiving, hey?' He stroked his short beard and pointed a finger at her as he backed away. 'Anyway, drop by and see the show if you have time. See how it's really done.' He rolled his shoulders, snorted a short laugh and nodded at her. 'That really is a great outfit, shame it's not real.' He turned on his heel and strode away through the crowd.

Connie watched him go, feeling inexplicably hurt. 'Swagger yourself,' she muttered, pocketing his card and making her way toward the balloon.

Connie emerged from the rings of tents into the open space surrounding the balloon. It was swaying gently in a light breeze, its shadow wafting across the grass. The scaffold frame was just off to her left, on the edge of the circular open space. Another pair of men, one in costume, one in t-shirt and shorts, were standing at the base of the ropes, holding them and looking at a man wearing flamboyant morning dress and carrying a bejewelled cane. He sounded a buzzer and the men began climbing.

'Come on, Daddy,' shouted a small boy, jumping up and down, his fist balled around his mother's shirt hem.

Connie wandered over to the scaffold, watching the two men haul themselves up, grimly clawing hand over hand, their legs wrapped on the rope.

A bell sounded. The men on the ropes were only about two thirds up, the one in the t- shirt closest to the top.

'Noooo!' called the boy, his shoulders dropping.

'Sorry gents,' called the balloon owner, adjusting his monocle and waving the cane at the pair. 'Not fast enough to crew my air-ship. If you wish to see the wonders of my air lab, you shall have to pay the entry fee. Down you come.' The men slid down the rope, obviously disappointed.

'Are there any here who might be speedy enough to join my crew?' the balloon owner called, casting looks at the people assembled on the lawn. A few of them laughed and waved their hands, declining his query.

'That's way too tough, mate,' said one of the men, his hands on his knees. 'No one can get up a rope that quick. You've rigged it.'

'I'll have a go,' said Connie. She was still stinging from Bartitsu's offhand dismissal.

The man who'd complained snorted.

'Ah, an intrepid adventurer. Fine spirit, fine spirit,' said the balloon owner, sweeping his top hat from his head and bowing to her. He ushered her to the scaffold. 'A compatriot for this young lady. Anyone?'

No one came to join Connie at the ropes.

The balloon owner replaced his hat. 'No matter. You shall be racing time itself. I shall only have the speediest aid me in my aeronautics. On my buzzer, you shall climb.' He raised a finger,

'But, you must reach the top before the bell if you wish to crew with me.'

'I get the rules,' Connie laughed, placing one foot under the rope and stepping onto it with the other, trapping the rope between her feet. She gripped the rope tightly with both hands.

'Ready?' asked the balloon owner.

'Yep,' said Connie, looking at the top of the scaffold. Her fingers itched in anticipation. From the corner of her eye she saw one of the men who had failed the climb rolling his eyes at her. Connie smirked, grasping the thick rope. *Just you watch.*

The buzzer sounded.

Connie heaved, pulling her knees up to her chest, her feet sliding along the rope. She pressed on her foot, trapping the rope between her feet again and stood up, sliding her hands upwards. Again. Tuck, stamp, stand.

'Fifteen seconds remaining,' called the balloon owner.

Tuck, stamp, stand. Connie kept her eyes on the top of the scaffold. She was over halfway. Tuck, stamp, stand. She took a deep breath. It was tiring, climbing with the knives. The cross belt limited her shoulders, but she was getting closer.

'Well, it seems that there may be someone proficient enough for my team, after all.' The balloonist glanced at his watch. 'Five seconds.'

One big push. Connie grunted and heaved, pulling her knees to her chin. She stood up, sliding her hands hard up the rope, wincing as the friction burned her skin.

'Three, two –'

Connie smacked the top of the scaffold with the tips of her fingers. A hollow metallic ring sounded.

'Bravo!'

Connie looked down to the ground, panting. The balloon owner was clapping enthusiastically, his cane tucked under his arm.

'Outstanding climb. Bravo. Come down; much slower, if you please, and we shall discuss the terms of your employment.'

Connie came down the rope hand over hand, her feet acting as a brake to slow her descent. The high ropes instructor would not approve, he'd told them never to cross hands, but it was something she'd never quite managed. She reached the ground and took the balloon owner's offered hand.

'That was a fix,' said the man who'd snorted at Connie. 'You gave her more time.'

'Are you accusing me of subterfuge, sir?' said the balloon owner, 'Because I assure you –'

'No he didn't,' Connie butted in, 'I just climbed with my brain. You stand on the rope. Only idiots climb with just their arms.'

'You saying I'm thick?' said the man, rounding on her.

'I think what my daughter is trying to say, is

that if you use your whole body rather than just your upper body strength – substantial though yours evidently is –'

Connie was irked that the man looked pleased at her mother's remark.

'Then you can climb faster. Strength differences notwithstanding,' her mother finished.

The man glowered at the rebuke.

Connie dabbed at her nose to hide her grin.

'Look mate,' said the balloon owner, dropping his act, 'no one here wants their day ruined. She had a good technique, that's how she made it up. But it doesn't matter. Here, free tickets for you and your family to go up on the basket, ok?'

The man snatched the tickets from the balloon owner's hand, mellowing. 'Thanks,' he said, walking over to his family.

The balloon owner sighed and looked at Connie, raising his eyebrows. 'And your tickets,' he said, presenting them to her, 'But maybe next time you could be a bit more polite. Costs a fortune to run this thing.'

Connie went to take the tickets, but her mother stopped her. 'Since you stepped in when you didn't have to, Connie will forego her free tickets, won't you?'

Connie huffed, 'Yeah,' she said. 'Thanks though.' She walked back across the lawn toward the tent village.

'Next time tell me, not Paul, that you're wandering off,' said Mum, catching up with her.

'What's that on your coat?' Connie asked, pressing her finger to a red blotch. It was blood.

'What? Oh, I don't know, must've caught myself at the stand,' Mum replied, 'Did you hear what I said?'

'Sorry, Mum,' said Connie, turning her head and smiling, her lips pinched together. 'And sorry, for that.' She waved at the balloon, 'Just hate it when people assume you get given extra just because you're a girl. That's cool.' She reached for the pendant hanging around her mum's neck. 'What is it?' Connie twirled the necklace in her fingers. It was a smooth, tapered, triangular obelisk, inscribed with a series of rune-like carvings that looked like they were faintly glowing despite the bright sunlight. Connie blinked. 'Are they really glowing?' she asked, twirling the pendant in her hand, and cocking her head to see how the light refracted off the metal and inscriptions.

'Just something I thought was interesting,' Mum shrugged and plucked the pendant from Connie's hand, 'And not something I'm going to let you pinch.'

Connie rolled her eyes, 'Jeez Mum, I was just asking, it's not like I stole your Henge Timekeeper or anything.'

'Umhmm,' said Mum. They walked toward the hall, skirting around groups of people in the walkways. 'Anything particular you want to see today, or do you want to wander on your own for a bit?' she asked, not looking at Connie.

'There's a weapons display in the Victorian Quarter. Thought I might check that out,' Connie said, shrugging.

'How'd you find out about that?'

'Bumped into the guy doing it.' Connie said, 'He asked me if I wanted to get involved with the knife display.'

Mum laughed. 'It's a Bartitsu display is it? If it's in the Victorian Quarter.'

'How did you know?'

'How'd I know what?'

'That the guy was John Bartitsu.'

Mum turned to look at her, frowning, her eyes slightly unfocussed. Some of her braids fell around her shoulders, catching on the collar of her coat. 'Bartitsu isn't a person, Connie, it's a style of fighting. Victorian martial arts.'

Connie shrugged, 'Oh, well, the guy said his name was John Bartitsu. It was on his card and everything. Think he thought I assumed he was creep at first when he spoke to me.'

'Can I see the card?' Mum asked.

'Sure,' Connie said, frowning. She reached the iridescent card out of her coin pouch and handed it to Mum.

Mum looked at it, spinning the plastic card between her thumb and index finger, her tongue rolling across her bottom lip. Her forehead was creased, she looked as if she was struggling with a thought process.

'I thought it was cool. In keeping with the festival, you know?' said Connie, a little disconcerted by the way her mum was looking at a business card.

Mum smiled, blinking. 'Yes, it is a nice gimmick.' She handed the card back to Connie, her brows still creased.

'You ok, Mum?' Connie asked, pushing the card back into the coin purse at her hip.

'Mmhmm,' Mum said. 'Shall we go see the display?'

4

1904, North Yorkshire

'Are you sure you'll be alright, Miss Gertrude?' the groom asked, bringing the chestnut mare across the yard, the horse's hooves clipping on wet flagstones. He lifted the reins over the mare's head and tickled her nose. The horse lipped at his fingers, snuffling contentedly.

'Of course,' Gertrude said, pulling her gloves on. 'And it's Miss Bell. Leg up, please.' She took the reins from the groom and grasped the saddle.

'Apologies, ma'am. You don't want to use the mounting block?'

'There aren't many mounting blocks in the desert. Come on.' She motioned to him with some irritation.

The groom bent and cupped his hands. Using him as a brace, Gertrude sprung off the ground and pulled herself lightly into the saddle. The groom stood upright and held her leg as she adjusted her riding skirts across the side pommel.

'It's changed quite a lot since you were away, ma'am,' he tried again. 'Perhaps you should take someone with you. It's not the best morning.' He squinted up at her, narrowing his eyes against the fine drizzle that was chilling the air. Around them, a light mist trailed grey tendrils across the yard, obscuring the gardens and turning Red Barns into a lumpen shadow.

'Nonsense,' Gertrude scoffed, turning the mare's head toward the gate. 'It'll burn off soon enough and an English woman is never afraid.' She nudged the horse into a walk and left the yard, turning right along the road. The horse stepped out and Gertrude could feel her energy through the saddle and bridle. She felt contentment wash over her as the hoof beats picked up a steady rhythm, ringing from a clop through to a thud as she turned off the highway and entered a dirt lane leading to the woods.

There was a peaceful silence over the grey morning as they walked along beside the hedge. Gertrude breathed in, enjoying the scent of damp earth and the sound of the first fallen leaves crunching under the horse's hooves as they passed by an old yew tree. She took another deep lungful of air, enjoying its stinging, pleasant freshness and admiring the way the scenery faded into the seemingly infinite mist. There was something wonderful about such early mornings, and though she loved the desert passionately, she always felt a tug for the forests and hills here. She urged the horse into a trot, keen to reach the woods.

5

1738, North Yorkshire

The boy reached a hand up onto the escarpment, hauling himself onto the rocky outcrop at the top of the sugarloaf hill. Sweat trailed in rivulets down between his shoulder blades into the cotton of his oversized school shirt. There was a damp patch along his spine after the climb and his mop of sandy hair had been blown into sticky spikes by the gusting breeze. The wind was much stronger at the summit than it had been down in the lea of the hill, though the boy found it welcome.

He stood, heaving, his hands on his hips. 'Always worth the climb, Roseberry,' he said staring out to the west, the wind at his back. He strained his eyes, shading them against the afternoon sun to see if the Pennines were in sight. Faint lines on the distant horizon hinted at a far-off set of hills but nothing substantial. The boy felt a small prick of disappointment. Despite the bright and cloudless afternoon, the light wasn't as good as he'd hoped. His view over the moors was hazier than he'd expected, and he'd been so sure that he'd see across the world today. At least, he liked to think it was across the world.

The boy turned to look east, toward the sea, his face into the wind. He breathed in deeply, sniffing for the salt tang that would sometimes lace the air, his anxiety at the school master's confrontation and the unusual dullness of his mind swept away by the tranquillity on top of the hill. He inhaled deeply as the wind gusted. There! A faint sea smell reached him and he smiled, his fingers dancing by his sides as the breeze streamed around them. All the while he looked out at the glistening blue-green sea. He breathed, again and again, a small smile playing over his lips and his eyes closing as he basked in the sun, the sweat on his back beginning to dry.

A loud crack jolted his attention and he snapped his eyes open, searching the hilltop for the source of the sound. Seeing nothing he spun, eyes wide. Still nothing. He stepped back and his foot slipped and wedged into a crack. The boy panicked. Roseberry had no crack there, he'd climbed it often enough to know that. He knew every inch of this sugarloaf summit. Yet, there was a crack and the space around his trapped foot had become a strange purplish shadow pricked with light. The boy shuddered, disconcerted.

Suddenly, the smell in the air changed. The boy flared his nostrils and took short, sharp breaths, testing the new odour. Not salt now, something more acrid, akin to the smell of iron in a forge. He opened his mouth, rolling his tongue forward, trying to expel the oily, metallic taste that was layering on his tongue. Around him the air darkened, as if a storm were approaching. *Where has this come from?* He reached down and tried to extract his foot from the shimmering, purplish crack-that-shouldn't-exist and let out a strangled scream. The hilltop, his much beloved refuge, was shearing amongst the foul metallic mist. The crack became a fissure; the rock to the east crashing away; down the hill and into it in a cloud of dirt, dust and purple-black fog. The boy screamed in terror as rocks crumbled beneath his feet and crashed about him. He tried to scramble away but to no avail. The hilltop sheared into the iridescent fog, and the boy fell with it.

6

'Not that way, Mum,' Connie said, grabbing her mum's arm as she headed toward the Victorian Street gates, a beautiful mismatched pair of tall, decorative wrought iron gates half way along the Victorian Quarter, which had been opened for the festival. 'We have to go over the clock.'

Mum turned, letting out an exasperated, but happy sigh. 'Please don't ever get too old for that, will you?' she asked.

For a moment, Connie thought she saw sadness flicker across her mum's face, but then she grinned, a perfect row of gleaming white teeth.

'Come on, you big kid,' she said, laughing.

Connie shrugged off her concern and walked beside her mum, under the portico into the museum, passing the winter garden on the right. They headed through the museum shop, Connie's boots making no noise on the tiled floor. She strode past the ornate hearth, complete with false fire glowing, on one side of the shop; a relic left in place from when the room had been one of the hall's principle sitting rooms. Beyond the shop, just before the entrance to the Victorian street and embedded into the floor was a beautiful clock face, similar to the one on

Big Ben, but with one key difference. This clock ran backwards. Ever since she could remember, Connie had been fascinated by this simple device, counting back the years to enable you to emerge in a Victorian simulation. Walking over the clock had always felt magical to her and the magic hadn't faded as she'd grown. She smiled, automatically buoyed, as she stepped over the glowing white face, its hands dutifully ticking backwards, out into the street.

Today, the effect was spectacular. The clock was inlaid in the floor of a quiet, modern atrium inside the body of the hall, with a lift discreetly installed on one side. Connie stepped through this modern space, through an automatic door and out into an entirely different world. At the centre of the tiny courtyard that comprised the entrance to the Victorian Quarter, there were two women dressed in bustles and short coats, each with a set of phials and conical flasks hanging about them, and multi-layered glasses perched on their noses. They were demonstrating their latest invention to a crowd that more or less filled the open space. The machine was a barrel-like contraption on wheels, with a glass cylinder bound in brass on the top. It was puffing purple smoke from between the wooden slats of the barrel and whirred busily at odd intervals, making crashing sounds periodically. The smell wafting about the yard along with the smoke was of burning chemicals. One of the women, dressed in red, was discussing advances in the sciences and how they were seeking to contain electricity with their device so it could be used as needed, while the other, dressed in blue, recruited an overawed child of about seven with long wavy brown hair from the small gaggle of spectators. This was ostensibly to manage a series of levers on the side of the contraption.

'Now, don't be alarmed,' the woman in blue said in a loud imperious voice to the little girl, who looked ready to bolt. She placed the girl's hand on a lever at the front of the barrel. 'This is quite safe.'

'If it goes as we expect,' said the other, putting a gloved hand out and cocking her head, grinning at the little girl. The crowd laughed. The little girl drew back her hand.

'Don't say that!' the woman in blue admonished her partner, flapping her hand above the little girl's head. 'It'll be fine, dear,' she said, putting the girl's hand back on the lever. 'Just pull it down when we tell you.' She nodded and turned away from the little girl, a comical frown on her face. This drew another laugh from the crowd and Connie paused to watch.

'Now, what you'll see here, is that electricity, when properly stored and utilised, can produce wondrous effects on the human anatomy. When we activate the current, watch what happens to our little friend here,' the woman in red said. She smiled at her partner over the little girl's head and mouthed, *It will go right, won't it?* Her partner nodded furiously, her eyes wide. The crowd laughed again. Connie cracked a smile, leaning on a drain pipe. The little girl looked about nervously as the two women hustled away, leaving her alone in the middle of the courtyard with the contraption, which was still belching out acrid purple smoke.

'Now, child!' the one in the red called, cringing backwards and lifting a hand in front of her face, her fingers splayed.

The little girl shook her head, jumping as another puff of purple smoke appeared and a dramatic crackle sounded from inside the barrel.

The woman in red gesticulated toward the girl, 'Pull the lever. Go on.'

The little girl looked about the crowd, took in the looks of expectation and swallowed before pulling the lever down.

'Keep hold! Keep hold!' said the woman in red, her eyes maniacally wide, her hand shaking in front of her.

The machine whirred and electric static leapt in blue lightning lines across a glass canister on the top of the barrel. The little girl jumped, staring at the flashes of light, but she kept hold of the lever and slowly her hair began to stand on end, creating a brown static halo about her head. The two steampunk scientists began clapping exaggeratedly, 'Bravo, bravo,' cried the woman in blue. 'I knew you were the one.'

Connie cocked her head, smiling as she saw the woman in blue drop a palm-sized remote control back into her skirt pocket.

'Ladies and gentlemen, the static charge from contained lightning,' the woman in red said striding in a tight circle around the courtyard like a manic circus master. She beamed at the audience and the little girl, the edges of her lips turned down despite her smile. 'I'm so pleased that worked,' she whispered loudly to her partner, who nodded enthusiastically.

'You didn't think it would?' asked the little girl, horror etched all over her face. The crowd laughed again and the two women looked at each other, the mirror of pantomime villains caught out in their plans. Connie laughed and ducked away from the scene through the alleyway into the street proper. Her mum had disappeared. She mustn't have realised that Connie had stopped to watch the mad steampunk scientists, but it didn't matter, Connie knew where she was headed.

Connie walked out into the main street of the Victorian Quarter, which was made up of repurposed outbuildings and stables of the original hall, along with its kitchen garden. She was dazzled by the array of costumes and artefacts; the commitment and intricacy of the participants at this year's festival was incredible. A man with a tattered tweed jacket, complete with wiring sticking out, a bright waistcoat and fingerless gloves jumped in front of her with a huge bellows camera on a stick and took her photograph. There was a flash of light and a puff of black smoke jetted upwards before a little whirr sounded and a polaroid print appeared from the front. 'Marvels these photographic devices, you know, especially with the adjustments I've made. Have it, a souvenir!' He pushed the print into Connie's hands and darted behind her, catching the next people to emerge from the alleyway.

Connie walked on past a tailor shop and print works, blinking away the light echoes and trying to take in the happy chaos of the festival as well as trying to catch sight of her mum, who was nowhere to be seen. All around her, just like on the lawns to the front of the hall, were people, both children and adults, dressed in a wide array of steampunk outfits. There were cowboys, people manifesting the heroic age of exploration, Regency aristocrats decked out with bejewelled muskets and lace sleeves, and a variety of takes on Victorian dresses and colonial outfits. The whole street had a carnival feeling, with laughter echoing between the rows of shops.

Connie slid between groups of people as she walked along the street, jumping neatly out of the way of two kids playing hoops outside the toy shop. All the time she kept an eye out for her mum. She headed toward the orchard, which was accessed by the wrought iron gates she'd pulled her mum away from so they could go over the clock. The gates were half way up the street and Connie thought Mum may have gone to collect some of the fruit that the museum allowed visitors to pick. As she reached the orchard gates, Connie noticed the tandem that had nearly knocked her over in the festival village outside. It was leaned against the wall opposite the tea shop, unchained and minus its solitary pith-helmeted rider. She walked over to the bike, drawn to the profusion of superfluous cogs and chains in the spaces of the frame, although as she got closer, she realised that they weren't superfluous at all. Flicking several levers stashed along the main struts of the bike would connect them to enable a set of panniers behind the second seat to open. It was a quietly ingenious mechanism and Connie crouched down in front of the bike, tracing her fingers along the lines to work out how to engage the cogs. It was complex, almost like a mechanical version of a Japanese puzzle box; she could see that some levers would undo the movement of others, meaning exactly the right sequence had to be pushed to engage the mechanism to open the panniers. She became so engrossed that she didn't notice a pair of feet, clad in long, shiny cavalry boots, stop beside her.

'And what would you be doing, adventurer?'

The crisp voice cut into Connie's consideration

of the tandem and she whipped her head around and craned her neck to look up into the face of the tandem's pith-helmeted owner. He was tall and strikingly good-looking, perhaps in his early forties, with dark hair, tanned skin, green eyes and a mottle of stubble across his jaw. His cream game hunter's outfit, worn under the blue jacket, was richly detailed and included a long, fine, slightly curved sword that emerged from an incongruously pedestrian grey cylindrical hilt with a lone lever placed for the thumb. The patterns on the steel showed myriad intricate folds and the blade looked keen. It was either an excellent paint job, or the real thing. The sword was hung from a cross belt filled with tiny blue-fletched darts, which shouldn't have fit with the ensemble, but somehow did. On the other side, folded into his jacket, Connie could see a matching cylinder hilt, though without a blade. Perhaps it had fallen off.

Connie caught the man's eye, smiling uncertainly. The man smiled back at her, but did not look pleased.

'I, er, was, just, admiring your bike,' Connie said, standing up and flourishing her hand toward the tandem. The man was at least eight inches taller than she was. She gulped.

'It's a tandem,' he said, flashing her an odd look. 'And not suitable for amateur explorers.'

Connie's eyes bulged. She couldn't tell if the man was serious. 'I was, just, admiring the craftsmanship,' she stammered. 'It must've taken you ages to work out that system.' She motioned to the intricate cog and lever work inside the frame.

The man raised an eyebrow, 'It's a good way to deter would-be thieves,' he said, 'But it makes it rather difficult to pilot without my Amelia. Have you seen her?'

'I didn't realise you piloted a tandem.' Connie frowned. He'd slurred the name Amelia pretty badly, and he didn't look too steady on his feet now she was looking more closely.

'What else would you do with it?' he asked, looking over her head into the street.

'Right,' Connie replied. 'You're bleeding.' She pointed to a small rivulet of blood running across the back of his hand.

He looked down and squinted at it, disconcerted. 'Hmm,' he said. 'Do you have a handkerchief I might borrow?'

Connie handed him one silently. The man was making her feel uncomfortable. He was really throwing everything into his character, and it was disconcerting because Connie couldn't see where the character stopped and the man began. She wasn't sure he could, either. The man seemed addled, maybe drunk. There was a hint of alcohol about him.

He wrapped the handkerchief over his cut, tying it off neatly across his palm. 'Excuse me, adventurer, I must find my Amelia. There is a storm coming. She must not be caught alone in it, as she has been these many years.'

Connie looked up at the clear, sunny sky. 'Doesn't look like it to me,' she said, eyeing the man.

'You do not see far enough, young adventurer. It is in the air. Please stand aside.' He put his wrapped hand on Connie's shoulder and pushed her gently to one side, striding past her into the street, scanning as he went. Connie watched him pause in the middle of the street, stutter to the right and then stride off to the left, his sword bouncing off his leg briefly before he caught the pommel and steadied it. He looked distracted, lost. Maybe he was just sloshed. Connie frowned and took a last look at the tandem, it was definitely unique. She shook her head and looked up as the sound of steel clanging rhythmically on steel signalled an ongoing sword fight. The Bartitsu display, by John Bartitsu – she shook her head, raising her eyebrows, it was a ridiculous affectation really – must've started. She hurried back into the street, following the sound of the steel.

7

Connie approached the back of a small crowd huddled at the far end of the Victorian street, beyond the mock police station and forge. The rhythmic beat of swords rang through the air and Connie dipped and wove to try and see the display, but there was no clear view through the array of heads and headgear.

'They've improved since last year,' she heard one man dressed as a Western bartender comment.

'Yes, they seem much more co-ordinated. Like his patter between fights, too,' replied his friend.

'Excuse me, do you think you could just let me dip through?' Connie asked the backs of the two men.

One glanced at her over his shoulder. 'There's no room in front of us, petal,' he said before returning his attention to the ongoing battle. Connie huffed and looked for another way through, or at least someone short enough she could see over them. No such luck. Just as she resigned herself to missing the action she spotted an empty bench over to one side and leapt nimbly onto the seat, leaning her elbow on a low tiled roof at the end of the replica forge, resting her head on her hand, and kicking one foot out in front of her so she was leaning on the edge of her heel. Somehow, the explorer outfit had enhanced her confidence. Connie smiled and craned her neck to look over the crowd, scanning for Mum as she took in the display.

Three men were battling inside a chalked circle, two with a single blade were co- ordinating their efforts against a large man whose face was obscured by his mass of whirling, almost waist length, dreadlocks. It was John Bartitsu, the man who'd accosted her in the tent village, sparring against two men and demonstrating impeccable footwork and timing. He lunged at one of the assailants and spun his blade, knocking the man's sword from his hand. His eyes glowed and he grinned, his nose wrinkling. The crowd cheered. Connie winced, Bartitsu had disarmed one opponent by leaving himself open to the other. The other man lunged. His sword point was set to skewer Bartitsu's waist. It didn't make contact. Bartitsu whipped up his other hand without looking and parried. The sword clattered harmlessly in front of Bartitsu, the man overstepping as his lunge went too far. Bartitsu reversed his sword blade and the man froze, the tip of Bartitsu's blade at his throat. The crowd burst into a huge round of applause.

'And that's why, despite it being considered ungentlemanly, a naval commander would often carry a long knife as well as his sword,' Bartitsu said, breathing hard and looking at his opponent. 'Pirates, buccaneers, enemy sailors: they'd all try and stab you in the back, because the aim is to stay alive. If you can parry the blade, you can stab them through the throat and really ruin their day. But, you might not have much room to move, so a short blade or cudgel gives you much more flexibility.' He smiled at his opponent, 'And you can hide it more easily, letting your enemy overextend. Thanks Matt.' He pulled his blade away from the other man's throat. The man stood, nodding to Bartitsu. He picked up the sword from the floor and took it over to a large bag under a wooden hoarding, where the second assailant offered him a canister of water. John Bartitsu took a bow, enjoying the continued applause of the crowd.

'Thank you,' he said, raising a hand. 'That was a demonstration of the heavy sabre. For those of you that have just joined us –' Connie could swear he glanced at her, but he didn't acknowledge her, just carried on speaking.

'My name is John Bartitsu and I run Bartitsu Arts, a nationwide martial arts school dedicated to the Victorian British Martial Art, Bartitsu, of which I am also the extremely well-aged founder.' He took a mock bow and grinned at the crowd. People tittered appreciatively.

'That would make you nearly one hundred and twenty,' shouted a little boy dressed in a top hat and tails and sporting a mechanical overlay on one of his arms.

'Yes, it would,' said Bartitsu, raising his eyebrows.

'You aren't that old,' said the boy dismissively. His dad put a hand on his shoulder.

Bartitsu crouched in front of him, his beaked headdress almost pecking at the boy's face. 'Nah,' he said, 'I'm much older. Or maybe it's younger.'

Connie could see a look of apprehension wash over the boy in the face of Bartitsu's stare. He bit his lip and stepped back into the shadow of his dad. Bartitsu grinned again and stood up. 'I never can remember, one of the problems with being young and old.'

His eyes flicked up to Connie again before he spun around and handed his sword and long knife to one of his helpers. Connie felt a flush run along her spine, leaving her tingling. He'd definitely looked at her that time. She shook it off. He'd probably glanced at everyone in the crowd twenty times, and she was the only one wearing a set of long knives. Maybe she shouldn't have put on that part of the costume.

She looked over to the three men. Bartitsu had tied his dreadlocks up into a mass ponytail and was motioning to one of his assistants. As he did the light caught the back of his black uniform, and Connie noticed that the back of his coat had a set of wings brocaded into it, with feathers extending all the way down the back and to the end of the sleeve. It was subtle, but unmistakeable. *Must've been an expensive costume*, she thought.

One assistant handed John Bartitsu a cane while the other walked about the chalk circle making slashing motions with his lightweight sword. He bounced back and forth on his feet.

Bartitsu turned back to the crowd, grinning beguilingly again before looking back down at the little boy in the top hat. 'Of course, I'm joking,' he said his arms open wide, the cane pointed down. The crowd chuckled appreciatively.

'I took on the name Bartitsu to try and reinvigorate the art. My school combines traditional Bartitsu with historical weapons fighting. Now, you might think that this match,' he pointed to his assistant, who was still bouncing up and down looking pleased with himself, his sabre glinting, 'Is uneven, since I have just a cane,' he pushed the cane forward for emphasis, 'And Matt is using a cavalry sabre, also known as a light sabre.' The crowd laughed again. A few people made whooshing sounds.

'Yep, fastest way to lose a class, tell them you're training them to use light sabres.' Bartitsu shook his head, smiling. 'It's not uneven, though, and light sabres,' he said, turning to face his opponent, 'Are overrated.'

Matt's features dropped into a comical frown. Bartitsu stepped back and lifted the cane into a guard position. The crowd seemed to take a collective breath and lean in closer.

'A cane is just as dangerous as a sword in the right hands, and this one is pretty special.' Bartitsu nodded to his assistant. 'En guard.'

Matt lunged, his body upright, sabre flashing out. Bartitsu whirled and parried, dancing around him. The man slashed, casting theatrical glances at the crowd. Connie frowned again. The clangs ringing from the sword and cane sounded odd. The cane was wooden, surely? So why was it ringing against the sword, not thudding? Why were no splinters appearing on the shaft? Bartitsu swept to the side as his assistant lunged. He pushed the sabre away and jabbed the cane's handle into his attacker's forehead. The man stumbled back, stunned. His hand flew to his head. The crowd laughed, but Connie bit her lip, disconcerted. That time it hadn't seemed theatrical and she could swear she saw a splash of blood between the man's fingers.

Bartitsu exhaled gruffly and turned to the crowd, his arms spread wide again, drawing attention back to himself. 'The carbon cane,' he said, holding it aloft on his palms. He clapped his hands together and the cane collapsed on itself, folding to a quarter of its extended length. 'More concealable and tougher than a light sabre. A gentleman's weapon, from a civilised age.' Connie squinted at the cylinder Bartitsu was holding between his hands. It looked very similar to the one she'd just seen on the colonial hunter.

The crowd guffawed and broke into a round of applause. Bartitsu spun away, the cylinder disappearing in the whirl of his coat.

'Now, for the next segment of the display, I'm going to need some volunteers,' said Bartitsu, rubbing his hands together, the definition of showmanship. Hands shot into the air. Connie paid little attention, still looking to see if the assistant was hurt.

'You, Explorer Girl with the knives, come join the show.'

Connie looked back over at Bartitsu, who was staring straight at her, his head cocked to one side. Around him were three other audience participants. 'I think you've got plenty,' she said, shaking her head.

'Need four,' Bartitsu replied, 'Or are those knives just for show?'

The crowd turned to look at Connie and she felt herself shrink in front of them, not keen on being the centre of attention.

'The best fight is one you're never in,' she said, trying to keep the quaver out of her voice.

'Then maybe you shouldn't wear an outfit with weapons that shouts, *Come and take me on.*' Bartitsu raised an eyebrow and rolled his tongue in his mouth. 'If you're going to carry knives, Explorer Girl, you should be prepared to use them. Come on, join us. I promise I don't bite.' He motioned to the other audience members. Two of them beckoned her, excitedly. She cast a look over the crowd, hoping Mum would appear. No such luck.

She shrugged and hopped down. 'Sure,' she said, making her way through the crowd to an enthusiastic, if scattered, applause.

'So, Phil, Ahmed, Jonathan and Explorer Girl, for this demonstration I need you all to learn some basic steps,' Bartitsu said, handing the three other audience members each a long and short blade, which were dulled for safety. 'Just follow me.' He settled into a stance, short blade reversed along his arm, the shiny pommel glinting in the afternoon sun. The long blade was out across his body in a guard. The three men followed suit.

'You forgot me,' said Connie, her arms folded across her chest.

Bartitsu looked over his shoulder at her, 'You've got knives. Same principle, Explorer Girl.' He turned away. 'Follow me.'

He set off in a quick-step motion across the yard. The three men followed him, one, Jonathan, moving more nimbly than Connie thought he should. She pulled her mum's dulled knives out and, spinning them to mimic Bartitsu, raced to catch up, skipping over the cobbled surface lightly. At the other side, Bartitsu paused. 'Now,' he said, 'we do it backwards.' He began stepping back. Connie followed, keeping half an eye on Jonathan. They went back and forth several times. Phil and Ahmed began to lose pace, though Connie noticed that Jonathan was moving ahead of Bartitsu at times. A plant then. That was good, she would be thrown out of the demonstration shortly.

She began to relax, letting herself flow through the movements. They set off again, Bartitsu moving quickly now. Connie smirked. The speed was designed to catch his three stooges out. Phil went first, stumbling on the cobbled surface and stuttering to a finish, raising his blade haphazardly. Bartitsu didn't pause, he just commenced the backward portion of the display, forcing both men to overwork and flail. Connie flowed back alongside Jonathan, her arms moving smoothly, modifying the movement to suit her shorter blades.

'And stop,' Bartitsu said as they finished the backwards movement. Phil and Ahmed looked thoroughly relieved, though they were staring at Connie and Jonathan. Connie shrugged. Bartitsu sheathed his weapons and put a hand over the pommel of the shorter blade. He cricked his neck and heaved out a sigh. 'Phil, Ahmed, sorry gents, but you're dead,' Bartitsu said without turning. They blanched. Jonathan however puffed out his chest. Connie smiled at the act.

'How'd I know?' Bartitsu asked, a feline grin spread wide across his face.

Connie creased her brows and looked at the floor, thinking. He hadn't mentioned her, so he'd seen something. The audience shouted out answers.

'You heard him stumble.'

Bartitsu shook his head. 'Yard's too loud.'

'You've got a mirror set up in the alcove.'

'Yeah, because you always have time to set up mirrors before a duel.' Bartitsu shook his head, laughing.

Connie glanced up, a glint catching her eye. 'But he's right,' she said.

'What's that, Explorer Girl?'

'He's right,' Connie pointed to Bartitsu's hand. 'But the mirror is your overly shiny pommel, there.'

Bartitsu lifted his chin and looked at her, his eyes narrowing against the sunlight.

Connie smiled apologetically, suddenly aware of everyone looking at her.

'Not bad, Explorer Girl. Not bad at all.' He turned back to Phil and Ahmed. 'So, unfortunately, you two aren't agile enough.' He shooed them away, all theatrics once more. 'And you, not sharp enough,' he said to Jonathan, the plant. 'She got it and you didn't.'

The plant slunk off, a smirk flickering across his face. Connie felt an uncomfortable knot in her stomach.

'You though,' Bartitsu said, turning back to Connie. 'Little surprised, I'll admit. But how much can you keep up?' He smiled at her and drew his sabre, settling into a guard position.

Connie suddenly felt played. She stepped back, not sure she wanted to be part of whatever this was, but one look at the crowd made her pause. She swallowed.

'What's the matter?'

'I'm really not a show-off,' Connie said, sheathing the knives and feeling self- conscious.

'You're not showing off, Explorer Girl. You're making their day, isn't she folks?'

The crowd cheered their agreement and Bartitsu gave Connie a lopsided shrug. Connie paused, unwilling to disappear into the crowd. Slowly, she nodded. 'Ok, what do you want me to do?' she asked, pulling the knives back out. The crowd cheered.

'There's my girl,' Bartitsu said, circling his blade and lifting it into a guard, facing Connie.

'What're you doing?' she asked, feeling nervous.

'Putting that footwork into action. En guard.' Bartitsu lunged forward, his blade snaking toward Connie's face. She jumped back, flowing into the backward steps they'd just practised, shock flushing through her. That had come too fast.

Bartitsu kept coming. Connie raced to keep up, flashing the knives back and forth to keep Bartitsu at bay. His eyes glowed as he forced her back, his footwork faster and faster. Connie matched him, feeling the ring of steel and shouts from the crowd bolster her confidence.

Bartitsu paused. Connie took the invitation and switched to the forward motion.

'Good,' Bartitsu called above the din.

Connie flushed with pride despite herself. She lunged deep into the final motion, over-extending.

Bartitsu began the reverse steps. Connie rushed to respond. The tempo changed. Bartitsu began to push her backwards harder, his blade landing heavily against her knives. Connie deflected, but her arms rapidly began to feel bruised.

Bartitsu began the sequence again. No pause. He was pushing her back and back, striking hard. Connie moved rapidly, reacting. She felt the wall getting closer behind her. She gulped. Bartitsu wasn't stopping.

Without thinking, Connie dropped and rolled sideways, knife against her forearm. A slicing clang above her head told her the move had been necessary. She twisted to her feet and stumbled back again. Bartitsu kept coming. The crowd was cheering. She realised they thought this was choreographed. Connie's eyes widened. Bartitsu struck two bruising blows against the knives. Connie backed away, footwork forgotten, deflecting. Surely it was over now? Her moves became sloppier, shifting under the theatricised beating. She stumbled. Hit the ground hard. Looked up.

The tip of a blade was an inch from the bridge of her nose. It wasn't dull. Her breathing came in heavy pants. The sound of the crowd was just ambient cacophony. The blade tip filled her vision.

'You were supposed to do the forward motion, not just keep going backwards.' Bartitsu was laughing, stoking the crowd. He sheathed the blade and reached down. Grabbing her arm and pulling her up, he swung her round to face the crowd. Ragdoll-like, Connie swung on the end of his arm. 'Ladies and gentleman, a hand for our Explorer Girl. Game, but still in over her head!'

8

'Three years, Imara. You disappeared. You left cryptic clues and snippets, barely enough to keep me going. You ran when I could have protected us. And now you bring me here and tell me I have to do this?' Marcus smacked his palm into a wooden crate and spun on his heel, his emotions rioting about his face. Sunlight drifted in through the window, showcasing the motes of dust spiralling in the weak golden glow. In the courtyard below a mock knife fight was taking place, he watched it half-heartedly before turning back to Imara.

'You really want to try that one? Three years was a bargain. Try living seventeen of them. Alone,' Imara replied, pushing her goggles further back on her head but otherwise remaining implacably still. 'Three years might feel like a lifetime to you, but believe me, it was interminably longer for me.'

'Then why go?' he asked, staring at her, his jaw jutted forward. He was seething but his head was spinning and he was struggling to focus. Imara was becoming an increasingly hazy blotch in front of him. She was leaning awkwardly too, her eyes scrunched against the light from the window.

'I told you why.'

'You left me the equivalent of a prophecy from the Delphic sodding Oracle. You didn't know that was what you had to do. You could have set this whole thing in motion.' He jabbed a finger at her chest, coming in close.

'You set it in motion when you wouldn't listen. When you forced the Chamber.'

Marcus flexed hands on Imara's upper arms, his anger unexpectedly subsiding. He breathed in the scent of her hair and was catapulted back. Days, months, years spent with her, watching, learning, investigating. It was almost more real than now. He yearned for those simple days. He'd had no idea just how easy they were, ironic given how complicated they'd seemed at the time.

He gripped her shoulders, all tension falling away, lost in the scent of her. He leaned forward, his lips brushing her hair, nose butting against her goggles. 'I've missed you,' he said, breathing the words out quietly. Outside a cheer rose, the crowd assembled in the courtyard below the storeroom bursting into a round of enthusiastic applause. He sneered into Imara's hair. Damn showman.

Imara pushed him back toward the other side of the room. 'No reminiscing, no distractions,' she said. 'You need to focus. We only have this one chance. Bell is key. I am trusting you with her life.'

'Well, that would be a first,' he said, slumping away from her into the shadows toward the door, stumbling into boxes as he left.

'Ladies and gentleman, give it up for our fabulous Explorer Girl!' Bartitsu flourished a mock bow toward Connie, who was standing, still winded, in the middle of the yard. The crowd erupted in cheers. 'Smile, Explorer Girl,' he said, pushing her forward, one hand gripping her upper arm. 'They think you're great despite your sloppy footwork.'

Connie winced and raised a half-hearted hand at the crowd, glancing at Bartitsu out of the corner of her eye.

'Not a bad effort, Explorer Girl.' He grinned at her.

Connie bristled, 'I could've done better. You set rules, then changed them.'

'That happens in a fight, Explorer Girl. Only thing worse than wearing weapons is not knowing how to use them.'

'Do you hit every volunteer that hard?'

'Not everyone parades around with knives.' Bartitsu shrugged and turned away. 'So, that concludes our volunteer demo. Next up we have a fantastically unusual weapon.'

Connie turned away and stalked over to where her knives lay on the flagstones. She sheathed them as smoothly as she was able, wincing at the effort. The muscles in her shoulders were seriously sore. She made her way along the edge of the display area, Bartitsu's showmanship just a buzzing in her ears.

'Ignore him, Connie. He's a tit. Last year's bloke was much better.'

Connie looked up to see Paul, the lab tech from Boulby, leaning against the forge doorway.

'You ok?'

Connie nodded, rubbing her arm. 'Have you seen Mum? She was in front of me, headed this way, but...' Connie trailed off and spread her arms, glancing at the crowd. 'Having said that, I'm kinda glad she didn't see me just then.'

'Your mum would say exactly the same as me,' said Paul. 'He hit you hard because he didn't expect you to keep up. He was showing off for his captive audience. You put a wrinkle in his efforts.'

'I guess. Have you seen her?'

''Fraid not.' Paul shook his head. 'You two seem to keep missing each other today.'

'Yeah, I'm gonna go look for her. I just get voice-mail on her phone.'

'You know your Mum, she's probably switched it off.'

'Yeah, and yet I get grief if I do that.' Connie shrugged, 'Tell her to give me a call if you see her?'

Paul nodded and Connie headed for the archway back to the main street. As she passed a doorway beside the fish shop, it was flung open and the tandem-owning hunter collided with her, knocking her down.

'You need to watch it,' she said, climbing to her feet.

He was leaning against the archway where he'd bounced after running into her. He looked over his shoulder and squinted at her, his eyes struggling to focus. Connie was too annoyed to care.

'And you need to figure out your own footwork.' He slurred, his eyes unfocussed. 'Sword Master taught you a losing pattern. You should've trusted your instincts.'

'Found Amelia yet?' Connie sneered, piqued at his retort.

The hunter stared blankly at her. 'My business is my own,' he said, and staggered away.

Connie stared after him, agape.

9

1904, North Yorkshire

Gertrude and the mare wound through the woodland, the mare picking its way delicately amongst the fallen autumn leaves. Mist trailed lazily between the trees, obscuring from view the rodents and other small animals she could hear in the undergrowth. She smiled as the horse walked on. No matter how far she travelled, nothing quite matched a dewy Yorkshire sunrise, but then, when she was amongst the sand and oases of the desert she felt the same. The horse meandered out of the woodland into a long open field, the mist laying lightly on the grass and lacing the air, turning the world a hazy, grey-toned wonderland where hedges and trees had indistinct, ephemeral shapes. Gertrude pushed the horse into a canter, enjoying the whip of cold, damp air across her cheeks. This, you did not get in the desert.

She leaned forward, the pommel of the side-saddle wedging uncomfortably against her knee as the horse raced over the damp turf. The proper way of riding was becoming tiresome to her, to ride astride would really be much more suitable. She pushed the horse on into a gallop, laughing before sitting up and deftly reining the horse back to a trot.

'Good girl,' she murmured, patting the mare's neck and looking about her, giving the horse a long rein to relax. They walked on, the mist becoming denser and darker. Gertrude frowned. The mist wasn't burning off. That was odd. A crackling sound caught her attention and she spun as far as the saddle would allow. Yes, side-saddle was getting tiresome.

A flash of light, like a fork of lightning, bristled through the mist and a tang of electrified earth reached her nose. *Lightning?* The horse whinnied and began pawing at the leaves. Gertrude gathered up the reins. Calmness began to evade her as her eyes darted left and right. The crackles came again, increasing in intensity.

The horse began jogging nervously on the spot, spinning about, jangling the bit in its mouth. Despite herself, Gertrude tensed. The mist was getting thicker, more fog than mist now, and she had lost her sense of direction. 'Come on,' she said soothingly to the horse, 'let's not get silly. Nothing to worry about.'

A huge crack of lightning lanced in front of them, gouging a thick, jagged purple line in the air. The light echo left in its wake was somehow iridescent and there was an acrid smell of burning. Gertrude let out a startled shout. The horse reared and spun, clattering back the way they'd come. The fog intensified, crackling all around them. Gertrude grabbed the strap around the mare's neck to keep her seat as the horse raced away from the lightning, unheeding of the reins. A chemical taste of oil saturated her mouth and a fetid, metallic smell assaulted her nose as the fog turned an inky, purplish black. She choked, holding on to the panicked horse with grim determination as it careened forward in the blackness. Gertrude opened her eyes wide, trying to catch sight of something, anything that would tell her where she was. There was nothing but choking blackness. The horse surged forward relentlessly.

And then the fog was gone. Just gone. The mare clattered to a stop and Gertrude cursed as she bounced up its neck. She pushed herself back into the saddle and looked around. The horse shivered, breathing great heaving puffs of air through wide nostrils. Its head swung left and right, it was evidently as confused as Gertrude herself. Then, in a change that made Gertrude laugh, it whickered softly and began grazing. Gertrude shook her head. 'Damn animal,' she said, before disentangling herself and dismounting.

She gathered the reins and stood by the horse's shoulder, stroking it gently and clucking, looking around her while the mare grazed. They had stopped by a large, wide river at the base of a long sloping bank. Above her, at the top of the slope, she could see a short, white spire; the tip of a winter garden glass house. She walked along the bank a little further, an inkling of her location starting to stir, only to see the domed roof of what appeared to be a giant bird cage at the top of the bank. Myriad bird calls floated down the slope on the breeze. None were native. She frowned. *Surely not? What on earth is Ropner up to now?* And how was she here? Preston Hall was miles away from Red Barns and on the other side of the river. Gertrude sighed. With no sign of the fog she needed to work out where she was and how she could get some help. Ropner, at the very least, would be able to contact her father. She tugged on the horse's reins and began walking up the hill, the mare trailing behind her.

10

Connie walked back into the main street and looked up and down it, frowning. She couldn't see her mum anywhere. She pulled her phone from the coin purse and tried calling again. It went straight to voicemail. Connie growled under her breath, replacing the phone. She'd never get away with being so uncontactable. Parents. She set off at a rapid walk across the cobbles past the mock police station, brushing against peeling old posters that had been pasted to the wall. She sniffed. The air smelled acrid, as if the pair of pantomime scientists who'd been in the entrance alleyway had brought their theatre piece further into the Victorian Quarter.

Connie coughed, trying to dislodge the metallic taste from her mouth. She was surprised to see the street was virtually empty. The shops were closing and the festivities seemed to be moving out into the tent village on the front lawns. She checked her watch, it was just after four. Connie raised her eyebrows, she hadn't expected it to be that late, but when she looked up, there was a greyish edge to the sky. She frowned. It was quite an abrupt change.

Scanning the empty street, she still could not

see her mum, nor the sloshed pith-helmeted man she'd been arguing with. That was weird, Connie was sure she couldn't have been that far behind and the street was relatively short. She walked to the mismatched gates over at the orchard. Pith Helmet's tandem was gone and the gates were being locked.

'Excuse me,' Connie said to the woman, who was dressed in a blue fleece with the museum logo on. 'Did you let a woman dressed as an aviator out before you locked the gates? Petite, with braids?'

'No, not seen anyone like that,' the woman said, pocketing the keys and dropping a bolt into the floor. 'Sorry.'

'Never mind, she's probably in the tent village.'

'That's where most people are headed, but you'll have to go out through the shop.'

'Thanks,' Connie said. She set off at a jog down the street, back past the print works and tailors, toward the alleyway and entrance courtyard. As she approached, she saw the alleyway was filled with patchy purplish smoke. The two scientists must've overdone it with the barrel gimmick. She walked through the alley, wrinkling her nose as the chemical smell crowded it. They really had overdone it. The hairs on her arms stood on end and she felt her skin begin to tingle as the air crackled.

When Connie emerged into the courtyard, the light was poor, even the glow from the automatic door that led back into the house and museum was muted. Smoke hung in large clumps around the courtyard, belched out from the barrel contraption. Connie could just make out the shape of it in the corner of the yard. The steampunk scientists were nowhere to be seen.

Wow, this is too much. Connie wrinkled her nose and tried to breathe shallowly, the stink was awful. They must have mixed sulphur into the smoke to make it smell like this. Connie coughed and gagged; the taste layered on her tongue with every tentative breath and it was giving her an intense headache. She hoped that the museum didn't cancel future festivals because of a couple of idiots. The May Day Steampunk and Victoriana Festival had just started to become this amazing event; it would be a shame if it was cancelled.

She strode across the courtyard amidst crackles and flashes of light. Connie shook her head and blinked rapidly, annoyed. The barrel had been a good gimmick, why had those two fools ruined it by not looking after the damn thing. She bumped into the automatic door and cursed, rubbing her head and eyes to clear away the blotches that were clouding her vision. Now the door wasn't working either. Connie huffed and pushed on the door, squinting against the stinging smoke as she walked back through the atrium. On the floor, she could make out the bright circle of the clock, a long shadow on it showing the minute hand ticking backwards.

Connie paused on the threshold of the shop. She blinked rapidly and rubbed her eyes, unable to clear the retina echoes that had blurred her vision to somewhere just short of blindness. She could hear the sound of static electricity, and the deep echoing sound of the sea, as though she was listening to the air currents in a sea shell. She shook her head, trying to clear the sound. *What the hell did they put in that barrel concoction?*
She walked forward, sniffing and shaking her head, her vision gradually clearing. Her eyes watered painfully as she tried to focus, willing the neon blotches that were blurring her vision out of existence, breathing heavily in relief as shapes became gradually clearer. She took two steps forward and stopped short. Under foot she could feel the springy texture of carpet.

Connie looked down as her vision began to clear. It was painfully slow. The rug, and it was a rug not tiles as it should have been, was a rich, patterned blue that extended virtually wall to wall. Connie looked around her, her head bobbing. The walls were papered with a cobalt blue and gold hand-printed motif wallpaper, and where previously there had been stacks of books, picnic blankets and replica Victorian toys, there were now mahogany-framed chairs, one upholstered in cream and the other matching the wall decor. A plump sofa was tucked beneath the window and warmth radiated from the hearth.

'What the...?' Connie said, her jaw dropping. She looked around the room uncertainly, taking in the brand new fixtures and fittings, the gleaming fireplace, lacquered woodwork and sumptuous fabrics. She sucked in a huge breath, unaware until that moment that she'd been holding it.

This didn't make sense. On the wall in front of her, next to a wide, heavy door, hung a magnificent oil painting in an ornate gilded frame. Connie stumbled over to it, staring at the Victorian subject. She didn't recognise him, but at the bottom of the frame, in the centre, was a small coat of arms. Black and yellow with three stag heads and three stars. Connie reached out and traced a finger along the motto, belatedly recognising the portrait as one that was occasionally hung in the main gallery on the other side of the house. 'Fides et Fortitudo,' she murmured and looked back up at the man. 'Robert Ropner.' *What is it doing in here?* She whirled round. *What is any of this doing in here?*

The decor throughout the sitting room, which should have been the museum shop, was Victorian, or maybe Edwardian, she wasn't sure. Mum would have known. Connie felt her fingers clench and unclench as she looked around the room. Suddenly she wished she'd paid more attention to her mum's irritating preciseness. Connie bit her lip and ran a shaky hand through her hair. 'Focus, Connie,' she said to the empty room. 'What's going on?'

She took another look around and stopped dead, licking her lips and gulping as she registered the heat coming from the hearth. 'The fire is lit,' she said, staring at the flames. No one was in the room with her, but if the fire was lit, it was unlikely to be long before she was discovered. As if on cue, the sound of voices came from the other side of the door of a room off to her right. The voices were getting louder, two equals, either servants or members of the household. Either way, Connie didn't want to get caught. She stalked for the opposite door, the only exit from the room now open to her. She wanted to get out of the house.

Connie pulled the heavy studded door closed behind her, her arms shaking. She'd only walked through the hall but that had been enough. The reception desk had gone, replaced by a Victorian, or Edwardian, side table and other fixtures and fittings. At least the door had been unlocked. She looked out hoping to see the tent village and slid down the door feeling defeated.

In front of her the lawns were empty, a great sweeping expanse of green scattered with fallen leaves. There wasn't even a hint of the huge festival village that had been there this morning. No litter, no track marks showing where the walkways had been between the tents and stalls, no evidence that only an hour or so ago the place had been teeming with about a five thousand people. Connie felt her heart thump in her chest, louder and more insistent. She scraped her fingers along the flagstones, closed her eyes and breathed in, her lower lip trembling.

'Get it together, Connie,' she said forcing herself to look out at the empty space, scanning from right to left. She gulped again. The car park, cafe and play area were gone, and there was no sign of the butterfly house. It was just green open lawns, with a few wire enclosures, each with a shelter in them, spotted about. This was beyond weird. She took a deep breath and leaned forward, heaving herself onto her feet and walking to the edge of the porch, staying hidden inside the stonework. She glanced at the winter garden to her left, noting the frost etched on the corners of the glass panes. 'Stranger and stranger,' she said, recoiling at the cloud of steam that billowed from her mouth. It was then that she felt the cold and noticed the shadows. They were in the wrong place. In the afternoon, the shadows should have been to the rear of the hall, down towards the river, but they weren't. That meant it was morning. 'But how?'

A rattling sound distracted Connie from her question and she looked down. Caught on her boot was a russet coloured leaf, brittle and dying. There was also the frost. Connie picked up the leaf and frowned.

It was morning, and it was autumn, and judging by the two rooms she'd seen of the Hall behind her, it was also apparently around the beginning of the twentieth century.

'What the hell is going on?' Connie said, staring at the leaf.

A loud cawing sound came from her left and Connie spun toward it, her eyes widening at the sight of the gleaming, enormous aviary. It looked new. More cawing sounded and Connie stared. Shifting patterns and excited jabbering from inside the aviary told her that it was stocked. Connie raised her eyebrows and exhaled a long, disbelieving breath. This was unreal.

11

Connie crouched in the bushes on the edge of the hilltop. To her left, the lawns rolled away to a wide, flat expanse of river, the Tees winding down its final miles to the estuary. Across from her was the aviary, its burnished steel, fresh from the works, glinting in the morning sunlight. Connie gulped back her fear, her fingers twirling the pendant hanging around her neck. The bird cage was stocked. Thirty or forty birds were fluttering around it, cawing, singing and otherwise making a racket. On top of that, standing in front of the aviary, her back to Connie's hiding spot, was a woman dressed in Victorian riding skirts, her auburn hair piled up on top of her head and tucked beneath a huge floppy felt hat. Beside her was a chestnut mare tacked up with a side-saddle and double bridle.

Connie crouched closer, squinting at the woman's clothes. It was a fantastic costume, the detail and precision of the tailoring was exquisite, she wouldn't be surprised if it was from a prop and costumes department for some upmarket theatre or film company.

'Are you going to come out from those bushes, little thing?' the woman said, not turning around.

Connie trembled and looked all around her, not quite believing what she'd just heard.

'Oh, I do mean you,' the woman said turning to face her.

Connie gasped. This was no costume. There was no mistaking the woman's strong nose and wide mouth, or her auburn hair. The ruddiness in her cheeks also betrayed time spent out in the sun. The woman standing in front of her was as familiar to Connie as her own reflection. The postcard of her portrait had been stuck above her desk for months.

'You're Gertrude Bell,' Connie said, standing up.

'Indeed,' Bell replied, her mouth twitching upwards into a wry smile. 'Though, it is still a strange thing to be considered a Person of renown.' She cocked her head at Connie, 'That is a strange manner of attire,' she said, waving her hand at Connie's steampunk outfit.

Connie fiddled with the cuff of one of her fingerless gloves, suddenly self-conscious of her outfit. 'Yeah, I guess it would look a little odd to you,' she said, not meeting Bell's eye.

'But comfortable for riding astride I would expect?' Bell asked walking over to inspect Connie more closely.

The wind blew up from the river and Connie shivered. 'I don't know, I don't ride.'

'Not very practical for warmth though, it would seem. Hmm.'

Connie rubbed her arms, 'Would you believe that it was a lot warmer this morning when I left my house?' she tried to inject a note of humour into her voice, but felt it fall flat on her tongue.

Bell frowned. 'It is morning, child. And early, at that.'

'Yes, I've been trying to work that out.' Connie smiled uncertainly and then stopped. 'And why aren't you more surprised by all this? You seem pretty calm given this isn't your house, and I'm dressed, how did you put it? In a "strange manner of attire."'

'Ah, you do have a mind. Delightful.' Bell smiled widely, taking Connie aback. 'It's been a rather strange morning, I'll admit, and I'll wager you've had one, too. Come.' She motioned to Connie and walked back to the horse, patting it soothingly on the neck.

Connie followed her haltingly across the gravel pathway to the aviary, stopping beside Bell to stare at the structure, her arms wrapped around her in an attempt to shield herself from the cold.

'What is it that you do, that you are attired so?' Bell asked, scratching her horse's neck. The mare snuffled contentedly.

'I, er,' Connie stopped, how on earth would she explain steampunk to Gertrude Bell? 'I'm an, explorer, of sorts,' she said, pushing her tongue into her cheek.

'You are an explorer?' Bell asked, raising an eyebrow.

'Yes,' Connie replied, feeling her shoulders tighten.

'And what is it that you explore?'

Connie bristled at the note of laughter in Bell's tone, 'I, er,' she stalled, pursing her lips.

'You don't know?'

Connie smiled tightly and ran her tongue over her teeth. She took a big breath and licked her lips, 'Never mind. So, what happened in your strange morning?' she said.

'I took a morning ride. It was rather drizzly and dank, very different to desert mornings, but refreshing. Anyway,' Bell waved her hand, dismissing her aside before continuing. 'There was a spot of lightning and some awful smelling cloud, probably from the steel works. Dorman really needs to be doing something about that. Anyway, we emerged here, on the banks of the Tees. I don't like this new aviary of Ropner's much.' Bell wrinkled her nose as she surveyed the noisy structure again.

'There was a spot of lightning associated with the steel works that left you, what, ten miles from where you started? And you're going to pretend that's somehow normal? Surely that's strange by anyone's standards?'

This time Bell grinned, though she was studiously focussed on the aviary. 'Delightful mind, indeed,' she said before turning to gaze at Connie. 'But it's closer to seventeen miles, little thing.'

'My name is Connie.'

'A pleasure to make your acquaintance. Connie?' Bell asked, extending a hand.

'Rees. Connie Rees.'

The two women shook hands. Bell's hand felt warm beneath the supple leather of her riding gloves. Connie could see freckles across her face, along with the ruddy glow that came from spending long periods out in hot, dry conditions. A face far too detailed for her mind to be dreaming it up. Connie felt a small thrill run up her spine. Whatever was going on – bizarre and strange as it was – right now she was talking to, shaking hands with, THE Gertrude Bell. It was incredible. Unbelievable, but incredible.

'So, Connie Rees, what is it you think is occurring to us this strange morning?' Bell asked, pulling the reins over the head of the mare and motioning that they should begin walking toward the wire enclosures.

Connie fell in beside her and took a gulp, thinking. 'You don't have any thoughts?'

'This place is not as I remember it, though it is a fair number of years since I have visited. Ropner and my father share interests in the rail industry.'

'I'm aware,' Connie said.

'Yes, he is a rather brilliant man, my Papa. I am interested in your theories, however. Do you have a hypothesis?'

Connie bit her lip, considering her own appearance at an Edwardian or Victorian Preston Hall, comparing it to the account Bell had given. 'You mentioned a foul fog,' she said at last. 'What did it smell of?'

'Hmm,' Bell considered. 'Sulphur, I would say. That's why I connected it to the steel works. Though it would have had to travel a substantial distance to have come from there.'

'I don't think it was the steel works. There was a contraption in the hall,' Connie jerked her thumb over her shoulder and shook her head, she'd almost said "Victorian Quarter" and she didn't really feel up to telling Gertrude Bell that Preston Hall had become a beloved museum rather than a family home. She glanced sideways. Bell had come to a stop next to one of the enclosures and was watching her with a raised eyebrow.

'Well, in the courtyard, anyway,' Connie went on. 'This thing was belching out purple smoke and it smelled of sulphur. It was rank.'

'That's not what that word means, little thing.'

Connie waved the comment away, her mind racing as she scuffed her boot back and forth on a clod of earth by the root of a tree. 'I think it was the twins. Maybe they did this.' She frowned. Somehow it didn't seem right, the two had been far too theatrical for their machine to have been real. Hadn't they?

Bell cocked her head. 'And who are these

twins?'

'They were doing experiments. It was a festival.'

'Festival?' Bell laughed. 'My dear girl, Robert Ropner may host parties, many of them, and boisterous at that. He likes to display his acquisitions.' She motioned to the enclosure.

Connie started; there was an unusual, small and evidently exotic animal hidden away in the recesses of the shelter at the rear of the pen. She had no idea what it was, it was too much in shadow, but it certainly wasn't native to the UK.

'But he does not,' Bell paused for emphasis, her gaze burning into the side of Connie's face, 'Host festivals in his home.'

Connie sighed and bit her lip, scratching at her temple. How did she explain this? She stopped.

'Stumped?'

'No.' Connie stuck out her bottom lip, 'Just thinking.' She paused. 'What if I were to tell you that you and I live in different times? That's why my clothing looks odd to you. Where I come from, we're a couple of decades beyond the twentieth century. I don't know if we're in the nineteenth century or the twentieth here, but my clothing is suitable for a much different time.' She shivered as a crisp breeze whipped her hair about her face, 'And season.'

'And how would we then have met, Miss Rees? Are you suggesting that the thing you couldn't remember exploring just now, is time? All our best minds agree such travel is impossible. Your proposal is preposterous.'

Connie glanced up to see Bell staring down her imperious nose at her. Connie's shoulders slumped. 'Any sufficiently advanced technology is indistinguishable from magic.'

'Speak up, child. Do not mumble. And put away that pet lip.'

Connie looked up, feeling suddenly aggrieved that Gertrude Bell was chastising her, though she had to admit, she had been feeling petulant. She huffed out a breath and fixed her lips into a wooden grin. 'I said, any sufficiently advanced technology is indistinguishable from magic. Who are we to say what is possible? We're both here.'

Bell nodded. Connie thought it might even be approval, but she couldn't be sure.

'But you could yet be a jape of one of my father's friends,' said Bell.

'Do you think I look and talk, even remotely, like a Victorian woman?'

'Speak.' Bell said. 'Look and speak. But no, you do not. Not even one of the worker women's children would speak like you. They lack the schooling you seem to have had?' She raised her eyebrows.

'Yes, I go to school. I study physics, mathematics, mechanical engineering and astronomy.'

'Don't boast, dear.'

Connie deflated. 'Look,' she said. 'This morning, you were out riding in,' she glanced at Bell's clothing, 'October, somewhere near Red Barns, correct?'

Bell inclined her head.

'I was sitting at home in Stokesley, in April.'

'Decades after the twentieth century?'

'Yes. I spent the day with my mum at a festival here. It exists in my time.'

'Ropner's descendants invite people onto the property?' Bell considered the possibility. 'A grand scale of philanthropy.'

'Something like that,' Connie said, deciding it was best to leave it. 'You seem to have ridden through some sulphur-tainted fog that brought you out miles from where you began but in the same or a similar time. I seem to have gone through the same thing, but for some reason I remained in the same place but a different time.'

'A reasonable summation, though you neglected to mention the lightning.' Bell patted her horse's neck. The animal nickered.

'What lightning?' Connie asked. 'There was no lightning for me.'

'Odd,' Bell said, pulling at the mare's mane and teasing out a cotter. 'Just before the fog became impenetrable and Manāt here entirely lost her senses, there was some…' She paused, working her fingers through another tangle in the chestnut mane. 'Some rather incandescent violet lightning. Striking in its beauty and danger.'

Connie stared at her open mouthed. 'Why

didn't you mention it?'

'Oh, I just assumed you'd have had the same.'

'No. And I'd have mentioned it. I'd have been terrified. Weren't you scared?'

Bell snorted and smiled, her expression amused. 'My dear Miss Rees. I have dined with desert tribes and been caught out on the face of Finsteraahorn in a terrible storm. For forty-eight hours my life literally hung on a rope.'

'So you weren't afraid?' Connie asked uncertainly, calculating Bell must be at least thirty-three if she'd already been stuck on the Finsteraahorn. That storm had nearly cost her her life.

'An English woman is never afraid, Miss Rees,' Bell replied, raising her chin.

'Sure,' Connie looked down, thinking. 'Maybe we had different experiences because of the lightning.'

Connie paced back and forth, thinking about Bell's recollection of the fog. Bell scratched Manāt's ears, singing softly beneath her breath.

A shot rang through the cold air. Connie instinctively ducked, her eyes and nostrils flaring, her hands covering her head. Manāt squealed and reared.

'Miss Rees!'

Connie felt something stinging in her neck and she touched it, finding a shard of wood caught against her skin. Wind blew her hair about her face, it tangled on the wood, tugging it. Shaking, Connie pulled it out and inspected it, the bloodied shard twitching in her trembling fingers.

'Did you see the shooter?' Bell yelled over the wind.

Connie stared at the splinter blankly, barely even registering the commotion. Still shaking, she looked at the tree trunk. There was a nasty gash on it, an open wound of freshly-revealed pale heartwood about six inches to the left of where she'd been standing. The bullet must've just missed her.

'Miss Rees,' Bell shouted, 'Concentrate on me! Did you see the shooter?'

The anger in Bell's voice cut through to Connie and she twisted her head round to look at the woman, ready to scream at her. The rebuke died on Connie's lips as she looked beyond Bell, who was struggling to regain control of Manāt. The horse was rearing and squealing, stirrup jangling against her side and causing more panic, but that was not what had caught Connie's attention. She stared, horrified, not at the angry-looking man wielding what looked like a musket rather than a rifle, but at the cloud of roiling, electric fog that was closing in about him, rising steadily from the embankment down to the river Tees. 'I can see the shooter, but we have bigger things to worry about,' Connie shouted, throwing the shard of wood to the ground and racing over to Bell, helping her to soothe her flailing horse.

Furious shouts echoed around the two, accusations hurled by the man racing toward them, all meaning lost on the wind. Connie saw him pause and raise his musket, the fog beginning to swirl around him. 'We need to go, now!' she shouted at Bell, who had finally managed to get all four of her horse's hooves on the ground.

Bell cast a quick glance at the man and pulled Manāt over to a low tree stump, heaving herself into the side-saddle. She reached an arm down to Connie. 'Up. Now.'

Another shot rang out. Connie repressed a scream. She jumped up onto the stump, grabbed Bell's arm and scrambled as best she could up onto the horse's back, behind Bell.

'Do you not know how to mount a horse?'

'Can you be disdainful about my horsemanship later, please?'

Bell urged Manāt into a canter. The horse raced forward and Connie clung to Bell's waist, her heart pounding. She blinked hard, trying to control her breathing. Something flickered in the corner of her eye. Connie turned her head, stray hairs whipping into her eyes as they were blown about. She rubbed them clear of her face, staring at the trees. In the wood line to her left she caught sight of it again and she craned her neck to look properly as Manāt carried them at a dash toward the entrance gate.

It was a shadow with flashes of cream and, was that a bike? It was too indistinct. Connie leaned back, her hands loosening on Bell's waist as she twisted to look back over her shoulder, the fog was reaching tendrils toward them now, its coils seeming to speed up as they did. The shooter was long since lost inside it but Connie had no desire to end up wherever he went.

'Stay still, Miss Rees!'

There was no mistaking the fear in Bell's voice. Connie felt a hand grab at her arm, steadying her as the horse took a half-leap over a low branch. She swung back, gripping Bell with both hands. 'Sorry, I thought I saw –'

'You can look around later. Hold on.' Bell leaned forward, urging her horse to go faster as thin tendrils of fog began to coil around them. The mare responded, the sound of her hooves thudding in an urgent rhythm on the damp grass, racing headlong toward the wrought iron gates at the end of the drive.

They crossed onto the gravel driveway, crunching taking over the sound of thudding as Manāt galloped toward the gate. Connie's eyes widened. Only one of the wrought iron gates was open. The gap was narrow. She held her breath, willing herself smaller despite the lunacy of it. They passed the gate posts. Connie exhaled loudly and Bell turned Manāt along the road, keeping the horse racing between it and a small gauge railway.

'There's no fog,' Connie said, suddenly realising that the smell of sulphur and crackle of the purple lightning hadn't followed them beyond the gates. Bell pulled Manāt up to a trot.

'How strange,' she said. She slowed Manāt to a halt, patting the mare's neck and soothing her with gentle clucks of her tongue. 'Dismount, please,' she said over her shoulder.

Connie slid off Manāt gratefully, her groin was sore from bouncing on the horse's hindquarters and her hips were aching. She rubbed her thighs vigorously and winced, huffing.

'You really aren't a horsewoman, are you?' Bell asked, amused, as she slid to the ground.

Connie gave her a sidelong look and said nothing, digging the heel of her palm into her leg to try and ease the muscles.

'This way.' Bell crossed the railway line carefully and began marching down the side of the track. She didn't look back.

'Where are you going?' Connie asked, forcing her legs into motion.

'Ropner doesn't have a station at the house – he really should – but there is a station just up ahead. Eaglescliffe. We'll take passage on a train there back to Red Barns. We may even get Manāt on board.'

'You can't take a horse on a train, and why would we go to Red Barns?'

Bell stopped and turned, Connie had to pull up sharply to avoid bumping into her. Manāt whickered, calm again.

'I am a Bell, Miss Rees. My father is a rail magnate and very cognisant of current affairs. We can take the train to Red Barns, most likely with Manāt, because of the former, and ask my father's counsel when he returns from London this evening because of the latter. Unless you would like to investigate time for the answers?' She didn't wait for a response, but turned away and began her march once more.

For a moment Connie stood, bewildered. She watched Bell striding away, her gait tense and felt a sudden bloom of anger mixed in with fear. Bell could not go searching out her father. 'I actually think investigating time might be more useful than consulting a rail magnate.' The words blurted out, more angrily than she'd intended, and there was a waver too that she disliked. It had the intended effect though. Bell paused. Connie didn't know how to broach the subject of time paradoxes, so she decided to attack Bell's sense of independence. 'Just because you're afraid, doesn't mean we should run to Daddy.'

Bell glanced back over her shoulder, looking Connie up and down. The distain was palpable on her face 'An English woman is –'

'Never afraid. I heard you the first time.' Connie walked along the tracks, stepping from pylon to pylon toward Bell, her mind racing. 'The thing is, Gertrude –'

'Miss Bell, please.'

Connie smiled tightly, 'Fine. Miss Bell. This is

beyond either of us. We need to be pooling our experience of the phenomenon to work out how we get through this, and we can't involve others, it could cause all kinds of unintended effects.'

'How so?'

'It's physics, and I'm very good at physics. So can we please find somewhere safe, well safer, and figure out what's happening before we go racing off to a place that might be further from where we need to be to get home.'

'My home is seventeen miles that way,' Bell said, pointing toward the east.

'But is it the year you left it this morning?' asked Connie, frustrated at herself for her barbed comments. *Not exactly constructive, Connie. Control your temper.* She took a deep breath 'Remember, you'd never seen the aviary before.'

'I've only recently returned to the country,' Bell said, though with hesitation. Connie took her opportunity.

'And you and I were born over a hundred years apart. Yet here we are. Together. We don't know what year this is. The man in the fog, that wasn't a rifle he was carrying, it looked more like a musket.'

'Lucky for you.' Bell pursed her lips.

Connie ploughed on, ignoring Bell. 'You may know where we are, but you cannot be certain of *when* we are. You can't go home. What if there is a younger, or an older version of you there? What would happen then? How would your father react? Is he really likely to believe that you are you?'

Bell opened her mouth to reply, then paused. The thought clearly hadn't occurred to her. She frowned.

'Please,' said Connie, 'Let's find somewhere we can start figuring this out.'

Bell considered, then she gave a single curt nod. 'I seem to recall there being a thicket with a clearing at its centre, just over there. It should be safe enough.' Without a backward glance, she started walking away from the road and railway toward the trees. Connie heaved a sigh of relief and followed her.

'So, you see, when you appear here, that doesn't necessarily mean that the you that should properly exist in this time disappears, but that there are two of you, and you can't interact. One of you knows more than the other about your life, so you could either ensure that you do the things you tell yourself you do, or – and this is important – you could so terrify yourself, that you never do the things that allow you to be here now.'

'Then how could I tell myself about them?' Bell asked, frowning. 'If I am here, and I speak to myself, I must always have spoken to myself, so what's the problem?'

Connie leaned her head back against the trunk of a tree and looked up through a roof of loosely woven sapling branches to the multi-coloured canopy above, smiling. She loved autumn. They were sitting inside a roughly made hide. The shelter, with its cut tree stump stools, old box containing rough waxed blankets and a battered storm lantern filled with oil had been something else that was new to Bell. As soon as they'd discovered it she'd wanted to leave, saying it must be in more regular use since her last visit to Ropner's estate. Connie had refused to move, saying they needed to work out as much as they could.

Bell had reluctantly agreed. Relieved, Connie had flopped down on the ground and was now sitting under the oil lamp that they'd hung from a branch of the central tree trunk, her back resting against the bark. The lamp offered a very weak source of heat as well as light, but Connie was starting to feel the cold. Nevertheless, this was the best place they'd found to regroup and Connie was conscious that her clothing would attract significant attention if they were out in public, it was nowhere near Victorian enough to pass. A warm, golden-tinted glow filled the little hide from the light of the lantern.

'That is the principle of a time paradox,' she said looking across at Bell. 'Have you ever had a conversation with yourself about time travel?'

'That is irrelevant. As you said, the myself I meet could be older than I am now.'

'True.'

'So, even if Papa could not assist us, it is entirely possible that I could.' Bell stood, hunched under the low roof of the hide and began to walk to the doorway.

'Where are you going?' Connie asked, panic rising.

'To ask me for help,' Bell replied.

'No!'

'Why ever not?' Bell was cross. 'As you have repeatedly said, we need to find out more about our situation.'

'We don't know what year it is for a start.'

'We'll ask someone.'

'Were you even listening to me? Or just the parts that fitted with your original plan of running home?'

Bell looked at Connie, furious.

Connie brushed a strand of hair back over her head and held out a placating hand. 'I'm sorry, but it's not that simple.' She licked her lips. Paradoxes were difficult things to understand anyway, and now she needed to explain to Gertrude Bell, of all people, what the problems were that they could encounter. 'Look, you've already said you've never spoken to yourself, right?'

Bell nodded.

'So, if we aren't in your future, then we already know we can't go to Red Barns.'

'And if we are, we are wasting valuable time arguing.'

Connie put out a hand, 'If you'd known that

climbing the Finsteraahorn would nearly cost you your life, would you have done it?'

'Of course,' Bell replied. She seemed confused by the question.

'Of course you would, you're Gertrude Bell.' Connie looked up at the branches again, sighing.

'And you would not have done so? One of the greatest feats of your life and you know beforehand that you will survive? You would not undertake the task in those circumstances?'

Connie pushed out her jaw. Bell was impossible, the woman had an answer for everything. A logical one at that. It was extraordinarily difficult to reason with her and Connie was exhausted, she felt like she'd been awake for around thirty hours.

Bell continued, 'Yet you would take on a task unknowing, without that surety that you will survive? It is not my logic at fault here, Miss Rees.'

Connie looked over at Bell. 'You cannot interact with yourself.' She tried very hard to keep her tone measured. 'We don't know enough, and before you say it, the you that exists in this time is not here to help us, she's likely not even in the country.' Connie suddenly seized on that. She knew Bell's life. 'You haven't asked me about what happens to you. And I know what you do in your life.'

'You aren't me.'

'But I know,' Connie smiled. 'I know that you

spend more and more time travelling, research-ing, exploring.'

'I have no intention of so doing,' Bell said.

'But you do, and possibly you do it because I've told you that's your life. Do you see the problem now?'

'Just because you tell me something, doesn't make it so.'

'Gertrude, please. I think we have both been pulled here for a reason, I don't know what yet, but you explore. You are extraordinary; you change things. You inspire people.'

'And what do you do that we two should be in this together?'

Connie paused. The rejection letter was fixed firmly in her mind. *It is with regret... Was it just wishful thinking, or was it more?* 'I want to explore,' she said. 'I want to be an astronaut. It's all I've ever wanted. We are bound by exploration.'

'And this, aeronaut business. You are trained in it?'

'Not aeronaut. Astronaut. Exploring space.' Connie pointed upwards.

'Space?' Bell looked incredulous.

'Not now, please. Gertrude, I'm certain of this. We, the two of us, need to work this out to-gether. Neither the you of this time, or the me of my time – if we somehow end up there – can help us. We are the ones out of time. We need to find our way home, not disrupt our own futures.' Connie could feel a small bubble of hope returning, the pain of rejection receding. This had to be it. She was going to be an astronaut after all. She was desperate not to have Bell crush it.

'Or past selves? Hmm?'

'Sure.' Connie did not want to get into that argument again.

'You look tired, little thing,' Bell said, taking a seat on one of the stump stools again. This time Connie caught a note of kindness in the expression. Outside Manāt whickered. Bell had tied her to a sapling on the edge of the thicket clearing. 'Perhaps we should rest a while. I can keep watch, I believe I have been awake for fewer hours than you.'

Connie smiled gratefully. 'I really could use a nap.'

'Sleep. We can discuss our strategy when you wake.'

Connie nodded and pulled a blanket from the box, frowning at the waxiness of the material.

'Lay it on the ground, wax side outermost and wrap yourself in it. The wax creates a barrier between you and damp earth. Helps to keep you dry.'

'Thanks,' Connie said, laying the blanket out and wrapping it over herself. 'Promise you aren't going to do anything daft.'

'I promise,' said Bell.

12

'Miss Rees, wake up. Miss Rees.'

Connie felt a hand on her shoulder, shaking her. She blinked. Her bones felt cold and her muscles ached. It seemed she'd only been asleep five minutes. 'What? What is it?' she asked blearily, rubbing her eyes and pushing herself up from the ground. Her side was damp. The blanket had obviously needed re-waxing, but that at least explained why she still felt bone-weary. Her mind was groggy too. She looked at Bell.

'We need to leave.'

Connie could hear Manāt's hooves pawing at the leaf strewn ground outside. She glanced through the woven saplings. The clearing was hazy. It must be twilight. 'Why?'

'The fog. It has reached us. Again.'

'What?' Connie leapt up and ducked out into the little clearing. Sure enough, tendrils of crackling, sulphur-smelling fog were curling out from under bushes, wrapping around tree trunks. She spun round, it seemed to be coming from three directions.

Bell appeared beside her. 'I told you. It came most quickly. I was surprised.' She strode over to Manāt and began tucking away the stirrup and checking the martingale, tightening the straps where she could, then she loosed the reins from the sapling, stroking the horse's neck before returning to Connie. 'We'll have to go out that way,' Bell motioned to a narrow pathway, barely wide enough to take a single person, that wove away through the bushes. It was the only way unimpeded by fog. There was no way they could use Manāt's speed to escape this time. The horse would struggle to get through the bushes.

'Maybe we should leave Manāt, she's going to slow us down.'

'Certainly not. I'd no more leave her than you. Are you coming?' Bell strode off into the bushes, pausing to wait for Connie. 'It's not good practice to walk behind a horse, Miss Rees.'

Connie pulled a face and walked past Bell onto the tiny track. She wasn't sure she was happy at Bell equating her to her horse, but now was not the time to argue.

'You need to move faster, Miss Rees.'

Connie stumbled on, thorns on the bushes catching on her jacket. She pushed them aside as best she could but the path only narrowed. The bushes started encroaching, undergrowth began obscuring the track. Connie looked around. 'It's gone.' She swallowed. She felt Bell stop immediately behind her.

'What has gone?'

Behind them came the sound of crackling lightning. Connie shivered. 'The path. It's a not a path anymore. We need to go back.'

'We cannot go back, Miss Rees. It is almost upon us. Use your weapons.'

Connie turned to look at Bell, not bothering to unsheathe the knives. 'There is no path,' she said. 'I can't cut one in ten seconds.' She stopped suddenly, her eyes widened and her mouth dropped open. A wall of thick fog, crackling with iridescent purple lightning was advancing on them with a slow and forbidding heaviness. Manāt was struggling in the narrow space between bushes, frightened whinnies coming more frequently as the first curls of the sulphur-tainted fog licked at her hind quarters.

'Is that what it was like the first time you came through?' Connie asked, paralysed by the sight. It was quite a distinction from the pale, lilac haze she'd passed through at the hall.

'Indeed,' replied Bell, who had also turned to look at the fog. She had a grim, resigned expression on her face. She removed a neckerchief and stepped forward, wrapping the scarf around Manāt's eyes and taking hold of the horse's forelock, whispering soothingly to her, her back to Connie. Bell reached an arm out behind her. 'Take my hand, Miss Rees. Perhaps if we all maintain contact we shall not be separated by this devilishness.'

Connie grabbed the offered hand, her skin crawling as the fog swelled up around Manāt. Bell remained focussed on her horse, issuing a constant stream of calming sounds.

'What language is that?'

'Persian,' Bell said, before returning to the stream of words.

Connie shivered and looked about, straining her eyes to see in the fog. A flit of blue-black caught her attention and she craned her neck, straining her eyes as she tried to see through the flickering purple lightning that scattered through the fog. She saw it again, like a wing fluttering, but huge.

'What is that?' She pointed to where the wing-thing had disappeared in the fog.

Bell didn't respond, her fingers had whitened, so hard was her grip on her horse's forelock. Manāt was prancing, snorting, panicking. Bell kept up her stream of Persian. The fog obliterated the bushes and trees. Connie put a hand on Manāt's neck and began making soothing sounds. She hunched toward the horse as the three began to float in the dark, dankness of the fog. Connie stared at the bright chestnut neck. Beside the disquieting purple flashes, it was the only colour she could see and the warm smell of the horse was comforting amidst the fetid sulphur smell. She glanced at Bell, who squeezed her hand, never stopping her murmuring in the horse's ear.

Connie touched her forehead to Manāt's neck and kept up her own stream of cooing, breathing in the musky, comforting stench of the horse's sweat. Where would they find themselves when the fog cleared?

13

Connie wasn't sure how long she breathed in the smell of Manāt, nor how long she uttered calming nonsense noises as the fog sparked and swirled about them. She concentrated on her breath and on the sounds she made even as the grey-purple fog clouded into her vision, obscuring Bell and Manāt. It was only because she could feel Bell's hand in hers, feel Manāt's warm, reassuring bulk under her hand, that Connie knew she wasn't alone in this miserable violet grey.

Eventually, and so slowly at first that it was almost imperceptible, the fog began to recede. Connie's first realisation of this came when Manāt stilled. She felt, rather than saw the horse's ears twitching as the mare tried to distinguish sounds. It was still dark. Her hand, grasping Bell's tightly, was going numb. Connie looked about her, shapes began forming in the gloom.

'I think we are, wherever we are,' she said. 'The fog is gone at any rate.' She let go of Bell and Manāt and stepped back, cracking her neck as she looked around. The ground crunched beneath her feet, she looked down to see a newly laid covering of gravel stretching away in both directions. Connie turned her head, following the roadway all the way to a huge building. She started, surprised. They were definitely not at Preston Park anymore.

A full moon emerged from behind some scudding clouds, bathing the building in a silvery glow and illuminating the façade. A huge stained glass window glimmered in the pale light. The wall of glass rose into a gothic arch, the mosaic of colour glinting mutedly in the moonlight. A smaller, similarly gothic window was perched immediately above it, extending into the point of the stonework. The smaller window was stone bound between the panes of glass, a small rondel sitting in the pointed arch piece. The window itself, had large stonework between panes, but its panes were larger and it was bound on either side by carefully finished square towers. On either side of these towers were two further windows, each flanked by another tower, which reached to about two thirds the height of the central arch. Behind the façade, a huge ecclesiastical building disappeared out of sight. Small outbuildings bounded it, the grey shadows flowering along them indicating lush foliage growing up the walls.

'It can't be,' said Connie. The building in front of her was eerily similar to artist's impressions she'd seen not a month ago. Mum had insisted on visiting the new exhibition, said she'd seen signs about it every day on her way to work and wanted to see what all the fuss was about.

'It cannot be what?' said Bell, coming to a stop beside her, adjusting the scarf back around her neck. Manāt was standing peacefully beside her, the horse much calmer in the clear night landscape.

'That's Gisborough Priory,' said Connie.

'Nonsense. The Priory has been a ruin since the reformation. Has the fog addled your mind?'

Connie sighed, 'No, Gertrude, the time and location altering fog has not addled my mind. We must be here before the monastery was destroyed. The question though, isn't really when or where we are, but *why* we are when and where we are.' Connie suddenly wished she'd paid more attention at the exhibition. 'What do you know about the Priory?'

Bell huffed. 'Established in the early twelfth century, it became one of the richest religious houses in Yorkshire by the time of Henry the Eighth. Although Gisborough itself did not take part in the Pilgrimage of Grace –'

Bell paused at Connie's lost look, raising one eyebrow and frowning at her. 'The Pilgrimage of Grace,' she continued, 'the rebellion of monasteries in the north against Henry's Act of Supremacy. The act that broke with Rome, when Henry declared himself Head under God of the Church in England. Do they not teach you history as well as physics at your school?'

'I'm better at science.'

'History, culture and science are not mutually exclusive, Miss Rees. We prioritise one over the others only at our own expense. Anyhow, despite being more acquiescent, Gisborough was nevertheless signed over to the Crown as part of Henry's reforms. The king disposed of it to one of his supporters who dismantled it, perhaps we should say destroyed it, more or less immediately. This is all very well-chronicled history.'

'I'm sure,' said Connie, drifting off toward the Priory. It was stunning. 'But that doesn't really tell us much about why we might be here. Are we well before, or upon, the eve of destruction?'

'Well,' said Bell, overtaking her, Manāt trailing behind. 'There is a definitive way to find out.'

'At least it's warmer,' Connie said, relieved that the damp coldness of Preston Park seemed to have been left behind in the fog. Flowers in the vines climbing along the priory walls were closed but evidently in full bloom. Connie stopped and inspected one of them, turning to Bell. 'What do you think, summer?'

'It seems likely. That particular plant blooms in early July.'

'Ok,' replied Connie nodding. 'Third season in three days.'

'Two days,' said Bell, walking ahead.

'Sure, let's go with your count,' Connie muttered, letting go of the flower.

'What did you say?' Bell asked.

'Nothing.' Connie smiled and walked on, patting Manāt on the hindquarter as she passed. The horse snuffled contentedly. Connie came to a stop about twenty feet further on and took a deep breath. 'I think we're post, what did you call it, the Act of?'

'Supremacy. Why?'

'The priory isn't entirely whole anymore.' Connie gestured toward the interior of the building. It was partially deconstructed, piles of roof tiles, stonework and statuary, all with their heads removed, were laid about. 'They must be salvaging anything except the icons.'

'Yes,' Bell stood next to Connie. 'The Iconoclasm was a great disgrace. A great deal of history and artwork was damaged, sometimes irreparably, in this scourge.' She sounded angry.

'Aren't you Anglican?'

'I am a scholar first and foremost, Miss Rees. I dislike – intensely – such wanton and unnecessary destruction.'

'Fair enough.' Connie shrugged and wandered off into the courtyard, trailing her fingers along some of the broken statues. Bell was right, some of the damage here was criminal.

'If your assertion about the fog is correct, that we are being transported by it for a purpose as yet undisclosed, why do you think it has brought us here? I have no connection to this place. Do you?'

'I visited once. Didn't pay much attention,' Connie said, catching sight of something flickering inside one of the cloisters, like a lamp quickly shielded. 'Kinda wishing I had now.' She tried to catch Bell's attention whilst keeping one eye on the cloister, searching the shadows for movement. The moonlight, unhelpfully, was casting shadows from that end of the courtyard. Connie peered into the darkness.

'What is it?' Bell asked, appearing at her shoulder.

'I could have sworn I saw a light.' Connie breathed the words out so quietly she could barely hear them herself.

'I don't believe we'll find answers in here. We should return to town.' Bell placed a firm hand on Connie's elbow and pulled her away.

'What?' Connie didn't understand why Bell was ignoring her. She was about to insist they take a look in the cloister when Bell gave her elbow three sharp squeezes in quick succession. Connie glanced at her and saw the pointed look. *Oh.*

Outside the courtyard, close to one of the flowering plants that was spidering along the wall, Bell stopped. She climbed fluidly into the saddle and held out a hand silently to Connie. Connie took it and swung up behind Bell. It was marginally better than her attempt at Preston Park.

'You're really not a horsewoman, are you?' Bell asked.

'Still not the time,' Connie replied. 'Why are we riding?'

'I saw the candle flame, further along than you were looking. It disappeared through an archway on the far side. And, it is usually best not to disturb thieves when one has other options. In this case, following discreetly.' Bell turned Manāt along the priory wall and urged her into an active walk. Fortunately the lush grass deadened the sound of her hoofbeats.

'Two women riding Manāt around a half-dismantled priory at midnight isn't what I would call discreet,' Connie said.

'We shall see. Manāt is also much fleeter than we alone, should that become necessary. Now hush.'

Connie pursed her lips and held onto Bell. There was no reason to argue the point. They approached the corner of the priory and Bell slowed Manāt down. They crept forward, Bell leaning over the horse's neck to see further. Connie cursed herself as she realised she was holding her breath. Bell straightened and pushed Manāt forward again.

As they rounded the corner, Connie felt a profound disappointment. The landscape was deserted. Lawns rolled away from the walls of the cloister courtyard, silvered in the light of the full moon. About two hundred metres away, the wood line was a hazy grey, darker blotches showing where the tree canopy was thicker. Connie looked left and right as Bell walked Manāt slowly forward. There was nowhere for the moonlighter to have hidden, and they couldn't have crossed the entirety of the space without being seen. At the very least they should have seen him – or her – Connie supposed, entering the trees. She let out a disappointed sigh and looked down. She jolted in disbelief, sliding off Manāt without pause.

'What are you doing?' Bell asked in a hushed whisper. 'Climb back up.' She held out a hand.

Connie ignored her. 'Stop Manāt from trampling this, give me some space,' she said, her hands trailing along the dewy grass, following a long, constant line about an inch in width.

Bell pulled Manāt back, standing her square about ten feet away. 'What is it?' she asked.

Connie bear-walked on her hands and toes, following the line. Occasionally there would be a faint widening that quickly resumed a single, inch wide track. 'I think it's bike tracks,' she said, looking up to follow the trail into the distance. It looked as though it was disappearing into the wood to the west.

'More likely a cart track. Bicycles have not yet been invented, if we are shortly post Act of Supremacy, as the dismantlement in the cloisters suggests.'

'I disagree,' said Connie. 'There's only one track.'

'Wheelbarrow then.'

Connie shook her head, pointing to where there was a brief widening of the track. 'Where it's wider there on that slight bend, that's where the wheels weren't quite aligned behind each other. The track is of two wheels arranged one ahead of the other.'

'So, now you are not only an explorer of time, but a master tracker?'

'No, my neighbour's kid just likes to make trails through puddles with his bike.' Connie looked up and shrugged. 'It's a lead and it explains why we didn't catch sight of our moonlighter out here. Also, if bikes haven't been invented yet, there's a good chance whoever it is, is like us. We should follow this.' She reached out a hand.

Bell stared at her, unconvinced.

'Do you have a better idea?' Connie asked.

Bell extended her arm wordlessly, her lips pursed.

Connie clambered up again and pointed her arm in front of Bell. 'The tracks head that way.'

'I can see that,' Bell replied. 'Hold on.'

The trees rushed by in a grey-blue blur as Connie and Bell entered the woods to the west of the priory. Cool night air whipped about Connie's face, and Bell's large felt hat obscured her vision.

'Slow down, you'll lose the trail,' she called.

'Not so, if there is a bicycle, the woods are narrow enough to either side to prevent the rider diverging,' Bell called back.

Connie seriously doubted it, the trees were not so crammed in that a bike couldn't be man-handled through them, but there was no denying they were following some sort of trail through the woods, so it would make sense for the moonlighter, whoever they were, to stick to the track. Manāt cantered on, Connie ducked her head as sapling branches threatened to poke her eyes, trying to adjust herself on the horse's hindquarters. This was not comfortable. Why on earth would anyone want to ride horses? Connie jangled about behind Bell, feeling annoyed and sore as they travelled deeper into the woods. Moonlight filtered down through the leaves and the woodland shone with a waxy halo, all the colour muted.

All at once Connie felt herself falling through the air. She crashed in a heap onto the ground. The wind was knocked from her lungs and she gasped. Lifting her head as much as she could manage, she saw a low branch blocking the path. Bell must have jumped Manāt over it. All she could see beyond the branch, through hazy vision, was Manāt's orangey rump, the bright tone deadened by the moonlight, disappearing into the trees.

'Wait,' she called hoarsely, coughing as she tried to get more air into her lungs. *Idiot, Bell. How would a bike get over that branch?* Her vision blurred and she laid her head back. 'Ow,' she said, feeling the hard rounded lump of a stone, half-buried in the dirt, digging into her crown. *Could be manhandled,* her own voice chided inside her head. 'You're no help,' she muttered, rubbing at the spot on her head and feeling blood. Her vision blurred again. She must have hit her...

'Careful. Careful, Conn. It's a nasty bump.'

Connie felt large, gentle hands around her shoulders, pushing her up into a sitting position. Her head throbbed. The unseen owner of the hands kept repeating her name. Connie's ears were ringing, but she was sure the voice was odd.

'Who're you? Gertrude?' she mumbled.

'You're here with Gertrude Bell? You lucky duck, I always wanted to meet her. Not allowed to of course.'

'What,' Connie tried to look over her shoulder. The hands pushed her head back to face forward. There was dirt on the person's hands, and they were big. A man's hands. Connie started.

'Don't move too much. Let me just check this, don't want you falling unconscious again.'

Connie rubbed her hands over her eyes, squeezing them shut and trying to concentrate on the voice. She'd heard it before. She made to look over her shoulder again.

'Stay still.' The hands were firmer this time. Holding her head in place.

Connie resisted for a moment then sagged forward, dropping her head into one hand, the other fiddling with the front of her cross belt.

'That's better. I think this should be fine, just let me clean it up.'

Connie released a small hand mirror from the bindings on the cross belt and angled it through the crook of her arm. It didn't do much, all she could see was blur of greyish clothes, but everything in this damn wood looked grey.

'Who are you?' she tried again.

'There. All done,' the man said.

A rustle of bushes made Connie look up. Behind her, she felt her rescuer – there didn't seem to be a better term for it – do the same. 'Gertrude?' Connie asked, unsure why she was so relieved at the thought of Bell reappearing. This person hadn't tried to hurt her.

'Stay here,' said the man. 'I need to resolve this.'

'Resolve what?' Connie asked. She was feeling dizzy again. Sitting up hurt. She heard the man stand and move off at a pace away from her. She didn't want to be woozy and alone in a sixteenth century wood. 'Wait!' she shouted, turning, her arm outstretched. The world spun and she crashed to the ground, her chin bashing into the same half-buried rock that had made her crown bleed. All she should see was a pair of long, muddied black leather boots disappearing into the trees.

'Wait,' she called again, groggily. Her vision began to blur. Her jaw hurt. Actually, everything hurt. She rested her head. 'Just for a moment,' she whispered.

'Connie. Connie. Wake up, child.'

Connie blinked. Her jaw was jangling against that damn rock again. 'What? What?' she said, batting the hand away.

'Thank heavens. I tried to return immediately, but there was a damn crackle of lightning. Manāt panicked. Are you hurt?' Bell sounded worried.

'I was,' Connie said, pushing herself up to her hands and knees. 'Did you bring the man?' she asked, looking at Bell through a dirty tangle of hair.

'What man?'

Connie sat back on her haunches, pushing down a wave of nausea. 'The man that treated my cut.' She motioned to the back of her head and gagged, choking down a wave of vomit.

Bell inspected her head. 'It has been treated,' she said, sounding astounded.

'Yeah. It was a man,' Connie repeated, sucking in a huge lungful of air. 'He knew my name. Shortened it. Ran off that way.' She pointed. 'I think there was someone else in the trees. He said –' She frowned, trying to remember his words. 'He said, he needed to resolve something.'

'Now there are two unknown persons running about these woods, potentially neither from this time period?' Bell stood and immediately began casting her eyes about the grey wood.

'I don't know. But I don't think he wanted to hurt me,' Connie said. She'd collapsed back into a sitting position, her head tucked between her knees. She felt like crap. She could hear Bell pacing around her. A snuffling nose pushed at her shoulder. 'No, Manāt, I'm not friends with you,' Connie grumbled, pushing the horse away. 'Wait, did you say you heard more lightning?'

'Yes.' Bell was still pacing around Connie, looking everywhere about them. 'I can't see anyone.'

Connie looked up, 'I don't think you, uh oh...'

'What? What?' Bell spun to look at her.

Connie stared back at her, her eyes wide. She pointed one finger to the canopy above them.

Bell raised her head, her lips parted as she sucked in a lungful of air.

Above them, the branches were clouded with sulphur-smelling fog. It crackled and pulsed an iridescent purple, swirling like a great inverted whirlpool above them, extending in all directions. The forest around them greyed further. Shards of rock and earth began tumbling out of the flashing purple maw, along with a great rumbling sound that could be mistaken for thunder if it weren't for the clods of earth and stone hailing down on Connie and Bell.

Manāt squealed and ran, bucking her rear legs against the falling debris.

Connie threw her arms over her head to protect it. Above the thunderous sound of the rockfall, Connie heard a thin, childish scream. The next thing she knew a body had landed on top of her, crushing the wind from her lungs again.

14

'Get off me,' Connie groaned, trying to pull herself out from under the lump. She felt sick and dizzy. The body snagged on the cross belt holding her knives, and Connie grated her teeth. Suddenly, wearing this outfit didn't seem like it had been the best idea.

The body, dressed in an oversized, grubby white shirt and loose-fitting blue trousers, groaned and sniffed, but remained a lump on top of Connie.

'I said, get off me.' Connie pushed at the lump, straining her arm to get some leverage.

'What is happening?' The voice was thin, uncertain. A mop of dusty light brown hair shifted and Connie found herself looking into the face of a frightened boy. He could be no more than ten or eleven.

'Kid, for the last time, get off me.' She pushed down another wave of nausea and grimaced gratefully at Bell, who grasped the boy's upper arm and pulled him off Connie.

'Let go of me. Who are you?' He kicked out at Bell, the panic audible in his voice.

'We shan't hurt you, child,' Bell said.

Connie grimaced again. It was the same tone Bell used on Manāt when the mare was misbehaving or frightened. She gulped down another wave of nausea and pushed herself off the ground. Her head was throbbing. 'Who are you?' she blurted out between the waves of sickness, leaning forward, her hands on her knees.

'I, I, I –' The boy looked at her, panic stricken. 'I don't know.'

'What do you mean, you don't know?' Bell asked. She shared a worried glance with Connie.

'I, I, I don't know.' He gulped, his eyes fairly popping out of his head. 'I, I can't remember. Why are we in a wood?'

'What do you remember?' Connie asked, pushing herself upright, nausea at last beginning to recede.

'I was climbing the Topping. The master, he'd been angry with me for not paying attention. I went, but I should have gone straight to the farm. I must get back. Let go.' He tried to pull his arm out of Bell's grasp, but she held firm.

'You cannot go running off, child. In case you had not noticed, we are not near any hills here. You are not where you believe.'

'I am at Gisborough Priory. The woods outside it at least,' the boy said, still pulling.

'Wait, you know where you are, but you don't know your name?' Connie asked.

'Let go. I must get home.'

Connie grabbed the boy by the shoulders and crouched in front of him, catching his attention. 'Hey, hey. Listen to me. How did you get here?

How did you go from Roseberry – that's the Topping, isn't it? – to here? How?'

The boy blinked, taking in Connie and her strange outfit for the first time. 'Who are you?' he asked.

'I'm Connie, Connie Rees. How did you get here?'

'I fell,' the boy said. 'There was a crack in the stone, and it all broke apart around me and I fell. It felt like I was falling forever and then I was here.'

'Did you experience a delay in the passage of time before you passed through the fog, Connie?' Bell asked, her voice unnaturally calm.

'No. I didn't.' Connie let go of the boy, who had become very still. She sat back on her haunches. 'You don't think the fog causes amnesia?'

'What's amnesia?' the boy asked.

'It's where you can't remember anything personal, like your name, but you can remember other things, like locations.' Connie motioned to the woods around them.

'Is that what I have?' the boy asked, uncertainly.

'I don't know,' Connie said, shaking her head. 'You might have just had a big fright.' She stood up and immediately wished that she hadn't. Her head started swimming. 'Maybe if we get some rest, you might remember.' She gulped her way through the sentence, blinking.

'You are still not well, are you, Miss Rees?' Bell asked.

Connie shook her head.

'We're going back to the Priory. We can shelter in the cloister and make a plan there. Come.' Bell motioned to the boy and caught Connie by the arm, helping her over to Manāt. 'Hold her martingale, it will help keep you steady,' Bell said, placing Connie's hand on the leather strap about Manāt's neck. Connie nodded weakly and took a deep breath. Bell took hold of Manāt's reins and turned to the boy, who was sidling off into the trees.

'Boy, it is better if you remain with us. The cloud you fell through was unnatural but we two have had a similar experience. It is safer you remain with us.'

'I want to go home.'

'Trust me, kid, we all do,' said Connie. 'Come keep me company though. Please?'

'You were angry with me,' he said, shuffling from one foot to the other.

'No, my head was hurting. Come on.'

He walked uncertainly toward her, his shoes scuffing across the ground. Connie held out her hand and waited until he took it. 'Lead the way,' she said to Bell.

Connie sat with her back to a cold stone wall and stared out at the empty space from the shadow of the cloister. The boy lay beside her, his head resting on her knee. Connie rhythmically stroked his tawny hair, her eyes glazing over periodically. Bell had settled them all down in the shadow of the cloisters, or what was left of them, before taking Manāt off to a wooden lean-to that had been erected by the south transept. Connie didn't like this new development. The priory was more ruin now than when she and Bell had first arrived, the mounds of stone and broken statuary long since cleared. It seemed time had shifted again.

Connie sighed, looking out at the moonlit cloister courtyard, now tinted red in the light of a blood moon. She felt adrift and groggy. She was exhausted, but the pounding of her head suggested it wasn't a good idea for her to sleep. The boy probably shouldn't sleep either. What had happened to him when he'd fallen from Roseberry Topping into the fog Connie wasn't sure, but the amnesia worried her. It could be linked to a head injury. He'd passed out shortly after Bell left, his thin body relaxing as he drifted off. There was a comforting feeling to the warmth of him, curled up next to her like a younger brother.

Connie swallowed. Family. She was worrying about this kid and she had no idea where her own mother was. Mum was probably frantic, there was definitely no phone reception in the sixteenth – or whatever – century. Not that Mum would accept that as an excuse, she was going to be really pissed off. Connie snorted, looking down at the sleeping boy. How Mum reacted didn't matter, she had bigger things to worry about right now. 'I'll take care of you, kiddo' she said, stroking his hair. 'We'll work out who you are and how to get you home.'

She leaned her head back against the cool stone and let her mind drift back to the stranger in the woods. He'd definitely used her name, shortened it, too. That was odd. No one called her Conn.

'What is going on inside that head of yours, Miss Rees?' Bell said quietly, dropping down beside her.

'Call me Connie, please. And I'd really prefer to call you Gertrude. I think we're beyond formality in this, don't you?

Bell smiled. 'And yet that is a very formal way of phrasing your request.' She paused. 'Connie.'

Connie chuckled. 'Yeah. You took a while, has it completely changed?'

'I rode Manāt once around the footprint of the building, just a quick check, the poor animal is in desperate need of a good long rest. The stone is weathered and unkempt. Whenever we are now, it seems the priory has been abandoned for quite some time.'

'Well, at least that means we're less likely to be disturbed.'

'Indeed.' Bell nodded agreement. 'So, you were pensive when I arrived just now. A penny for your thoughts?'

'I was just thinking about my fall. There is someone here who knows me, or knows enough to use my name at any rate. But I didn't know them. I'm definitely not familiar with the voice. I keep playing it over, again and again in my head.'

'They may no longer be with us, Connie. We've passed through another rift on acquiring the boy. Anyhow, it's possible you misremember the voice. You had just taken a bad fall,' Bell replied, suppressing a yawn.

'I guess, on both counts.' Connie twisted her head to look at Bell and winced as she caught the bump against the stone.

'Careful.' Bell bit back another yawn.

'You should get some rest, Gertrude. I can keep watch. I shouldn't be sleeping anyway.' Connie motioned to her head.

Bell nodded. 'You must wake us before sunrise though, Connie. We do not know the year and it would not do for us to be caught here.'

'I'll keep watch, Gertrude. Rest.'

Bell smiled and leaned back against the wall, closing her eyes. 'Whatever is going on tonight, this is still much more comfortable than the nights I spent on the Finsteraahorn,' she said.

Connie laughed.

Connie blinked, shaking herself awake. She couldn't believe she'd dozed off. Next to her, Bell was still sleeping soundly, propped up against the wall of the cloister. The boy was still curled up, his head on her lap. She scanned the courtyard in front of her, her eyes rapidly adjusting. The red light of the moon had disappeared, replaced by a low rolling mist. *No!*

Connie caught her panic. It wasn't the sulphur fog, just a normal morning mist shimmering in the grey hour between night and day. Connie exhaled a long sigh of relief.

'Did you think you'd seen something?' Bell asked, leaning forward and rubbing at the small of her back.

'No,' Connie said, too brightly. 'Just the mist shifting.'

Bell gave her a sidelong glance.

'Are you ok?' Connie nodded to Bell's back.

Bell grimaced. 'I do not recall being so sore when we came down from the mountains, though I did sleep for near forty-eight hours following that excitement.' She cocked her head from left to right, easing the muscles, before pushing herself to her feet. 'Can you wake the boy?'

Connie shook the boy's shoulder. 'Hey, you need to get up, we need to leave.'

'What?' The boy sat up and rubbed his eyes, his hair sticking up at unruly angles. A fine coating of grey stone dust and mud ran in thin lines down one side of his shirt, made into whorls where he'd been curled on the floor. He stifled a yawn and uncovered his eyes, freezing as he took in the mist.

'It's ok,' said Connie. 'Just bog standard morning

mist.' She pushed herself up and held out a hand to him. 'Do you remember your name yet?'

He took her hand and shook his head, his lower lip protruding.

'Anything?'

He shook his head again. 'Nothing about myself. Where we are and what has happened. All too clearly.'

'Do you remember the year it was when you climbed the hill?' asked Bell. She was standing next to a pillar on the outer edge of the cloister, staring into the mist.

'Seventeen thirty-eight.' He said each word carefully, as though he was testing it to be sure.

'You're certain?' Connie asked.

'Yes, because I am ten. Seventeen thirty-eight.' This time, he had a huge grin on his face. 'I am ten. I am ten. I have been going to school for two years. I like school. I do not like the master.'

'Hey, that's great,' Connie beamed at the boy. 'You remembered how old you are. Keep trying. It'll come.' She patted him on the shoulder and walked over to Bell, who was still staring out into the mist.

'You could congratulate him you know, it must be terrifying, on top of all of this, to not know your own name.'

'I would,' said Bell, still peering out into the mist, 'If it weren't for the fact someone has just run across the priory lawns, and I don't know if they saw us.' She pulled on a pair of tan leather gloves. 'Bring the boy. I shall get Manāt. We'll need to follow this stranger.'

'Why?'

'To ascertain our current situation, Connie. We do not know the year, season or whether we'll soon be in our respective homes. Nor do we know if your erstwhile nursemaid is still roaming the woods. It's time we took charge of the situation. Quickly, before we lose our opportunity to trail them.' She strode off into the mist, tucking stray strands of hair under her floppy hat, her skirts swirling about her legs.

'Where is she going?' the boy asked, coming up beside Connie.

'She's gone to get her horse. She thinks there's someone we need to follow. Come on.' Connie set off across the courtyard.

'It's not Crispin Tocketts, is it?'

Connie turned. The boy was standing, half-hidden behind the cloister pillar, his eyes wide. She frowned at him. 'Is that someone you go to school with?'

The boy shook his head.

'Then who is he?' Connie asked, concerned.

'They said he was a cobbler.'

'Ok,' Connie said, uncertainly. She walked back toward the boy. He was shaking. 'Why are you frightened of someone who was a cobbler?'

'I'm not. I'm frightened of who Crispin Tocketts finds in the priory.' The boy gulped.

'Who does he find?'

'Connie, we need to go.' Bell had reappeared in the cloister entrance. In her hands

were Manāt's reins. The horse's head was just visible behind her. 'Our stranger is making toward the wood. Precisely where we met our young friend here. It's too much a coincidence. We need to follow. Hurry.'

'In a moment, he's frightened,' Connie said, not turning her head and not entirely agreeing with Bell's summation of the situation. It could be entirely coincidental. She crouched down in front of the boy, 'Who does he find?'

The boy gulped again. 'He finds the Devil.' The boy choked on the last word.

Connie's eyes widened. 'Oh kiddo, you don't need to worry about that. There's no such thing.' She put a hand on his shoulder and smiled reassuringly, but the boy kept shaking.

'Until yesterday, I did not think I could fall through a hill and end up five miles from it with a strangely dressed girl wearing swords.'

'Knives,' said Connie, a smile flickering across her face.

'What is going on?' Bell asked, appearing behind them. 'We need to go, or we shall lose our chance.'

'I don't want to go looking for the Devil.' The boy stared at the two women, his jaw set.

'And we shall not be so doing, child. But we must go. Come.' Bell's imperious attitude seemed to stir a sense of compliance in the boy and he moved slowly out into the courtyard. Connie smiled encouragingly and held out her hand. The boy took it. 'You'll protect me, won't you?' he asked.

'Of course,' Connie said.

He squeezed her hand and they followed Bell out onto the lawns.

15

Bell moved cautiously through the deep grey of the wood, skirting close around the edge of nebulous thickets of briar. Manāt trailed sedately behind her, her head low, ears relaxed. Bell was walking in an impressive half crouch, a feat that Connie found even more admirable since she was doing it in heavy Victorian skirts. Connie and the boy walked along behind Manāt's tail, stooped over to keep themselves lower than the surrounding bushes. Neither of them was being particularly cautious about the way they walked and the occasional twig got trodden underfoot. They had lost sight of the mystery man about five minutes earlier and were now relying on Bell's ability to follow his trail. The woods were still a haze of varying depths of grey, a low breeze billowing the mist into patchy clouds, though the weak sunrise was starting to burn it away.

Suddenly Bell stopped, holding up a hand as a signal to the others. Connie pulled up, releasing the boy's hand and reflexively reaching for her knives. Somehow the further they had followed the distant stranger into the wood, the more nervous she had become. The boy's fear of the Devil had been too real, and despite knowing it was unfounded – she didn't believe in some fiery demon presiding over Hell, though there was perhaps some merit in the concept of alienation and estrangement leaving oneself in a form of eternal torture – Connie was still disturbed. Legends, after all, usually relied on some level of truth. She held her breath, searching through the shifting mist until she caught sight of a bulky shadow in the shape of a man about fifty feet ahead of them. He was just visible over the bushes, which should be providing the three, and Manāt, with some cover. Connie released her breath and shuffled forward to Bell. 'What's he doing?' she whispered.

'I'm not certain,' Bell replied, 'He seems to be checking something though. You see in his hands?'

Connie took another look. She could just make out a large square of something. 'A map?' she asked, feeling tension leave her shoulders. A map meant a lost traveller, not a devil. Though he could still be dangerous of course. She rolled her eyes. Now she was winding herself up.

The shadowy figure moved off again, this time more certainly. Bell paused, counting levelly under her breath, a single finger held aloft. 'Ok, now we move.'

She set off, stepping carefully over the ground to ensure she didn't break any twigs. Connie waited for the boy and then followed along, bringing up the rear.

Soon, the figure was back in sight, always just far enough away to be no more than an indistinct blur in the trees. It took a while for Connie to realise that Bell was deliberately keeping them at a distance from him. She tucked in behind scrub and brush at every opportunity, moving impressively stealthily despite her bulky attire. The boy, too, was unexpectedly adept at sneaking along between the trees. He seemed to have relaxed a little. Connie meanwhile was getting increasingly annoyed at the multiple snags on her costume. She was struggling not to catch her mum's outfit on the thorns and was getting irritated at the cloak and dagger performance. It was so frustrating.

They carried on, Bell increasing their pace to a light jog as the mist burned almost fully away, uncovering a morning lit light green through the tree branches. They ran on. Connie noticed the boy hesitate momentarily. She extended her legs and caught up to him, 'What's wrong?'

'The woods are different,' he said, looking left and right. 'There should be more trees.'

'Ok. Maybe we're not in seventeen-thirty-eight anymore. Perhaps we're in an earlier year.'

'I don't like it. It's strange'

'I know.' Connie turned to smile at him and her arm caught on a low branch, tearing the sleeve of her costume. 'Do we really need to be acting like Jason Bourne, here?' Connie hissed at Bell's back, her frustration getting the better of her.

Bell stopped suddenly and waved a hand at her, peering around a bush on the edge of a clearing. She stood upright. 'He's gone,' she said, walking out into the glade, all sense of stealth gone. 'Just gone.' She sounded perplexed.

Connie inspected the tear, luckily it was repairable. Mum was likely to have a fit though. She grimaced, *Strange thought to have when you're stuck in the wrong century, Conn.* She laughed. She'd never called herself Conn before. She kind of liked it.

'Well, where did he go?' asked the boy. He'd joined Bell in the clearing. It was rimmed with scrubby bushes, a few gnarly trees and broken stones. The stones could have been part of an ancient circle, but Connie had never heard of anything like that in the area, so she dismissed it, looking around to see where their stranger might have gone. There were no obvious hiding places. The boy wandered to the edge of the clearing, looking about him.

'Don't go too far, I don't want to lose you,' Connie said, turning about in the centre once more to see if she'd missed anything.

'What's that smell?'

Connie looked back at the boy. He'd frozen next to a standing stone covered in lichen. 'It's like the smell when I was on top of Roseberry.'

Connie felt her skin crawl. She shared a look with Bell.

'No fog,' said Bell, shaking her head.

'There was barely any fog the first time I went through,' said Connie, walking over to the boy. She sniffed. There was a sulphurous tang to the air, but it was faint, fading. 'Maybe our mystery man went through the fog?'

'I think he went into the tunnel,' the boy said. 'We should leave the woods. Now.' His hands were clenched around his shirt, twisting the fabric into knots.

'What tunnel?' Connie asked.

'The Tocketts Tunnel.' The boy pointed to a hawthorn bush, shaking.

'How utterly bizarre. If I'd not seen it, I should not have believed it,' said Bell, walking over to the bush and picking up the end of a twine string, which had been tied neatly around a branch. Bell looped her finger and thumb around the twine and followed it a small distance. She gave a short laugh. 'I thought this was nothing more than idle town gossip.'

'Can one of you two catch me up, please?' said Connie, looking from the frightened boy to Bell, who was staring at something just behind the stone.

'Can we go, please?' the boy asked, tugging at Connie's arm.

'Not until I know what you two are talking about.' Connie put a hand on his. She was fed up of not knowing what was happening.

'It's the tunnel, the Devil's tunnel. Please, I want

to go.'

'Nonsense,' said Bell, walking over to a sapling, producing some twine from a pocket hidden in her skirt and tying it to a tree. 'It's just a cave, and the only likely place we may find our mysterious friend.' She looped Manāt's reins through the twine and patted the horse on the neck.

'What are you doing?' Connie asked her.

'Well, Manāt won't fit through the opening and it's fairly obvious that is where we need to go.'

'I'm not going in there.' The boy stamped his foot and stared at Bell.

'I have to say, I had no idea that the legend went back that far.' Bell scratched her ear, looking at the boy with curiosity. 'Let's go.' She set off toward the stone.

'Stop,' said Connie.

Bell turned to look at her, one eyebrow raised.

'No one is going anywhere, until one of you tells me what both of you are talking about.'

Connie stared first at Bell then at the boy, her face set. She felt self-conscious, but she wasn't just going to tag along, she wanted to know what had them both worked up; Bell was excited, the boy terrified, she needed to know why.

The boy shook his head and remained silent, rooted to the spot.

Bell rolled her eyes. 'It's a silly superstition, "The Chest of the Raven."'

'No, it's "The Raven's Gold,"' said the boy, swallowing audibly. He was still twisting the hem of his shirt, his knuckles white.

Bell scoffed, 'Whatever it's called, it's a story designed to frighten children and stop them from playing in the ruins and surrounding woodland. That's all.'

'But what is the legend?' Connie asked, exasperated.

Bell turned to face her. She pursed her lips. 'We are wasting time, Connie.'

Connie stared back and Bell huffed out a sigh. 'Very well. According to legend, there is a tunnel that runs under the priory. It has existed for as long as the priory has, or perhaps longer.'

Connie walked around the stone. A narrow passageway, half covered by scrub appeared. The line of twine disappeared inside. She walked back to Bell and pointed behind her. 'That looks like an actual, real life tunnel to me,' she said.

'I've not yet finished,' replied Bell, 'Might I continue?'

Connie forced a smile on to her face.

Bell tutted, but carried on. 'As I was saying, the tunnel itself was known, but people never ventured into it for fear of the raven.'

'You missed out the gold,' said the boy.

'I was getting to that part, and I'd be able to relate the tale much faster if I was not constantly interrupted,' Bell said, looking first at the boy, who looked down sheepishly, and then at Connie, who smiled blandly at her. A cloud drifted over the sun above the trees, diffusing the green light to a murky shade and giving Bell an eerie cast. The boy huddled closer to Connie.

'So, the gold,' Bell continued as though nothing had changed. 'The raven is said to guard a huge chest of gold that is lodged halfway along this passage, but, it attacks anyone who tries to take it, attempting to blind them. So no one ever goes looking for it.'

'So, we're not going into the tunnel because of a hypothetical bird?' Connie asked. 'I think we can get past it.'

'It's not a bird,' said the boy, 'You're telling it wrong.'

Bell stared at him.

Connie frowned. 'What do you mean?' she asked.

'It's called the Tocketts Tunnel for a reason, Connie,' said Bell. 'Crispin Tocketts, who was supposedly a cobbler in Guisborough, is said to have ventured into the tunnel and faced the raven. I imagine it was Tocketts we three were following through the woods just now, since there is twine at the entrance here.'

'Why?' Connie asked.

'We three are from different times and the priory is in a different state than when we first found ourselves inside it. It stands to reason we've just pursued someone from yet another period of history. I'm not sure why you are contesting this, wasn't that what you were trying

143

to convince me of with all of your talk of paradoxes?' Bell shrugged. 'Anyway, Tocketts, too, decided that the raven was just a bird and he set out to find the tunnel and retrieve the chest. Not knowing whether the tunnel would branch or not, he brought with him a stack of long, tallow candles and a ball of wool.' Bell paused and motioned to the twine tied to the branches of the hawthorn bush closest to the tunnel entrance. 'Tocketts followed the tunnel and found it did not branch, but it was dark and narrow, overgrown in places by tree roots. He pressed on, climbing and hacking his way through as he needed, certain he would find the treasure and claim it for his own.

'Before too long, he was rewarded. The legend says he emerged from the tunnel into a cavern aflame with an unearthly but captivating light, and at its centre was a chest of shining treasure. There was no sign of the raven.

'Tocketts raced toward it, amazed by the chest's size. So large it must contain a fortune that would take several lifetimes to spend, if that were even possible. He ran his hands over the bindings, which were carved with lettering that was unfamiliar to him, excited that the chest had no lock. Overcome by greed he placed his candle down on the plinth on which the chest stood and tried to open it.

'It was not a normal chest like one might find in a house however, since it required the would-be opener to find hidden latches, levers and switches to unlock it.'

Connie stared at Bell, simultaneously fascinated by the story and amazed she'd never heard of it.

'Tocketts marvelled as he worked through the sequences, feeling his excitement grow as he unlocked more and more of the chest, the prize coming ever closer to his grasp. When he found the final lever and lifted the lid he was amazed. There were gemstones, chains of silver and gold, strange orbs that danced as though they contained fire, and mounds of precious jewels. Tocketts could barely take it all in and, so astounded was he that he almost didn't feel the buffer of air and swish of wings as a huge, almost man-sized raven appeared above him, glaring at him and pushing down on the lid of the chest.'

'The raven was real?' Connie asked, her eyes wide despite herself. Beside her, the boy had begun rocking back and forth. Without thinking, Connie put an arm around his shoulder. He huddled closer.

'It's a legend, Connie,' Bell stared at her, waiting until Connie blinked before continuing. 'Anyhow, the story goes that Tocketts backed away in the face of the raven, his courage wilting under its glare. The bird leaned forward, extending its huge wings as if to wrap Tocketts into them, preventing him from fleeing. Tocketts leapt back and stumbled, frightened. He heard the lid of the chest crash shut and when he looked up, the raven had transformed into the Devil and was climbing over the chest toward him, angry and domineering, the very figure of terror.

'So of course, Crispin Tocketts screamed and ran, cursing his greed and stupidity as he fled back up the tunnel, tripping and flailing in the dark, since he had forgotten his candle in his flight. All the while he could hear the Devil's voice sounding in his wake and smell the foul, acrid stench of Hell – for that is what he assumed he had found beneath the priory – curling in his nostrils.

'When he emerged from the tunnel, Tocketts was a changed man. So much so that it was many years before he told anyone of his ordeal, and when he did, the people of Guisborough made sure to tell the story as a warning, lest anyone else be foolish enough to go searching for the Chest of the Raven,' Bell finished with a flourish. 'But it's just a story, as I said, made up to frighten children.'

Connie stared at Bell, at a loss as to what to say.

'How can you say that?' asked the boy, his eyes wide. 'The tunnel is right there and you said yourself that we've probably just followed Crispin Tocketts here.' He turned to Connie, looking for support. 'We shouldn't go in. We should leave.'

Connie squeezed her arm on his shoulder. He was still shaking and though the rocking had stopped the boy evidently believed the story Bell had just related was true. 'You know,' she said to him, 'Stories like this, most of the time they're just the way people explain things they can't really understand. I don't think the Devil is at the end of that tunnel, not really. Something strange, maybe, like a, a, geothermal fissure with a quartz cavern. It would be something Crispin Tocketts couldn't make sense of, but that doesn't mean it was Hell, or that he met the Devil.'

'There's only ironstone at Guisborough,' said the boy. 'Everyone knows that.'

Connie shook her head. Ironstone. Another thing that everyone, except her, seemed to know.

'And what's a geothermal fissure?'

Connie sighed, smiling crookedly. 'It's where hot water and steam escape from the ground. The water's heated up by the earth and pushed to the surface through cracks.'

The boy wrinkled his brow, thinking. 'We don't have any of those either,' he said, chewing his lip and frowning. 'How does the earth heat up all the water?'

Connie laughed and ruffled his head. Having him around was nice, she'd always wanted a sibling and she liked the kid, he couldn't remember his own name, but he was still trying to puzzle out geothermal fissures. 'That's a really good question. You see –'

'Are you two quite finished?' asked Bell. 'We need to get going.' She took up the cord of twine, her hands still in the tan riding gloves. At that moment the cloud above drifted away from the sun and the forest lit again, friendly and inviting as the warmth of the day seeped under the canopy. Connie felt the boy stiffen and his breathing became shallow.

'I want to stay out here,' he said. He gulped and Connie squeezed his shoulder again to reassure him.

'I don't think you get to dictate this decision,' she said to Bell. 'We're all in this, we should agree on what we're going to do and we have no idea what's down there.' She didn't say it, but Connie wasn't overly keen on going into the dank, fetid tunnel herself.

'And what other choices do we have, little thing?' Bell asked. 'As you pointed out only a few hours ago, we have no idea what is happening, but we do know that we've all been through the strange fog and that fog brought us all together. Further, we know that the very odour we can smell at the mouth of this tunnel is the same as that which we smelled in the fog. We all agreed this.'

'Don't patronise me, and that's not the point. There are too many variables, we don't know what going through the fog does to us. Another exposure could kill us. My mum would say –'

'Your mother isn't here, Connie,' Bell cut across her, waving a hand dismissively. 'We are going to go into this tunnel. All three of us.' Bell looked at the boy, who was frozen to the spot. She sighed and softened her shoulders. 'I've already been through the fog twice, as has Connie. It does not seem to have any effect.'

'No, I –' Connie stopped. There hadn't been much in the way of fog, just smoke when she'd stepped over the clock, but the smell had been present, definitely. She could recall the taste in her mouth that had accompanied it. There had been a very brief flash of grey. She's assumed it was light on the glass. Maybe not.

Bell smiled at the boy, 'It shall be fine,' she said, reaching a hand out to him, 'I've been caught in many a storm while mountaineering. I've been accosted in the desert by tribes whose legend said they killed their captives. They were, to a man, incredibly hospitable and kind. Most undeserving of their vicious reputations. The short of it is that I have survived. We can all manage the foul-stench fog, but none of us, if Miss Rees here is to be believed and I do believe her, can get home until we find out what has happened. Come.' She beckoned him over and the boy took a hesitant step toward her before looking back at Connie. 'You're sure it's not the Devil down there?' he asked her.

'Positive,' Connie replied, smiling reassuringly

and pulling the torch from the front of her cross belt. She flicked it on and tested the beam.

'What's that?' asked Bell, curious.

'Little light to guide us,' Connie said, walking past them to the tunnel entrance and shining the torch into the passageway. The light it provided was dim, but enough that they wouldn't trip over any protrusions. The boy gazed into the tunnel, fascinated by the torch beam. 'You're sure about this?' Connie asked Bell over his head.

'We cannot go back, Connie. You said as much yourself. We must go forward if we are to find our way home.'

'And you're not afraid?'

'An English woman, Connie Rees, is never afraid.' Bell smiled and Connie turned away, stepping into the tunnel mouth.

'That's not really true though, is it?' she asked over her shoulder, pushing down a sudden image of a raven engulfing her. She rubbed her nose with the back of her hand to hide her gulp of panic.

Bell smiled, Connie could hear it in her voice when she spoke. 'Even if it is not true, we never let them see it, Connie. Not ever.' She picked up the cord of wool and handed it to Connie.

'Right, then,' Connie said, setting off. 'Let's go find our Theseus. Stay between me and Gertrude, kiddo.' She gave the boy what she hoped was a cheery grin and set off into the tunnel.

'As long as we don't find a raven,' he muttered,

grasping the wool and following along behind her.

16

Connie leaned forward to duck under a root, feeling her way forward with her feet and glad of the grip of her Spanish boots. The torch beam lit a small patch of darkness ahead of her, enough to see where the tunnel bent, was overgrown or descended sharply, but not enough to give much more detail than that. She kept a tight hold of the twine in her hand, using it like a bannister to guide her along the tunnel. Behind her she could hear the muffled sounds of the boy and Bell, each of them finding the walk harder than Connie as they had no light to guide them.

So far, and consistent with the legend, there had been only a single tunnel and Connie had been surprised to discover it was man-made, edged neatly in an odd mix of brick and stone. It was roughly five and a half feet high, which meant she had to walk slightly stooped and in some places the roof was semi-collapsed with roots dangling down, which was a handy marker for the accompanying fallen stonework. However, despite these trip hazards, it had been reasonably easy to follow, certainly not the twisted mess of Bell's retelling of the legend.

'Getting a steep downward bend here,' Connie

called over her shoulder, the stonework causing her voice to echo softly around them. Behind her she heard the boy grunt in pain. She paused. 'You ok, kiddo?'

'Stubbed my toe,' he grumbled.

'Yeah, that was a bad one,' Connie replied, ducking forward and adjusting the beam as she began descending. Her head brushed the ceiling and she flicked the torch around, the tunnel ceiling had lowered. 'Ok, now the tunnel is shrinking. Great.' She stooped lower, keeping a slow steady pace so as not to get too far ahead of the others.

They descended deeper into the tunnel, the air around them growing warmer and drier. Connie felt a little light headed. She sniffed but couldn't smell anything other than the faint, but pervasive, odour of sulphur. She paused, blinking rapidly, her head beginning to ache. The boy bumped into her.

'What's wrong?' asked Bell from behind her. 'Is it blocked?'

'No,' said Connie. 'I just feel faint and I have a headache. I'm worried there might not be enough oxygen down here for us all.'

'I feel fine. How about you, boy?' came Bell's voice. It was imperious even in the shadows of the tunnel.

'I can breathe. I'm not happy that we're eagerly walking into Hell,' he grumbled.

'This is not a pathway to Hell.'

Connie was about to intervene when her torch

beam began to flicker. 'Oh no.' She bashed the head of the torch, jostling the batteries inside. Now was not the time for the batteries to give up. The torch beam flickered out, plunging the trio into darkness. The boy screamed. The sound reverberated off the walls and disappeared down the tunnel, a haunting wail. Connie shivered. That had sounded hellish, and she knew where it had come from.

'What's happened?'

'The batteries have run out.'

'I don't understand?' said Bell.

'Never mind,' said Connie, swallowing back a rising sense of fear. 'I think we should go back. We know the way back is safe.'

'No,' said Bell. 'It was safe when we passed. It may not be so now. We go on, we find our stranger and we find a way home.'

'I want to go back,' said the boy.

'I can't see anything,' Connie replied. 'It's absolute darkness. It's madness to keep going.'

'Do you not have any more of these batteries?' Bell asked.

'No, I'd have already used them if I did.'

'Can you feel the twine continuing?'

'Well, yes, but –'

'Then we can go on. We are following a trail, not making our own way.'

An indistinct sound, like feet shuffling, drifted down the tunnel toward them. 'Seriously? We can't see anything,' Connie said.

'We should go back.' The boy had started shaking again.

'Miss Rees,' Bell said, her imperiousness reasserting itself. 'We do not give up half way through a journey. We must continue.'

Connie felt her skin crawl and she got the distinct feeling they were not alone in the tunnel. *Don't be idiotic Connie, of course we aren't, we're following someone else who left twine behind.* 'Seriously?' she hissed at herself, feeling frustration and fear intermingle. She hit her hand against her hip, trying to control her rising sense of panic. She stopped. Her hand had hit something. She reached into the pouch on her wide, leather belt and pulled out her phone. She'd completely forgotten it was in there. The screen lit up at her touch. No signal of course.

'I thought you had no more batteries? And why is the light different?' asked Bell.

'Never mind,' said Connie, flicking the phone's torch beam on and closing her eyes. Suddenly she was terrified the light would bring her face to face with a devil. She exhaled deeply and opened her eyes. A white halogen glow lit the tunnel for about five feet ahead of her. It was completely empty and she could actually see better than with the torch. 'Ok, way ahead is clear,' Connie said, gulping and taking another step into the tunnel.

'We're not going back, are we?' the boy muttered.

'Sorry, kiddo. The lady is right, we do need to keep going. Stay close behind me.' They continued on.

The tunnel became warmer and warmer. It twisted on, though the roots were fewer and the stonework appeared in better condition. Connie trailed fingers along the wall, the twine hooked on her thumb. It was unbelievably smooth, almost like sheet metal rather than stone. The heat continued to rise and Connie began to sweat. She wiped her brow with the back of her hand. The glow from her phone darted about the passage, up onto the ceiling. Connie stopped short, peering ahead.

The passageway in front of her was still lit. A soft, hazy glow illuminated a gentle curve in the tunnel. Connie stared at it, becoming aware of a low hum and vibration reaching them from ahead. 'I think we're almost there,' she said quietly over her shoulder.

'Almost where?' asked the boy.

'Wherever the tunnel ends,' Connie said, tiptoeing forward and realising that the tunnel had grown again. It was now at least eight feet high. She switched off her light and put the phone back into her waist pouch. Clinging to the nearside wall to stay hidden as long as possible, she inched around the bend, dropping the twine as she saw the ball on the floor at the end of the passageway.

Her jaw dropped. She walked forward. There was a slight momentary pressure as she left the tunnel, followed by a decisive drop in temperature. Connie shivered and rubbed her arms, staring around her. The space was vast and shimmering. Connie squinted into the distance, but she couldn't see the far side of what she assumed was a cavern, though the walls she could see were honed to an improbable level of smoothness for something natural. The cavern was also glowing with an iridescent purple light and was filled with myriad droplets, motes, and orbs of varying sizes, all of which hung suspended in the air, sparkling like otherworldly chandeliers. On the cavern floor – Connie thought of it that way for lack of a better word – was a network of shifting walkways of various widths that bled into and out of each other seamlessly. Some were raised, others lowered, and between them was a deep infinite blackness through which long, spire-like columns that supported several ephemeral concentric rings drifted upwards into a swirling, crackling violet haze. The pathways rippled and eddied about the spires, dancing over the black chasm. Combined with the shimmering room, it was disturbingly beautiful.

Connie gazed up at the crackling ceiling, transfixed. Here, where it was not so threatening, the fog and lights gleamed like stars. Connie felt as though she could be on a spacewalk, dangling on the edge of infinity. It was breathtaking. 'I think we may have found the source of the fog,' she said. Her breath misted in front of her, curling away as though she was outside on a chilly morning. Connie frowned, cocking her head.

'I am minded to agree, but what is it?' asked Bell leaving the tunnel to stand beside her. She shivered involuntarily.

'It's Hell.' The boy pointed to the centre of the room. Connie followed his extended finger and saw a tall monolith on a raised dais, scuds of crackling mist around it. It pulsed with a cool silvery glow that diffused to a calm shade of lavender as it passed through the mist. It could almost be the deepest circle of Dante's Hell, yet counterintuitively it was soothing.

'That's the Raven's Chest. We need to go. Please,' said the boy, dragging on Connie's arm.

'I don't think so,' Connie said, patting his hand and crouching down. She inspected the floor. It was icy cold to the touch, smooth, flecked with crystalline pieces and seamless. Silvery pulsing light drifted under the surface, like a regular flow of blood. 'This isn't a cavern. Not a natural one at least. And it's definitely not Hell.'

'Then what is it?' the boy asked, gripping Connie's arm again.

'I think it's a laboratory. My mum works at a subterranean lab not far from here investigating dark matter. This could be another one.'

'They have technology like this in your time?' Bell sounded incredulous.

'That's irrelevant. We don't know for certain what time we're in. Let's go and look at that plinth.' Connie pushed herself up from her knees and set off across one of the walkways, flexing her fingers. The floor had been cooler than she expected in a subterranean cavern, but she found she was more curious than fearful. Whatever this place was, it was like nothing she'd even heard theorised, let alone seen. The closest thing she could think of was an art installation that used mirrors and lights to create a sense of infinity, but faced with this space that now seemed very much finite.

Testing a theory, she placed one foot half on the walkway and half on the darkness. Her toes found no purchase. 'Stay clear of the black patches, they're holes,' she said, following the flowing path out into the centre of the cavern or laboratory – whatever it was – and ducking her head as she passed the concentric rings. They seemed completely insubstantial, but she didn't think it wise to take the risk.

She reached the dais faster than she'd expected; the pathways had seemed to converge, speeding her passage to the centre, at least she assumed it was the centre, of the room. In front of her the monolith, which appeared to be a vast crystal, continued to pulse, a regular heartbeat-like rhythm that sent beams of light out into the cavern structures in an indescribably complex pattern. A wave of cold air washed off it with every pulse. That was evidently where the refrigerator-like conditions were coming from. The monolith was about seven feet high and decorated with a strange set of symbols. Connie stepped in to get a closer look and inhaled sharply. 'Oh, that's icy,' she said, pulling her face back. She peered at the runes from a distance. Some appeared to be scientific symbols and others pictograms.

'That's Sumerian Cuneiform,' said Bell. 'How curious.'

'And those are Futhark Runes.' Connie pointed to the inscription.

Bell raised an eyebrow at her.

'We did a project at school,' Connie shrugged. 'I liked them.'

'Indeed, but how have Futhark Runes and Sumerian Cuneiform come together. They are languages separated by distance and millennia.'

'This place doesn't seem to much care about time,' replied Connie.

The boy poked his head between them.

'Not so frightening up close, is it?' Connie said to him.

'No, but there is a raven, though,' he said, staring at the base of the monolith.

'What?' Connie turned to look and jolted. Sticking out from the side of the monolith was a cap, worked in black to look like a beaked bird. Underneath the cap was a set of long dreadlocks. Connie felt her skin crawl. The ensemble was familiar. 'That's not a raven or a devil,' she said, pushing the boy behind her. She gulped and walked slowly around the plinth to get a better view. The crumpled form of a man with waist length dreadlocks and a well-tooled black militia-style uniform was sprawled across the dais, his overcoat missing. He was unconscious, his hands in shackles attached to the base of the plinth.

'Is it Crispin Tocketts?' asked the boy, 'Has the Devil got him?'

Connie's eyes widened. 'No,' she said kneeling down to push the dreadlocks aside. His skin had taken on a sickly paleness, more beige than taupe, but the chained man was unmistakeable despite the blue tinge about his lips. It was John Bartitsu.

17

'I know this man,' Connie said, staring at the prone form.

'How?' asked Bell.

'He was at the festival, a sword master doing a display. I helped him.' She was taken aback to see Bartitsu here, but someone had helped her in the fog at Gisborough. A man who had known her name. 'I think he might be the person who helped me when I fell off Manāt.'

'Hmm.' Bell knelt beside Bartitsu, pushing his dreadlocks to one side. 'Rather alluring, actually,' she said, reaching a gloved hand to his neck. She nodded. 'A pulse, good.' She pulled her fingers away, rubbing them together. 'But he is cold, and there is blood. He appears to have been beaten quite savagely.' She looked up at Connie, one hand still resting on the floor. 'You said he was a master at arms?'

'Yeah,' Connie frowned. 'Who would hurt him?'

'A more pertinent question, if he is indeed skilled at arms, is how would they succeed in hurting him?' Bell stood and scanned the room. 'I do not think there is anyone else here, for now. But it may be best not to linger. So, do we try to remove this man?'

'John,' Connie said. 'And yes. He's as stuck as we are.'

'You don't know that, Connie. You said yourself, you only met him at a festival. Taking him will alert his captor to our presence, and will slow us down. He's a large man. It will take two of us to support him. And that is only if we are able to release him from his chains.'

'We're not leaving him,' Connie said.

Bartitsu groaned. It was a long, painful sound, though there was no echo around the chamber. He shifted on the floor, pushing his arms under his body and lifting his head. 'How'd you get in here, kid?' he said, his voice croaking and dry. He moved stiffly.

The boy had crouched in front of him and was staring at him intently. 'You're not scary,' he said eventually. 'And I don't think you're Crispin Tocketts either.' He lifted the raven cap from Bartitsu's head and inspected it. 'You have funny hair though, and a strange hat. Why?'

Bartitsu coughed out a rough laugh, heaving himself into a hunched sitting position, trying to keep away from the monolith. His arms stuck out awkwardly in front of him, the chains too short to allow him to relax his shoulders. He smiled lopsidedly, his eyes creased in pain. 'I'm not the one running around in an oversized shirt, kid. How'd you –' he paused, shifting his jaw from side to side. He was slurring badly. It reminded Connie of the drunk hunter with the bleeding hand from the festival. She frowned, leaning forward. Bartitsu looked up at the movement and he caught sight of Connie and Bell behind the boy. 'Three. Three of you.' He seemed shocked and dizzy all at once. He rubbed his eyes and grimaced. 'How'd you get in here?'

'I could ask you the same question,' Connie replied.

'Never mind,' Bartitsu said, 'Don't suppose you're any good at picking locks, Explorer Girl?'

'I am,' said the boy. 'If someone can give me some picks.' He seemed excited to be able to help.

'Whoa,' Connie said, 'I'm not untying you until I know what's going on. Why are you here? What is this place? Why are you chained and bleeding? And why do you sound like you're drunk?'

'That's a lot of questions, Explorer Girl.' Bartitsu grinned at her.

'Start answering them.'

'What makes you think I have the answers?' He cocked his head. 'Why shouldn't these two believe you're the one causing all of this. I mean, look at the way you're dressed, and I bet you know more about this place than they do.'

'I don't believe that for a moment. I have been with Miss Rees throughout,' said Bell, stepping in front of Connie. 'Answer her questions, or we shall leave you here.'

'Gertrude Bell, as I live and breathe. More beautiful in person, I have to say.'

Connie rolled her eyes.

Bartitsu flashed Bell a wide smile. Bell flushed. Connie had to admit it, his smile was dazzlingly disarming.

'You won't leave me. She doesn't want to do that.' Bartitsu nodded at Connie. He was slurring less.

'And your story, sir, is already inconsistent,' replied Bell, recovering herself. 'Or were you not unconscious when Connie and I had that debate.'

Bartitsu leaned forward and rubbed his thumbnail along his top lip. He sniffed and looked up, still grinning. 'I was not.' He inclined his head to Bell and then looked over at Connie. 'Forgive me, but I wasn't sure if you were with Marcus or not. It's what I was trying to figure out at the festival.'

'What?' Connie frowned. 'I don't know anyone called Marcus.'

'But you spent quite a lot of time talking to him, Explorer Girl. Guy with a pith helmet? Tandem? Little too pleased with himself. One might say, peacocky.'

Connie guffawed. 'That bloke? He's not my friend. I thought he was creepy.'

'Yeah, he does a good line in that.' Bartitsu smiled.

'Who is this Marcus?' Bell asked.

'He's my partner. Or he was until he broke the Raven's Code. Now, he's wanted for crimes against history, and I have to catch him, a task at which I seem to be failing since he managed to lock me up in here.' He lifted his shackled hands, wincing as if pain was lancing through his arms.

'Does this Marcus have a surname?'

'That's your question?' Connie was astounded at Bell. The boy, too, was staring at her in disbelief.

'And what would your question be, Explorer Girl?' Bartitsu said, leaning his head back. It brushed the monolith. He winced and leaned forward, breathing out heavily.

'Crimes against history? Raven's Code? And you still haven't answered my first question. Who are you and what is this place? Oh, and why are you drunk?'

'Drugged, not drunk, Explorer Girl.' Bartitsu pointed to a small nick under his chin, and continued, 'I'm a Raven. Chosen by the Temporal Council to guard one of the network of Infinity Chambers.' He nodded around at the room. 'That would be this place. You might call it a time machine, but it's much more complicated than that.'

'Yeah, I'll bet,' Connie muttered.

Bartitsu continued, 'Our Code, the Raven's Code, is to safeguard time, because the Infinity Chambers allow us to access any and all moments of it. At will.

'Marcus, my ex-partner at this Chamber, is the one who drugged me at that damn festival, then left me chained and bleeding so he can finalise his exploitation of the Chamber and steal the futures of this region's greatest explorers. He wants their notoriety to improve his own miserable existence. Apparently being a rarefied keeper of time isn't good enough for him.'

Connie felt a sudden warmth flush through her body. She smiled to herself. Of all the things she'd expected to hear Bartitsu say, the theft of the futures of famous explorers was not one. And she was here. Connie felt hope swell inside her chest. A great explorer. This was amazing. Marcus wanted the futures of explorers. Bell already was a notable character, then there was the boy who had something about him and a lot of developing to do, and she was here too, that must mean...

'Not you, Explorer Girl.' Bartitsu broke into Connie's revelation. 'Those two.' He nodded to Bell and the boy. 'Gertrude Bell, James Cook and myself. That's his aim.'

'James Cook?' Connie could barely believe it.

'Yes! That is my name.' The boy was elated. 'James Cook, born in Marton. I remember my name.' He danced a jig on the spot, crying tears of relief and laughter. He stopped. 'How do you know my name, Mr Raven?'

Connie looked at Bartitsu. A fleeting look she couldn't quite make out glanced over his face as he stared at Cook. He became very intent for a moment and then it passed.

'John,' said Bartitsu, inclining his head to the boy, still smiling his Cheshire Cat smile. He seemed incapable of much more movement. Connie was beginning to dislike his grin, as disarming as it was. It seemed to be reflexive rather than genuine.

'I know it because I'm a Raven. That's my job,' he said.

'Then why am I here?' Connie asked.

'Dunno, Explorer Girl. You must've gotten caught in the trail as Marcus left Preston Hall. You really have no business here. You see anything that looked like his ridiculous tandem after you got lost in time?'

Connie deflated. She had, on the escape from Preston Park and in the woods outside the priory, just before she'd fallen from Manāt and Bartitsu had helped her. *Crap.*

Bartitsu jangled the shackles and raised his eyebrows, bringing her back into the chamber. 'You could still help though,' he said. 'Might even be fun.'

Connie stared out at the glinting orbs and crackling mist, her back to the other three. Cook was using some hair grips and a narrow file she'd found in her cross belt to manipulate the lock on Bartitsu's shackles. Bell was hovering over them, watching intently.

Connie growled under her breath. Bartitsu's brash statement had come like a gut punch. She'd just allowed herself to enjoy the moment, the Chamber, the feeling of the infinite, and now it seemed this was as close to her dream as she was ever going to get. Here she was standing alongside James Cook, Gertrude Bell and John Bartitsu, Guardian of Time, and she was just excess baggage. She sighed, looking out at the gleaming pinpricks, droplets and orbs of light, imagining them as stars. In front of her, the pathways extending out from the dais shifted, rising, falling, widening and thinning, some appeared no wider than a strand of hair. They were in constant motion. Connie smiled sadly as she watched the pathways. Her mum would have loved to see this. Connections between dimensions, the building blocks that stitched time and place together.

She wandered to the other side of the plinth, looking for the tunnel entrance that had brought them to the room. There was nothing there, no hint of a bridge leading to the entrance. Just a mass of strands twisting like spaghetti out into the infinite space around her. Connie felt a rising panic. She looked left and right, stalking the edge of the dais, but the pathways simply disappeared into an infinite tangle, each one making a twisted pathway toward an orb. Some were close, others were mere pinpricks of light at an indeterminate distance. She could only step out onto a very small number of the pathways extending away and none led to the tunnel they'd followed to get in.

'Where is the path out?' she asked, striding

around the pulsating monolith to Bartitsu. Bell was helping him to his feet.

Bartitsu reached into a pocket and pulled out a small vial, unstoppering it and holding it to his nostrils. He inhaled deeply, his eyes widening. He replaced the vial and sniffed, coughing lightly. 'Thank you,' he said to Bell, his voice no longer slurring.

She smiled at him.

'What was that?' Connie asked.

'A little pick-me-up. Clears the toxin.' Bartitsu stretched his arms above his head, his back to Connie. Across the back of his jacket and along the length of the arms Connie could make out the same pattern that had adorned his great coat, subtle wings woven into the sturdy fabric. No wonder the legend had said there was a man-sized raven in the cave. She pushed the thought aside.

'Did you hear me?' she asked.

'Relax, Explorer Girl,' he said. 'The pathways do that. I can get you all out. I'm the Chamber's guardian, remember?' He cricked his neck and rolled his shoulders. 'God, it's good to be able to stand up again,' he said.

'How is your head?' Bell asked.

'Pounding.' Bartitsu smiled his wide Cheshire Cat grin. 'But we need to stop Marcus.' He turned to the monolith and stumbled. Bell and Cook caught him.

'Be careful,' Bell said. 'I really think you should

rest a little more. Perhaps the toxin is taking longer to be expelled from your system.'

'No time,' Bartitsu said. 'But I am going to have to ask for your help.' He looked at Connie. 'All three of you. I'm not fit enough – now – to take out Marcus alone.' He touched his temple, wincing.

Connie stared at him and scuffed her foot along the dais. Bartitsu punched her gently on the arm. 'Come on, Explorer Girl. You got the knives, you got the outfit. Don't you want to be a hero?'

'That depends on what you're proposing.'

18

'So, you're saying that you are the reason that they have ravens at the Tower of London?' Bell asked Bartitsu. She was laughing. Connie couldn't believe what she was hearing, but Cook and Bell were staring avidly at Bartitsu, absorbing everything he was saying. Cook had warmed to Bartitsu as soon as he'd learned his own name. That was understandable, but Connie got the impression that Bell was impressed because he was older and confident in his approach. That and the fact Bartitsu had been flattering her for the last half hour. Bartitsu was fiddling with the monolith, using some sort of control element to move subsurface crystals and symbols across it, altering the path of the lasers that bounced around the interior. He seemed to be recalibrating it.

'Well, not me specifically, but Ravens, sure.' Bartitsu shrugged. He was still focussed on the monolith, but he had a lopsided grin on his face. 'I mean, they got the wrong sort of raven, but there's a reason they picked that bird. We stop things from disintegrating.'

'That's just ridiculous,' Connie said. She was standing a little apart from the other three, her thumbs tucked over her belt. She was rolling one leg left and right on the heel of her boot. There was definitely flirting going on between Bell and Bartitsu. It was weird.

'Why?' Bartitsu asked her.

'No, no it's actually very logical, little thing. We see it often in cultural cross- translation,' Bell said. She was smiling at Bartitsu. He glanced across at her, not bothering to hide his attraction. 'I expect this is one of many Infinity Chambers in the world. Am I correct?'

'You are indeed,' he nodded.

'So, the Ravens would be known across millennia and multiple civilisations, and as such we find it throughout global mythologies, but always associated with the same qualities.' She gazed at Bartitsu. 'Marvellous.'

Connie huffed.

'Why don't you join us, Explorer Girl? We could go another round with those knives?' Bartitsu said, finalising his work on the monolith and stepping back from it. Connie smiled tightly at him.

'Why are you dawdling? I thought we had to stop this Marcus?'

'I had to fix the TQC.' Bartitsu nodded at the monolith. 'Time isn't something you just go barging around in, you know. It's delicate.'

'TQC?' Connie asked.

Bartitsu jerked his thumb at the monolith. 'Tactile Quantum Computer. It controls the time points, monitors the fabric of time.' He waved toward the glistening orbs.

'A quantum computer? That's why it's so cold in here.' Connie walked over to the console – it seemed odd to call it a monolith now she knew it was a computer. 'But the crystal would have to be multi-laminated, with a cold infusion constantly running through each layer for it to not overheat. I'm guessing liquid nitrogen?' said Connie.

Bartitsu looked surprised.

Connie ignored him, inspecting the console, her fingers hovering over the crystal. It was intensely cold. 'And there must be some sort of cold absorption in the outer layers, because otherwise we'd need pressurised suits just to be in here. What are the internal crystals for?' she asked, looking over her shoulder at Bartitsu.

'They change the refraction and reflection rates to modulate the time strands,' Bartitsu said. 'Who taught you all this stuff?'

Connie shrugged. 'I'm a physics geek,' she said. 'And, you're gonna need to tell us more than that.' Connie wasn't really sure why she felt so angry that Bartitsu was surprised by her knowledge, but it was there, bubbling away in the pit of her stomach. Maybe because Bell had started to treat her like a child again instead of an equal. That and Bartitsu constantly referred to her as Explorer Girl.

'Like what?'

'Like if time is so delicate, why are you messing with it at all?' She pointed to the pulsing light coming from the console. It was more erratic now, bouncing along the walkways that tethered the time points to the dais.

Bartitsu frowned at her, scratching at the back of his neck. 'We study critical moments in time. There are several that occur here. I had to recalibrate the console because Marcus is trying to subvert one of those moments, which is why the console is struggling. If he succeeds in destroying it, it'll rend time, change history. He'll reweave it, but if we follow him along the path he's begun to set, we're playing catch-up, and we'll lose.'

'This is helping?' Connie pointed to the drifting orbs spiralling around the Infinity Chamber. They'd changed. Several were drifting, with no connecting strand, however narrow, visible amongst the shifting mass of pathways.

'It's complicated.'

'Try me.'

'What's going on?' Bell asked, peering over at them.

'I want our new friend to tell me why, since he's been messing about with the Tactile Quantum Computer,' Connie pointed to the console, 'several pathways from this dais have disappeared.'

'Miss Rees, John is the guardian of this fascinating device. I'm sure he understands its workings much better than you.'

Connie felt herself flush and she looked down. Cook was looking at her from where he was sitting, cross-legged, on the floor. 'I'd like to know,' he said, before shooting her a quick smile.

Bartitsu glanced at him and shrugged again. He swept his dreadlocks over his shoulder. 'Marcus messed up. You two,' he pointed to Bell and Cook, 'Should have been thrown out of your times, isolated beyond help, and certainly you should never have found your way here.'

'Myself and Master Cook, but not Miss Rees?'

'No,' Bartitsu said, smiling apologetically at Connie. 'Sorry, Explorer Girl, but like I said, nothing I know about you says you're special. You're just caught in the cross winds.'

'But why me?' asked Cook.

'You'll see, my friend, you'll see. You'll live it. After we catch Marcus.'

Cook considered and sat back, watching the swirling mists and lights in the wider Chamber. 'They are very much like the night sky,' he commented.

'I don't believe I was just in the cross winds?' Connie felt battered, she was grasping. Surely there was a reason she was here? She at least had a grasp on this technology. Cook and Bell didn't. She couldn't just be tagging along, could she? 'Marcus bumped into me just before I got pulled in. He knocked me down.'

'He did? Huh.' Bartitsu rolled his tongue around his jaw, he seemed to be considering something, then he shrugged. 'Maybe he tagged you accidentally. That could make the Infinity Chamber pull you in. Is there anything in your cross belt? Jacket?'

Connie checked. 'Just your fake business card,' she said, twirling the holographic rectangle between her thumb and forefinger.

'That's just a business card, Explorer Girl, and I don't like your insinuation.'

'I'm not insinuating anything,' Connie said, her cheeks colouring. 'And –'

'Look, Explorer Girl,' Bartitsu cut in. 'Whatever it was probably dropped out at the thicket or the priory. Once you were with Gertrude, you got pulled along with her.'

From behind Bartitsu, Bell gave Connie a conciliatory smile.

'But –' Connie said, grasping.

'You were in the wrong place at the wrong time.' Bartitsu was struggling to contain his frustration. 'I'm sorry, but that's all. You need to stop pretending to be somebody else, looking for anything to feel important.'

Connie felt like she'd been slapped. It must have shown on her face because Bell smiled kindly at her again, which just made Connie want to punch her.

'Did you need to be so abrupt, John?'

Bartitsu looked over at Connie. 'I'm really sorry you were pulled into this. You were having a great day at the hall.'

'You remember me?' Connie asked, surprised.

'Sure, you danced along with the footwork during the demo section. You seemed to know your way around it.'

'Thanks, I do Wado Ryu and fence, it's similar.' Connie laughed, she was rarely complimented on her skill set.

'Wado Ryu?'

'It's a style of karate.'

'Then why not just say karate?' Bartitsu shrugged. 'Anyway, I know you like to have your questions answered, so the reason that some of the strands have gone,' he flicked a finger at the points of light, 'That's because Marcus is causing time implosions. Points where the fabric rends, so he can patch it up with his new version of history. I've isolated those moments for now, but time in this area is fracturing. You'll know about it, though you won't have correctly attributed it until now. The Shearing of Odinsberg? The Day of Great Darkness?'

Connie's eyes went wide. 'Oh, those,' she pointed down at the dais. 'Those are from here, now? Even though they are from years ago?' It was mindboggling.

Bartitsu nodded.

'What is Odinsberg?' asked Cook.

'We call it Roseberry Topping now, kiddo,' said Connie, still staring at Bartitsu. 'You're saying those happened because of Marcus? Because of what he's doing now?'

'Future history.' Bartitsu nodded. 'Some of it's already firm. What do you know about Katherine Routledge?'

'She did a range of important archaeological and anthropological work. Her Easter Island studies are still used by anthropologists today.'

'What about her personal life?' Bartitsu stared at Connie. She frowned. He was evidently angling at something.

'Well,' Connie considered. 'She suffered from paranoid schizophrenia. It was a lifelong condition. In the end she was institutionalised.'

Bartitsu shook his head. 'She wasn't a schizophrenic. I know that from the annals, but I can't undo it now. Your memories – they feel so real, don't they? – But they are new. What you remember as history, is how the shattering of Katherine Routledge's time strand manifested.' For the first time Bartitsu was solemn. He stared at Connie intently. It was mesmerising and terrifying in equal measure. 'There is always an effect, and we don't know where the ripples end. That's why we have to stop Marcus.'

'Dear God,' said Bell.

'I don't want either of you to worry,' Bartitsu said, looking from Bell to Cook. 'We have a chance, a small one, to stop the rest from cementing in the timeline and I need your help. It's not glamorous, but as you can see from Routledge, it's important. And,' Bartitsu spread his arms, 'He killed my team. I could use that footwork of yours' he nodded at Connie before looking at Bell, 'And that brain of yours. What do you say?'

'Can't you just go and pull your team in from a time where that hasn't happened yet?' Bell asked.

'No,' Bartitsu said, shaking his head. 'Some things can't be undone. Threads end, you know?'

'You can count on me, John,' Bell said. 'Connie? Master Cook?'

'I'll help,' Cook said. 'If I can.'

'Absolutely,' Bartitsu grinned. 'Kids can get in anywhere.'

Everyone stared at Connie. 'Sure,' she said, though she was not entirely sure at all.

Bartitsu stood at the console. He'd discarded the control element and had donned a pair of thin gloves covered in filigree wirework. He was using the gloves and the beaked point of his hat, which on closer inspection was an inlaid piece of obsidian, to manipulate the crystals and lights under the surface of the stone. It was far more rapid than his actions with the control element. Connie was fascinated. 'So, it's not just that crystal that can manipulate the control panel?' she asked.

'TQC,' Bartitsu corrected her, 'And no, we can use both. The element is a fine instrument, it allows us to be extremely precise.'

'So, why aren't you using that? Precision seems

to be paramount,' Connie said, rolling the words around, exaggerating them.

'Don't get clever, Explorer Girl. Marcus has screwed the timeline. The gloves allow for more large scale manipulation. It's why we rarely use them, but in this instance it's very necessary.' His hands never stopped moving as he spoke, but the effort it took to make the movements seemed to be increasing. 'I know this machine, you don't.' Bartitsu focussed his attention on the TQC. He tapped a sequence rapidly with his fingertips in a diagonal line at head height, finishing with the point of his cap. It was easy to imagine him as a giant bird, though watching him work on the console was more like watching a potter at work with a piece of clay. He was manipulating elements that laid beneath the surface and the crystals were altering the internal lasers. Connections were breaking and reconnecting under his touch.

'What's happening?'

Connie spun round at the tone in Cook's voice. She'd been so focussed on Bartitsu working the TQC that she'd not given the wider Chamber a second glance. The time points were flickering, blinking and merging. The lights and their associated pathways – time strands – had begun roiling, like a stormy sea crashing about the platform. Transfixed, Connie walked to the edge, staring out at the rapidly shifting points of light.

'It's getting harder to manipulate the time

strands, too many are being cross-drawn,' said Bartitsu.

Connie looked back at him, under the fabric of his jacket, she could see his muscles bulging. Sweat beaded across his forehead. There was a rising sound of wind echoing about the chamber. 'What does that mean?' she shouted, pushing her hair back from her face and grasping it behind her neck.

'It means the best moment for us to exit the Chamber isn't accessible. Marcus – and you three, being where you shouldn't – have damaged the time plane. We're going to have to improvise.' He swept his arm in a wide arc across the glowing stone. It began to pulse quickly. A gust swept across the platform. Connie instinctively pushed Cook, who rolled inward to the centre of the dais, but Connie found herself repelled the opposite way. She landed in a heap on the edge of the platform, her head hanging in the abyss. For a moment she froze, staring at the swirling mass of light. There was something painful now about the mass of tangled pathways, no longer flowing, but puckered and stretched unnaturally. She heaved her head back onto the platform.

'Get to the centre,' Bartitsu shouted above the gale.

Connie felt her extremities flood with adrenaline. She cast another quick look at the roiling pathways, some now thread thin and shearing.

The Chamber itself seemed to be fragmenting.

'What are you doing? It's getting worse!' she shouted.

'Move it, Explorer Girl.' Bartitsu grunted, his face contorted with the effort of controlling the TQC. The lights inside it were flickering faster and more angrily, wheeling and snapping in a syncopated rhythm. Connie tried to pull herself toward the centre. Cook and Bell were huddled at Bartitsu's feet, his great coat between them and the icy console. Bell was holding her great, floppy hat tightly against her head. Connie struggled toward them on all fours, unable to get a strong purchase in the rising wind. She was buffeted by the increasing gale, her feet and hands slipping as she tried to crawl across the smooth stone surface. Inch by inch, Connie wormed her way toward the other three, her belly almost running across the floor.

'Faster,' Bartitsu said, heaving against the monolithic console. 'This is going to get worse before it gets better.'

As if on cue, the stone platform began to shake, tremors running from the TQC and jolting the dais. Light belched out of it in jagged arcs, racing along the time strands erratically. Connie froze. Bell reached out a leg, extending her foot as far toward Connie as she could. Gratefully, Connie stretched out a hand and grabbed Bell's boot. She breathed a sigh of relief, even as the platform began to shake more violently. Bell's boot acted as an anchor, and with one hand firm on it, Connie moved more confidently, pushing herself toward Bell and Cook and dragging herself into the relative calm at the centre of the Chamber. She leaned back against the TQC without thinking. Before she could pull away her back touched crystal. There was warmth emanating from it. Connie sat forward. That had been lucky, but there was no way that console should be warm. It must be perilously close to overheating. She pulled her curly hair back into a rough knot behind her head, jabbing the beak clip into to hold it.

'You couldn't have warned me?' she asked Bartitsu, her voice getting lost in the howling wind.

'I didn't know it was going to be this bad,' he said, his back still to the three.

Connie stared out at the roiling mass of time points. This was nuts. She twisted to see what Bartitsu was doing. His dreadlocks were whipping about in the wind, thudding across his back and into his face. He looked like he was struggling to manipulate the console, his hands kept shifting back and forth, as though he couldn't move the coloured crystals beneath the surface any further. He was breathing raggedly and Connie saw sweat beading on his face. He tensed. Suddenly, he wrenched his whole body to the side, away from the three, his hands dragged along the surface and his fingers tapped out a sequence on the TQC, embedding under-surface crystals into place. Connie blinked at the syncopated rhythm. She wasn't sure why, but the inversion didn't seem to correlate with his earlier manipulation. Connie stared at the fluctuating lasers under the laminated crystal. She could have sworn they were trapped, forced into that space.

The gale dropped. 'What?' Connie looked around the Chamber. It had stilled. Somehow, that was even more unsettling than the storminess that had preceded. The time points waited, blinking as though on standby. It felt wrong.

'Phew. That was a close thing.' Bartitsu let out a harsh laugh, leaning forward, his hands on his knees. 'He must be really going some. I hope you three have your wits about you.'

'Why are they still like that?' Connie asked, a sense of unease rising up her throat as she stared at the shivering time points, the time strands to them evidently straining to continue their complex flow.

'Because it was the only way I could open up the time point that takes us where and when we need to go.' Bartitsu brushed past Connie.

'That's not really an answer though is it?' Connie stared at Bartitsu. 'What's going on?'

'Whatever are you talking about, Connie?' Bell asked.

'We may not have been here long, but this is wrong.' Connie gestured about at the unnaturally still Chamber. 'You talked about a complex weave of time. This entire Chamber seemed to exist as a constantly interweaving mesh. Nothing here is weaving now. Why?'

Bartitsu rolled his shoulders. He let out an exasperated sigh. 'Because Marcus, who knocked me out and chained me up, if you recall,' he said, staring at Connie. 'Has damaged time, damaged time strands and limited our opportunities to intervene. I had to identify *when* he went to, and then fight to find us a way there. Best I could do was to arrive twenty-four hours ahead of him. Ok with you?'

'What you've done sounds damaging.'

Bartitsu raised an eyebrow and laughed. 'It is, Explorer Girl. But what he's doing is worse. You gonna help me stop him or not?' He looked back at Connie. She stared at him.

'What aren't you telling us?'

'Connie, I know how exciting this must be for someone so adept at physics as you,' Bell cut in, 'But do you really think you understand more of the quantum theory that underpins this machine than John? We do not have time to argue.'

'No time?' Connie threw her arms out, 'We're in a damn time machine. I can't think of a better time to get answers than when we have literally all of time at our disposal.'

'Ms Bell's right.'

'Gertrude, please.' Bell flashed a smile at Bartitsu.

He inclined his head toward her. 'Gertrude's right, Explorer Girl,' he said. 'Ordinarily, you'd be right too, but not now. I've – well it's complicated – but effectively, I've paused time so we can exit the Chamber *when* we need to be. But it'll only hold for so long.'

Out of the corner of her eye, Connie saw a flicker. She glanced out at the time points. Several were beginning to vibrate and the time strands out to them, shadow lines spiralling away from the dais, were beginning to shift and glow again.

'See?' Bartitsu said. 'We need to go, now.' He turned on his heel. 'This way.'

They followed him to the other side of the platform, where a pathway, no more than six inches wide, snaked out over the abyss, lit on either side by a glowing sliver light.

'Narrower than I'd hoped, but it's open.' Bartitsu cocked his head to either side. 'Hope you all have good balance.'

Without another word he stepped out onto the pathway, arms extended. He walked with surprising agility across the void to the time point, disappearing through the silvery orb. Connie couldn't tell if the orb had grown to accommodate him, or if he'd shrunk to fit it. He'd not been on the pathway long enough for it to be a vanishing point.

'Next he'll be telling us Lewis Carroll has been to one of these things,' she muttered.

Bell frowned at her. 'I shall go first, then you, Master Cook. Connie, you'll follow Master Cook.'

'Wait, I'm not sure –'

'Miss Rees.' Bell spun to look at her. 'We have work to do. It's not just about our futures,' she gestured to herself and Cook. 'It is about your history, the world you live in and know. Please, no more arguments.' Bell turned back to the path and walked out. She moved with a confident grace despite her skirts, unsurprising for a seasoned mountaineer. Soon, she too had been swallowed by the time point. Cook gave Connie a wan smile.

'I'll be right behind you, kiddo,' she said, grimacing and following him out onto the pathway.

19

Connie stepped out onto a sweeping lawn, lit a silvery grey by a full, bright moon. Behind her, the time point remained, a narrow rend in the air, hazy with a purplish glow. She looked at it for a moment. That must be what the Chamber did when it was under control. There was a beauty to it, much more restful than the electric fog she'd been going through up to this point.

Connie turned away from the time point, looking about her. A light breeze blew through the grass, sending it washing in waves away from Connie. She followed the movement all the way up a low rise and gaped. Standing tall in the moonlight, on top of the small rise, was a stunning manor house. A set of shallow steps led up to the impressive façade, which was split in two by a rounded tower about one third of the way along the building's front. To the left of the tower, the house was two storeys high, with long Georgian style windows set at regular intervals on both floors. To the right of the tower, the house had been extended to three storeys in height, the second floor windows set into a steeply sloping, black-tiled roof. The main entrance was a deep portico, set in the centre of this taller section, and on the far right hand side of the house was a beautiful white painted orangery with four tall arches set in a cross pattern. It was almost two storeys high and glinted in the moonlight. 'Is that Marton Manor?' Connie asked.

'Yes,' replied Bell. 'Though not as I remember it. You seem surprised.'

'It burned down in nineteen-sixty, before my mum was born.'

'Pity,' replied Bell. 'Though I never particularly admired the architecture.'

'We're not here to admire the architecture,' said Bartitsu, pushing something back into his jacket pocket.

'What was that?' asked Connie.

'Just something I use to monitor the time plane.'

'You keep calling it that. Why plane? Why not dimension?'

'Because that's what it is. A plane of existence; we cross it, we monitor it, we protect it, and when we need to, we repair it,' Bartitsu said, scanning the open meadow.

'Why are the trees broken?' Cook asked. Connie looked over at him, he was pointing to a small stand of trees, some of which had been snapped almost clean in half. Craters and gouges ran across the scrubby copse, great gashes in the landscape.

'I had no idea the bombing had been so bad

here,' Connie said.

'Bombing?' asked Bell, 'I'm not familiar with that term.'

'From the war,' Connie said distracted, staring at the splintered trees. She turned to Bartitsu, 'Please tell me you didn't bring us here during the war?'

'That's not something you need to worry about, Explorer Girl.' He sliced his hand across his throat. 'And less of the future history please.'

'What year is it?' Connie asked.

'Nineteen-forty-three, ok?'

'What?'

'Is this year during the war you mentioned, Connie? There is to be a war within Great Britain?' Bell's eyes had widened.

'Gertrude,' Bartitsu caught her arm and looked at her, 'You can't ask too many questions about the near future, ok. You shouldn't be here, shouldn't be seeing this. I know it's hard for an enquiring mind like yours, but please, we need to focus on Marcus.'

'I am not convinced ignorance is a good way for us to proceed, John. What if we are accosted?'

'You won't be. I can promise that.'

'Bartitsu.' Connie was annoyed. 'Why nineteen-forty-three?'

'Because this is *when* he is!' Bartitsu wheeled on Connie. 'Why are you trying to make this something it isn't?'

Connie, Bell and Cook stared at Bartitsu. The

outburst had evidently taken all three of them by surprise. Connie's eyes widened and her jaw went slack. She'd hit a nerve.

Bartitsu pulled himself up and stopped. He closed his eyes and pinched the top of his nose between his thumb and forefinger. 'I apologise,' he said, the words muffled by his hand. He looked up at Connie. 'I don't have time to explain every tiny detail to you. Marcus is here. I don't know why he is here, there is no future for him to steal, but this moment was not one I could access – ever – until you three were there in the Chamber with me. Ravens can only access times like this moment when there is a need. The Chamber self-calibrates. You saw how difficult it was for me to open this path. Whatever happens, you three, and me and Marcus, we're part of history – not observers of it – in this exact moment.'

Connie nodded. Bartitsu had been shaking by the time he'd finished manipulating the TQC, it had cost him a huge amount of effort. 'What do you need us to do?' she asked, feeling embarrassed, though she wasn't sure why.

'Thank you.' Bartitsu inclined his head, before shifting to look behind her. Connie spun, hands reaching for her knives. Her heart was in her mouth. Was Marcus behind her? There was nothing, just a flickering quality to the rend that showed where the time point cut an opening back to the Infinity Chamber.

Bartitsu cursed. 'We don't have much time,' he said, striding past Connie to the opening. 'He must be remotely recalibrating the Chamber. I need to go and hold the strands together. You three need to find him and relieve him of whatever control element he's using.'

'How the hell are we supposed to do that? What does it even look like?' Connie asked, exasperated.

'Figure it out. The control will look like the element I used on the TQC. Marcus is a trained fighter, but lazy with it. Between the three of you, I think you can take him. Gertrude knows how to handle herself and you're pretty handy with those knives, Explorer Girl.'

The rend shuddered, purple electric began to flicker about it and a smell of sulphur permeated the air. Bartitsu strode toward it.

'But Marcus got the better of you,' Connie said to his back, appalled at Bartitsu's attitude.

'So don't let him drug you.' Bartitsu disappeared inside the rend, his hand raised above his head. It sealed rapidly behind him, catching the tail end of his coat. A frayed piece of fabric floated to the floor, loose threads dangling uselessly from frayed edges.

'Would that happen to us if we didn't get through the tear in time?' Cook asked, stooping to pick up the piece of black fabric.

'Let's not find out,' Connie said, extending a hand to him.

'Quite,' said Bell.

Connie looked at her, she seemed disturbed.

'I think we should get out of the open,' said Bell. 'Find somewhere we can rest and plan. John said Marcus would not arrive for twenty-four hours, but we must be ready.' She began walking south across the grass toward the tree line beside the manor house.

'Where are you going?' Connie asked.

'Bolckow's arboretum will provide us with somewhere safe to wait for this Marcus to arrive. Besides which, we need to sleep. Come.'

'Gertrude, we don't know –'

'Which is why we need to take a decision, Connie.' Bell cut across her. 'Whatever year this is, whatever is happening in this beautiful country of ours, no decision is still a decision. I prefer action over cowardice and we are most exposed in the open.'

'It's not cowardice to consider your options,' Connie replied.

'But we should consider them under cover of the trees. Come.' Bell set off again. Connie rolled her eyes and looked at Cook. 'It would feel safer in the trees,' he said.

Connie exhaled a long, slow breath and looked up at the moon. Something caught her attention, but she couldn't quite work it out. 'Yeah,' she said, squeezing her lips into an approximation of a smile as she looked at Cook. 'Come on then, kiddo. I'm sure Gertrude will have a plan.'

Connie sat with her back to a tree. It had a substantial girth and lots of low-hanging, twisted branches. They were sitting in a circular, man-made stand of trees on the southern side of the arboretum, not far from the main house. There was a pleasant coolness to the air, a comfortable summer temperature that was neither humid nor chilly. It should have been peaceful. Instead, Connie's mind was working overtime. She looked up through the branches and reams of thin, spiny leaves, staring at the moon and the stars. The sky was still bothering her and she couldn't quite work out why.

'So, we shall each monitor an aspect of the property. It seems certain to me that Marcus must be seeking something in the manor to achieve his aim. When one of us discovers him, they shall signal the other two and we shall apprehend him.' Bell seemed pleased.

'How?' asked Connie. She looked at Bell. 'We have nothing to apprehend him with. We have nothing to signal each other with, and only I know what he actually looks like.'

'Well, we must work out the details. History depends upon it,' replied Bell. She seemed full of energy, revitalised by having a task to achieve and plan to make. 'Perhaps we would benefit from you making a contribution rather than staring at the heavens, Connie.'

'Contribution?' Connie scoffed and stood. She

began pacing. 'Don't you see how ridiculous this is? We've been abandoned in a time none of us is familiar with, by a man who couldn't wait to leave. He hasn't given us the faintest idea of Marcus's skill set or goal here, but somehow we're supposed to catch him? How do we even know he's coming to the manor house?'

'Henry Bolckow is a titan in Middlesbrough. I imagine there are many things in the manor that Marcus may require to execute his plan.'

'You imagine?' Connie stared at Bell. 'Imagining isn't going to help us. We need to know. Bartitsu should have given us more information.'

'He couldn't anticipate the damage to the time plane.' Bell waved a hand dismissively.

'Now you're an expert?' Connie asked, disbelief colouring her voice.

'You agreed to this in the Chamber, along with the two of us.'

'I thought we were going to help Bartitsu, not do it for him. He, supposedly, knew what we needed to do when we got here. So why didn't he tell us before he left?' Connie was feeling increasingly angry.

'Miss Rees, you've been called to a great task. Are you really going to shy from it because someone didn't tell you exactly what to do?'

'This task is not achievable! Your plan, such as it is, doesn't give us the faintest chance of success. Spot him, catch him. That's not a plan.'

'It is a more concrete plan than you have thus

far offered. We must work it out.'

Connie's nostrils flared. *Work it out.* 'That's about the ninth time you've said that.'

'Please don't argue,' said Cook. 'I'm worried, and I don't want you two to be angry with each other.'

Connie leaned forward and rubbed her hands across her eyes.

'Do you have a better idea, Miss Rees?'

'No,' Connie said. 'But we can't afford to split up. Marcus took down Bartitsu. How did he manage that? Bartitsu is an accomplished fighter – I have first hand experience of it.' She rubbed her arms as she recalled the clanging numbness she'd felt when Bartitsu had battered her during the demonstration at Preston Hall. She huffed out a breath. 'One of us, alone, has no chance of successfully accosting Marcus. We need to work out why he might access the manor and which entry he's likely to use.' She looked over at the manor. It was a great grey shadow in the moonlight, the moon gradually aligning with the weather vane atop the tower. Cook looked too, his face a half grimace, the look of a child trying to show concentration.

'What's that?' he pointed up to the weather vane. With the moon illuminating it, a series of rune-like cut-outs in the steel stanchion had become visible.

Bell looked. 'Oh,' she said, 'Those markings are similar to the ones we saw on –'

'The TQC.' Connie stopped her pacing as she finished Bell's sentence. She turned to Bell, 'Gertrude, was Bolckow involved in anything that might have been called mysticism, or the occult, or even just plain old antiquities?'

'Not as far as I'm aware,' Bell said. 'But I was barely ten when the man died.'

'Still, it's too coincidental,' Connie said, rubbing her lip, her gaze fixed on the runes. 'So, maybe there's something in the tower, or on that weather vane, that Marcus needs.'

'That's a stretch,' Bell said.

'It's the best hypothesis we've got. I think he wants something in that tower.' Connie gestured to the dome, just visible beyond the steep grooves of the west side of the house.

'The ground to the front of the manor is too open. I doubt he would approach the front entrance if that's where he's going,' Cook said.

'Agreed,' Bell said. The two of them seemed to be latching on to Connie's idea. Connie gulped. It was just a hypothesis.

'And I believe that door there under the loggia is ajar.' Bell pointed to a door in the shadow of an ornate stone colonnade.

Connie squinted. Bell was right. 'Yes, looks like it's broken.'

'So, Connie. Do you have a contribution?' Bell asked.

Connie took a deep breath. *No point complaining and then staying quiet, Connie.* 'Ok. Yes, we can get in via that entrance. Gertrude, do you know the internal layout at all?'

'I recall visiting once with Papa.' For the first time Bell was hesitant. 'Of what

relevance would this knowledge be?'

Connie gulped again. Gertrude Bell was deferring to her. It was a strange feeling. She looked back at the stanchion of the weather vane. It was the only possible thing they'd seen here that gave them a handle. She cocked her chin toward it. 'It's not just the markings. The base of that vane looks like a silhouette of the TQC,' she said. 'I don't think we need to stake out the house. I think we need to stake out the tower, and that means we can hide inside, set a trap and wait for Marcus to walk right into it. We set it right, we won't need to fight him at all. Fight your enemy where he is not.' She looked at Cook. 'Can you set a snare trap? Catch rabbits?'

The boy nodded. 'Never caught a man before though,' he said.

'Just think of him as a big rabbit.' Connie smiled tightly and looked across at Bell, 'What do you think?'

Bell pursed her lips. 'I'm not comfortable with us being trapped inside a ruin. I've spent some time studying ancient monuments. Architecture left to ruin can be very dangerous.'

'This whole situation is dangerous, Gertrude, but I think we're safer concentrating our efforts than spreading them thin.'

Bell nodded. 'We should get inside, then. I estimate a maximum of nineteen hours before Marcus should arrive.'

20

Connie pulled hard on the cord. It came away from the curtain rail with a cloud of dust. The house was in extremely bad repair. In the next room she could hear Bell's feet clipping across the exposed wooden floors. A shadow appeared through the gloaming and Bell coughed into view. 'Well, this is most depressing,' she said walking back into the room, her arms full of re-covered cord.

'What is?' Connie kept pulling on her length of rope, heaving it clear of the curtain rail. It fell to the floor, along with a large section of plaster work.

'The disrepair of this house. It was once very fine. A great shame.'

There was a loud crashing sound as more plaster shattered across the floor, cracking three of the floorboards. A cloud of white dust floated up and coated Connie. She coughed and patted herself down, brushing off as much as she could. The wafting dust sent her into a fit of sneezes again.

'Nicely done,' said Bell. She reached past Connie and pulled the cord rope out of the shattered plaster, coiling it roughly into a bundle. 'Do dust that out of your hair, Connie. It looks ridiculous.' Bell walked across the galleried room and out onto the landing. Connie leaned forward and rifled her hands through her hair. The dislodged dust sent her into another coughing fit and it was a couple of minutes before she could follow Bell.

She crossed the landing to the stairs to the top floor. Half way up, six stairs had rotted away, leaving the top floor of the building inaccessible. Connie looked at the gap. Definitely too far to jump, even from above. Satisfied, she jogged back down the stairs to the tower, all that was left now was to make the tower room the most appealing route for Marcus to get to the domed roof.

Three thuds broke her train of thought. Connie turned her head, frowning. Plasterboard halfway down the landing was puckered and split outwards, wallpaper torn around it. Connie crept toward it, wondering what could have caused it. She pressed her fingers to the plaster, glancing behind her to make sure there was no one there. She looked at the marks on the wall. 'Bullets?' she said, using her finger to scrape one of them out of the plasterwork. The crushed bullet laid in her hand, a brassy, dented mess. Connie looked across the light well to the other side of the landing, where the stairs were. There was nothing there. She closed her fingers around the bullet and went to join the others.

Connie sidled through the door into the tower room. The hinges had long since broken and the door was wedged firmly in place. Cook was sitting cross-legged in the centre of the floor, deftly weaving the cord into a thicker rope. He tied off a section and passed it to Bell. 'Can you cut the loose ends, please?'

Bell looked at Connie. 'Are your knives sharp?'

Connie nodded. 'Enough. I used the whetstone you found.'

Bell held the ends taut and Connie sliced carefully through them. 'Good work on that, kiddo,' she said, sheathing the knife. 'How are we getting on? We must've been going for a few hours now.' She looked out of the window. The north lawns were colouring, the grey hue filling out with green as the night waned. Connie stifled a yawn.

'I just need to set the spring and coil the rope,' Cook said, leaping up and dragging a chair across to where he'd balanced a make-shift snare frame. He was excited. Connie could hear it in his voice. It worried her. He was only ten. She watched the stars begin to fade from the sky. There was that, too. The setting moon, the fading stars. She wasn't sure why the sky was bothering her, and the fact she couldn't work it out bothered her more.

'What's concerning you?' Bell asked, joining her at the window.

Connie sighed. Now was not the time to lose Bell's trust by rambling on chaotically about a weird sky. She opened her fist, revealing the battered bullet. She looked at Bell and swallowed.

'Oh,' said Bell. 'Was there any sign of the shooter?'

Connie shook her head.

'Then it could have been here for years, Connie. This house, much to my chagrin, has been derelict for decades.'

'I heard them thump into the wall, Gertrude,' Connie said quietly. 'What if he's already here?'

Bell took the bullet out of Connie's hand and patted it, 'Even if you are right, we must still proceed. It is our only way home.'

Connie pushed her tongue into her cheek. Bell was right, they had no other options, but it just seemed insane. The sound of Cook humming floated across the room to them. Connie took a deep, juddering breath.

'Anything else?' Bell said, cocking her head.

'Him.' Connie nodded toward Cook. 'He's ten. He shouldn't be doing this. Any of it.'

Bell shrugged. 'In his time, children not much older than he go to sea. They are ships boys, apprenticed early to make a living. They work. Cook himself labours alongside his father at the farm. Besides which, you are not much older, Connie. And you are here, trying, like us, to get home.'

'It's gone a bit further than that, wouldn't you

say?'

'You're doubting your plan?' Bell asked.

Connie glanced at Bell. She was studiously gazing out of the window. 'Yep,' she said.

'You do not have the luxury of doubt, Connie.' Bell fixed her with a calm stare. 'We are here. We must do as we can to achieve our aim, with the tools and information at our disposal. Your plan fits with the information we have and makes best use of it. It can do no more. Do not expect it to.'

'You approve of my plan?'

'I would not have co-operated if I had not, Connie.'

Connie couldn't quite believe it. She'd thought Bell had only gone along with her because she was at least agreeing to do something.

'It's ready,' Cook said.

Connie smiled at Cook. He was standing in the middle of the room twisting his shirt about his hands. He was watching them anxiously, waiting for approval.

'Looks great, kiddo,' Connie said, inspecting the snare trap carefully. It wasn't visible from the doorway and the ground rope was concealed amongst some wood on the floor. 'And it'll trigger as soon as Marcus comes in the room?'

'It should, it's hard to scale it up.' Cook looked worried.

'That's ok, you did better than either of us could,' Connie said.

'Now what?' he asked.

'Now, we wait, and hope I guessed right. This way.' Connie led them out of the room, carefully skirting the trap. Once Bell and Cook were clear she pulled a broken chair across the open space, making the trapped, rubble laden floor the only traversable area. Hopefully, that would be enough for Marcus to walk across it and get himself snared. If not, well, Connie didn't want to think about that.

She gulped and turned to face the other two. 'Come on,' she said, guiding them across the landing and into a room opposite the tower. It was dark and dusty inside. The windows in this room had been covered with drapes. Connie let her eyes adjust to the gloom and the shapes of bedroom furniture began to materialise. A bed, chaise longue, easy chair, dressing mannequin and several chests of drawers took shape in the halflight. Connie jumped at the sight of the mannequin, but a closer look showed it was headless, so nothing to worry about. She looked back out of the door, across the landing. They had a good view of the tower room, but with their door partly shut they should be obscured from view. 'This should do,' she said.

'I agree,' said Bell, inspecting the thick layer of dust with her finger. 'Although Marcus may realise we have been tramping about the house. The dust is quite thick where it has been undisturbed.'

Cook yawned.

'Get some sleep, kiddo,' said Connie, pushing him toward the bed. She looked at Bell, 'Good point. You watch him. I'll go see what I can do about our tracks.'

'I can do it,' said Bell.

'No.' Connie shook her head. 'I'm not the one history needs to get back.' She walked out of the room.

Marcus flowed through the trees and bushes to the southern side of the house. The three out-of-times had entered it some forty minutes ago. They'd made a beeline for the tower room, directly beneath the marker. He knew the girl was smart, but he'd not expected her to be able to convince the others, particularly Bell. That one had a reputation for stubbornness that matched her bravery, and it was a reputation well-earned from what he'd seen.

He crouched in the shadows of a huge tree, checking each window on the first storey methodically, searching for any sign of movement. It was possible they weren't heading for the tower, but he couldn't risk checking from the front of the building, where their location would be most obvious. The lawns were open, he'd be spotted instantly if any of them glanced out of a window. For once, he wasn't pleased by the brightness of the moon, though usually he loved it. Because of Imara. She adored the stars and everything associated with astronomy. He remembered first meeting her, five years ago. They would never have met of course, if they had lived their lives linearly. But they did not. Unconsciously, he twisted the wedding band on his left hand.

Imara had astounded him from the first moment he'd seen her, sitting atop this very house, staring avidly at the moon, her skin shining under its light like some glistening obsidian jewel. He'd never quite understood how her skin, with its rich mahogany tints, glowed like that. Maybe it was just the way he'd been drawn to her, an echo in his mind, but it was so clear. From the moment he'd first spoken to her, convinced she was another Raven, for no black woman would have been sitting atop a nineteenth century English industrialist's house as she had been, her intelligence, her grasp of fundamental quantum mechanics, her innate sense of fun, had absorbed him. What he'd been doing for near two decades, she claimed she'd been doing for only two or three years, yet she'd been the one to show him how to explore the wonders of a non-linear existence. The possibility had never occurred to him before Imara came along.

For two blissful years they had wandered all of time through the Gisborough Chamber and discovered how humanity had turned, the minor moments that had shaped lives, which in turn shaped millennia and the trajectory of human development. Imara had shared it all unhesitatingly, taught him so much more than the Temporal Council. She was a savant of the Infinity Chamber, unusual, but not unheard of for someone who, linearly, predated him. The way she manipulated the Infinity Chamber was light and harmonious. It was beyond anything any Raven he'd met was able to achieve, and the only way by which an Antiquarian – the term for those whose lives predated the Chambers – could join the Order. No member of the Temporal Council would have turned Imara away.

Yet even she could not access certain time points. She'd said only that those felt solid to her, like they were part of her own path, or maybe his, or maybe both. It made sense in a way. While the Order didn't really understand it, they had known for some years that although time wasn't linear, humans were. The Infinity Chambers, sometimes frustratingly, accounted for human limitations. Imara hadn't worried about it though, and his concern had dissipated as she absorbed him, distracted him, made him too confident in his role.

And then, it had happened. He'd had the sense she'd known it was coming. She met with him less frequently. Avoided him, tried to disentangle from him, never once denying how much she loved him, and when she'd told him why, it had ripped him apart. That she would exclude him from this. Go through a vortex that he could not reach. Leave him, when they had so much. He'd returned to the TQC, and forced it, with as much strength as he was able to muster with his partner, to connect to one of his chronological time points. To try and reach Imara. He'd seen her. Briefly. For one moment he'd thought he could have it back. But it was a mistake. One he paid for and was still paying for. One others would pay for if he didn't correct it.

Now, everything he'd tried to prevent was playing out as Imara had told him it would. Prophecy. He'd thought it a superstition, an ancient way of explaining the chaos that could sometimes result from misuse of the Chambers. Now he knew better; it was the anticipation of the points of his future history that were set, unchangeable, points that he'd been given the tools to navigate, if he would just pay attention and flow. Imara had given him the key, to go with the current of time, accept its pattern and shape only what was malleable. But the girl was the only way he could succeed, and she was already one step ahead of him. What did she know? How precarious was his mission now?

He shook himself out of the reverie, there was movement on the landing, a flit of grey as someone headed to the stairs. He pulled the control element into his hand. It crackled, sending electric jolts up his arm. The moment of flow was ebbing. He did not have much time to push the girl through. He set off toward the house.

Connie made her way gingerly down the main staircase. It had once been very grand, but now was seriously dilapidated. As she walked she was horrified by the evidence of their passing. Great swathes of dust and debris had been shifted, it was as though some large animal had been flailing about in the hall. A good thing then that Gertrude had noticed the problem otherwise Marcus would have been aware of their arrival before he ever got to the tower room. She reached the bottom of the stairs and looked about her. A great stone mantlepiece stood on one side of the room, its yawning hearth a black pit filled with feathers. Connie shivered. She didn't like being in the deserted house alone, it was dark and shadowy. It would be very easy for Marcus to hide in here.

There was a scuffle down the hall behind her. Connie spun, her chest tightening at the unexpected sound. A lone butterfly with bright blue wings fluttered across her line of vision. Connie shook her head at the bizarre sight. *What on earth?* The butterfly floated away amidst the dust and Connie disregarded it. It wasn't important.

She peered into the gloomy passageway where she'd heard the sound. There were no windows in it, it must've led to the kitchens or servants' quarters. Connie pursed her lips. That was likely where she'd find a broom, or something else to try and swirl the dust about anyway. She set off into the passage feeling furtive, resisting the urge to put on her phone light. If Marcus was in here, it would be stupid to highlight exactly where she was. The only concession she made to her unease was to draw one of the knives. She held it low against her thigh and tiptoed on, passing closed doors on either side. She checked each one but they were stiff, clearly unmoved for decades. The air in the passageway was thick with dust. She sniffed, her nose itching badly. She shook her head, trying hard to hold her sneeze and walked on, the tension in her shoulders easing as she stepped across the threshold at the end of the passage, out into the kitchen. The air here was much clearer. She blew out three times to clear her nose and scanned the room.

Silvery light from the moon filtered through dusty windows. There was no sign of anyone else in the room. It was still, abandoned like the rest of the house. Against a far wall Connie spied a dilapidated broom. She breathed a sigh of relief and strode across to it, sheathing her knife and collecting it from where it was hung near a stained and pitted mirror. As she turned away something caught her eye. She spun back to look in the mirror, adrenaline pumping freely through her veins. There was nothing, but Connie was frozen. The mirror surface was virtually useless it was so browned, and yet, she knew she'd seen something. She kept staring at it, willing the black depths to show her what had moved.

'Please don't be him, please don't be him,' she muttered quietly beneath her breath. She could feel herself bouncing on her toes, a tiny action that would allow her to shift quickly, but it also gave a rhythm to her movements. A predictability. Conscious of the problem, she willed herself to stillness, remaining completely focussed on the mirror.

She stared. It felt an eternity, like staring into an abyss. The dark patterns on it remained resolutely still. Connie was beginning to think she'd imagined the whole thing when a shadow moved. Connie's breath, a silent scream, caught in her throat.

She exhaled. It was a pigeon. The bird shuffled out from the Aga, head bobbing as it pecked through the dust. Connie turned and looked at it. 'Don't skulk in shadows,' she said to the bird, letting out a rattling breath. She was way too jumpy.

Shaking her head, Connie strode out of the kitchen, an idea forming as she caught sight of the swirls the pigeon made in the dust.

21

Did you manage to erase the signs of our passage?' asked Bell. She was reclining in the arm chair having moved it to give her a better view of the entrance to the tower room.

Connie nodded. It had been a difficult task. 'Not sure how well I've done. I got some inspiration from a pigeon, but it was harder than I expected it to be. Provided he's focussed on whatever it is he's after, he'll miss it.'

'And if he's not?' asked Bell, cocking her head.

'I shouldn't expect my plan to do more than it's able.'

Bell nodded silently.

Connie looked over at Cook. He was curled on his side on the bed, breathing steadily. 'How long has he been sleeping?'

'A while,' replied Bell.

Connie stifled a yawn and flopped down on the chaise longue at the end of the bed opposite Bell. Bell glanced at her.

'You really should take the opportunity to rest, Connie,' Bell said. 'I have energy enough to take the first watch, and I estimate approximately nine hours before Marcus arrives, if John was correct that we are here twenty-four hours ahead of him.'

'There's something odd about the sky,' Connie said, staring out of the window and frowning. The moon was rising behind the house. It hung in the sky, fat and low. Connie lifted her hand and traced a finger between the moon and its nearest constellation, using the upright lines of the window to gauge the angles of intersection. There were more stars than she was used to. It was difficult, as the window was smeared and pitted. She did it again, shifting her hands about to frame the moon and the stars, squinting. There was something strange about the profusion of stars, but her brain was bugging up with exhaustion.

'What do you mean?'

'The constellations, the moon' Connie said, still twisting her hands about to try and make sense of the sky. She dropped her hands. *How did you not realise sooner, Connie?* 'The moon is in the wrong place. It was setting when we left the tower room. Now it's rising behind the house.' She squinted at the stars. 'And there are twice as many stars as there should be, some are in the wrong place.'

'The stars move relative to the earth each year,' Bell said. 'Perhaps you have a different sky in your time.'

'I know that,' Connie shook her head, 'But the tangents are all wrong. The arc of the moon. This is wrong.' She yawned, unable to stifle it this time and pushed herself out of the chair.

'Where are you going?' Bell asked.

'I have a bad feeling,' said Connie, slipping out of the room and heading for the front of the house.

Connie peeked through the tower room door and gulped. The moon was setting over the open parkland to the west of the house. Connie walked back to the bedroom, sliding through the door. 'We have a problem, Gertrude,' she said, rubbing her forehead.

Bell raised a quizzical eyebrow.

'There are two moons,' Connie said.

'Pardon?' Bell sounded confused, 'What do you mean?'

'I have no idea,' Connie said. 'Maybe time is overlaying itself?' She rubbed her head and yawned.

'You need to sleep, Connie, you are imagining things.'

Connie shook her head, 'No, I'm not. I think we should leave. I don't trust Bartitsu, our plan is precarious, and now there are two moons. One either side of this house, so low in the sky that we didn't see them both until we were right in the middle, here.'

'You don't trust John? Why ever not?' Bell seemed genuinely surprised.

'You do? And you aren't worried about the extra moon in the sky?'

'I can do nothing about an additional celestial body, Connie, but John explained that Marcus ruptured time. His explanation fits with everything we have experienced, including this new phenomenon. Even your earlier encounter with this Marcus at the festival. You yourself have identified the marker Marcus must be seeking here. We have responded to the situation, we must not falter now.'

'Bartitsu's explanation fits the known facts. He didn't want to answer questions about anything beyond that. Doesn't that bother you?'

'That is an oddly disingenuous way of phrasing the matter.' Bell's voice was stern.

Connie took a deep breath, which quickly turned into another stifled yawn. 'Why am I so tired? We were at Gisborough Priory only –' She checked her watch. It had stopped. 'Never mind. It doesn't feel too long ago though, does it?'

'Sleep,' said Bell. 'Perhaps you are feeling the effects of the Infinity Chamber. It may be affecting your judgement.'

'Maybe Bartitsu's flattery is affecting yours.'

'I will put that ignoble slur down to exhaustion, Connie,' said Bell. 'I will not do so again. Rest, please.'

Even in the dark, Connie could see that Bell had become rigid, her mouth a thin line. She looked at the moon again, taking long, slow blinks. 'Wake me for a watch, will you?' she asked, her head drooping.

'Of course,' said Bell.

'Connie, wake up. You were right, something is

wrong.'

Connie blinked rapidly. Bell's concerned face took focus close to her own, she looked uncharacteristically shaken. 'What's,' Connie stifled a yawn, 'What's wrong?' she said, pushing her hair back behind her head and freezing. She could hear an unsettling crackling sound coming from beneath them from roughly where the huge mantlepiece in the hall would be. Slowly, she turned her head to look for the fireplace in the bedroom. There was a faint, reddish glow emanating from it and there was a warmth in the air accompanied by the smell of burning. Connie sat up. 'The house is on fire.'

'I realise that,' said Bell. 'What year did you say the manor burned down?'

Connie did not like the anxiety she could hear in Bell's voice. 'Nineteen-sixty.'

'That is what I feared. I believe I know the reason for your two moons. Look.' Bell stumbled over the words as she pulled Connie over to the doorway.

Connie gasped. Marton Manor was in full blaze. Fire was licking up the woodwork on the landing, rising rapidly toward the roof. A crashing sound made Connie crouch low, and the sound of glass splintering in the heat was followed by a shower of broken shards falling down the stair well, shattering even more on the tiled floor of the hall below. 'I thought he said we were in nineteen-forty-three,' Connie said.

'John did say that, yes.'

'Well, we aren't now. We've shifted time again.'

'How? John –'

'I don't care about bloody John Bartitsu.' Connie pushed herself to her feet and stalked to the window, assessing whether they could escape that way. The southern loggia, where they'd found the open door was about eight feet away. Too far to jump. Connie cursed. 'We were never in nineteen-forty-three. The house wasn't damaged in the war. That came after. We shouldn't have been in a damaged house if we had ever been in nineteen-forty- three.' The heat of the fire burned Connie's cheeks. If the air in this room was this hot, the manor had evidently been on fire for some time. There were great belching clouds of black smoke rising around the building, obliterating the sky. Connie inhaled and coughed, the smoke burning on her throat and eyes. 'We need to get out. Down the main stairs, it's the only option. Where's Cook?'

Bell looked at the bed, frowning. Her eyes were unfocussed. The bed was empty. 'I have no idea.'

'What do you mean, you have no idea? You were the one keeping watch.'

'I, I was.'

It was the first time Connie had heard Bell stutter. The woman was shaken. *No time, Connie.* She strode across the room to the bed and placed a hand on the mattress, breathing a sigh of relief. It was warm. 'At least he's in this time, somewhere

in the house. Or the grounds,' she said looking at the indentation on the mattress. 'And he's
only just left.' Connie spun around. Cook was nowhere to be seen. 'Why wouldn't he wake us?'

A flaming rafter crashed down on the far side of
the bed. The dusty sheets were alight
in moments.

'No time to consider, Connie. The house is unstable.' Bell pulled her toward the door.

'What about Cook?'

'We can't find him if we get trapped in the
blaze,' Bell said, lifting her scarf about her face,
covering her nose against the smoke. Her eyes
had a strange haze about them, or maybe it was
the smoke. Before Connie could check, Bell disappeared through the door, hunkering down as
she ran across the landing to the stairs.

Connie followed her, her hand over her mouth
to protect herself. The heat was intense, beads of
sweat rolled into Connie's eyes. She blinked furiously, stumbling behind Bell, who was edging
down the first flight of stairs, as close to the bannister as she could be. It made sense, the wooden
struts there would be stronger. Connie followed
her, acutely aware of the licking flames all about
her. The smoke was getting thicker.

Connie stumbled on, barely able to see until
she felt something crunch under her feet. Shattered glass. She must be at the base of the stairs.
That meant the exit door was about fifteen feet
diagonally to her left. She squinted through the

smoke, she couldn't believe the heat in here, most of the house was rubble, how was it burning so intensely? A tiny gap appeared in the smoke. It was venting through a door, eddying around the gap. Connie coughed and lunged toward it, hoping Bell was still ahead of her.

Connie emerged into the loggia, running for the south lawn, coughing and sputtering. At the base of a shallow flight of stairs she stopped. Bell was hunched over, panting, her hand clutched at her throat, her red hair in unkempt strands. Her hat was missing.

'Breathe, Gertrude. Breathe.' Connie panted the words out through great lungfuls of air, hands on her knees.

Bell glanced over at her, coughed and dragged her hand down over her face, scratching at her throat. 'What's this?' Bell pulled something out of the neck of her dress, holding it out and studying it in the moonlight.

Connie heaved herself over to get a look at the thing. Her heart sank. On Bell's palm was a tiny blow dart, fletched with blue feathers. Connie recalled that dart, it was just like the ones on Marcus's costume. The ones that shouldn't have fit with his colonial hunter outfit, but somehow had. Connie thought back to their first encounter with Bartitsu in the Infinity Chamber. He'd shown Connie the mark on his throat where Marcus had drugged him, and Bell had pulled her dart from the same spot. Bartitsu's parting warning rang in her head, *So don't let him drug you. Oh no.* She suddenly felt guilty for doubting Bartitsu. He'd saved her life at the priory, probably from the man who'd set the blaze. 'I think I was wrong,' she said, picking up the dart. 'We are in nineteen-forty-three, and so is Marcus. Worse, he knows we're here, and I think he set that blaze to kill us.'

'I thought you said the manor doesn't burn down for another decade or so.' Bell coughed loudly.

'Maybe he decided history needed to change to tie up some loose ends.' Connie stood up and inspected the tip of the tiny dart, holding it up to the moon. There was only one moon now, whenever they were, it was a single moment in time. She hoped Cook was still trapped with them.

She inspected the dart. Its point glistened, slick with a clear substance, like it was varnished. 'I'm gonna guess this knocked you out. Do you have a handkerchief?'

Bell handed her one silently. Connie wrapped the dart and put it into her waist pouch. She turned to look at the burning manor house.

'That's odd,' she said.

'I agree, a building burning down years before it is supposed to is very odd,' said Bell.

'No, it doesn't look like the fire has caught as much as it felt like it had inside, look.'

Bell turned to the building. The way she started

convinced Connie she was right. The house was no longer billowing black smoke, the orange glow was contained to the central hall, and the blaze had barely left the ground elevation. 'Are we watching a fire go backwards?' asked Connie, unable to process what she was seeing.

'I have no idea,' replied Bell, her mouth slightly open as she stared at the derelict building. She blinked and turned to Connie. 'You said that dart was likely from Marcus. That must be how I missed this blaze that seems to have never been.' She waved a hand at the derelict, but unburned manor house. 'If you're right, Connie, that means Marcus is here and we have no idea where Master Cook is. Do you think Marcus could have absconded with him after he drugged me?'

'Marcus is here?'

Connie spun round. Cook was standing behind them, looking confused. 'How did you get down here? Are you alright?' she asked, running to him and grabbing him by the shoulders. Relief flooded through her when she saw he was unhurt.

'I'm ok. I saw that and wondered what it was.' He swung round and pointed behind him to an urn set on a pink granite plinth. The whole thing was placed on a circular set of flagstones. Connie grimaced. She'd forgotten about the urn.

'Why did you leave the room, kiddo? We were supposed to lie in wait for Marcus.'

Cook looked abashed. 'I'm sorry Connie, I

looked out of the window and saw the urn. I wondered what it was, so I went to look.' He looked at her, wide-eyed. 'I was going to tell you, but you were both sleeping and I thought it was safe, that we had ten or so hours. I didn't know he was already here.' The boy hung his head, shoulders slumped.

'Dear child,' said Gertrude, gesturing behind herself to the not-burning house. 'Did you not think? Anything could have happened to you. We could have been separated by another visitation of that noxious fog.'

'I'm sorry, Miss Bell. I didn't mean any harm.' Cook couldn't meet Bell's eyes.

Connie gave him a one-armed hug. 'Leave off him,' she said to Bell. She squeezed Cook's shoulder and whispered conspiratorially, 'Never mind. Turns out you were safer out here.' She tried to guide him away from the urn.

'It has my name on,' said Cook.

Connie froze. 'What does?' she asked, knowing the answer.

'The urn, and the flagstones. It says "I had ambition not only to go farther than any man had ever been before, but as far as it was possible for a man to go. Captain James Cook, seventeen-twenty-eight to seventeen-seventy-nine." That's me, isn't it? I become a captain, and I die when I'm fifty one?'

'Yes.' Connie nodded. There was no point lying about it.

'Oh. Do I join the army?'

Connie smiled. Kids had a weird way of looking at the world sometimes. 'I can't tell you that, kiddo, you'll have to figure it out yourself. Come on, we need to get under cover.' Connie looked up at the sky. It was starting to get light. What on earth was going on with the hours of the day? Embers floated on the air and the sound of a fire crackling rose and fell behind her.

She started across the lawn, her arm still around Cook's skinny shoulders, 'Gertrude?' she called when she didn't hear Bell move behind them. 'Gertrude?' Connie turned.

Bell was frozen, staring at the manor. Connie followed her gaze up to the loggia and felt her heart skip a beat. Standing on the flat roof of the colonnade was a tall, striking silhouette. The man was no longer wearing a pith helmet, but his frame was clearly outlined, the costume of a colonial hunter, complete with long, mud-splattered cavalry boots. Marcus was staring at them, dual pistols trained on both Connie and Gertrude.

'What do we do now?' Cook whispered to Connie.

'Exactly as I say, Master Cook, and everything shall be fine,' said Marcus.

22

Connie stared at the man on the loggia. She swallowed.

'Are you scared?' whispered Cook.

'Terrified,' Connie replied.

'Miss Rees, Master Cook, come and stand alongside Miss Bell, please.' Marcus flicked the pistol, ushering the two of them back toward Bell.

Connie complied silently, pushing Cook behind her as she walked forward.

'No, no. Three abreast.'

They reached Bell. Connie cast her an anxious sideways glance. Bell shook her head almost imperceptibly. Connie understood. *Don't do anything stupid.*

'What are you doing up there?' Bell asked. Connie couldn't help but be impressed by the woman's imperious tone, though she had no idea how Bell was managing it.

Marcus shrugged, 'Safest place to be really, until you three kindly exited.' He walked to the end of the colonnade roof and sat on the edge, holstering one pistol. The other remained steady on Bell.

'Why?' she asked.

'Because this part doesn't burn down, does it

Connie?' Marcus flashed Connie a grin. Connie shivered. Marcus was behaving as though the two of them were friends. It was disturbing. She looked at Bell. The other woman was staring daggers at her.

'How does he know your name? John said you were not of consequence to his plans.'

Connie shook her head furiously. 'It's not what you're thinking. I know because the loggia is the only part of the house that exists in my time. It doesn't burn and it's never demolished.'

'But how does he know your name?' Bell hissed the words out between clenched teeth.

'Good question,' Connie said, nodding at Bell, desperately trying to maintain eye contact. She looked at Marcus. He had his head cocked to one side and the way he was holding the pistol was almost lazy. 'How do you know my name?'

He grinned. 'I liked your trap,' he said to Cook, levering himself over the edge of the roof and dropping nimbly down into the bushes beside the loggia. 'Little obvious, but points for effort.'

Cook was staring wide-eyed at Marcus, who jogged down the grass slope toward them. His sabre was gone. In its place was a dark grey cylinder, smooth at one end and leather bound closest to his hip, approximately one foot in length and an inch in diameter. It mirrored another cylinder on his other hip. They both bounced at his sides as he came down the hill toward them. Connie stared at them, transfixed. When she looked up, somehow, he had two pistols in his hands again. Connie hadn't even seen him move to redraw the second. He was slick. That was worth knowing.

'And I know a lot about you as it happens, Connie Rees.' He gazed at her, fascinated.

'What are you doing?' Connie shuffled back, disturbed by his gaze and the pistol pointing at her sternum.

Bell stepped in front of her. 'Do not stare at her so lasciviously, sir. She is little more than a child.' Bell jutted out her chin.

Connie was stung and grateful in equal measure. She didn't like Bell thinking of her as a child, but she was glad Bell was standing between her and Marcus's unsettling gaze and never-wavering pistol. At least it meant Bell didn't think she was in cahoots with Marcus. Probably.

She peeked around Bell, Marcus was frowning at her. He flicked the pistol. 'Back over.'

'I shall not,' said Bell.

'It's ok, Gertrude,' Connie said. 'Don't do anything stupid.'

'Are you sure?' Bell asked, not taking her eyes from Marcus.

'Yes.'

Bell stepped back beside Connie.

'Thank you.' Marcus inclined his head toward her. 'Well, we should probably talk, all of us.' He seemed unreasonably chirpy, but, Connie reasoned, that might just be a side-effect of the kind of megalomania needed to reweave history about yourself.

'You know the way to the temple, Conn?'

Connie started. Marcus looked at her inquisitively. She gulped back a sudden, rising fear. 'Yes,' she said.

'Lead on, then. And no tricks, please. I'd prefer not to shoot anyone. It's a nightmare for history.'

Bell scoffed. 'Why would a brigand like you care for the rights and wherefores of history?'

'That, my dear Miss Bell, is one of the things we must discuss,' Marcus replied, ushering them across the lawn. 'Lead on, Connie Rees.'

Connie led the way along the tree lined path to the temple folly. It stood in an octagonal glade in the arboretum about three hundred metres to the west of the house. Connie made a beeline for it, her shoulders slumped. Cook trailed behind her, Bell was behind him and Marcus brought up the rear, humming. Connie hated hummers.

'Here we are,' she said, waving her arm at the small ornamental garden with three trees growing in the middle of a planted area of flowers in front of the folly. The temple was not much more than a sheltered bench area, fronted by a pastiche temple with doubled-up Doric columns on either side and a low-sloping triangular roof over a tiled floor. The façade was styled more after St Paul's than an actual Greek temple, but it was pretty enough. Connie looked around and nodded.

'You approve?' Marcus asked.

Connie looked at him, he was frowning at her again. 'Looks better without the graffiti,' she said, shrugging.

'Most things do,' he agreed.

'Yeah, we're not friends,' Connie said, sloping over to the bench and sitting on it, her arms crossed.

'What is the purpose of bringing us here?' asked Bell. She stood outside the temple, her arms folded. She looked haughty despite her hair sticking out in tufts and the smoke stains on her cheeks.

Marcus shrugged. 'It's less obvious to prying eyes, and like I said, we have things to discuss. Take a seat.'

'We are already aware of your attempted subversion, Mr Marcus.'

'Marcus is my first name, Bell.'

'Oh,' Bell flushed.

Connie shook her head. All this going on and the thing that had so far most disturbed Bell seemed to be her own lack of manners.

'Shall I start?' Marcus asked.

'Might be an idea,' said Connie.

He flashed her an unsettling grin again. Connie sniffed. Somehow, he'd been less disconcerting when he was stumbling. And a drunken Marcus might have been easier to best.

'So, you three are out-of-time.'

Connie felt her throat tighten. *Oh no.*

'Not like that, Connie,' he laughed.

Connie felt her skin crawl.

'I could have killed you all at the loggia if that was my intention.' He holstered his pistols.

Connie swallowed, she wasn't falling for that, he'd been way too quick on the draw earlier. Fluid.

'What I mean is you are literally out of your time. None of you should be here, and all of you must be here if we are to correct the time plane.'

'The time plane that you have ruined.' Bell's tone was accusatory.

'Solidified, actually. As best I can right now, anyway.'

Bell scoffed. 'John told me you would likely attempt this ruse if I let you speak, but it is not likely that we shall believe your fanciful tale, Marcus,' she rolled her tongue over his name derisively, 'Since we have already been aptly apprised of the situation by Mr Bartitsu, the Raven you sought to capture to ensure your destruction of my future.' Bell gestured to herself pointedly. Connie frowned, the movement was unlike anything she'd seen of Bell prior to this. It didn't fit with her manner, and anyway, it was Bell and Cook who had a stake in this, why hadn't Bell mentioned him? She glanced about, not daring to move her head. Where was Cook? She licked her lips. *Oh.* She looked at Marcus who had an incredulous expression on his face.

'Bartitsu? Well, that explains why it took me longer to track the bastard down. Low tech change. Easy deception. Well, that and his propensity to, erm –' He tapped his bandaged hand, 'Drug people.'

Connie frowned. It was the one he'd dressed after she'd noticed a puncture mark on it at the festival. Marcus laughed. Weirdly, Connie found the sound oddly warming, wholly inappropriate given the situation.

'What do you mean?' Bell was haughty, staring down her nose at Marcus. An impressive feat given she was substantially shorter than him.

'You of all people, Miss Bell, should know that Bartitsu is a bastardised martial art. John Bartholomew,' he said, placing emphasis on the words, 'Didn't even give you his actual name. Why are you so keen to believe him?'

'He is a man of principle,' replied Bell, raising her chin. 'One that you left bleeding in the Infinity Chamber so you could steal the futures of notable Persons. He told us what you did to poor Katherine Routledge.'

'What?' Marcus asked.

'Your destruction of her time strand left her institutionalised,' Connie said, angry at his callousness. 'Don't you care what you do to people?'

Marcus frowned. 'Routledge suffered from paranoid schizophrenia her whole life. Her time strand hasn't been touched.'

Bell let out an angry, shaky breath. 'You'd like

us to believe such, I am sure,' she said. 'But you shall not do likewise to me. John Bartitsu has assured me –'

'Would it surprise you to learn that he lied?' Marcus cut across her.

'Liars often accuse others of lying,' said Bell. 'John is a man of principle, preserving history from the shenanigans of cads like you.'

'Weren't you once persuaded into an engagement with a penniless man who gave a good front to being wealthy? Your father had to step in didn't he?'

Bell blanched, but recovered her composure quickly. 'Of what consequence would that be?'

'It's of consequence, Miss Bell, because it shows that you are, rather famously, a poor judge of a man's character, and easily swayed. Sit down.' Marcus motioned to the stone seat in the temple folly.

Bell placed her hands on her hips, refusing to move, her nostrils flared. She glowered at Marcus. 'Incorrect as you are on many things, Mr Marcus, it is unsurprising that you would think that.'

Marcus waved his hand in a decisive line. 'That's not important right now. Bell, do you remember Frank Wild? Do you know the name?'

Connie drew in a breath and felt it hold in her chest. A rustle of leaves behind Marcus betrayed Cook. They couldn't let the ex-Raven spot the boy. 'What has Wild got to do with anything?'

she blurted out, injecting her voice with anger that sounded more panicked than anything. She grimaced.

Luckily, Marcus didn't look at her. 'Not now Connie,' he said. He was staring at Bell, who was frowning. 'Do you know the name Frank Wild?' he asked again.

Bell frowned, cocked her head and turned to look at Connie. Unexpectedly, she winked. Connie closed her eyes. Bell was playing for time, giving Cook opportunity to sneak up on Marcus while he was focussed on her. Connie hoped she wasn't about to overdo it.

'Mr Wild,' she said slowly. 'Yes, I believe he's a local man who assisted with the nineteen-oh-one Scott expedition to Antarctica. My father remarked upon it in one of his missives. A young man from the area participating in heroic endeavour. What of it?'

Marcus sighed, his shoulders visibly relaxing. Connie could have sworn it was a sigh of relief. Her curiosity was piquing. 'Why is it important that Gertrude can remember Frank Wild?' she asked, leaning forward on the bench.

'It's important,' Marcus said, still heaving relieved breaths. He was nodding to himself, but glanced up and looked at Connie. The smile on his face faltered. Then he was upright, pistols drawn, levelled at the two women. 'Well done,' he said, his face contorting. 'Where is he?' He was glowering at them.

'I have no idea. Honestly.' Connie raised her hands and shifted uncomfortably on her seat.

'What have you done?' he asked. He was furious.

'Nothing!' Connie was alarmed at his change in attitude.

A stick swung into the back of Marcus's head, the heavy, gnarled end making a thick-sounding thunk against his skull. Marcus crumpled, his eyes spinning comically back into his head.

'Well done, Master Cook,' Gertrude said, stepping over Marcus's prone form and picking up the pistols. 'Odd design,' she said, pointing one of them into the arboretum, 'But I believe I shall be able to make use of it at close range.'

Cook dragged two long pieces of timber into the garden, hauling them over to Marcus and dropping them on the flower bed. He looked very pleased with himself.

Bell looked up from where she was plaiting vines. 'Excellent Master Cook, they will make good sidebars for the sled.'

'Thank you, Miss Gertrude,' Cook bounced on the balls of his feet, looking for anything else he could do to help.

'Take a vine, start plaiting,' said Bell. Cook sat beside her in the early dawn and began work.

Connie paid the other two little attention. She was sitting next the unconscious Marcus, going through his satchel. She'd found it hidden at his back, attached to his cross belt like a cavalry message pouch. Laid out next to her was a small blow dart, obviously the thing he'd used to knock Bell unconscious in the house, an intricate game box that looked like a Viking strategy game Connie had seen in a National Geographic article on the Uppsala Warrior, a Viking chieftain who'd been recently determined, by genetic analysis, to have been a woman. It had sent ripples through the archaeological community with many archaeologists trying to relabel the chieftain a spouse. Connie had been fascinated by the determination to impose modern standards on Viking culture. There was also a piece of split and inlaid obsidian attached roughly to a long black leather thong and a notebook. Connie continued rummaging in the satchel and found the thing she'd been looking for. She glanced over at Bell and Cook. They seemed absorbed in their work, but she shifted round anyway, her heart pounding. She turned her hand over, keeping it inside the satchel, and smiled. She was holding a TQC control element. The stone was warm under her touch, which she found curious, and there was a very faint, purplish glow about it. Without pausing to consider what she was doing, Connie dropped the element into her waist pouch and picked up the notebook, flicking it open to a random page. She exhaled a sigh of relief. Beside her, Marcus breathed evenly.

'Did you find anything of interest, or the control element?' Bell asked, appearing beside her.

Connie glanced at her. 'Lots of equations,' she said, forcing herself to focus on the calculations on the page. She frowned. They looked familiar, like she'd seen them recently.

'Something wrong?' asked Bell, leaning over Connie to get a better view of the book.

'I, I've seen something like this.' Connie shook her head and flicked through another couple of pages.

'Perhaps in the Infinity Chamber?' said Bell, 'Did John present anything to you, perhaps?'

'No.' Connie frowned, still flicking through the notebook. There was a frightening quality to the equations, precise and deft in a way that was surprisingly reminiscent to her. 'We need to wake him,' she said, turning to shake Marcus.

'Absolutely not.' Bell caught Connie's arm. 'He's a dangerous criminal, Connie. Whatever has possessed you?'

Connie wrenched her arm. Bell held tighter. Connie gasped at her strength. 'Let go, I have to ask him about these.' She flapped the notebook about uselessly.

'You can ask John about them,' said Bell, releasing her. 'Now, enough. We need to tie him before he wakes. You will help?'

The way she said it told Connie she was expected to comply. She stole a glance at the pistol, which Bell had managed to holster at the waist of her skirt. No point starting a fight when Bell was armed. She didn't think Bell would shoot her, but the woman had exhibited some zeal after Cook had bashed Marcus on the head.

'I really think,' she said, taking her time and phrasing her thoughts carefully. 'That we should incapacitate Marcus, wake him, and ask him some questions. He wanted to know if you remembered Frank Wild, why? He could have killed us, and didn't, why? If he wants your future, why not just shoot you, and Cook? If we don't like his answers, we can take him back to Bartitsu. But I think we need to ask him.'

'He may have intended to kill me. Or have you forgotten the dart?' Bell asked. 'And anyhow, I think we need to be getting ourselves home, don't you?' She walked away. 'Master Cook, can you begin threading the timbers as we discussed.'

Connie growled beneath her breath and crouched next to Marcus. She didn't dare wake him, not with Bell behaving like a prima donna, but the notebook had shaken her. She swallowed as the reason came to her. She flicked back to the notebook, double checking the calculations. She didn't understand what they denoted, there was a lot about movement and variables, but the rhythm of the equations was increasingly familiar. Her heart began racing and her mouth dropped open. 'Oh, no. No, no, no, no.' She didn't understand all of the calculations, but she recognised the forms, the mathematical language, even this way of working through the problems.

Connie began shaking Marcus, leaning over him to try and conceal what she was doing. 'Hey, wake up,' she hissed in his ear. He groaned, shifted and slumped again. There was a glistening patch in his hair, at his temple where Cook had made contact with the stick.

'What are you doing, Connie? I explicitly told you not to wake him.'

'He's bleeding,' Connie said, wrenching Bell's scarf from around her neck and using it to dab at the wound. 'And his calculations. They're familiar to me. We need to know what he knows.' She shook Marcus again, jerking away from Bell, who was trying to pull her away.

Bell humphed. 'He is a criminal, you cannot trust a word he says. We shall return him to John and rejoin our own times. All will be well.'

'What if he's not a criminal? What if he's the one telling the truth?' Connie rounded on Bell. 'We're going on the word of a stranger. One who left us here alone.'

'This mad faith in the honesty of a criminal is because you do not trust John? Don't be so ludicrous Connie. John entrusted us to manage our own fates, to reclaim our destinies. And we have done so.'

'Indeed you have.'

Connie spun around. Bartitsu was leaning against a tree, leering at the prone figure on the floor. 'I knew I could count on you, Gertrude.' He flashed her a wide, lopsided smile as he sauntered over to Marcus. He nodded approvingly at the makeshift sled Cook was finishing. 'Nice work.' He toed Marcus with one hobnail boot and crouched down, emptying the satchel. 'Where's the TQC element?' he asked, standing up again.

'Everything I found is there.' Connie bit her lip. 'I thought it might be the necklace?'

Bartitsu picked up the leather strung piece of obsidian. 'This is a piece of junk,' he said throwing it over his shoulder. 'Nothing else in here?'

Connie shook her head.

'He must've stashed it. I can find it later. Come on, we need to get him back. The Temporal Council have a few questions for Marcus and they don't like to be kept waiting.'

'If we're using an Infinity Chamber to take him to them, how are they kept waiting?' Connie asked.

Bartitsu looked over his shoulder at her. 'It's all relative, Explorer Girl. Don't start blowing things out of proportion again.'

Connie stared at him open-mouthed.

'Do not gawp, Connie. It is unbecoming of a lady, and I did rather think you had more sense,' said Bell. She gave Connie a pointed look and flicked her eyes at Bartitsu. Connie scowled at her.

Bartitsu grinned, 'Nice pistol,' he said to Bell. 'Hand it over.'

'I'd rather not,' replied Bell.

'You can't have future technology, Gertrude. It looks like a nineteenth century pistol, but trust me, it's not.' He motioned with his fingers. 'Give it to me.'

Bell did.

'And the other one.'

Bell rolled her jaw and handed over the other pistol.

Connie could feel her fists clenching and un-clenching. She stared at Marcus, his face only partially visible in the dirt. Bartitsu had knelt down and was lashing Marcus to the makeshift sled.

Connie stood back, watching, thinking. The cal-culations, the way he'd been looking at her. It was more than a little disturbing. She didn't buy that she was here by accident. She bit her tongue, concentrating. She needed to talk to Marcus, a few questions would give her the in-formation she needed, she was sure of it, but how when Bartitsu was here now, and Bell was being obstinate?

Bartitsu stood up, hefting the sled with him. He rolled his shoulders and set off, trudging along the dirt path. 'Vortex is this way. Come on,' he said.

Connie trudged behind the sled. She was keep-ing a wary eye on Bartitsu, but she had no idea how she was going to speak to Marcus without him hearing, nor how she was going to wake him to speak to him. The four filed to the edge of the tree line, where Bartitsu, who was leading, stopped abruptly. He dropped the sled, it crashed heavily to the ground. Bartitsu ignored it, rolling his shoulders. The sun was rising on the far side of the lawn, sending long shadows across the grass. Everything was very still.

'Why are you stopping, John?' Bell asked.

'We're going into the Chamber here,' he said. He pulled a TQC element from his coat pocket and began manipulating it, running his fingers along the stone. 'Come see how this is done.' He flashed Bell a wide smile as she joined him.

'Why here?' asked Connie. She didn't want to admit it, but she was angry that Bell was getting the lesson. 'If you can open a vortex anywhere, why not just do it at the temple?'

'Because, Explorer Girl,' said Bartitsu, still focussed on the TQC, 'It's easier to open a vortex in an open space. Does she always question everything?' he asked Bell.

'Yes,' Bell said, her lips curling into a half smile.

Bartitsu continued working the TQC, but it seemed it was increasingly frustrating. He began to curse under his breath.

Cook sidled up to Connie and pulled the hem of her skirt.

'What?'

'The house is gone,' he whispered, staring at the ground, his feet shuffling uncertainly. 'Don't move too much.' There was a note of panic in his voice.

'What do you mean, the house is gone?' whispered Connie.

'There's a great big glass house where the manor house should be. You said –' he hesitated, still looking at the ground. 'You said that the house is gone in your time. Is this your time?'

Connie shifted to her right foot, tilting her head to see through the trees. Pale stonework shone in the rising dawn. 'The house is there, kiddo.'

'What?' Cook peered past her, frowning. 'It was gone, I swear it.'

Connie looked at him, he seemed genuinely confused. 'I believe you,' she said, recalling the two moons she'd seen earlier. 'But see?' She pointed an index finger through a gap in the trees where the dawn light glinted off the orangery.

'It's not on fire,' whispered Cook.

Connie frowned and looked again. He was right. The house was whole, well-maintained. There was no sign of dereliction or fire.

She strode toward Bell and Bartitsu, 'Hey, what's going on?' she blurted the words out before thinking.

Wood splintered next to her head. Connie ducked instinctively and spun behind the tree. She felt a warmth on her cheek and pressed her fingers to it. They came away red. Gingerly, she felt back at her temple, closing her eyes in relief as she felt a thick splinter of wood caught in her hair. Another shot rang out. More wood splintered. She cast about, looking for the others, pinning herself back against the tree trunk. She caught sight of Cook, he was lying prone behind a bush, indistinct in the shadows of the leaves but with no hard cover. Bell and Bartitsu were sheltered behind a wide, squat oak tree on the other side of the path.

Connie heard a groan and saw Marcus's hand lift and stop. He blinked, tried to lift his chin to see what was keeping him restrained. Groaned again. Another shot. More splintered wood, above her head this time. Connie squealed and crouched low, her head in her hands. When she looked up, Bartitsu was staring at her. He pointed silently, making sharp gestures at her. There was no mistaking his meaning. *You. Stay put.* She nodded fervently, her eyes and nostrils wide. She could smell her own fear. She didn't like it. Blood seeped into her eyes from her cut. She wiped it away, trying to keep a clear view of Bell and Bartitsu.

Bartitsu handed Bell a pistol, his overcoat, Marcus's satchel and his beaked cap. Connie watched in fascination as Bell put on the clothing and began to return fire. Bartitsu slipped back into the shadows and ran into the trees in a long, sloping lope, his mass of dreadlocks bouncing against his back as he disappeared into the gloom. Connie gulped. Under the bush, she could hear Cook whimpering. The boy must be terrified. She cursed, he couldn't stay where he was, it was only a matter of time before he was spotted.

She looked up. The tree trunk had been hit twice, both shots on the left hand side. Connie tried not to think about the exploded gouges, the pale heartwood shattered and open to the air. 'Stay right,' she muttered to herself, sliding onto her belly. She used her elbows and toes to push herself along, keeping her head ducked so low her nose almost trailed in the mud. Cook was less than ten feet away but it felt like it took her forever to reach him. She reached out an arm and tapped his ankle. He turned to look at her, wide-eyed. He was hyperventilating.

'Follow me,' she said. She shuffled back slowly, keeping herself low. At first, Cook didn't move, then slowly he began to shuffle backwards, mimicking Connie. She kept moving slowly until they were both behind a group of squat trees next to a low stone wall.

Cook threw his arms around Connie, his breathing still hard. Connie stroked his head, keeping her back hard up against the wall.

23

Connie wasn't sure how long she sat holding the frightened boy. It seemed forever and no time at all. So fixated was she with muttering nonsense to him in an attempt to keep him calm that she wasn't even aware of the pistol fire ceasing. Feet appeared in front of her and Connie looked up.

'A good idea to get out of the way, Connie,' Bell said.

'Is he back yet?'

'John? No, he has gone to accost our would-be assassin. He told me we are to meet him by the northern lake. He said you'd be familiar with it? I trust you now see the sense in listening to him?' Bell raised an eyebrow.

Connie nodded mutely, staring blindly ahead. The gunfire had shaken her more than she wanted to admit. 'It's over toward the north western gate, directly in front of the house,' she replied, pushing herself up.

'Then we'd best get our captive and get moving. It will be substantially harder for you and I to pull that sled, and as I am sure Master Cook will agree, I don't think we should linger here.' Bell extended a hand to Cook, who took it. He was still shaking. 'Up, up,' she said, pulling him to his feet.

Marcus was shifting when they arrived back at the sled. Low moans accompanied the movements.

'He's waking up.' Bell spun the pistol in her hand, raising the butt above Marcus's head.

'Don't do that,' said Connie, putting her hand out over Marcus. 'He's tied up, what does it matter if he's awake?'

Bell lowered the pistol. She narrowed her eyes at Connie and then pushed the gun into her waist belt. 'Very well,' she said. 'Lift the other side.'

Connie stepped over Marcus and grabbed the wooden pole, lifting it with some effort. She heaved forward, feeling the pole bounce and skid slowly into motion. Bell was right, this was going to be a slog.

They dragged Marcus out over the lawn toward the house, Connie facing toward the sled, leaning back to pull it along. Cook walked along behind them, looking uncertain. Connie did her best to smile at him, but from the look he gave her it seemed she'd only managed a grimace. She heaved on the wooden strut again, stumbling to keep up with Bell, who was using a length of plaited vine rope over her shoulder to haul the sled. It made sense, she'd get tangled in her own skirts any other way, though she cut quite a menacing figure in the Raven cap and overcoat.

They bounced across the lawn toward a low set of stairs, up to the manor. Marcus continued to wriggle and moan and Connie began to wonder if maybe she should have let Bell pistol whip him, every movement made it harder to drag the sled. But she needed him awake if she was going to question him about Bartitsu.

They bumped up the stairs, the rough sled bouncing wildly. Connie could feel the strain in her shoulders. It was exhausting and they still had to cross the park. Why the hell had Bartitsu made the rendezvous so far when he could open a damn vortex anywhere? They reached the top of the stairs, their footsteps crunching in the gravel.

'I told you it had gone,' said Cook, pointing behind her.

Connie craned her neck and her jaw dropped. There was no house. There was no ruin. The only sign that the building had ever been there at all was the loggia, one arch deep and seven long. In place of the house was a large, forlorn conservatory, the metal frame oxidised with rust. It towered above them, almost as high as the old house's roof, its windows were filled with condensation. It blocked their way entirely. On the air, Connie could smell a faint odour of humid fermentation and decay.

'Connie?' The tone in Bell's voice was one of carefully controlled shock. Connie glanced at her. Bell was likewise slack jawed and dismayed. Connie couldn't help a small smile. It was nice, amidst all of this, to see Bell wrong-footed.

'I've never seen it before,' she said.

'The fastest way to the northern lake is directly through this building.' There was an exhausted sense of frustration in Bell's tone, but Connie could tell she was not going to give up. 'Connie, any ideas?'

Connie stared at the glass house. There was a set of doors directly in front of them, the windows reinforced with a thin mesh of wire. Connie stared at them, trying to think whether she knew about this building. A shadow, tiny and light flittered across the condensation. Connie squinted at it. She took a couple of steps closer to the door. Behind her she heard the sled bang. Marcus was trying to break his ties. More faint shadows shifted across the condensed glass. Connie took a deep draught of air. The undertone of decay reached her again.

'Miss Rees,' Bell shouted across to her.

'Yeah,' said Connie, smiling. There had been a butterfly in the hall earlier, and now she thought about it, her mum had mentioned this place virtually every time they had visited the park. Bartitsu's initial desire to open the vortex on the south lawn made sense. 'I think there was a hothouse here for a while – after they demolished the manor – but they knocked that down too. A long time ago.'

'How does that help us?'

Connie walked back toward Bell, her boots no longer crunching. She looked down. The gravel was gone, replaced by tarmac. Her theory might just be right. 'This is the hot house,' she said to Bell, crouching down to grab the sled pole. 'All that's inside are exotic plants, a few quail and a kaleidoscope of butterflies.' She stood up, shifted her grip on the pole and smacked Marcus across the temple. 'Knock it off.' It was better than having him knocked out again.

Bell raised an eyebrow. Connie shrugged. 'My shoulders are already killing me. We go through, while we can. Straight across the top.'

'Is that wise? We would be entering another time period.'

Connie stamped her boot on the floor. 'Look down. We've already done that. And the northern lake is another newer addition to the park. Time is shifting around us. It has to be, otherwise none of this makes sense. We go through. Grab your rope.'

They dragged the sled over an ornamental bridge, its ends thudding rhythmically against the wooden slats. Around them, great thick leaves, some wide and flat, others sharply pointed, overhung the concrete pathway. Connie huffed and blew as she tried to keep a particularly sharp leaf out of her eye. The greenhouse was deceptively warm, even at this early hour. She could feel sweat beginning to trickle down her spine and her face felt puffed and bloated in the heat. Beside her Bell drew in ragged breaths, the layers of clothing she was wearing making it stiflingly hot for her.

Cook brought up the rear, gazing at the bushes and trees that rose up to the heights of the ceiling, foliage brushing against the glass panes on the roof near three storeys above them. He alone seemed unaffected by the humidity and heat, his blousy shirt and trousers lightweight enough that the microclimate didn't affect him.

Butterflies fluttered around them, alighting on tables of rotted fruit and floating in front of bright flowers, testing for a spot to land so they could feed. Connie thought it would have been pleasant if they weren't dragging a bound man, and she wasn't desperately trying to figure out how she could question him before Bartitsu reappeared.

'There's the front door,' she wheezed, leaning forward as she dragged Marcus. Her shoulders were crying in pain.

'Thank God,' said Bell, 'Master Cook, see if you can open it.'

Cook darted to the front, clambering through some orchids on the side of the pathway. He jangled the entry door but it didn't move. 'It seems to be locked.' He crouched down and began twiddling with the lock, picks appearing in his hands from nowhere.

'Where did you get those?' asked Connie, stopping for breath as he worked. She didn't dare release the stretcher though.

'Tower room,' he said. 'They're better than mine. Got it.' He pocketed the picks and stood, pulling the door and holding it open.

Connie looked at Bell and sighed. The two women heaved forward once more, managing – just – to squeeze through the door and drag Marcus out of the glass house.

24

'I need a moment,' said Bell, dropping the rope. The sled tipped and wrenched out of Connie's hands, dumping Marcus unceremoniously on the floor. Connie grunted in pain and grabbed her wrist. The sled had wrenched it badly and it was throbbing under her touch.

'You could be more careful,' grunted Marcus. He was face down on the floor. The sled had rolled on top of him. He shifted uselessly. Above them the sky was an angry, thunderous black.

'I thought it was dawn when we entered?' Cook said, looking up uncertainly.

'It was,' said Connie, looking around. 'But I don't think time is running smoothly now. I think it's layering. Look.' She pointed behind them. On the far side of the hot house, a beautiful, crisp dawn could be seen, the sky washed with gold and lavender tones. Above the conservatory, virtually at the apex of the building, the sky abruptly changed to an inky black. Connie turned to look across the rolling lawn to the northern lake. The grounds seemed to be flickering. Trees, pathways, sculptures and even drifts of snow hazed in and out of view. 'I don't like this,' she said. 'It's unstable. We cross that ground and it flickers we could be impaled or embedded in a tree or anything.'

'We've just come through that building and now you're making this assumption?' said Bell.

'Not the same,' said Connie. 'That land was either big entertaining rooms in the manor, the paths we walked on in the butterfly house, or an open lawn. It was a calculated risk, but I don't know what could happen out there.'

Lightning cracked across the sky, illuminating the parkland briefly before pitching them back into darkness. Connie was horrified. In the moment of illumination, she'd seen fluctuating ground right across the park. It shifted as though it were waves. Hillocks and ditches appearing and disappearing, trees, stumps and fences shimmering and then gone. Walls, plain brick at times, other times beautifully rendered, rose and fell with alarming frequency and precision.

Other features stayed; a tangle of wire, ponds, ditches and god knows what else, all of which could change or disappear at any moment. A noise caught Connie's attention and in the next flash of lightning she saw a tractor motoring across the grass dragging a massive lawn cutter attachment behind it. Connie gulped.

'What's that?' asked Cook, his eyes wide. The tractor promptly disappeared.

Connie gulped. 'This is not good,' she said, biting her lip, 'It's basically a time minefield. And it's at least five hundred metres to the gate. I don't think we can safely make it.'

'We have to try,' said Bell.

'Did you see that tractor?' Connie asked. 'Even if we manage all the natural obstacles, in this pitch black, dragging that sled, if one of those appears near or on top of us we'll be ripped to shreds.' She threw her arm out, gesturing to where the tractor disappeared. 'Ow,' she said catching her wrist. The gesture had damaged it again.

'We cannot stay here,' said Bell, picking up a sled arm and heaving Marcus back over. 'Connie, are you listening?'

Connie barely heard her. Flickering into view, leaping and bounding across the shattered landscape, she caught sight of John Bartitsu. Over his shoulder was a prone form, braids tangled with his dreadlocks, goggles askew atop her head. Connie took a few steps forward, her breath catching in her throat, wrist clutched to her chest.

'Connie, pick up the sled, we have to risk it, we must get to the vortex to reach John.'

Connie stared at the running figure of Bartitsu. He seemed fixed in the landscape, unlike anything else. Neither he, nor the woman over his shoulder, flickered at all. Connie stared, peering into the darkness, hoping for a flash of light. It came.

'No!' she screamed, her voice lost in the wind. She spun back and grabbed Marcus by the lapels. He grinned stupidly up at her. 'Why the hell does

Bartitsu have my mum?'

Bell was faster than Connie had expected. She grabbed Connie's wrists and wrenched them free of Marcus. Connie winced and Bell clenched hard on her bruised wrist. Her eyes began to water. The sled clattered to the floor again. Marcus grunted in pain.

'What on earth are you talking about?' Bell asked.

'Bartitsu just ran across that damn time-mine-field like he knew where to go and he had my mum over his shoulder.'

Bell frowned, staring at Connie from under the point of the Raven's cap beak, her grip loosening. Connie didn't care what it sounded like. She knew that was her mum. She had no idea why Mum was here, but that had been her mum. She was certain of it.

'I would imagine he understands the vagaries of the fluctuations better than we do,' Bell said.

'Or he's a liar who duped you into helping him rend history,' said Marcus from the sled. His voice was grating, like he was winded.

'Be silent,' said Bell. In front of them the blackened sky and the landscape continued to buck. Bell regrouped. 'We have to get to the lake.' She looked across the grounds toward a flickering lake, though she didn't seem certain.

'You cross that field and we'll all die. The planes are rupturing.'

All three spun, staring at Marcus.

'What do you mean?' asked Bell.

'I mean that John Bartholomew rigged the park.' Marcus was straining his neck to look at the three. Sweat beaded on his forehead. 'He wants you dead, if you're out of history he can take your place, claim it, maybe even convince the Temporal Council that his sudden appearance in history is warranted. Spin it so that he's a protector of history.'

Bell snorted. 'That, Marcus, is your plan. John said you'd attempt this ruse.' She nodded, breathing heavily.

'You're shaking, Bell,' said Marcus. 'Even you don't believe what you're saying.'

Bell raised a shivering hand, aiming the pistol in it at Marcus. Her finger hovered over the trigger, her expression dark. 'You shall not have my future.'

'Woah, woah, woah.' Connie moved before she had time to think, putting herself between Marcus and the pistol. 'Oh.' She gulped.

'Move, Connie. He's causing this.' Bell pursed her lips and glared at Marcus. 'Remember, John couldn't find his control element. He's doing this.'

Connie took a deep breath. 'Gertrude, keep your eyes on me.' She reached her hand to her waist belt.

'What are you doing?'

'Easy, I'm not a threat here, just going to show

you something.' Connie pulled the TQC control element out of her waist pouch. 'I took the element.' She laid it flat on her palm, a smooth, dark crystal, cool to the touch now. 'I don't think it's active,' Connie said, keeping her eyes fixed on Bell. 'Remember in the Chamber, the one Bartits –'

'Bartholomew,' Marcus cut in.

'You're not helping.'

'Sorry,' said Marcus, ducking his chin.

Connie bit her lip. Her throat was dry and cracking. She took a breath. 'In the Chamber, when Bartholomew was using a control element, when it was active, it glowed along the seams.' Connie traced a finger along the crystal seam. Her hand was shaking. 'No glow, see?'

Bell's shoulders slackened, but she didn't lower the pistol.

'And when he put it down to use the gloves, the wired ones –'

'Bartholomew had filigree gloves?'

Bell moved her head, focussing on Marcus. She began to tense again.

Connie shifted back into her line of vision. 'Not helping.' Connie raised her voice. What the hell was wrong with the man? 'Gertrude, look at me please.'

Bell looked back at her. There was a trace of confusion in her expression.

'Ok, when he, John, stopped using this he manipulated it so it stopped glowing. If this crystal isn't glowing, I don't think it's in use.'

'That is a guess, Connie.'

'She's right,' Marcus said. 'The element isn't active. I was trying to protect you. Imara intervened because it turns out you three are unexpectedly wily. But she was aiming to miss, she didn't want to kill you.'

'Preposterous,' said Bell. 'I forced the shooter into cover.'

Marcus laughed. 'Not Imara, you didn't. The woman has a thirty millimetre spread. At that range she hits her target every time. Unless she chooses not to.'

Connie felt a flush of cold up her spine. 'That name, what did you just say it was?' she asked, turning to look at Marcus.

He smiled at her, his head cocked awkwardly as he strained against the bindings. 'I said Imara is an outstanding markswoman.'

Connie stared at him open mouthed.

'And Imara is your comrade?' asked Cook. 'It's a funny name,' he considered, 'But so is Marcus.'

Connie blinked. He'd been so quiet she'd almost forgotten he was there.

Marcus ignored Cook, never braking eye contact with Connie.

Connie blew out a long breath. It whistled between her teeth. 'Marcus isn't doing this, Gertrude,' she said. 'Bartholomew spun us a lie.'

'What makes you so certain?' Bell asked.

Connie could hear the confusion in her voice.

She almost laughed, it was pretty close to how Connie was feeling herself. 'I'm certain because Imara is my mother's name.'

25

Connie pulled a knife from her brace and pushed the blade onto Marcus's jugular. 'How do you know my mother?' she asked. 'What have you got her involved in?'

'Your hand is shaking, Connie. Back that blade away, this plane isn't stable,' Marcus said. His voice was impressively calm.

Thunder rumbled above them, the ground shifted, flickering as it turned from grass to tarmac. Connie screamed. Bell and Cook had disappeared. There was a tightness about her ankles. She looked down. Her feet were embedded in tarmac.

'Connie stay calm. Don't move. Look at me.'

Connie looked at Marcus. He was half was buried in the tarmac, his face rising out of it like some macabre parody of a gang-inflicted torture, except he was still alive. 'It's a flickering temporal superimposition,' Marcus said. His breath was ragged. 'Different times overlaid on each other. It won't last, but if you struggle and break something, that will. So don't move.'

'Can you breathe?' asked Connie.

Marcus pursed his lips. 'Not well. When you're trapped out of time, you can get stuck, like we are now, in the substrates of the time you're,' he gulped and his breathing became shallower, 'Drifting through. The substrate fills any cavity it can, because you shouldn't exist there.'

Connie stared at him. He was evidently struggling to breathe. Half of his torso was beneath the concrete. She pulled the knife away from his neck.

'Thank you,' he said.

'So your lungs are?'

'At times partially filled with dirt.' Marcus blinked and coughed.

Connie glanced around them. It was dark, there were no discernible features, but she could hear someone shouting instructions. A marshal calling out rules for a run. 'I think we're in my time,' she said. 'It's the weekly park run.'

'We're in no time,' Marcus said. His breathing was getting increasingly shallow. 'You can hear echoes of your own time, that's all.'

'What do we do?' Connie could feel her throat constricting. Her head darted left and right. She tried pulling her ankles clear.

'Connie, look at me, don't move. You have to stay calm.'

'How?' she said, twisting and losing her balance. She toppled forward, her ankles didn't follow. Flailing, she jabbed the knife down, grabbing the hilt with both hands. It sank into something soft, jarring Connie's arms, but it held. There was a shout. Connie heard it as an echo, as though it was very distant. *Maybe it was the starting call for the race?* She exhaled shakily. She could feel a tight pinching pressure moving slowly up her shins. Her eyes watered and her breathing came in ragged gulps. She focussed on the tip of the blade below her and frowned. A red pool was slowly forming around the blade. That was odd. Connie stared at it blankly.

'When you've caught your breath, stand up slowly and leave that damn machete exactly where it is.'

Connie blinked and frowned. A red pool, a shout, a sinking blade. She looked across at Marcus, her eyes widening. Veins were standing out on his temple and every sinew in his throat was stretched. He huffed out breaths between clenched teeth, his nostrils flared. She could see him trying desperately not to strain against the black asphalt prison.

Connie pushed herself back upright, wincing as she used the hilt to lever herself backwards. Marcus groaned, his eyes rolling back.

'Sorry,' she said.

He ignored her, panting out short, sharp breaths. 'Stand. Still,' he said through clenched teeth.

Connie nodded. She looked about her, colours faded across the infinite murky grey that surrounded them. 'How do you know my mother?'

'You want to talk about that now?' Marcus laughed and immediately wheezed. 'You're just like her.'

'I get that a lot.' Connie said. 'You said she's your partner, but she's a physicist. I've met all her colleagues. Never you.'

Marcus coughed. 'Then you didn't meet all of them.'

Shapes drifted through the mist around them. Two, some twelve feet tall, one with long extended wings, solidified in the mist. 'Totems,' Connie said, feeling the pressure of the tarmac rising further up her legs. 'Oh no.'

'What?' asked Marcus.

'When they built the Captain Cook museum, they raised the level of the ground. And I can see the totems that stand outside the museum.' She stared at the eagle atop the highest totem. The paintwork on it was a dark blue, almost black. Its eyes glared back at her, claws extended, menacing. She blinked and steeled herself, then looked at Marcus. Sure enough he was disappearing under the ground, it bubbled and boiled around him.

'What do I do?' she said, panic rising.

Marcus's breathing was getting shallower. His legs disappeared entirely. 'Connie, don't move.' His breathing was distorted. The concrete rolled up his cheeks. Connie stared. It was like watching someone sink into quicksand. The tarmac just rolled up. It reached the corners of his lips. It was suffocating him. 'It'll pa –' He grunted a short breath, cut short as the concrete covered his face.

'No!' Connie crouched, shrieking as the pain in her shins intensified. She stood up, her mouth wide. The fog coiled around the eagle totem. It seemed alive. It twisted, the wings flexing in the shifting mist. Connie screamed, her hand covering her mouth. The fog coiled around her, thick and oppressive. It swirled, getting thicker. All Connie could see was the twisted claws of the eagle, talons stretched toward her. Everything disappeared in a haze. She wrapped her hands around her head, squeezing her eyes shut.

'Connie! Connie!'

Connie felt something gripping her arms, shaking her. Her whole body was shuddering. She pulled against the talons, batting them away. She opened her eyes. Between her arms she could see a great flapping black mass. The grip on her arms tightened.

'Get off me! Get off!' she screamed, clawing at the talons.

'Connie! Connie it's passed.' Coughing followed the voice. It was male. 'It's passed.' The words came out with some effort.

Connie stilled. She opened her eyes and peeked through a gap between her arms. Bell was staring back at her, Bartitsu's voluminous black coat flapping behind her. She released her grip on Connie's arms, stepping away uncertainly. 'What happened?' she asked.

'What do you mean?' Connie panted, anxiously patting her legs down. They were no longer trapped.

'You suddenly started screaming, talking about totems and changing ground.' Bell looked perplexed.

'You could see all that?' Connie asked. She'd had no idea Bell had been in the fog with them.

'And how did your knife end up in his leg?'

Connie spun. The wound on Marcus's leg was bleeding freely. She dropped beside him, wrapping her hands around the wound and putting pressure on it. She gulped, looking at the wound. It was on the side of his leg, just above the knee, a slice rather than a stab, but it was bleeding badly judging by the amount of blood. She had no idea how to fix it. 'Help me,' she said over her shoulder to Bell. Her hands were shaking.

Marcus was laid on his back, panting. 'I told you it would pass,' he said. He coughed. 'Could you untie me, please. I need to sit up, clear my lungs.'

Connie nodded. She looked at Cook. 'James, use my other knife, cut the ropes.'

'Absolutely not,' said Bell. 'It was difficult enough to apprehend him the first time.'

Connie set her jaw. 'Cook, slice the bindings. Bell, get over here and help, or shut up.'

Bell made a displeased sound but didn't move. Connie couldn't see what she was doing, but at this point, she didn't care. Cook slid the second knife out of the sheath on Connie's back and began carefully cutting the ropes binding Marcus to the sled. He was remarkably dexterous about it, despite the semi-dull edge on the blade.

Connie looked at Marcus. 'How do I stop the bleeding?' she asked.

Marcus pushed himself up onto his elbows. He coughed again and spat. Great gobs of dirty brown mucus thudded to the floor next to him. 'I hate it when that happens,' he said, heaving.

'This has happened to you before?' Connie couldn't believe it.

'A long time ago, just after your mother and I...' he trailed off.

'What?' said Connie.

He shook his head. 'That laser, on your cross belt.' He nodded to it. Connie looked down.

'This? It's a ratchet, a costume piece,' she said.

Marcus shook his head. 'No, it's a medical laser, used to repair torn tissue.'

Cook released the last of his ties and Marcus pushed himself to sitting, wrapping his hands over Connie's. He smiled at her. It was obvious it took some effort to do so. 'I've got this. You get the laser. Hand it to me.'

Connie slid her hands out from under his, wiping her palms on her leggings. They left behind red-brown streaks. She plucked the ratchet from her cross belt and held it out. 'You're wrong,' she said, holding it out to him.

He took it from her and fiddled with the dials, enlarging the circular aperture on the wrench end. He placed it over his wound. It began to glow, white hot. It began to hum. Connie stared. Marcus gritted his teeth, pushing air out in a long hiss as he slowly traced the aperture along the gash in his leg. 'Pull out the knife,' he said. 'Smoothly, straight up.'

Connie nodded. She stood up and gripped the knife hilt, pulling it up as smoothly as she could. Marcus grunted. His eyes rolled, but he kept the ratchet in place, working it slowly along the tear in his leg. Connie stared, fascinated, bending close to see what was happening. She squinted at the interior of the aperture, where the light was brightest. Sure enough, there were tiny lasers knitting across the wound, drawing flesh together, leaving a bright pink line of scar tissue behind them. There was also a distinct smell of burning flesh. 'Should it smell like that?'

Marcus laughed. It was a pained sound. 'No, but I've never done it myself before, I generally prefer not to get injured.' He grimaced. 'I'm probably doing a substandard job.' The whirring stopped and the light disappeared. He breathed heavily, closing his eyes.

'Well, this is all very pleasant, but you are still detained.' There was a sound of a pistol cocking. Connie looked behind her. Bell had the pistol levelled at Marcus. 'Connie, step back and explain. What is that device, and what is going on?'

Connie turned around slowly, raising her hands

and stepping to the side, setting herself between Bell and Marcus. 'I honestly have no idea,' she said, keeping eye contact. 'But I think we need to listen to Marcus.'

'He is a criminal.'

Lightning flashed around the sky. At the edge of her vision, Connie could see fog, thick and swirling, coming closer. She took a deep breath. If she was right, the plane was rupturing again. 'That's what John told us. Look around you, he doesn't seem particularly trustworthy to me right now. And I don't want to get stuck in no time in that fog again.' She pointed to the swirling mist. It had engulfed the butterfly house and was rolling slowly, menacingly toward them.

'That's a good choice,' said Marcus from behind her. 'Master Cook, take this to Miss Bell.'

Cook walked past Connie. He handed a leather thong to Bell. Dangling from it was a black triangular obelisk, seams glowing faintly. 'Press your thumb to the base,' he said to Bell.

Bell stared for a moment, then slid her thumb under the base of the pendant and pressed. The pistol never wavered from Marcus. Connie would have been impressed if it weren't for the mist.

The pendant glowed and shivered on Bell's palm. Points, pathways and dais flickered into the air around them, a miniature holographic representation of the Infinity Chamber. The orbs in the hologram were vibrating, shaking, col-

269

liding. Pathways tangled, fractured and twisted, some severed from their time points completely. It was like the whole Chamber was being shredded.

'What is this?' Bell asked.

'It's an Infinity Monitor. It shows the Chamber, in real time. Right now, what you're looking at is time shattering,' said Marcus. 'The Infinity Chamber is trying to hold it together, but it's under too much pressure. Look there,' he said, pointing his finger to a spot near the edge of the Infinity Chamber hologram. Connie cocked her head to one side and stared at the point. Three orbs floated, enmeshed together, two were severed from their pathways, which floated nearby, trailing around the third, which was hanging by a single strand, infinitesimally narrow.

'Follow the pathway back to the central dais.'

Connie stepped into the hologram, tracing the pathway with her finger, rolling and twisting. Marcus heaved and leaned forward overtaken by another fit of coughing. More gobs of brown-red mucus spewed from his mouth, staining his jacket. He wiped his mouth.

'Oh,' said Connie, coming to a stop. 'Is this what I think it is?' She pointed to a bulge in the pathway. Light spilled out of it, tiny shards, severing it strand by strand as the light coalesced. The light was running along the two severed pathways, slowly creeping toward the flaying end, growing in intensity as it travelled. One was almost as bright as the other time points.

'Depends what you think it is.'

'A new future, that's disconnecting all of you from your times,' she said, her hand dropping to her side.

Marcus nodded. 'You are bright,' he said. 'I'd like to think you get some of that from your father, but I know it's all Imara.'

Connie frowned at him.

Marcus stood up. 'This is Bartholomew inserting himself into your strands,' he said, glancing at Bell and Cook. 'Strands are the things that look like pathways. If we don't stop him before he severs this final pathway, you,' he looked at Bell, 'will lose your future.' He looked past Connie to Cook. 'We all will.'

Bell exhaled and shook her head. She still had the pistol raised.

'Time's ticking Miss Bell,' said Marcus. Connie couldn't believe how calm he was. 'You of all people should know, sometimes you only survive by knowing who to trust. Take a leap of faith.'

Bell shook her head, her lips pursed. 'I'm not sure about this. John –'

'Is a liar.' Connie cut across her. She walked over and put her hand over the barrel. 'Put the gun down, Gertrude. Please.' She looked at the fog. It was licking over the sled, which appeared to be dissolving into it. 'We can't stay here, and we can't cross that field. Marcus understands this better than we do. He kept me calm, safe, when we disappeared. He didn't have to do that.'

'Do you trust him, Connie? Because you said you did not trust John.' Bell was wavering.

Connie considered. She didn't want to lie to Bell, but they were out of time. 'I trust him more than I would trust Bartholomew,' she said.

'Thanks, Conn,' Marcus grumbled under his breath.

'Still not helping,' said Connie.

Bell lowered the pistol. 'I will be keeping this,' she said, stuffing it back into her belt. 'And I shall be keeping a close guard on you, Marcus.'

Connie sighed in relief.

'Fair enough,' Marcus said. 'This way, I set up a harbour at the temple. It's why I took the three of you there in the first place.' He jogged off across the indistinct ground. 'Stay right behind me,' he called.

Connie put her hands on her thighs, leaning forward to catch her breath. Her shins were sore. The run had been terrifying. She looked behind her, the fog stopped ten feet away, billowing gently against some invisible line. It was opaque now, but every so often a shadow would run through it. Connie shuddered.

Next to her the other three were panting. Cook flopped on the floor, laughing. 'That was the most fun thing I've ever done.'

Connie stared at him. 'That's not exactly how I would describe it.'

'It's just like when the fog – normal fog that is – rolls in on Roseberry and you find your way because you know your way. I loved it.'

Connie shook her head and stood upright. 'So this is a harbour?' she asked Marcus.

Marcus was making a circuit around the edge of the temple garden checking some ornamental spheres placed on top of decorative iron pyramid trellises. 'Yep, although I guess you might call it a temporal sanctuary.' He laughed, looking at the temple folly. 'Get it?'

Connie took a deep breath, shaking her head. This didn't seem like an appropriate moment to be joking.

'Time is stable in here?' Bell asked. She looked shaken. 'We are safe?'

'For now,' Marcus said, finishing his inspection and returning to the three. They were congregated near the folly.

'Then tell us what in God's name is going on,' said Bell. She looked dishevelled and angry.

'John Bartholomew was a senior Raven,' said Marcus, emphasising the past tense. 'He's been assigned to Infinity Chambers all over the world.'

'There are more Infinity Chambers?' asked Connie. 'I thought Bartholomew was just trying to impress Gertrude.'

Marcus frowned at her, 'Of course there are

more. You seriously thought it was just Gisborough?'

'Focus, please,' said Bell. 'John – Bartholomew –' She seemed to struggle with the name, 'is, by your own admission, a senior Raven, but you want us to trust you, an outlaw?'

'Bartholomew was a senior Raven,' said Marcus, 'Until five months ago when he was excommunicated. Linearly speaking.'

'You make it sound like a religion,' said Bell.

Marcus grimaced, 'It's something we dedicate our lives to.' He looked at Connie, 'At great personal expense. Excommunication is torturous, we lose everything.'

'So why would John,' Bell huffed, 'I mean, Bartholomew, be excommunicated?'

'He decided he wanted to be notable in history. That's not our role. We should be invisible. Legend, myth, nothing more.'

'You're a secret society?' Connie blurted it out.

Marcus laughed. 'No, Conn. Not in my time, just in history.'

'Oh,' Connie felt disappointed and stupid at the same time. 'Hang on,' she said, 'You said, linearly speaking. What does that mean?'

'Well, surely you've realised by now that time isn't linear? It's more of a fabric, strands entwine in different ways at different points. Like an embroidery or a tapestry,' replied Marcus. He was leaning against one of the temple columns watching Connie closely.

Connie paused. Suddenly the rhythm of the time points in the Chamber and the syncopated rhythm Bartitsu, or Bartholomew, had tapped popped back into her head. The points had been fighting to free themselves, as though they were trapped. She'd assumed it was because Bartholomew was correcting the damage Marcus had done, as he'd claimed, but what if...? Connie began pacing, excitement and fear flooding through her together, the nervous energy making her shiver. 'Bartholomew was distorting the fabric, trying to embed his own line into the plane where it shouldn't exist,' she said coming to a stop, staring blankly ahead of herself. She felt stupid for being so easily duped.

'Well-reasoned,' said Marcus, 'but not quite.' Connie could feel his eyes burning into the side of her face, but she didn't want to look. First time fell apart, then Bartholomew stole Mum, and now she'd helped Bartitsu, Bartholomew, whatever the hell his name was, damage the time plane. She didn't want to see the look in Marcus's eyes. Connie set her jaw. Beside her, she heard Marcus sigh.

'Just like your mum. It shouldn't have been a surprise. Bartholomew's life line – strand, actually, but terminology aside – is like mine. It floats across the plane because we exist in all times and none. My linear time is like a,' he paused to consider, 'Like a repair to the plane. I investigate time, monitor it, keep history on track and measure future impact. I, and other Ravens, very rarely exist in our own linear time.'

'I don't understand.' Connie said, frowning. She dared a glance at Marcus. Surprisingly, he didn't look angry, just calm, like her teacher explaining a complex concept in physics.

'I'd be shocked if you did. Very few linearly historic people, even kids as bright as you are, Conn, can conceptually understand the concept of floating time.' He shrugged. 'Those who do, or did, passed into legend long ago.'

'Like who?'

'Morgana-le-Fey, Merlin – contrary to legend, they were actually twins,' he said. 'Cassandra of Troy, Nanshe.'

'The Sumerian Nanshe?' Bell asked.

'The very same.' Marcus inclined his head toward Bell.

'That's insane,' said Connie. 'These people are myth. One is part of the Sumerian pantheon. They didn't exist.'

'Imara taught you the pantheons.' Marcus nodded approvingly.

Connie found it odd to hear Marcus use her mum's name. There was a warmth in his tone that was almost like a caress.

'Of course she did,' he smiled at Connie, considering her. 'But, come on Conn, you know better than that. All myth is an explanation of human experience. It's rooted in facts that are often inexplicable to the people experiencing them. The stories of sorcery and prophecy explain away the unknown. Make it manageable.' Marcus cocked his head. 'But as with so much in life, reality is stranger than the fiction we produce to explain it, wouldn't you agree?'

Connie stared at him, her mind reeling.

Marcus crouched down near a rhododendron bush at the edge of the harbour and reached under it. His head and upper body disappeared into the foliage.

'You're saying that mythology is people explaining away the existence of Infinity Chambers all over the world?' said Connie, walking over to him.

'Well, not all mythology. That would be ludicrous,' said Marcus from inside the bush. The branches rustled around him. Bell arrived next to Connie and drew the pistol again, training it on his back.

'Do you really have to do that?' Connie asked her.

'Do what?' asked Marcus, re-emerging with twigs in his hair. He took in Bell's pistol. 'Oh.' He lifted a box the size of a briefcase up in front of him. 'I was just getting this.'

'And what is that?' asked Bell, not moving.

'A plane recalibration tool.' Marcus squatted down, laid out the machine and began flicking switches. Holograms flitted across it, indistinct and ephemeral. Marcus shook his head, twisting knobs and dials on the machine.

'Stop that.' Bell cocked the pistol.

He sighed, his shoulders dropping. 'I don't have time, Bell. This fog, this is the worst I've ever seen a storm like this, so many temporal moments bleeding across the physical plane. And I thought last year's incident at the Rann of Kutch was bad.' He kept moving levers.

'This has happened before?' Connie asked, surprised.

Marcus nodded, continuing to twist dials and knobs. 'Guarding history tempts some people to try and become it. A few Ravens have gone rogue.' He shrugged. 'Unfortunately it happens. Usually we manage to contain it, sometimes you get changes.'

'Changes to the timeline?'

'Or the physical plane.'

'Like?' Connie asked. She was baffled.

'The Allah Bund in Gujarat.'

'Impossible,' said Bell. 'The Dam of God has been in existence since the Rann of Kutch earthquake. It's been there for over eighty years.'

'Well, since last year, yeah, that's right,' Marcus sat back on his haunches and looked at Bell. He sighed, scratching his head. 'Sometimes we can't correct time, the best we can do is smooth over the damage. Bartholomew is counting on that. So, if you don't want it to happen to you, you need to let me work.' He shrugged, returning his attention to the device.

Connie watched him. It was like he was tuning some strange radio, trying to find an image in the static. His movements became more precise, tiny corrections. Roseberry Topping shimmered into view. Marcus hit a button and a purple glow emanated from the machine. A smooth, circular metallic blue pebble, cross-marked like a compass, rose out of a cylinder, materialising from some shimmering, mercury-like liquid.

'Cook, take this.' Marcus held out the stone to Cook, who took it hesitantly.

'It's warm,' he said. 'And glowing.'

'Keep hold of it,' Marcus said. 'It's your keystone. You fell from Roseberry, didn't you?'

Cook nodded.

'You need to place it at the point that you fell to reconnect your time strand to your future. You need to do it when it glows bright purple. Ok?'

'I can do that.' Cook turned away, walking toward the south.

'Where are you going?' asked Marcus looking up from the device, alarmed.

'Roseberry Topping is a long walk, Mr Marcus,' Cook said. He was staring at his stone, as if afraid it would suddenly glow brightly and he would have failed.

'I'll open a vortex to send you there when it's time. I still have some control of the TQC. If you walk, you'll never make it. Unstable intersection of the temporal and physical planes remember?'

'Oh, yes.' Cook looked down. He shuffled off into the folly and flopped onto the bench inside, cradling his stone.

'Why is my home appearing on that device?' asked Bell. 'I was not at Red Barns when I went through the fog. Vortex?' She'd lowered her pistol and was staring at the machine, which was producing another stone. This one was a yellowish bevelled rectangle, long and smooth, and covered in cuneiform writing overlaid on an etched, irregularly shaped rectangle.

Marcus pulled the stone from the machine and handed it to Bell. 'You weren't at Red Barns?'

She shook her head. She traced the outline on the stone. 'This could be Arabia. Curious,' she said.

'What was the vortex like?' asked Marcus. 'Smooth, like walking through a mist?'

'No, it was rather unpleasant, like being caught in a vast electrical storm,' Bell said, still peering at the stone.

Marcus looked at the machine. It had whirred on, the images on it shifting.

'What's it doing?' asked Connie.

'It's scanning for the last focal point,' said Marcus turning his attention back to Bell. 'Did you leave Red Barns unexpectedly?'

I decided quite abruptly that I wanted to ride. It was a beautiful chilly morning.'

'Good,' Marcus nodded. 'You still need to go to Red Barns. The machine isn't wrong. Bartholomew expected to pull you away from Red Barns. He had to recalibrate for you being in motion away from the house, that's why the vortex was a storm.'

'The last point is the manor house, here,' said Connie. She was crouched in front of the machine, fascinated by it. It was producing another stone, this one different, translucent and filled with myriad imperfections, like dirt and bubbles suspended inside the material. 'Is it broken?' she asked.

Marcus crouched next to her. 'No,' he said, lifting it out carefully. 'The keystones – they're anchors – they correspond to the person they're relevant to, and the location they need to be set. I met your mother on top of Marton Manor – linearly – five years ago. That's where this stone needs to be placed.' He put the stone in his pocket and stood, facing them. 'So, here's what we need to do.'

26

The vortex shimmered. Roseberry Topping, its sugar loaf summit disconcerting to Connie, began to haze. Cook looked back at them from the wood line at the base of the hill, his arm raised. The vortex winked shut.

'Will he be alright?' asked Connie.

'If he gets to the summit in time, yes,' said Marcus, his fingers tracing over the TQC control element.

'What if he doesn't?'

Marcus paused his work and looked at her, 'Let's focus on him getting there, ok? Kid's a good climber, he'll be fine.'

'I still don't understand why you could not send him directly to the summit. Particularly when we are, according to you, so short of time,' said Bell. She was pacing. It was the only sign of nervousness Connie could see in her, but then, what Marcus had just explained to them had sent a cold flush through Connie. It was something that had left her aching. It was as if she'd been sucked into the deep cold of the TQC interior, as if her lungs were shards of ice. The situation was ridiculously precarious. 'I agree with Gertrude,' she said. 'It would have been better to send Cook directly to the summit.'

Marcus sighed. 'I explained I couldn't do that. Too close to where Bartholomew stripped him out of his time, and he could be alerted to our play. We can't afford that.'

'It's an eight hundred foot climb, and he hasn't slept in about forty hours,' said Connie.

'He's more tenacious than you give him credit for, Conn.' Marcus finished his calibration. 'Anyway, it's too late. He's already climbing. Miss Bell, you're next.'

Bell nodded, taking a shaky breath. A swirling vortex opened over the low staircase that led away from the ornamental garden. Through it, a modest, yet lovely red brick building appeared.

'Remember, you need to place the keystone at the spot you made that decision.'

'I am far from dim, Marcus,' said Bell, swallowing and looking at the vortex. It hovered above the first step. 'I shall not miss my footing?'

'You're not going down the steps, you're going through the vortex,' said Marcus.

Bell nodded. 'You're sure you shall be fine alone with him?' she asked Connie.

'Yes, Gertrude,' said Connie, squeezing her hand, 'An English woman is never afraid, right?'

Bell smiled at her. 'Indeed.'

'Good luck,' said Connie.

Bell inclined her head.

'Come on,' said Marcus, 'Time's wasting.'

Bell walked into the vortex.

'Do not be seen, not in that state.'

Bell gave him a sharp look and put a hand to her unkempt hair. She looked down at her stained and dirty clothing and let out a short laugh. 'Perhaps you're right,' she said. 'Good luck to you, Raven,' she said to Marcus over her shoulder.

'And you,' he said.

The vortex closed behind her, winking out, only a drift of mist identifying it had ever been there.

'This stuff is surreal,' said Connie, shaking her head. 'How do you manage it? What is the Infinity Chamber, exactly? How do you, that machine, the console, make the computations that say this plan will work?' She threw her arms up, 'That it has any chance of working? I just don't see it.'

Marcus raised an eyebrow. 'Saved that until after Bell left.' He nodded, 'Thanks for that. She'd never have gone if you'd shown such a lack of faith while she was here. In fact, I think she still wants to shoot me.'

'Don't patronise me.'

'I'm not,' he said, checking the spheres again. The fog was clouding more densely around the harbour, blotting any sense of place beyond their little garden. 'She agreed because she thought you understood better than she did, and you agreed to my plan.'

'I'm aware of that,' said Connie.

Marcus shook his head. 'You're right, the Infinity Chamber is immense. I wasn't much older than you when I first went inside one and I knew they existed. I was overwhelmed.'

Connie stared at him.

'How's your quantum mechanics?' he said.

'Patchy.'

He frowned, disbelieving. 'Ok, the paths and points within the Infinity Chamber are peculiar. All of time exists within the room. The pinpricks, diamond stars, are access points to moments of time, but not all paths can be accessed at all times. We don't really understand why. Your mother suggested it could be because we must come to our own futures unknowing. She's an outlier though.'

'Yeah,' said Connie. 'In the twenty-first century, that would be pretty outlandish thinking.'

Marcus cocked his head at her, a quizzical expression on his face. 'Right. Anyway, the Chamber isn't sentient, but it does seem to coordinate a balance between the threads and access points and that is what Bartholomew is trying to change. The Chamber's internal management of the time plane.'

Connie felt a cold sensation wash over her. 'You didn't think to build a failsafe into the machine to stop that from happening?'

'We didn't build them, Conn. We found them, but the technology is way beyond our understanding. Best we could tell, they'd been there for millennia, but were built millennia after we discovered them. It's like they exist in all times regardless of when they were built. We can manipulate the technology, but we don't fully understand it.'

Connie puffed out a long stream of breath. It condensed in front of her face. 'So you just cannonball about in history, with no clue what you're doing?' She couldn't believe what she was hearing.

'No, we've learned enough that we can investigate history, and enough that people like Bartholomew can try and overwrite it, damage the fabric. The threads you saw floating in the hologram?'

Connie nodded understanding. 'If you didn't make the Chambers, why do you guard them? Surely the people who built them should do that?'

He shrugged, 'Maybe they should, but they don't. We never used to guard them, just investigate the past, but that had complications.'

'Like the Allah Bund? The earthquake that created that was fall out from a Chamber?'

'Yes. We contained the damage of that storm, which is why we know the Allah Bund is a new addition to the time fabric, what we don't know is if anyone has previously successfully shifted the fabric. So we guard the Chambers.'

'But why?'

'The Chambers are a known technology in my time,' he said. 'It was considered politically expedient.'

Connie shook her head. 'What does that mean? Why wouldn't you just stop using them? If you didn't build them, they weren't meant for you, surely?'

Marcus took a deep breath. He opened and closed his mouth a couple of times before responding. 'When I come from, people know about the Chambers but most are still frightened of them, much like Crispin Tocketts. It's understandable, we don't know who built them, what they really do or how they work. But, they also contain all of this knowledge and a window, a real window, into the past and future. That's a powerful tool. No government was going to give up that kind of apparent omnipotence. So they created the Order of the Raven. We research the Chambers, past and future. It makes people feel safe. I'm a temporal archaeologist, kind of like Indiana Jones.' He grinned.

Connie rolled her eyes. 'That film is really old, even in my time.'

'And it's still a classic in mine.' He smiled. 'You should rest. We don't have much longer before Bartholomew comes for the keystone.'

Connie blinked awake. She was hunched in the corner of the folly, Marcus's blue jacket laid over her. It still smelled faintly of alcohol. She got up stiffly and swung her arms uncomfortably. She felt tense. Marcus was sitting on the step between the columns, his back to her. She sidled over to him. 'So,' she said, elongating the word. 'What do we do now?'

'You're awake, good,' Marcus said, not turning around. He was concentrating on something on the floor in front of him. Connie craned her neck, looking over his shoulder to see what he was doing.

'Why do you have the Uppsala Warrior's strategy game in your bag?' she asked, watching him set the board. 'How is ancient technology going to help us?'

Marcus ignored her, moving pieces into place. 'Friya's rift board was a revelation when she produced it. I'm not surprised she was buried with one, but it's not ancient technology, and it only works when connected to an Infinity Monitor, which was not buried in the mound for security reasons.'

'But she was a Viking?' Connie said, uncertainly.

Marcus shook his head, twiddled with his Infinity Monitor and set it in the centre of the board. The pieces began to move, drifting in patterns, toward an inner threshold on the board. He kept his eyes on the moving pieces. At the threshold one of them disappeared and rematerialised in its initial location. The other turned a matte black. It seemed cold and dead. 'Didn't you notice in that list of historical names I gave you that three were women?' he said, shifting the two pieces into different positions. The matte black shifted back to a metallic hue and they began moving again. Marcus watched, his shoulders hunching.

'Yes,' replied Connie. 'What's that got to do with anything?'

'That's not an accident,' he said. 'Some of our best Ravens, particularly those from the distant past, are women.' The pieces reached the threshold again. The same piece solidified to the dead black. He shifted them again, huffing. Connie didn't understand what he was doing. Marcus continued, his eyes never leaving the board, 'Women seem to have a more innate understanding of time. Friya, the chieftain you're talking about, was a legend in her time, and in my linear time. She found me, told me I was non-linear, that I should become a Raven. On her death she chose to return to the site of her *When*. Her linear time. Said it was important.'

Connie rocked back on her heels, astounded. 'Do you know why?'

Marcus shrugged and shook his head, his face creased in a frown. 'No. Might be for reasons that come along long after I'm dead.' The piece vanished again.

'That one doesn't seem to want to go to that section of the board,' Connie said, deciding to concentrate on something that might eventually make sense.

'No, and I was hoping to avoid that,' said Marcus. He glanced up at her, his lips pressed together. He reset the pieces again, switching the two of them. They began to move.

Connie watched with baited breath. The switched piece reached the threshold and crossed it. Marks began to appear on its surface as it came closer and closer to the centre of the board. It shook and bubbled.

Marcus sat back, tendons in his neck standing out, his expression grim. The piece juddered to the centre of the board; part matte, part metallic, and scarred.

'That's not good, is it?' Connie asked, looking at him.

'No,' he said. 'It's not.' He sighed. 'But we're going to have to try, and I'm going to need your help.'

Connie nodded. 'If I'm here, I might as well help. Gertrude Bell and James Cook were inspirations to me. I don't want them to become John Bartholomew.' Bile rose in her throat as she realised that if Bartholomew succeeded, that was exactly what would happen.

Marcus sat back on his heels, watching her.

'What?' she asked.

He shook his head, seeming to reach a decision. 'Guess we'd better see what he's up to then,' he said.

Marcus set the Infinity Monitor into one of the spheres at the edge of the temporal harbour.

'What are you doing?' Connie asked.

He ran the leather thong dangling from it down either side of the trellis pyramid, connecting the ends into two discreet ports. Connie was surprised to see the leather emit a soft purple glow. Marcus caught her expression. 'Not everything is what it looks like,' he said.

'So, what is it?'

Marcus ran his finger across a piece of the trellis. 'This will make it life-size,' he said. A hologram appeared from the Infinity Monitor, the simulation surrounding them. Connie shivered. It still felt odd to her. In the centre of the ornamental garden was a life-size emulation of the Infinity Chamber. Connie felt queasy. She was floating between the pathways and had a sudden sense of vertigo. She looked over at Marcus and started. Standing beside him, as a holographic representation, was John Bartholomew. He was manipulating the TQC console, one hand wrapped in a filigree glove, the other wrapped so tightly around the control element that his knuckles were white. His teeth were bared in frustration. Connie shivered.

'Why is he only using one filigree glove?'

Marcus frowned. 'Not sure. The gloves allow greater manipulation, but they are for Ravens beyond my time. Beyond his time, too.'

'Don't all Ravens use the same tools?' asked Connie. 'It would make sense if you did.'

'You'd think, wouldn't you?' Marcus said, peering at the TQC. 'Good, it's working.'

'What is?' Connie wrapped her arms around her. The garden was frosting over and she felt bone cold.

'By sending Cook and Bell through earlier than he anticipated we've disrupted the quantum stream he was building. He's struggling to contain it.' Marcus shook his head. 'You know, he was formidable. Tipped for the Temporal Council. I will never understand why that wasn't enough.'

Connie frowned at him. 'You weren't just partners, were you?' she said. 'You were friends.'

Marcus nodded. 'He was best man at my wedding.' He grasped a ring on his finger, turning it round.

'You're married?'

'Mmm,' Marcus said, squinting at the holographic TQC, watching Bartholomew's movements. 'Although we only got to spend two years together afterwards before time and tide tore us apart. Good, he's losing the ability to control it from the Chamber. He'll have to come for the keystones.'

Connie stared at Marcus. 'What did you just say?' she asked. Puffs of white air streamed out of her open mouth. Marcus glanced at her. He picked up the coat from where she'd discarded it on the bench and wrapped it around her shoulders, rubbing them. He stepped back and winced. His leg buckled.

'What's wrong?' Connie asked, grabbing his

arm. He was dangerously close to the edge of the temporal harbour.

He grimaced. 'Thanks. I'm not as good with that laser as I should be, that's all. Get me to the bench.'

Connie looped his arm over her shoulders and helped him to the bench. Marcus dropped onto it heavily. There was fresh blood on his trouser leg. 'Laser,' he said, holding his hand out.

Connie unclipped it and handed it to him. He flicked it on and grunted. The smell of searing flesh was worse this time. He hissed, his hand shuddering over the end of the gash. 'You picked a hell of a time to impale me.' He grimaced.

'It wasn't intentional,' replied Connie.

He shook his head and flicked the laser off, leaning back against the stone wall of the folly. Connie waited, staring at him. His breathing was heavy. 'She always made it look so easy,' he said.

'You often end up injured like this?'

He shook his head, gulped and laughed. 'Not often, but enough.' He looked at the hologram. Bartholomew was still struggling with the console on the dais. Connie followed his gaze.

'Can't we just go in there and stop him?' she said. It seemed odd to be watching him rend the Chamber.

Marcus shook his head. 'No. I tried. Somehow he's sealed it.'

'So we just wait? We're risking a lot on him coming here first. What if he tries to stop one of the others?'

'He'll come here first. This pathway, this keystone, it's never been available before – to him or me – this is *when* he needs to be.'

'If you say so,' Connie flopped down beside him, the oversize jacket flapping around her. 'Where is my Mum?'

'I'm not sure,' said Marcus, staring at the hologram. 'Oh no.'

Connie saw it too. She froze. John Bartholomew had hauled an unconscious figure into view and was tying her to the TQC. Once the figure was secure, he pulled the filigree gloves onto her hands and moved them across the surface of the console. The woman's braids flopped and clattered silently against the quantum stone. Connie stared at her unconscious mother, uncomprehending. 'What's he doing?' she asked as Bartholomew secured her mother's wrists in place.

'He's using her to secure the internal laser processors. She'll be the one to hold his new time strand in place until it knits into the fabric.' Marcus was breathing heavily, his shoulders stuck in a brittle hunch.

'What? What will happen to her?' Connie could barely get the words out.

'If we don't correct the plane, and the processors overwhelm the quantum stone, she'll die.' Marcus said staring at the hologram. He took a shaky breath, his jaw set.

'We have to get in there, get her down!' Connie

was panicked. She had never felt so helpless.

'We can't, Conn. Our only chance is to stop Bartholomew.' Marcus looked toward Marton Manor, the temporal fog was thinning and there was a narrow concourse through it toward the house. 'We need to get into position, come on.' He plucked the Infinity Monitor from the sphere and set off toward the house without waiting for Connie.

'Hey, what the hell do you think you're doing?' Connie raced after Marcus along the narrow open path toward Marton Manor. It materialised slowly through the fog, with the butterfly house overlaid on top of it. Marcus pulled up so sharply Connie ran into his back and fell down.

He frowned at her. 'You weren't paying much attention, there. If you'd fallen into the fog you could have been lost.' He looked at the banks of shimmering, enveloping fog. 'It's barely breaking at all now.'

Connie glared up at him from the floor. 'I said, where the hell are you going? We have to go and get my mum.' She pushed herself up, brushing down her increasingly battered dress. She didn't care anymore. Mum could scream. Connie would welcome it.

'The only way to save your mother is to stop Bartholomew. I know it's tough, but you have to focus. We need to place the keystone.'

Connie's jaw dropped open. He couldn't be serious. 'Did you see what he did to her?' she asked. 'He strung her up like some temporal Andromeda.'

'I saw, Connie,' Marcus said, his jaw clenched. He stalked away scanning the buildings in front of them. 'This is bad,' he said, stopping at the junction of the conservatory and loggia. The iron framework and glass panels twisted in with the house, flowing and melding into one single lump. Through the house windows banana trees and ferns were visible, as well as flitting butterflies. Humid condensation rolled about the buildings, distinguishable from the fog only by its lack of iridescence. 'The buildings are actually intertwined,' Marcus said, tracing a finger along one of the iron struts. 'I've never seen anything like it.'

Connie grabbed his arm and pulled him round. 'I don't care what you've seen, or not seen, before,' she said, her heart pulsing. 'You are finding a way to get me into that Chamber to get my mother.'

He wrenched his arm down and away. 'Don't be childish,' he said. 'We have a job to do.' He turned back to the house, studying the intersection.

'Easy for you to say.' Connie thought she spoke, but even in her own ears she could hear her voice yelling frantically. 'If those lasers breach the console she'll burn. You know that. You didn't just watch that happen to your mum!'

'No,' Marcus rounded on her. 'I watched that happen to my wife. It doesn't change anything.'

Connie stopped short. All of her anger drained away. She felt dizzy. Seconds seemed like an eternity. She could feel the blood pumping in her ears.

When she eventually looked back at Marcus his shoulders were slack, a look of pain was etched across his face. He threw his arms out to the side. 'Do you want the Star Wars moment?' he asked her, his shoulders hunching. There was a sense of forlorn hopelessness about him. 'Connie, I am your father.'

Connie realised he'd never meant to tell her. Or at least, not tell her like this. She stared at him. He stared back. All Connie could do was count her breaths. They were shallow. In. Out. One, two, three, four.

'Say something, Conn, please.' He swallowed. He looked more terrified than she'd ever seen him in the brief time they'd been acquainted, even when he'd been getting buried in the foundations of the Cook Museum. Connie pushed her hair back, scratching at her temple. She bit her lip.

'You,' she swallowed, making an effort to look up at him. 'Know a lot about late twentieth, and early twenty-first century pop culture for someone from the distant future,' she said. Her eyes darted away. She swallowed again, uncomfortable. That had been a stupid thing to say.

Marcus laughed and rubbed the back of his neck, looking at his feet. Connie followed his gaze to his boots. Long, mud-splattered, cavalry boots. Just like the ones of the stranger who had helped her at Gisborough Priory. So that had been Marcus, not Bartholomew. *Oh.*

'Yeah, when I realised your mum had based in the twenty-first century, and that I couldn't follow the two of you there, I learned everything I could about the things kids liked to do then.'

Connie broke from her reverie and looked up. He was watching her. He forced out a smile and shrugged. 'I couldn't be there with you, so I found out about all the things you might like. With your mother being who she is, Star Wars seemed a dead cert.'

'And Indiana Jones?' Connie asked.

Marcus laughed nervously. 'Ok, I like Indiana Jones. Feels like a cooler version of me.'

Connie felt a smile inch across her face. It was absurd. 'Time travelling, what did you call it? Temporal archaeology. That's much cooler than fighting Nazis.'

Marcus raised his eyebrows, 'Glad you think so. I mean, you're wrong, but now's not the time to debate that.' He turned back to the wall abruptly, examining it.

Connie joined him, taking a huge steadying breath. 'Guess not. What's the problem with this?'

He gave her a sidelong glance. 'It's a stable temporal superimposition.'

'Like before?' asked Connie, shuddering at the

memory of Marcus half-buried in tarmac.

He shook his head, 'No, it's different than when we were pushed into the flicker. Stable superimpositions are a deliberate intermeshing of two different times. This one's been well grafted, but it's still dangerous. Bartholomew has risked a lot to keep these times parallel. Something that shouldn't happen.' Marcus sighed. 'It means he doesn't know which one is the temporal-locality.' He sat back on his haunches, one hand on the melded iron and stonework. 'And I don't know why.'

'Does it matter?' asked Connie. 'We're the ones placing the keystone.'

'I don't like the variables,' Marcus said. 'But we're out of time. Come on.'

27

'You said, "when you realised you couldn't follow us there,"' Connie said, staring out over the
south lawn. 'What does that mean?' She was feeling increasingly jumpy, something made worse
by Marcus's latest revelation, and the fact that it
was impossible to think of him as her father.

Marcus was crouched down beside her, picking the lock on the south door of the massive,
rusted glass house. It seemed to be taking him
a while. He carried on, ignoring her question.
His face – what Connie could see of it at least –
was pinched in concentration. It didn't seem he
had much experience with lock picking. It was a
shame they'd already sent Cook off, the kid had
been a natural.

'What does that mean?' she asked the back of
his head again.

Marcus paused in his work and leaned his head
into his hand, wiping his brow. 'It means,' he
said, manipulating his picks delicately, 'That I
tried, and failed, to reach you, and in doing so, I
brought all of this about.' The lock clicked and
he opened the door. 'After you,' he said, waving
her in.

'I thought Bartholomew was the one doing

all of this,' Connie said, walking into the hot house, glancing at the thick, tropical foliage that crowded onto and over the concrete paths. The humid air smelled of mulching foliage and rotten fruit, a sickly sweetness that was both appealing and awful. Perspiration beaded across Connie's brow almost instantly in the artificial heat. Her hands felt clammy. She flexed her fingers and looked around. Butterflies fluttered everywhere: some tiny, with sharp, pointed wings; others huge and shimmery. Blues, reds, yellows and whites intermingled easily. It was a beautiful sight.

Marcus slid past her, jolting her back into the moment. 'Come on. We need to get out of sight.'

Connie followed him into the centre of the artificial jungle, crouching down onto her hands and knees to crawl behind him under some thick, waxy bushes into a concealed clearing. Marcus sat on his haunches, sweat trickling down the side of his face. His blue coat, which Connie belatedly realised also had the Raven embroidery on it, was far too thick for the indoor climate of the conservatory.

'You didn't answer my question,' she said, flopping down onto the mud and wiping her hands on her trousers. 'I hate it when people ignore my questions.'

Marcus looked down at the soil and took a deep breath, his jaw jutted out. 'When Imara told me she was pregnant, I was happier than I could have believed. Ecstatic. Ravens don't often have children, Conn.'

'Why?'

'That's a complicated question, for another time, when we're not –' he motioned to the foliage, but kept his eyes focussed on the ground.

Connie nodded, though she wasn't sure he saw her response. 'So, you were happy. Mum was happy. What went wrong?'

Marcus looked up, 'In the middle of the second trimester Imara told me she was leaving, to keep you safe. That I wasn't to follow, that my path wouldn't let me. She didn't wait. Wouldn't discuss it. She just walked through a rend, and like that,' he clicked his fingers, 'You were both gone.'

'What?' Connie could barely believe it. It was callous. Cold. Unlike anything she'd ever seen or heard of her mother. 'Mum just left?'

'Yes,' Marcus said. He was looking at the floor again, his jaw tight. He picked up some soil between thumb and forefinger and rubbed it into tiny grains. 'John found me shortly after. We were partnered here, at Gisborough. I was desperate to find you both, to be there no matter what it cost. John said he would help me.'

The way he said it set Connie's teeth on edge. A shiver ran up her spine and she could feel goose bumps rising on her arms. 'What did you do?'

Marcus grimaced and swallowed. 'There is Lore about the Chambers and Law, as created by the Temporal Council. Lore is tricky and dangerous, so it's restricted to Senior Ravens.'

'Like Bartholomew?'

Marcus nodded. He let out a long breath. 'We began researching Chamber Lore surreptitiously. We discovered that the Chambers closed different time points for different Ravens, and deduced that meant the Chambers were self-calibrating for the individuals inside them, though some time points were universally inaccessible, or so it seemed. We found that if we increased the number of manipulations we could make to the internal lasers, that we could force some of these inaccessible points to open. So instead of one control element, we used four.'

'You embedded control elements in gloves?' Connie said, thinking back to Bartholomew's huge, wrenching movements and the unnatural, syncopated rhythm of the Chamber once he'd finished manipulating it. More than one control element seemed to be a problem.

Marcus frowned, 'No. We do not have access to those gloves, I told you that. We used the crystal elements.'

'Then how come Bartholomew has a set?'

'I do not want to speculate.' He waved a hand. 'But there were pathways we couldn't even get close to when we were running our tests with four elements. Just four contacts made the Chamber hugely unstable.'

'But you kept running the tests anyway?' Connie said, incredulous.

'I wanted my family, Connie,' he said, looking directly at her. 'You and your mother. Desperately. I didn't care about the Chamber, or the consequences. And I should have. But all I could think about was finding you and Imara.'

'Did you?'

Marcus nodded. 'Once. Briefly. But the vortex was small and unstable. I only just had long enough to throw a sweater in the bottom of your pushchair.'

'My NASA sweater?'

'My NASA sweater,' he corrected her. 'You were three, and it was cold. I wanted to warm you up. The jumper was a souvenir from my first Chamber appointment. It was all I could fit through the vortex.'

Connie looked down, an itching feeling across her shoulders, almost like a tingle. She'd been wearing Marcus's jumper to connect with him all these years, as a way to connect with her father, but now he was here, it just didn't feel – anything. It was all too strange. She swallowed. 'But how is this, the time storm, Bartholomew's megalomania for other people's futures, your fault?'

Marcus trailed his fingers through the soil. 'I was so focussed on finding you and Imara that I didn't see everything else he was doing when we were manipulating the time strands,' he said. 'The research we did; it was illegal for a reason. Bartholomew used the Lore to learn how to manipulate time in a way no one had ever dreamed possible. He took it, took my desire, my loss, and twisted it. He used me. And I let him. He couldn't have done it alone.'

Connie reached a hand out to comfort him and stopped midway. It was a natural reaction for her, but it felt odd when she considered who Marcus was. She pulled her hand back, cradling it on her lap.

Marcus glanced at her. 'The Temporal Council were not happy with us when we were discovered, but John disappeared. He left me to – I think – take the fall for everything.'

'Were you punished?' Connie could feel her heart pounding, blood pumping through her ears.

'Yes. And no.' He lapsed into silence.

'Marcus?' Connie asked.

A blankness dropped down over Marcus's face. He pulled out the keystone, rolling it across his hand, deliberating. Connie watched in silence.

'Take this and keep hold of it,' he said, handing it to her and closing the conversation.

Connie could feel sweat running down between her shoulder blades. Her eyes were heavy. It seemed they'd been waiting in the small clearing under the foliage forever, though it couldn't have been more than half an hour.

Marcus waved a small vial under her nose. She sat bolt upright and gagged.

'What was that?' she asked. She wanted to vomit.

'Pick-me-up,' he said, screwing a cap on and putting the vial in his pocket. 'Shifting through time is taxing, but I need you to stay awake.'

Connie shook her head and sniffed hard, even the slightly fetid smell of rotting fruit was better than the stinging smell from that vial. She wriggled her nose. 'You couldn't have just punched my arm?'

Marcus looked hurt. Connie wasn't sure why. She looked down, embarrassed. 'Never mind,' she muttered, shifting her back against a tree. The only sounds Connie could hear was the splash of the artificial waterfall and under that, the sound of the mechanical pump running it. She wiped her brow. It was hot and sticky.

She fidgeted with her cross belt and chanced another glance at Marcus. He was sweating too. He'd removed his blue coat, but his shirt was starting to stain at the collar. He was staring up at the jewel green foliage, watching it sway against the glass roof. Connie wondered what the Temporal Council had done to him. She opened her mouth to ask, but stopped herself. He'd barely looked at her since admitting to his part in unwittingly helping Bartholomew and it didn't seem like now was the best time to press the matter.

Outside, the sunlight gave way to an encroaching bank of unnatural iridescent fog. It hadn't moved any closer since they'd entered, but the way it hung over the glasshouse was oppressive.

'Why is it so still?' Connie asked.

'The gloves Bartholomew forced on Im, your mum, are holding it in place,' he said, then he shrugged. 'Best guess.' He lapsed back into silence, staring at the canopy, preoccupied.

'Isn't there something we should be doing?' Connie prompted.

He shook his head and lifted the Infinity Monitor from his chest. 'This'll light up when Bartholomew arrives. Until then, we stay put.'

'We couldn't wait in the house?'

Marcus took a deep breath and looked back at her. He shook his head. 'He'll come through this way. Eliminate it as a site of importance. We, or more specifically, I, need to stop him here.'

'And what do I do?' Connie asked.

'Stay out of the way, Conn. Once I've contained him, you place the keystone, and this is all over.'

Connie wrapped her hand around the translucent stone in her waist pouch. 'There's some stuff I don't understand, Marcus,' she said. He winced and she gritted her teeth. She couldn't really call him Dad, she barely knew him. 'Can you, maybe explain it?'

He sat up, stretching his back. 'What do you want to know?'

'Why does Bartholomew want three futures? Why not just one? And why yours?'

'Why do you th–' he cut himself short and grimaced.

Connie frowned at him.

He waved his hand. 'Never mind.' He shook his head, smiling. 'You're just like Imara, do you know that?' He sighed, considering. 'Ravens are like any other human being, Connie. We're fallible. Some are seduced by the power of infinite knowledge that comes with control of an Infinity Chamber, which is why Chamber Lore is restricted. It's been abused even before Bartholomew's actions; Ravens making themselves mages and soothsayers for more primitive ages.'

'Like Merlin and Morgana?' Connie asked.

Marcus weighed her question, his head shifting from side to side. 'Their story has been corrupted. Yes, they broke the rules, but only for the purposes of guiding their *When*. The twins – that's how I know them – were pulled into the Order from the age in which they eventually gave their prophecies. The result of that was fame, acclaim even, but it's not as cut and dried as the kind of abuse I mean, the kind Bartholomew is trying to wreak.'

'I don't understand,' Connie said. 'If they manipulated people around them, how is it not the same?'

'They were sensible enough to be opaque about the predictions and they only intervened when –' he paused, searching for the right word. 'When unique pathways opened inside the Chamber.'

'You can't access them all?' Connie said. She was

surprised. The thought hadn't occurred to her.

Marcus shook his head. 'I already told you that, when I explained about our research.'

Connie winced at his abrupt rebuttal. It wasn't like this stuff was easy to figure out, and she struggled with Physics. Or did she? That didn't seem right.

Marcus wiped a hand across his mouth, stifling a yawn.

'Maybe I should vial you,' Connie suggested, reaching for his pocket.

Marcus batted away her hand, but he seemed pleased with the joke. 'Anyway,' he said. 'In the end they had minimal impact on history, they made room for themselves, they didn't change history materially. We can see this in the temporal annals which the Council hold.'

'But Bartholomew is different because he wants multiple futures?'

Marcus shook his head. 'He's dangerous because he wants futures not his own, from times he never existed. He's not manipulating the temporal plane, not guiding history. His aim is to supplant it.'

Connie felt the hairs on her arms stand on end. She took a shaky breath. It was a lot to take in. 'But why?' she said. 'What does he get from it?'

Marcus rubbed at his eye and swatted a fly from his ear. He coughed. 'What does who get from what?' he asked.

Connie frowned. 'John Bartholomew. What

does he get from it?'

Marcus looked at her blankly. He blinked several times. 'Bartholomew?'

'Marcus, are you ok?' Connie asked, concerned.

His eyes snapped back into focus. 'Notoriety,' he said. 'He claims these moments as his own and eradicates the rightful owners of the strands from history. Then, if and when the annals correct, his crime will cease to exist too. We'll have no record of Bell or Cook.'

'Or you,' said Connie, beginning to panic. Bartholomew was stealing three futures. She clenched the stone in her pocket. Marcus had told Gertrude and Cook that it would help to anchor them in their times until they could reclaim their strands, but she had Marcus's stone. 'You remember who you are, right?'

'Of course, Conn,' Marcus said. He sat up and puffed out his chest, coughing and testing out a deep tone. 'I am your father.' He grinned.

Dad jokes. In spite of herself, Connie smiled.

Marcus looked around her, frowning.

'What is it?' she asked, suddenly feeling tense.

'The manor is on fire,' Marcus said. He pushed himself up onto all fours and crouched into the undergrowth, stalking toward the spot where the manor meshed with the greenhouse.

28

Connie shuffled through the undergrowth, pushing fronds away as she came to a stop beside Marcus. In front of them was a wall that looked like a wrecking ball had been swung through it. On the far side of the torn wall was a dated, but expensively furnished drawing room. It was on fire. Smoke billowed upwards, concealing the ceiling of the room and flames licked across the floorboards. In some areas they had caught and were burning strongly, in others, they were barely taking hold. It was like the fire had been blazing for hours and had only just ignited.

Connie reached a hand in front of her. A butterfly landed on it, darting its proboscis down to her skin, taking in the salt and sweat on her hands. It seemed totally oblivious to the flames. 'There's no heat,' she whispered to Marcus.

'No,' he replied, scanning the flames.

'Why is there no heat?' Connie asked, flexing her leg. Her muscles were beginning to cramp.

'Because we are in a different temporal moment to the manor,' Marcus said, crawling closer to the flames and peering into the smoky drawing room. 'This complicates things.'

'Great.' Connie flopped back onto the damp

hothouse soil and rubbed her calf. "Cos this was feeling way too easy.'

'Sarcasm does not suit you, Connie Rees,' said Marcus, still peering into the house. He picked up a rock from the edge of the plant bed and tossed it, overarm, into the burning manor, directly into one of the widest flaming areas of floor. He nodded and picked up another stone, repeating the throw to a different area.

'What are you doing?' Connie asked. She rubbed her head. The heat in the conservatory was getting to her, she felt fuggy.

'Testing a theory.'

'And?'

'And, it was good.' He pointed to the fire raging across most of the floor. 'The fire is another temporal superimposition. An additional layer on top of the main physical realities.'

Connie stared at him. She felt totally out of her depth. 'Talk like I'm someone who doesn't know. Because I don't.'

Marcus smiled. 'In this situation, the layering of the superimposition is where one event that directly follows another event – in this case, dereliction followed by fire – co-exist in the time storm, but the earlier time, dereliction, takes base form on the physical plane.' He pressed one hand on top of another to make his point.

Connie looked at his hands, her brow creased. 'I don't understand. Why is that good?'

Marcus looked at her, concerned. 'Because it

means we can safely run across the floorboards. The fire hasn't corrupted them. It's superimposed.'

Connie frowned. That seemed complex. 'Superimposed?' she asked.

'Superimposition, yes.' Marcus leaned forward, 'Look at me, Connie,' he said. She blinked at him, not wanting to disappoint him, though she wasn't sure why.

'Connie,' he said, his tone worried. 'These are simple terms. You were understanding much more complex quantum theory earlier today. What's wrong?'

Connie blinked at him. 'Nothing,' she said. Immediately she winced. That had been too sing-song bright.

Marcus raised his eyebrow. 'Tell me how you met Gertrude. At the start of all this. I saw the pair of you riding away from the militia man but I didn't see you meet.'

'Gertrude?' Connie was puzzled.

'Gertrude Bell, the woman who you told me not an hour ago was an inspiration to you.' Marcus pronounced each word carefully, slowly.

Connie nodded along with him. He'd never struck her as stupid, but this was ridiculous.

'Bell, the famous explorer. The woman who mapped Arabia, who helped to found your modern state of Iraq.' Marcus was still speaking in that slow, over-pronounced way.

'No,' Connie frowned. 'That was Bartholomew

of Arabia. He was the cartographer whose skill enabled T.H. Lawrence to conduct his campaigns. Why are you looking at me like that?'

Marcus looked astounded, as though he'd never heard anything so stupid. 'Shit,' he said. 'He must've gone to Red Barns first.' He placed a hand on her head. Connie wasn't sure why, but it felt familiar, almost paternal. She stiffened and shook his hand away. She didn't know her dad, he'd abandoned her and her mum before she was even born.

'Where's the keystone?' Marcus asked her.

'The what?'

'The translucent stone I asked you to hold.'

'In the pouch where I left it, why?' Connie said. This was getting boring.

Marcus opened the pouch and pulled it out. He placed it on her left palm and closed her fingers around it.

'What are you doing?'

'Hold it,' he said.

'It's just a stone.'

'Hold it.' He clasped his hands around hers, keeping her fingers tight against the smooth translucent stone.

'Hey,' Connie pulled her hand away. She didn't know this person. Why was she on the floor in bushes with him? He was stronger than she was. His hands remained clenched around hers.

'Hold it, Connie. Don't fight it.' His voice was strangely calm.

The stone heated in her hand. The warmth began to seep up her arm, flowing across her, flickering at the edges of her brain. Her lip trembled. It was like a heavy oilcloth was being lifted from her mind. Memories bloomed. The electric fog. Bell, Cook. Gisborough Priory. Her eyes widened. Images rushed by. Bartitsu and the Chamber. Marton Manor. Marcus. Bartholomew and his theft of futures.

'Dad?' she said, shaking.

Marcus closed his eyes and swallowed, visibly relieved. 'You'll probably regret calling me that in a bit,' he said. 'You've been very studiously staying away from the word.'

Connie curled in on herself. He was right. She kept tight hold of the stone though. Strange as it was to think of Marcus as her father, she much preferred it to being terrified of him as a stranger.

Marcus smiled sadly and patted her hand. He stood, searching across the conservatory. 'Bartholomew must've known. Something must've tipped him.' He stopped, staring through the glass. It was heavy with condensation. Connie followed his gaze. Someone was prowling along the edge of the conservatory.

'Is that him?' Connie asked.

Marcus pulled one of the strange grey cylinders off his belt, rolling it in his hand. 'I believe so,' he said. 'I need to get you somewhere safe. Whatever you do, do not let go of that stone.'

Marcus dragged Connie along a pathway inside the hothouse, glancing all about him. He was evidently looking for something, but as she flumped along behind him, Connie had no idea what it was. When he spotted a kaleidoscope of butterflies fluttering over a patch of ferns, he pulled Connie off the path and pushed her into them. 'Why can't I let go of the stone?' she asked, feeling uneasy and rubbing her arm. She was still feeling sick from the surge of memory that had come when he pushed the stone into her hand. She didn't really want to keep hold of it.

'Why do I have to hold it?' she said.

'Because I need you to anchor the other two,' Marcus said. 'Just in case this goes south. You are a reservoir of memory, adrift in the temporal rift. Hold the stone, keep your memories, and we hold onto the temporal plane as it should be.'

'Individually, those words make sense. But what does it mean?'

'Whatever happens, stay hidden,' Marcus said. He began rearranging the fern fronds in front of her.

'What are you going to do?' asked Connie. 'Why must I keep hold of the stone?'

'What I came here to do,' he said. 'Do not let go of that stone, skin contact with it will help you to preserve reality. Focus on Bell and Cook. You remember them?'

Connie nodded, her eyes wide. 'It's hard.'

'Bell or Cook?' asked Marcus.

Connie squeezed her eyes shut. 'Both.'

Marcus cursed and glanced over his shoulder. 'He must've guessed I'd be here with you. Too late to change it now. Connie, listen, if you feel your memories get patchy –'

'Mine, or the ones I have of James and Gertrude.'

'Any,' said Marcus. 'If it happens, you need to follow the stone.' He pulled some banana leaves down, rearranging them to better conceal Connie. He stepped back, inspecting his work, the matte grey cylinder still in his hand, off to one side as though he was holding a weapon.

'What does that mean?' Connie asked, straining to see him through the fronds. She moved one of the leaves.

Marcus batted her hand away. 'You need to be concealed,' he said, rearranging the frond. 'If you can't remember Cook or Bell, or both, then Bartholomew is close to succeeding. His manufactured timeline will supersede their reality and they'll be lost. You can anchor them for a little longer, but only if you keep hold of that stone. That's your part in this, Conn, ok? You are future memory.'

He glanced over his shoulder again. His breathing was getting faster. On the other side of the glass, a dense shadow was stalking toward the conservatory door. 'I need to go and stop Bartholomew,' said Marcus, peering through the leaves at her. 'Remember, stay put, I'll come back for you, but if your memories of Cook and Bell start to go fuzzy, follow the stone.'

'What do you mean, follow the stone?' Connie hissed.

There was a sound of iron scraping on concrete and a cool breeze washed through the hot house, blowing spiky fern fronds into Connie's eyes. They watered and she blinked rapidly, her hand clenched tightly around the stone. Marcus craned his neck and looked over the foliage toward the door, then jumped onto the path and sped away.

'What does that mean?' Connie hissed toward his disappearing back.

Marcus ran lightly along the concrete path toward the entry. He was half crouched and moving fluidly, rotating the cylinder in his hand. He dipped off the path and into the bushes at a stand of orchids, dropping into a squat and edging through the foliage to get a view of the doorway. It was open and outside the physical plane was becoming ever more fragmented. Marcus didn't want to think about the pressure Imara must be under. Holding the TQC pulses so that the conservatory and the house would remain steady when there was this much strain on the temporal plane would be next to impossible. It could be killing her.

He looked about, adrenaline beginning to pump through his veins. There was no sign of

Bartholomew. Marcus scanned the concrete. On the floor there were three faint boot prints heading off to the right. He crept forward slowly, making his way toward the waterfall on the far side of the hot house.

Connie leaned out from her hiding spot, staring at the space where Marcus had disappeared. 'Great,' she said, sitting back on her haunches and fidgeting with the neck of her dress. She was beginning to sweat profusely, rivulets ran down her back and there was a sheen on her arms and hands. Some of it must be fear, the conservatory was humid, but not oppressive, and her heart was pounding. She squeezed her eyes shut, trying to block out everything unnecessary, her features clenched in concentration, her fingers white around the stone. Her memories of Bell and Cook were getting harder to hold onto. She swallowed and breathed. Sweat trickled along the inside of her arm. The stone slipped from her hand.

Connie's eyes flew open and she let out a short, sharp breath, scrabbling in the dirt for the stone; memories, not just of Cook and Bell, but of her own childhood, were beginning to slip away. Her fingers brushed the stone. A memory ignited. In her relief, Connie let go again. It was like curtains, sheer and gauzy, falling, layer after layer, hazing and shutting off part of her mind. She lunged for the stone, grabbed it and felt relief flood through her. The curtains lifted. She opened her hand. It was such a small thing, but as she inspected it she noticed that like the TQC it had tiny filaments of light pulsing under its surface. Where they touched her skin, warmth spread. She frowned at it, unsure what to make of it. The TQC had been cooled by some bizarre, stone embedded nitrogen infusion, the intense cold mitigated by the heat the TQC generated. This was far too small to have anything similar embedded. She turned it over in her hands. She began looking through the dirt, searching for a pebble, anything similar to the stone in her hand. Working out what it was exactly wasn't any use, she needed to make sure she could keep hold of it. Finding a likely stone, she pocketed it, then pulled a length of leather cord from her cross belt and wrapped the stone in it.

29

Connie sat in her makeshift hiding place rocking gently back and forth, the stone gripped tightly in her fingers. 'Gertrude Margaret Lowthian Bell, cartographer and explorer, of pivotal importance to the endeavours of T.H. Lawrence, helped found modern day Iraq, died in Baghdad nineteen-twenty-six. James Cook, son of a labourer, became an explorer, cartographer and Captain in the Royal Navy, a place he gained on merit after going to sea with the Merchant Navy. As a child he showed intellect and dedication through his schooling and a lack of aptitude for shop work.'

'That won't work.'

Connie felt the flat of a blade slide along her throat. It was like a caress, barely touching her skin. She gulped and froze. The upward tilt on the blade placed pressure under her chin. Connie pushed up to a half squat to relieve it.

'What I really want to know though,' said Bartholomew, his breath warming her ear. 'Is how can you remember them at all?' He raked his hand into her hair and dragged her upright. Connie could feel herself shaking. She let out an involuntary cry. Bartholomew pressed the blade closer to her throat. 'I cut them loose before I came looking for you, so how can you recall them?'

'I thought you said I wasn't important?' Connie said, over her shoulder. Her hand was clenched tightly around the stone and she was trying hard to get her breathing under control.

'You aren't,' Bartholomew said, pulling her around. Connie stared down the length of a strange, matte blade, the same colour as Marcus's cylinder, its tip grazing her windpipe. 'You wanted to be involved, Explorer Girl,' he said, staring at her. 'Maybe you should have stayed where this was all just a game.'

Connie could see why Crispin Tocketts had panicked and thought Bartholomew was the Devil. The man was an immense wall of righteous fury. She stared at the blade, intensely aware of the keen edge, needle sharp, against her windpipe. The sword wasn't moving at all. Bartholomew's hands were perfectly steady. She had to at least try to delay him. The greenhouse wasn't so big that Marcus could take forever to search it. *Unless he's already dealt with Marcus?* Connie blinked the thought away. If that was true, then it was up to her anyway. 'Not using your pistols?' she asked.

'Bullets don't mix well with a temporal rift. You never know if they'll go through to some-*When* you don't want them,' he said, scanning her. 'Open your hand.'

'You did before,' Connie said. 'On the south lawn.'

Bartholomew scoffed, 'Storm wasn't so bad then. Open your hand.' He pushed the edge of his sword harder against her throat.

Connie complied. She wished she wasn't shaking so much.

'Other one.'

Connie opened her other hand. The stone shivered on it.

'Scared, Explorer Girl?' Bartholomew said.

Connie opened her mouth and closed it again.

Bartholomew shrugged. 'Works for me. Throw the stone on the floor, near my feet.'

Connie held out her hand. The stone dropped onto the concrete with a hollow clatter, rolling toward Bartholomew. He crunched it under his heel. 'These things never look the way you expect,' he said. He drew the blade back from Connie's throat. 'I think I should send you home,' he said, sliding a lever on the hilt of the blade. It collapsed in on itself with a metallic whoosh.

Connie swallowed, 'What is that?' she asked, shuffling back.

'It's a sword, Explorer Girl,' he replied, clipping it onto his belt. 'A Raven's Blade. Highly honed tungsten, collapsible, discrete. Not for amateurs.'

'Specially designed for the Order?'

'Yeah, they –' Bartholomew stopped. His blade arced out, extending from his hip. Connie leapt backwards. She hadn't anticipated it extending like that. She just caught it with her knife, batting it down and away. She fell down, landing heavily. Her arm jangled. Bartholomew loomed over her, kicking one knife away and stepping on the other one. He pushed the tip of the tungsten blade forward. Connie stared at him. She was not going to close her eyes.

'What is that?' he said, nudging the point of the blade under a length of leather around Connie's neck. He lifted the cord and a translucent stone slid out from under her dress and nestled it in the cleft of her throat.

'Nice try,' he said, snapping it from her neck and holding it up. 'This is definitely more what I thought it would look like.'

'Why is that?' Connie said.

'Because,' Bartholomew said, dropping the stone onto the floor and stamping on it, 'A keystone ties to the person it anchors. Ties in to their potential, keeps it a possibility in the midst of a temporal rift. Very unique items.' He frowned at the floor. The stone hadn't broken under his heel. 'Hmm.' He picked up a rock and smashed it down on the stone.

Connie began shifting backwards. The man in front of her was behaving very oddly and she didn't recognise this part of Preston Park. Her knife rang on the floor. She blinked at it. Why did she have a knife out? The man pointed his sword at her. A scratchy feeling on her neck made her feel like it wasn't the first time he'd done it.

'Don't move,' he said.

'John, Bartitsu?' she said, staring at him. 'What's happening?'

He scowled at her. 'Shut up.' He crouched down and hit a small translucent stone with a rock.

Connie stared at it curiously. It was quite pretty, glowing, with a beautiful spiral pattern embedded in it. It also wasn't breaking under the force of the rock. Quality craftsmanship. It reminded her of the pendant her mum had bought earlier at the steampunk festival.

A blaze of images seared behind her eyes. Confused and blurry. Connie leaned forward. Her vision was hazy. She panted. A voice rang in her ears, fuzzy and indistinct, but familiar. The voice was cursing. There was a sound of stone being hit against stone. A man grunting harshly.

Connie saw none of it, she was trapped in a kaleidoscope of images. A fair, bustling and happy. A ruin and a strange woman, dressed as a Victorian, but not in costume. 'Gertrude,' Connie mouthed the word. Her throat was dry.

'I really hope, for your sake, that you haven't tried the same thing twice, Explorer Girl.' An arm grabbed her. She squealed.

'Get up,' said the voice.

'No,' Connie said, flinging herself away. She was reeling. Still assaulted by images that made no sense. One was like a spacewalk, she was floating in some strange nebula-like clouds, stars glinting all about her. Then a temple and a boy overjoyed to remember his name – 'James,' she whispered. Her hair stood up in goose bumps on her arms.

Her vision clouded. The shape of a man, huge and looming appeared behind a scrawl of images that whizzed by like a broken film. Connie shuddered. The hand grabbed her arm again. Pulled her roughly upright. At his touch, the images became sharper, overlaid moments that flickered. Sometimes the woman and the boy were more distinct, at others, they were replaced by a man, prowling and issuing orders. The arm shook her. Connie flailed.

'I said, how are you doing that?' The voice was angry, cold. Connie blinked toward it. It came from the looming man, dreadlocks were becoming visible hanging about his face. Slowly, he swam into focus.

'John Bartholomew,' Connie squeezed the words out with effort. She could barely dredge the name from her memory. She heaved with the concentration it took.

Bartholomew threw Connie past him, growling in anger. She landed heavily, jarring her wrists. She twisted to look over her shoulder to see the tungsten blade unfolding.

'I'd rather have done it properly,' he said, pocketing the stone in a concealed pouch on his hip. 'But this is unprecedented.' He raised the blade and aimed it at her heart.

Connie breathed. It was all she could hear. The sound of air being sucked through her nostrils. The tungsten sabre filled her vision. There were patterns in the matte metal, evidence of multiple folds to strengthen it. Connie stared at them. She could still hear the raspy sound of her breathing, but the blade patterns were drawing her attention. They were swirling and beautiful, and there were no marks at all where the blade slid into itself. The engineering was magnificent. Also, it was taking a long time for Bartitsu – no Bartholomew – to stab her. *Not that I'm complaining*, Connie thought, *it just seems odd.*

Connie frowned and looked up at Bartholomew. A man stood behind him, holding a pistol to the small of his back. 'Finished admiring the Muramasa?'

'You're joking?' Connie asked, glad to recognise a name if nothing else. She rubbed at her temple. The sick feeling was coming back. 'That's a Muramasa?'

The second man shrugged. 'Connie, forget about the Blade. Where did he put the stone?'

Connie shook her head. It was starting to feel fuzzy again.

'Don't tell him, Conn,' said the other man, the one who was being held at gunpoint. He pressed a lever on the hilt of his sword. It slid back into the hilt casing. That was cool, but why had he been pointing it at her?

'Shut up, Bartholomew.'

Connie raised her eyebrows, not sure what to make of it all. Her head hurt. She stood up and looked around her. 'Are we in Butterfly World?' she asked, dusting down her dress. There was a big tear on one side of it. 'Mum's going to kill me.'

'Connie,' said the second man, more firmly this time. He looked like the bloke in the pith helmet from the Victorian Quarter.

'Where's your hat gone?' Connie asked. 'Is this theatre? She looked around them. 'Some kind of who-done-it? I don't remember signing up.' She peered into the undergrowth and searched along the ceiling struts. A network of pipes shook and began sprinkling water down over the plants. Connie shivered and frowned. Behind the two men, and untouched by the water that was sprinkling over the hot house plants, were patches of rampant flames. Connie stared at them, uncomprehending.

'Connie, the stone. Where did he put the stone?' The second man sounded more frantic now. Connie kept staring at the flames. 'In his pocket, Dad, jeez.' She stopped short.

'What did you call me?' Marcus asked.

Memories blossomed. Connie was at the park with her mum and dad. Dad was running beside her as she balanced along on a bike. There was a strange haze about the scene, a flickering quality to it. Connie didn't care. It was beautiful.

'I'm going to let go now, darling, ok?'

'No, Daddy,' shrieked Connie, her childish laughter ringing across the open lawns.

Connie's lips spread into a wide smile. Tears welled in the corners of her eyes. The memory was real. It was right there. Of course her mum and dad were there. Nothing kept the three of them apart. She felt warmth spread through her body. Her finger tips tingled. She gazed at the memory, tears streaming down her face.

'Connie!' Marcus shouted, staring at Connie. She was standing six paces away, smiling vacantly, lost in some vision. Outside the greenhouse, the temporal rift worsened. Lightning streaked continually across the sky. Wind howled, rattling the glass panes. 'Connie!' Marcus pushed Bartholomew away from him, levelling the pistol at his chest. 'What did you do to my daughter?'

'I gave her a future and a past she never dreamed existed, buddy.' Bartholomew said, stepping back, his hands raised. 'Made it a pleasant one for you, too. All you have to do is let me pass. You, Imara, Connie. You can all be together.'

Marcus cocked his pistol. 'No, that's a lie, it's not her life. Why are you doing it, John? Was it really so bad being a Raven?'

Bartholomew snorted, sneering. 'Maybe it was enough for you, but you never were very good at reading the fabric. Even Imara fooled you.'

'Leave Imara out of this.'

Bartholomew flexed his shoulders. 'Let me pass, Marcus. I won't hurt her, I swear.'

'You had your Blade pointed at her heart.'

'I did,' Bartholomew raised his hands, placating. 'But I'm glad you stopped me. It would've been wrong. I'm not the bad guy here, Marcus, My future is tied up in this, too. You never saw it, you were too obsessed after losing Imara, but I am key to our future. Noteworthy. Not a Raven, a Person. I'm not rending the plane, I'm correcting it.' His eyes shone zealously.

'You're deranged,' said Marcus, wincing.

'Leg hurt?' asked Bartholomew, peering down at Marcus's lasered wound. 'I thought you'd be better at that.'

Marcus sucked in a hard breath, shifting his balance, raising the pistol.

'I wouldn't use that if I were you,' Bartholomew smiled.

'Why not?'

Bartholomew cocked his head to the side. 'You might hit your daughter.' He raised his eyebrows at Marcus and arranged his mouth into panto-mime shock.

Marcus looked over Bartholomew's shoulder. Behind him was a rend in the temporal plane. Through the sliver window he could see Connie shrieking in delight on the south lawn. His eyes teared up at the possibility laid before him. He'd never met his daughter before the steampunk festival, never existed in the same century as her. But here she was, with him, as if he'd always been there. He stared, entranced, at the memory-that-could-become.

Connie was about three years old, riding a bike and behind her, Marcus saw himself, holding the saddle, supporting her as she shakily pushed the pedals around. His shirt sleeves were rolled up, shirt tucked into jeans. A normal, twenty-first century father. He was laughing, calling encouragement as he released the saddle and Connie pedalled forward on her own, wobbling but delighted. Imara sat on a picnic blanket behind them, clapping. Bundled up next to her was an oversized grey NASA sweater. His sweater. Marcus took an unsteady breath.

'That's your future, partner, and your past,' Bartholomew said, 'Just let it be what it should always have been.'

Marcus could feel warm tears mingle with the water streaming down his cheeks. It would be so easy.

'No one would ever know,' said Bartholomew, his voice soft, enticing. 'Once I correct the fabric, this will be all anyone ever knew. A family life, buddy. My gift to you.'

Marcus stared at the scene. He was flopping down next to Imara, Connie was riding in circles around them. The whole scene was suffused in a soft, flickering golden glow. He tore his gaze away from the time sliver. 'That is not my life,' he said to Bartholomew. 'It's not hers either. I'm not taking what she has from her.'

Bartholomew shrugged. 'Worth a try,' he said, hurling a rock at Marcus's leg.

The rock struck Marcus first, a direct blow on his injury. Marcus grunted in pain, hunching forward. Blood began to stain his trousers. Bartholomew tackled him, slamming him into the ground. Winding him. Marcus coughed and sputtered. The sprinklers were working overtime, that meant that the heat from the fire must be bleeding through the temporal overlay. He blinked the water spray from his eyes. He could feel a massive weight on his chest. A fist crunched into his nose. He felt it break.

'Not this time, bud,' snarled Bartholomew. 'I'm too close.'

Marcus felt a hand grab his coat. He was pulled forward, his head was still reeling. Another fist, this one into his throat. He coughed. Felt Bartholomew preparing another hit. He brought his forearm in front of his face. The fist crunched into his elbow. Marcus exhaled. Blood was streaming into his mouth from his broken nose. He threw his legs up; one caught around Bartholomew's head. Bartholomew let go of his coat. Marcus smacked back down into a puddle.

'Aggh,' Marcus screamed. Pain sang from the gash on his thigh. Bartholomew twisted his thumb into it.

Marcus gritted his teeth, heaved his other leg. It made contact. Bartholomew's dreadlocks whirled forward, smacking him in the face. Marcus looped his legs and heaved again, sending Bartholomew whipping backwards, crashing down. Marcus sat up. He tried to roll to stand but his leg gave way. A lump rubbed his quad from a pouch on Bartholomew's pocket. Marcus leaned forward. A boot struck him hard on the cheek. He pushed the boot away. Everything faded except for the pocket. He grabbed at the stone through the material, ripping it out.

The boot struck him again. He hurled the keystone toward Connie. She was still standing vacantly, staring into a false memory. It just had to make contact.

'Connie!' he shouted.

Bartholomew escaped Marcus's legs. He sat up, one eye bloodied, his cheek cut. Marcus rolled away.

Connie watched the flickering little girl. She was riding in circles around the picnic blanket while her Mum and Dad cheered. It was such a happy moment.

Something hit her cheek. She raised her fingers and looked down. On the grass beside her, touching her boot was a translucent stone. It had a silvery purple glow. Connie crouched down, one eye on the stone, one on the memory. It was so vivid. Her fingers brushed the stone. She blinked. The memory had changed. Now it was just Connie and her Mum, and they were on the street outside her house, by the stream. The clouds above were grey, threatening rain. Connie was wobbling forward, her helmet askew on her head. Mum walked along beside her. Connie watched them, feeling the rain soak through her clothes. She frowned, looked up at the clouds. It wasn't raining, just overcast. Mum let go of the saddle. 'You can do this Connie, just concentrate on where you are going. The rest is about balance.'

Connie frowned. *Where she wanted to go?* Her fingers curled around the stone. It warmed in her hand, pulsing. Her breathing became laboured. She felt very aware that she'd been still for quite some time.

Connie closed her eyes, trying to recall the memory, pressing the stone to her chest. It was her mum who'd taught her to ride. Her dad was an unknown – at that point anyway. The sound of metal ringing on metal echoed in her ears. She breathed in, feeling the water from the sprinklers soak her. The hot house in Stewart Park. Marton Manor. The time storm. James. Gertrude. The keystone. Marcus. Mum strapped to the TQC. Connie gripped the stone harder. That had been close. She opened her eyes.

30

Blades clashed in front of her and Connie threw herself backwards. Neither man seemed to notice her move. Marcus and Bartholomew were too intent on each other. Both men wielded a Raven's Sabre and a carbon cane, blades collapsing and shooting out again as they wove in a complex figure eight.

The fighting was stylised. It was like nothing she'd ever seen before. Connie could barely follow the footwork. She stared at Bartholomew and Marcus. Bartholomew huge and whirling, his sword an extension of his arm, his cane twisting like a cudgel, barely extended. He folded through impossible gaps in Marcus's defence. Marcus was smaller than Bartholomew, not by much, but enough that Bartholomew shouldn't have been able to make those moves. Then she realised he could do it because his sword was extending and retracting as he flowed through a form. Connie watched in fascination, her lips apart.

Lunge, parry, feint.

Marcus stumbled back, his face etched in pain. Bartholomew landed a glancing blow on his thigh. Blood spread across the fabric faster from his injured leg. He kept moving. Bartholomew shadowed him.

Lunge, collapse the blade, twist.

Marcus shifted away, parrying with his cane and wrong-footing Bartholomew. His footwork was heavy, one-sided. Connie realised he could barely stand on his injured leg. Bartholomew whirled around, his sabre slicing down toward Marcus's neck. Marcus switched cane and sword – Connie couldn't follow how – his sword retracting and extending with lightning fluidity. Bartholomew's blade glanced by, slicing a red line on his ear.

Connie saw the error. Marcus was now front foot on his injured leg. He wasn't going to be able to move.

Bartholomew growled and speeded up, pressing his advantage.

Lunge, lunge, feint. Retract, spin. Bartholomew dropped into a cross-legged sit, and kept moving, spinning back to standing. He punched Marcus's leg as he rose.

Whoosh. The sword extended. Marcus lunged out of the way, rolling across one of the plant beds and using a tree to push himself up.

Bartholomew stalked toward him, teeth bared in a grimace. Again, Connie wasn't surprised that at times he'd been mistaken for the Devil.

Connie watched them circle. She was barely breathing. She was impressed, Marcus could really fight, but he was floundering, hampered by his injured leg. Blood seeped more freely through the thick fabric of his trousers, a red stain spreading across the material. Bartholomew was hacking at him. He'd disposed of the carbon cane and was using his Raven's Blade two-handed, like a katana. His blade rang clearly against blocks Marcus was barely managing to make. Marcus wasn't going to last much longer.

Swallowing, Connie tucked the stone inside her bra, it seemed as safe a place as any, and reached for her knives. She only found one. Scanning the ground around her, she saw the other knife under some low-lying foliage and reached for it. As she leaned down she felt a tug inside her clothes. The stone heated at the movement. She grabbed the knife and stepped back.

'Ow.' The stone had gone from warm to icy cold. Connie looked down. She saw a freeze mark on her skin. She looked up.

Bartholomew had knocked Marcus to the floor and was rounding on her, tungsten sabre extending. He looked incandescent.

Connie spun the knives, breathing hard.

'I'm going to skewer you, Explorer Girl.'

Connie was shaking, staring at the point of the Blade.

'Connie, run,' shouted Marcus. He was trying to limp to his feet. He couldn't put weight on his leg. 'Run.'

'I'm not leaving you,' she shouted.

Bartholomew snarled and leapt at her. Connie ducked away, barely aware of what she was doing. Bartholomew's blade flew at her and she whipped the knives about, clattering hard against it, knocking it back. Barely. Her arms tired quickly. Bartholomew was stronger than her. He was pushing her back. The stone was getting colder on her chest. She gasped. The blade skewered toward her sternum. She whipped the knives into a reverse grip, along her forearms, and swept sideways, doubling up her block. She kept moving, not trying to stop the blade, just guide it away from her like she'd learned with her Sai in class – before Bartholomew had mangled her footwork in the display.

The Raven's Blade wedged into a tree trunk. Connie shifted away, dropping lower. That had been lucky.

Bartholomew retracted the blade and swung round. Connie swung one knife forward again, keeping the other tucked along her forearm.

'I don't recall you being that neat in the park,' Bartholomew said. His sabre whooshed out again. It was disconcerting. The distance between them disappeared, just like that.

'I don't recall you paying much attention to my footwork,' said Connie. 'You just wanted to beat me into the ground.'

'Still do,' he said, lunging at her.

Connie moved back lightly. She stopped trying to block Bartholomew's attacks, instead letting them flow to either side. She curled in on herself, keeping her limbs compact, her movement minimal. She backed away, heading toward Marcus. The stone began to warm on her chest. *What the hell was going on with it?*

She raised her arm to deflect a blow. Bartholomew's strikes kept coming. Connie collapsed under the force of it. Knees to the ground she managed to send it slicing down diagonally, second knife set as a safeguard.

Retract. Bartholomew spun the hilt in his hand. She hadn't seen that coming.

Extend.

Marcus lunged in front of her, his arms across his chest. Bartholomew's blade sliced into them.

Connie was thrust back. The laser ratchet was knocked from her cross belt. 'Marcus!' Connie shouted. Bartholomew was trying to retract the blade. It wouldn't move. Marcus had separated his arms. Connie winced. He was using his own body as a wedge against the micro layers the blade used to retract.

'Follow the stone, Connie,' he gasped. 'Run.'

Connie stared at him. She could feel the water from the sprinklers spraying on her. The heat of the flames behind her. The stone tugging against her chest. *Follow the stone?*

'Run, Connie. Run!' Marcus shouted.

Connie looked up. Bartholomew had retracted his blade. Marcus collapsed to the floor.

Connie spun. The stone tugged at her chest, pulling her forward. She sheathed the knives and ran.

Connie stooped and grabbed at the smooth grey cylinder as she sprinted past. Marcus had dropped it and it wouldn't hurt to have another weapon. She clipped it to her belt and leapt over some low foliage, through a sliver rend and into the flaming drawing room of Marton Manor. There was a momentary pressure as she crossed the threshold between realities. It felt as though she was being crushed and released. She landed on the drawing room floor and heard a disquieting crack. She wobbled and wavered, her arms wheeling wildly until she stabilised. She looked down. The floorboards had sheared, crumbling away in the flaming intensity. The only reason she'd not fallen through them was because she'd landed on a supporting beam. The thicker wood of the strut had prevented the beam from warping so far. The rest of the floor though, had vanished.

'So much for temporal superimposition,' she said, then shook her head. *Where had that come from?*

She set off along the beam, shuffling forward, her arms outstretched. She was breathing hard and the air was getting hotter. The reality of a stable, derelict Marton Manor was bleeding away. She jumped for the floor at the end of the beam and hugged the wall, sliding along it toward the drawing room door.

John Bartholomew landed on the beam at the other side of the room. His arm whipped back and he threw the Raven's Blade hilt, the sword extending.

Connie ducked. One shuddering breath reassured her she hadn't been hit. She slid to the door and chanced a look at Bartholomew. He was surging across the beam. She ducked through the doors, slamming them shut behind her. She scrabbled for a baton laid by a broken chair and rammed it through the door handles. She backed away from the door. It wouldn't hold him for long. She looked about her, trying to work out where in the house she was. It took a moment for her to realise the room wasn't on fire. It was dark and cold. Coated in a thick layer of dust. Connie looked around her. 'This complicates things,' she said, pressing her hand to her chest. The stone was emitting a stronger tug now, pulling her onwards.

A sound caught her attention. She spun. The blade of Bartholomew's sword retracted through the wall. The doors rattled, dislodging the baton. Connie ran for the next door.

She skidded though the open door and into the hall. It was on fire. 'Great,' she said, taking in the flaming carpet and the wide staircase, which had been partially caved in by a fallen chandelier. It laid tattered and broken, massive splintered floorboards cocooning it.

She felt an inexorable need to climb, to get to the roof. 'Damn stone,' she said, testing the floorboards in front of her and walking cautiously toward the stairs. Smoke was billowing about the hall, rising through a broken skylight at the top of the stair well. Connie coughed and covered her mouth and nose. She could feel the heat on her skin. She was definitely in the same reality as the flames. She sped up, Bartholomew would cross the room behind her in no time, but his weight might be a problem in here. She reached the bottom of the stairs and sighed in relief, grabbing the bannister.

She began climbing, hugging the wood. Her foot crunched on something. She looked down to see thousands of chandelier crystals under her foot. They were all shapes and sizes. She picked one up. 'You never know, Conn,' she said. She made it to the half-landing and blinked in the thickening smoke. She crouched down, trying to breathe under the smoke. Bartholomew was climbing the stairs just behind her. He lunged for her.

Connie screamed and ran, choking into the smoke. She thundered up the stairs to the first floor landing, barely able to see anything except a grey haze of smoke backlit by a flickering red-orange glow. Wind whirled the smoke on the landing and a large rectangular object appeared. Connie scrabbled for the edge of the bookcase and heaved, toppling it toward the stairs. She flung herself out of the way, relief flooding through her as she heard floorboards crack under the weight of books. She coughed and spluttered, pulling herself up on the balustrade. She dragged herself along the landing, using the bannister as a guide. Her eyes were streaming with water, stinging from the smoke. She struggled blindly forward, the stone and the bannister her only guide.

'Give it up, Explorer Girl.' Bartholomew's voice hissed through the smoke, the crackling of the flames lending it an eerie tone. Connie couldn't tell how far away it was. She lumbered forward. Her lungs were burning.

'You saw what you could have. All you have to do is let me meet my destiny. I'm only here to claim what is already mine.'

Connie's foot thudded into a riser. She looked down. Stairs, up to the next floor. The stone in her bra was still tugging. She heard footsteps amid the flames. Running. Connie swallowed. Bartholomew definitely wasn't up there, but the bookcase hadn't stopped him. She ran upwards blindly, coughing. A hand grabbed her ankle. Connie smashed into the stairs, winded. She panicked, kicked behind her. Met air. The hand tightened on her ankle. She kicked again, angling her leg. She felt the crunch of a nose breaking. Bartholomew roared. He let go of her leg. There was a thud of a body rolling down the stairs.

Connie scrambled away, climbing another eight steps. She stopped. There were no more stairs. Cold washed through her as she remembered the gap from when they'd laid their snare trap. She blinked. She'd climbed into a derelict moment of time. The stairs she was on were firm, coated in a layer of grime and filth. But ahead, beyond the gap in the stairs, the house was an inferno. Even if she could jump, there was no way she'd survive that heat. She looked to the side, the bannister here had broken away long before the fire. Connie leaned out and peered down, wondering if she could swing back to the first floor. She gulped. It too was a raging inferno. She looked across the light well to the landing on the opposite side. It was a wide, gaping space. Even with a run up she wouldn't come close to making it. She heard footsteps again below her and swallowed. She turned. Bartholomew's head was rising out of the smoke in front of her.

Bartholomew paused when he saw Connie and creased his brow, cautious. Then he caught sight of her predicament and smiled. He was nothing more than a head and shoulders embedded in billowing smoke. Connie didn't think she'd ever seen anything more terrifying. Bartholomew reached a hand to his nose and felt along it, then snapped it back into place. He never took his eyes off her. Connie winced.

'That is going to cost you, Explorer Girl,' he said, climbing toward her.

'Connie,' Connie said, swallowing.

Bartholomew laughed. 'My apologies. Connie.' He touched his hand to his forehead, mocking her, then reached forward and grabbed her hair, pulling her up to face him. 'You definitely get your stubbornness from your Dad. Why couldn't you both have just gone to live happily ever after? Do you know how much effort that cost me? I didn't have to do it. I wanted to give Marcus something pleasant. He was my partner, until he stopped seeing the bigger picture.'

Connie stared at Bartholomew. 'There's no such thing as happily ever after,' she said, twisting her head. He tightened his grip on her roots. Connie stopped moving.

'There won't be now,' he said, pulling her to the edge of the stairs.

Connie grabbed at his wrist, digging her fingers in. Fear flooded through her. 'You're going to drop me?'

'No, Connie,' Bartholomew frowned. 'I'm going to throw you.' He rolled his shoulder.

Bartholomew pushed her back. Connie felt her heels cross the edge of the stairs. She gripped his arm tighter. 'I'd have preferred to lose you in time, Explorer Girl. It's neater, keeps my future more intact, but I'll settle for stopping your heart.'

'Wait,' Connie said, her eyes wide. Sweat was streaming down her back, she had no idea what to do.

'No,' said Bartholomew.

He wrenched her head forward, grabbed the front of her dress and threw her into the light well.

31

Connie felt the space around her open up. He'd actually thrown her. It was unreal. She arced across the light well, barely able to comprehend the flames and smoke below her.

A thin, black rope dropped down from the skylight three feet in front of her. Connie stared at it, sailing closer. A rope.

A rope, Connie. A literal lifeline. Connie grabbed for it reflexively, wrapping her legs around it and pressing one foot on top of the other, the rope safely clamped between them.

'What the –?'

Connie could hear Bartholomew cursing. She swung on the rope, not daring to look. The stone continued to tug at her, she could feel it was warmer at the top than the bottom. She still felt the need to go up. The swinging on the rope ebbed to a gentle sway. Connie opened one eye. Bartholomew was standing half a floor above her glaring down. He levelled a pistol at her, his teeth bared. He fired.

The air in front of Connie shimmered and the bullet disappeared. She blinked at the rippling air. It was like a mirage in the flames. Bartholomew cursed and fired again. More ripples. Connie clung to the rope, staring at the mirage. 'The bullet holes in the woodwork,' she said under her breath, recalling the oddity from her first foray into the manor. 'It's a rend.' She looked up, along the ripple. It shimmered along at least ten feet of the rope. Connie lifted her legs, keeping the rope clamped between her feet. Pre-training for Tirol had come in handy after all. She began to climb, ignoring the sweat beading on her brow and the clammy sensation on her hands, which mixed with a rough pain that felt like rope burn.

Curses and the sound of gun fire reached her amid the raging heat and crackle of the fire. She blotted them out and kept climbing. Hand over hand, lift legs, cock foot, stamp on rope. Repeat. She kept going, coming eye level with Bartholomew. He was grinning at her. Connie gulped. The ripples had ended. Her head was clear of the rend. Bartholomew raised the pistol.

Click.

Connie released a juddering breath.

Click.

Bartholomew looked at his pistol. It was empty.

Connie glanced at his sabre hilt and balked. She started climbing again, her abs aching from the effort of pulling her legs up and her foot sore from holding the cocked position that was letting her climb. She puffed hard. This rope was thinner than others she'd used. A climber's rope, rather than a rope for climbing. She gritted her teeth and heaved herself up. The broken skylight was just above her. She was almost there.

The rope began swinging wildly. She looked down. Bartholomew was hanging on the rope fifteen feet below her. He was swinging from side to side in the light well, his bulk acting as a pendulum. Connie squeezed her feet together and hung on.

Bartholomew began hauling himself up the rope hand over hand. Connie couldn't believe what she was seeing. Despite the swinging, he was gaining on her. She looked up, four feet between her and the broken skylight, give or take. Her shoulders were burning. Connie heaved on the rope, pulling herself up. Her muscles sang in pain and she felt her calf begin to cramp. She pulled and reached, wrapping her fingers over the iron window edge. Slowly, gruellingly, she crawled out onto the roof, rolling down the metal frame and onto the tiles on the top.

She laid on her back and looked into the sky. The roiling cloud bank, lightning and thunder of the time storm was gone. The sky was a deep violet blue, speckled with stars. The Milky Way arced over the house, a band of speckled light in the dark.

'Why on earth wouldn't you just use the stairs?'

Connie sat up, frowning. It was Marcus's voice.

'Because I felt like doing a spot of abseiling tonight. The light well is as good a choice as any.'

'Mum?' Connie said, pushing herself to her feet

and following the voice to the point of the gable.

'You can't find a better spot than a derelict manor house?' Marcus asked.

'Not for free abseiling locally.' Imara dropped a climber's bag onto the parapet. 'Skoosh over.'

Connie peeked over the point of the roof. Below her, sitting on the parapet were her mother and Marcus. His arm was draped around her shoulders and her head was leaning on his.

'Mum,' Connie shouted. Her mother was here, and she was ok. Connie was elated.

'I love these moments,' said Marcus. 'Just us and the stars.'

'Shame we won't get too many more of them,' said Imara.

'Mum,' Connie shouted again, frowning. It was quiet on the roof, there was no way her mother hadn't heard her.

'What do you mean, Im?' Marcus said.

'Don't worry about it.'

Connie could hear the smile in her mother's voice. It was a tone that she used only when she was feeling happily content. 'Mum?'

Imara and Marcus continued to stare out at the sky. Neither shifted, neither looked around. Connie got the strangest sensation that they had no idea she was there. She clambered over the roof and slid down to the parapet. It was a flat stone ledge about a foot wide. Loose stones dislodged and clattered off the edge. Connie watched them fall and gulped. It was a long way down.

'Always easier going up,' she said, cautiously pushing herself to her feet, one hand trailing along the tiles to her right. She glanced at her mother and Marcus. They still hadn't moved. Connie waved her hand slowly side to side. It should have been enough for one of them to spot her. They didn't. Connie crouched closer. On inspection, her mother looked younger by about a decade. Marcus though looked much the same as when she'd met him. Less bloody, but essentially the same. Connie frowned. Her mother's lips were moving, but Connie couldn't hear anything she was saying. She waved her hand in front of her mother's face. Imara didn't flinch, just laid her head on Marcus's shoulder.

They couldn't see her. Connie sat back on her haunches and sighed. 'Superimposition,' she said to herself, gulping back her disappointment. She stared at her mother, feeling alone and afraid.

Under her dress, the stone was getting hotter. It was uncomfortable on her skin now, burning her flesh, and still tugging her forward toward the tower room. Connie wiped her mouth and looked at her mum. She and Marcus were fading, insubstantial forms. The wind picked up. Lightning flashed across the sky. Connie jumped. One foot flailed over the edge. She threw herself toward the tiles, breathing a sigh of relief as she regained her footing. She looked up. The time storm was rolling across the sky once more. She looked back at her mum and Marcus. They began to fade, blown away on the wind. The last vestiges Connie saw was of her mum laughing at something Marcus had said.

'Bye Mum,' Connie said, pushing herself off the tiles and wiping her eye.

'Aw, that's sweet, Explorer Girl.'

Connie's shoulder's slumped. She looked up at the apex of the roof.

John Bartholomew, his face blackened with soot and smoke, was leering at her over the gable.

Connie backed away along the parapet, her eyes fixed on Bartholomew, her hand trailing on the tiles. He jumped over the apex and slid down to the parapet, stalking toward her.

Connie sped up, feeling for the windows, where the parapet narrowed. She knew there were two between her and the tower room. The tug of the stone was getting stronger. She slid around the first window, breathing hard as she gripped the turned stonework, her fingers slippery. Bartholomew sped up. Connie moved faster, shuffling her feet backwards but not daring to turn away from Bartholomew. He reached the first window.

'Give me the stone and I'll send you to your parents.'

Connie felt the second window behind her. 'You

tried to shoot me,' she shouted back.

'I didn't say where you'd meet them,' Bartholomew laughed, swarming past the first window and striding toward her. 'But you'll all be together.'

Connie grabbed the top of the window edging and swung herself, spinning, across the narrow gap, hauling herself to the far side. She felt finger tips on her knife hilt. She threw herself forward onto the parapet. To her right, she saw a gap in the rooftop, a drainage channel between this roof and the next. She scrambled for it, her knees scraping on the stone. She swept into the narrow channel and spun round, reaching for her knives. They weren't there.

'Looking for these?' Bartholomew appeared at the roof edge, obliterating everything behind him. Connie's eyes bulged. He had both of her knives and was spinning them idly, grinning at her. 'I never waste a weapon, Explorer Girl, and it's not like you are going to need them.'

Connie shuddered and gulped.

Lightning flashed, splitting the sky and leaving light echoes trailing behind it. The wind whipped Connie's hair about her face. She stared at Bartholomew and stepped back.

'Agh.' Cold seared at her chest. She clutched at it and froze, looking up. Something thunked against her thigh.

'Hurts doesn't it?' said Bartholomew, squeezing his broad frame into the channel and trailing the knives along the slate. They made a screeching sound that echoed down the man-made gully. Connie shivered. It was easy to imagine this was Hell.

'You're interfering with destiny, Explorer Girl. That stone is telling you to give it to me.'

Connie stepped back, gripped in pain. The thing thudded again. She looked down. Marcus's tungsten Raven's Blade, or maybe it was his carbon cane, was clipped to her belt. Connie shivered. She didn't care which one it was, it was a weapon. She pulled the hilt, settling in a double handed stance. She rolled her shoulders, dropping them into place.

Bartholomew raised an eyebrow and laughed. 'Got to admit, I did not see that coming.' He stood up, chuckling, Connie's knives lowered. 'Go ahead, give it your best shot.'

The wind gusted down the gully, blowing Connie's hair in front of her face. Strands whipped ahead of her. She pressed the lever on the hilt.

32

Nothing happened.

Connie looked down at the hilt. She pressed the lever again.

Still nothing.

Over the howl of the wind and thunder, Connie heard Bartholomew laughing. She looked up at him, aghast.

'Didn't see it coming, but knew it wouldn't help you.' He was chuckling, but there was a menacing undertone to the sound.

Connie gulped. She didn't believe it. She pressed the lever harder, again and again.

'It's bio-printed, Explorer Girl,' Bartholomew said, looking satisfied. 'Only extends for the Raven it's assigned to.' He spun her knives outwards, pointing them toward her. 'These, however, are not, and they're actually nicely weighted.'

'Muramasa.' Connie looked down at the sword hilt, curling her fingers around it. It was rumoured his blades were cursed. Now she knew why. She reached one hand into the pouch at her hip.

'Muramasa,' Bartholomew agreed, swinging his head in an exaggerated nod. 'Guess you weren't paying attention when good old Dad told you it was a Muramasa blade. All those superstitions.' He leered at her.

'Superstitions that came from the Order of the Raven.'

'Some blades get lost, or stuck extended, but they still can't be wielded unless you're a Raven.' Bartholomew smiled, stalking toward her.

'Wait, wait, wait.' Connie stumbled back. 'What if I give it to you?' she asked, holding out her clenched fist. 'You could send me, Mum and Dad to that future you showed us. It was beautiful.' She swallowed.

Bartholomew paused, considering. 'I think I'd rather take it. You've already caused too many problems.'

Connie shuffled back, her jaw set. 'Then take it,' she said, hurling the stone over his head.

Bartholomew whipped round, leaping and twisting. He grabbed the stone out of the air, landing closer to the roof edge facing away from her.

Connie got to her feet, gauging the distance. Further than she would like. She gripped the hilt of the Muramasa blade. It might be useful for something.

'This is a chandelier crystal.' Bartholomew turned around, throwing the crystal aside. He was seething. 'You did it again?'

Connie gulped. Now or Never. 'Well, you didn't seem too bright, Time Boy,' she said, hurling the

Muramasa hilt at his head.

Bartholomew threw his free arm out to ward off the sword.

Connie ran and leapt at him, kicking both of her feet into his chest. Bartholomew flew backwards. Connie landed on her back, her head smacked against the stone gutter. 'Ow,' she said, pushing herself up onto her elbows. Her heart sank. Her kick hadn't been hard enough. Bartholomew was only half off the roof, his torso and buttocks were hanging over the edge of the parapet, but his knees were wedged against the slate roof edging, stopping him from falling. She could hear him grunting, his stomach contracting as he tried to pull himself up.

The stone burned on her chest, pulling her upward.

Lightning flashed.

The weathervane illuminated, the markings on it clearer from the rooftop. It was the same mix of Sumerian and Futhark she'd seen on the TQC in the Infinity Chamber and there was a small oval indentation beneath the vane.

'Follow the stone,' Connie breathed, scrabbling up the roof. 'Couldn't have been somewhere easy, could it?' She glanced behind her, Bartholomew was heaving himself up, his hands reaching for a hold. She didn't have much time and she was out of ideas. Adrenaline flooded her body and she pulled herself onto the narrow apex, balancing along the moulded tin, which was greasy with rain. This was much harder than the high ropes. The tassels on her zips thrummed against her calves in the wind. She reached the end and leapt, two-footed, onto the tower dome.

Connie landed squarely, one foot in front of the other on the iron frame, her fingers hooked around the iron strut. The glass on either side cracked. Connie gritted her teeth and sidled up the iron, reaching the narrow cylinder formation below the weather vane. She pulled herself up it, using her arms and anything she could wedge her foot against to get to the base of the weather vane. She looked up, the hollow was just above her. She reached into her bra and pulled out the stone, feeling a sear on her chest where it had burned her.

A hand grabbed her ankle and wrenched. Connie clung on. 'Don't you ever give up?' she shouted through a mass of hair.

'That's why they'll write history about me, Explorer Girl,' Bartholomew shouted back, dragging on her foot and shaking her. The wind whipped Connie's hair again, clearing a tiny section below her. She looked down and saw Bartholomew wedged in the glass. It had shattered around him and he was bleeding freely. Below him, Marton Manor blazed. Smoke curled out through the broken shards, twisting around Bartholomew.

The wind blew again obliterating her view. Connie heaved a sigh of relief and clung to the tower. Tears streamed down her face. She hurt everywhere. Her hair was all over her face, she couldn't see anything. She reached up, tapping the stone toward the hollow. It didn't lodge. She was too low. It was burning hot now. Connie could barely hold onto it.

Bartholomew kept swinging on her leg. She could feel her strength fading. Around her the lighting had intensified to near constant. It tore across a dark sky, a menacing, rippling purple. Connie gritted her teeth. The stone was searing her palm and her face was bruised from the iron. She breathed hard and leaned into the arm wrapped around the tower, her fingers were clenched so tight she didn't think she'd be able to let go. She pressed her forearm to the other side, keeping her hand locked around the agonising stone, counting as Bartholomew shook her foot. She closed her eyes. One, two, three.

Connie pushed off her other foot and raked it down her leg toward Bartholomew's hand. She stamped. Iron twisted and glass shattered and Connie felt herself stretch. The damn man hadn't let go. Her arm started to slip. She kicked again, stamping on her own foot, flexing it down.

Bartholomew's fingers slipped and Connie felt her foot get lighter. Her body stopped stretching. Connie could feel her jaw trembling. She gripped the iron, trying to get a firm purchase on the rain-slicked metal. *Follow the stone.*

She tensed her arm around the tower and lifted

her leg slowly back onto the iron strut. It bent, but it didn't give.

Follow the stone. It burned in her hand. Connie shuffled up the iron strut bodily, shaking the whole way. *Follow the stone.*

At the top, she slid up the weathervane pole, reaching for the hollow. The stone cooled rapidly. Connie had no idea if that was good or bad. She slid it home.

33

Connie closed her eyes against the howling wind, flopping against the tower, her arms stiff and bruised. She was beyond tears. Only exhaustion washed over her. She closed her eyes and swallowed, steadying her breathing. Tremors shook the house. Connie clung on, her eyes squeezed tightly shut. She didn't have the energy to move. She shivered.

Connie cocked her head, listening. The wind had gone. The tremors had stopped. In fact, she couldn't even feel the iron beneath her and her arms seemed to be floating in an open circle where the tower should have been. She opened one eye, peering out into a vast, absolute dark. Connie swallowed. Around her, light streaked by, bright bolts across the black, but not lightning. There was a different quality to it. Connie watched it, awed, forgetting entirely that she'd been holding onto something. She felt as though she was floating. Her breathing was calm and rhythmic. She went to wipe her face but found she couldn't reach it.

'Am I dead?' Her voice echoed oddly around her. There was a faint hiss behind it.

She spun about, looking for anything that

might indicate where she was. A streak of light cut through the dark. It looked like the rends in time that had littered Marton Manor. Beyond it Connie could see a woman in a garden dressed in Victorian attire, her red hair pinned up neatly. She was placing a small yellow stone into the earth, covering it delicately.

'Gertrude.' Connie's voice hissed back at her.

The woman looked over her shoulder and her face broke into a wide smile. She raised her hand in greeting. Connie raised her hand and waved back. It was Bell. But Bell was looking past her. Her smile faltered and her eyes widened. Her hand flew to her mouth.

Connie rolled over. Somersaulting was a good word for it, but Connie wasn't sure how she was somersaulting. Behind her, there was another tear. Through it she could see a small boy fighting his way across a rocky outcrop, his hair whipped about him in a silent gale. A trig point flickered in front of him, sometimes complete, sometimes just a frame waiting for the concrete to be poured.

The boy dropped to his hands and knees, crawling forward against the gale.

Connie could see the whites of his eyes.

He reached a hand out for the trig point. It was clenched around something. He pushed up off his other arm and was blown backwards, his oversized shirt billowing and catching the wind like an enormous sail.

'Hold on, kiddo,' Connie breathed.

Cook bent his head into the wind and lunged for the trig point. His hand disappeared inside it as it flickered from a frame to a flaking old hulk, white paint peeling from decades of neglect. Cook leaned his head on his trapped arm, his sides heaving. Connie could swear he was laughing.

Pain blossomed on her chest again. Her arms began to ache and wind pulled at her hair. Instinctively, Connie curled in on herself, her arms grasping the unseen tower.

'Connie.' A voice called over the wind to her.

Connie blinked against the wind and rain and looked down. Beneath her the flames of the Manor fire were out. The house was just a blackened husk. Ironwork creaked. Connie clung tighter to the frame. Her entire body was wracked with pain. Her ankle was throbbing where Bartholomew had tried to drag her off the dome. The dome shifted sideways. Connie screamed.

'Connie, the loggia. Run.' There was an urgency in the voice.

Connie frowned and wiped rain from her face. Her brain felt foggy. There was a grey light in the sky. Dawn was coming. Connie blinked again. There was no smoke. The rain was light, more a smattering than rain fall. 'Not enough to put out the fire.' Connie said, pushing herself up, precariously. She surveyed the manor house. 'Oh no.'

Around her, the house was dematerialising. Rooftops, walls, windows were fading away at different rates. The weathervane creaked and fell, crashing to the floor forty feet below. The iron frame of the dome creaked. Connie pushed herself back along it, scrabbling for the rooftop. The iron warped and twisted before her eyes, dropping away in front of her. Her feet touched the stone parapet and Connie threw herself back, landing hard on tiles. The dome collapsed.

'Connie, get to the loggia. Hurry.' Marcus's voice was panicked.

Connie rolled over. She was on the north side. She needed to get over the top of the house. She looked up the gully. Marcus was standing at the far end of it, waving at her.

Stone and tiles dropped away into the house, some just disappeared. The whole rooftop was behaving like shifting sand. Connie gulped. One wrong move... She didn't want to think about it. An iron strut appeared along the gully. Connie stared at it. 'Bolckow was an iron master.'

'Connie, move!'

Connie gulped. She traced the line of the strut along the gully, saw junction welds on the metal. Beside it, the house still had a roof, though it was looking increasingly dilapidated. *The steel frame would hold even after a fire. Not stably, but maybe enough.* She took a deep breath and walked out onto the beam.

Marcus nodded encouragingly, motioning her toward him. Connie kept going, steadily sliding her feet forward, one behind the other.

Marcus stumbled. Looked down. 'Get to the loggia,' he shouted, placing his hands on the rooftop. Then he dropped.

'Marcus!' Connie screamed, stopping dead still.

The house had vanished from underneath him. He was gone. Connie stared at the spot Marcus had been just moments before. Underneath her the iron began to twist. Connie looked along the beam. The whole length was buckling, the weld where another beam connected was bulging. Connie ran, all thought of balance and care gone. She reached the weld and leapt for the secondary beam, heading for the south side of the building. It was a gamble, but a good one. Tiles and roofwork disappeared in front of her, revealing a beam that was still sturdy, if narrower than the primary beam she'd started on. Connie stopped, looking wildly about. The beam was taking her west. She needed another one. The roof fell away, disappearing in a cloud of dust. Laid out in front of her were series of beams parallel to her own, spread a metre apart, all the way to the south edge of the roof. 'You have got to be kidding me.' Connie swallowed. The beams began to weather before her eyes. In her head she heard the laughter of the high ropes instructor after the air rounds. *"Do it without ropes and then tell me it's easy."*

She bit the inside of her cheeks and took a deep breath. 'Challenge accepted.'

She jumped.

Connie landed in a squat, curling her hands over the beam for extra surety. The first beam held.

She took another wavering breath. Four more beams and she was at the south side. She swallowed and sprung again.

Shaking, she opened her eyes. The second beam held. She looked up at the next one. 'Come on, Connie, you can do this.' She leapt again.

The third beam buckled.

Connie swung wildly forward, overbalancing on the twisted beam. Her fingers gripped the rusty metal and she strained her arms, forcing herself back up on top of it. The beam shuddered under her weight. Connie steadied herself and looked at the last beam. Her mouth dropped open. The last beam was a buckled mess. The iron a tortured lump. Behind it was the remnants of a stone chimney. Connie closed her eyes. The blaze at the manor must've concentrated heat up the chimney. The iron of the final strut had warped in the heat. It had warped before the fire had ever gone out. Time had overtaken her.

She looked down. Most of the building had vanished. Rubble and plasterwork littered the ground below her. The south wall was crumbling away, revealing the very edge of the loggia. She stared at the stone work as her beam began to bend under her weight. The fire had compromised it, now decay was finishing the job. Connie suddenly felt envious of the solid stone loggia. She'd been so close. Two metres, if that, and a fifteen foot fall if she'd been dangling. So close.

Her beam twisted again, bowing at the point where Connie was crouching. She closed her eyes and steadied herself. She was going to fall, that was certain, so she might as well fall in the right direction. It was madness. It was only two metres. *And a twenty foot drop*, she screamed at herself. 'I'll take twenty feet over forty any day,' she said, and leapt.

The wall vanished in front of her. The loggia rushed toward her. She was heading for the edge, not the roof. Connie closed her eyes and braced for impact. She was going to break bones, she knew it.

A hand grabbed her cross belt, pulling her roughly onto the roof. Connie landed in a heap on top of the person. She rolled off them and stared up at the bleached dawn. A pair of sparrows flew overhead. She looked over at her rescuer. It was Marcus.

'Where did you come from?' she asked.

'You're welcome,' he said, groaning.

34

Marcus clambered down the side of the loggia and looked up at Connie. 'Your turn.' Above them the sky had turned from thunderous black to a bleached-out white.

She swung herself gingerly over the edge and slid down the stone, her feet feeling for the decorative lip at the top of the column. Her arms ached and her chest was sore. Her feet found purchase. Connie winced and crouched down. Her hands slipped and she fell backwards.

She landed on top of Marcus again.

'Thanks,' she grunted.

'At least you said "thank you" this time,' he said.

Connie laughed and climbed to her feet, offering him a hand. 'What now?'

'We get Bell and Cook, and your mother, and I send all of you home, you're all still stuck out-of-time,' Marcus said. 'You need to go back to your own futures.' He grinned. 'Seriously? I was born decades after that film was popular.'

'And yet, you knew what I meant.'

Connie rolled her eyes and looked through the loggia. Parkland rolled away from the hilltop and the totems outside the museum rose on the far side of the arches. 'I think we're in my time, aren't we?' Connie asked. She frowned. The land-scape of the park was greying, colour leaching from it. 'What's happening?' she asked.

Marcus looked around. 'The plane isn't re-asserting itself,' he said. 'I don't know why. We need to get back to the Chamber before Bar-tholomew's future construct collapses.'

Connie watched the landscape fade, a blank whiteness rolling toward them. 'Mum,' she said. 'Could she still be strapped to the TQC?'

Marcus scowled and pulled the Infinity Monitor from his pocket. 'Damn it.'

He jogged through the loggia, across the foot-print of the house, now a flat lawn planted with summer blooms, toward the steps down to the parkland, still working the monitor. Connie fol-lowed him. A groan sounded from the bushes near the front of the Captain Cook Museum. Con-nie shivered. It sounded familiar.

'It can't be?' she said, looking at Marcus.

He paused his calibration, looking at the bushes. 'Stranger things,' he said. He reached into the undergrowth and pulled out a blood-ied arm. The rest of John Bartholomew followed. Marcus crouched over him, rifling through his pockets. He pulled out an Infinity Monitor. It was glowing and whirring. 'Ow,' Marcus said, dropping it. He took a breath and picked it up again using his fingertips, manipulating it until it stopped glowing. He pocketed it. 'Nice trick,' he said.

Bartholomew guffawed a pained laugh. 'Layers upon layers my friend,' he said, wheezing.

Marcus checked Bartholomew again, this time using the laser to seal his injuries.

'Why are you helping him?' asked Connie.

'It won't last long,' Marcus said to Bartholomew, 'but it'll get you in front of the Temporal Council.'

'Great,' he replied.

Marcus stood and began calibrating his Infinity Monitor again. Connie looked at Bartholomew in disgust. She stamped toward him, anger boiling over. He'd tried to kill her.

Marcus caught hold of her. 'What are you doing?'

Connie sawed her jaw back and forth. On the ground, Bartholomew wheezed out a laugh. 'I wouldn't blame you, Explorer Girl,' he said.

Connie snarled. 'My name is Connie,' she said, shrugging away from Marcus. 'You aren't limping,' she said to him, surprised she hadn't noticed sooner.

'I might not use that laser well, but it's an amazing bit of kit.' He finished his calibration. Lavender mist swirled in front of them.

'Why are you helping him?' she asked again.

'Because I am a decent human being,' said Marcus. 'And because he has to stand trial for his crimes against history.' He glanced at her. 'There's a proper order to things, Connie. He's broken the most stringent oaths of a Raven. If

I didn't bring him in, I'd face charges myself. Would you have done anything different?'

'Might've thought about it,' Connie said, glaring at Bartholomew.

Marcus frowned at her.

'No,' she said, wrapping her arms across her front and hugging them close. She looked at the parkland. What little she could see of it was completely devoid of colour. The whiteness rolling ever closer. It was as though the landscape was being erased.

'Good,' Marcus said.

The mist stopped swirling and the vortex opened. Unlike her previous experiences, this portal looked calm and reassuring, a lavender passage fading into grey. Marcus pulled Bartholomew to his feet and helped him toward the vortex.

'What'll happen after his trial?' Connie asked, tearing her eyes away from the blankness.

'If he's convicted, ignominy,' said Marcus. 'He'll be erased from the annals. Set adrift in time. The fate he wanted for those whose futures he would have stolen. The worst fate possible for a Raven.'

'If?'

'Trial still works on innocent unless proven guilty *When* we come from,' Marcus said. 'Come on.' He set off toward the vortex, supporting Bartholomew. Connie followed behind.

Vortex portals opened along two time strands.

Connie watched as two figures, one in large skirts, the other a slip of a boy, materialised along them.

'Connie, you made it,' Cook shouted, running along the time strand toward her. He barrelled into her, wrapping his arms around her waist.

'Hi, kiddo,' Connie said, hugging him. She closed her eyes, relieved he was safe. It was definitely like having a younger brother.

'I'm glad to see you too, Connie,' said Bell, as they reached the dais.

'I didn't think you'd made it. I was worried. But you're here, so did you see it?' Cook asked. He looked upset.

'See what? And why?' Connie crouched down and looked at him.

'It seems Master Cook and I are in agreement,' said Bell. 'We failed to save one future. The Raven's future.' Her face was ashen.

Connie stared at Bell, perplexed and horrified. Marcus had said the Temporal Council both had and had not punished him. Was this part of his sentence for unwittingly abetting Bartholomew?

'Both Master Cook and I saw each other after we placed our stones. It was like looking through windows in our realities.'

'Ok,' said Connie. 'I saw both of you, too, so why do you think we lost Marcus's future?'

'Because we each saw another falling into blackness,' said Bell. 'Did neither of you see it?'

Connie frowned. 'No. Just you two. Marcus?' She turned to look for him.

Marcus was shackling Bartholomew to the floor by the TQC, his back to them.

Connie screamed. 'Mum!'

Imara was chained to the TQC, still holding the pulses she'd seen Bartholomew capture in the holographic image at the temporal harbour. Light from the TQC console illuminated Imara's face. There was a greyish hue to her mahogany skin and her head was pushed back at an awkward angle. Her arms were twitching and smoke was curling from the filigree gloves. Connie pushed past Bell and raced toward her mother. She could feel the heat pulsing off the TQC. Despite the laminated cooling system in the outer crystal shell, it was overheating. The machine was juddering, sending shockwaves through the platform.

Marcus grabbed her. 'Do not touch that machine,' he said, glaring at her. 'Use your brain.'

'She's dying up there, because you wouldn't come and get her.' Connie strained at his arm, sobbing. 'Mum.'

'Miss Bell. Hold her,' Marcus said. His voice was harsh.

Bell caught Connie's arm in a tight grip.

'What are you doing? Let me go,' Connie scratched at Bell, her fingers raking along her leather gloves.

'Let him work, Connie,' said Bell, catching her

other arm.

'Thank you,' Marcus said, spinning away toward the TQC and pulling gloves and a thick black coat embroidered with Raven's wings on over his clothes. He pulled a stubby knife from his belt, its blade a dull carbon black and stepped up to the crystal interface, pressed in close to Imara.

Connie watched with baited breath, half-heartedly pulling at Bell. Steam sizzled from her mother's trousers as Marcus leaned over her, pressing her limp body against the crystal. Marcus was sweating profusely. Connie could see the sheen on his skin. He reached up toward the cord holding one of Imara's hands, sliding his other hand between her face and the console, shielding it. He sawed at the cord, grunting and panting.

Connie could feel the heat rolling off the TQC. The quantum laser work inside it was overheating. She ground her teeth.

The cord snapped. The lights inside the TQC bounced erratically. The dais shook. Imara's head thudded toward the console, thumping into Marcus's gloved hand. Her other hand dropped away. Marcus pulled Imara backwards. The TQC pulsed, vibrated, stilled.

The heat in the chamber began to dissipate. The monolithic computer whirred quietly, its lasers pulsing in a complex and erratic rhythm. Time points glinted in a purple haze, lightning crackling quietly between them.

Connie exhaled slowly. She hadn't even realised she'd been holding her breath. She didn't care about the Chamber. She focussed on her mother, leaning against Bell's grip. Bell released her arm and she ran, collapsing next to her mother. Marcus was leaning over her, checking her vitals.

'Is she?'

'No,' he said, visibly relaxing. 'There's a pulse. She's just in shock.'

He pulled the tiny vial from his jacket and unstoppered it.

Connie wrinkled her nose. Even from this distance, the concoction made her want to gag.

Marcus waved it under Imara's nose.

Nothing happened.

'Come on, Im,' he said, picking her up. His eyes were watering. Connie found it odd. Despite everything, Marcus was still a virtual stranger to her, hearing him call her mum "Im" – no one did that – was strangely intimate. She shivered and sniffed. Marcus was holding the vial closer to Imara now, right under her nose.

Imara coughed.

Connie laughed in relief. 'Mum.' She placed a shaky hand on her mother's leg, holding her breath. *Open your eyes, Mum.*

'Take that thing away from me,' Imara spluttered, pushing Marcus's hand away.

Connie threw her arms around her mother, hugging her tight.

'Hi Connie,' she said, patting Connie on the back.

Connie wasn't sure how long she hugged her mother, all she knew was she didn't want to let go. She held tightly, breathing in the jasmine scent of her hair, not caring that one of Imara's braid cuffs was digging into her cheeks.

'Connie can we get up now please?' Imara asked her.

Connie pushed herself back, wiping tears from her eyes. 'Thought you were –' She couldn't bring herself to finish.

Imara smiled and shook her head. 'But I'm not. Best not to dwell.' Imara stood up and stretched her arms out, cricking her neck. She peeled the filigree glove from her hands, wincing as patches of skin came away with it. 'That was a little close,' she said, inspecting the damage.

Marcus looked over from the TQC. He was using two elements to control it, weaving the lasers into an intricate pattern of reflection and re-fraction against the crystal superstructure. The chamber was illuminating slowly, a gold-tinged violet pulsing softly all around them. Time points began shifting again, flowing in harmony about the cavern. 'It's done,' Marcus said. He looked at Imara, 'You ok?'

Imara nodded, her arm around Connie.

'Good,' he said, staring at her. He looked at Connie and turned away.

'I'm sorry, Marcus.' Imara said, letting go of Connie. 'She had to be born in her own time.'

'Mum, are you a Raven?' asked Connie.

'No,' Imara said, looking at her. She walked over to Marcus, placing a hand on his back. He glared at her.

'You played a dangerous game there, Im.'

She smiled benignly at him, then looked at Connie. 'I'm not a Raven. I just got lost one night. Wandered through a vortex.'

'What do you mean?' Marcus said, a confused look flickering across his face.

'I, might have bent the truth a little,' said Imara. 'There was too much I wanted to find out. And I liked you.' She shrugged and reached her hand around him tentatively. A look passed between them. Connie averted her eyes, the whole idea of Mum having a husband who was here was bizarre to her.

Marcus wrapped his arms around Imara, his chin resting on the top of her head. 'You still took her. I could have found a way.'

Imara leaned into him. 'You need to get everyone home, love.'

He released her and looked at Connie, Cook and Bell. Connie had her mouth open. Marcus smiled at her. 'Yep,' he said. 'I do.'

35

'This one will take you home,' Marcus said, pointing to a time strand extending from the dais. It was broad and thick, shining with the pulsing glow of the TQC. It disappeared into a wide, glimmering vortex, beyond which Connie could see glimpses of a stately red brick manor house. Other pathways and time points floated around it, weaving seamlessly.

'What about Manāt?' asked Bell. 'If I return without her there will be questions.'

'Manāt is already there. I opened a direct vortex around her.'

'That sounds difficult,' said Bell.

Marcus shrugged, an upside down smile on his face. 'It is.'

'Well, thank you,' said Bell, offering him a hand, 'And, apologies for, unthinkingly accepting a misrepresentation of you as fact.'

'Don't worry about it,' said Marcus.

'And also, for failing, in part, at the end.'

'You have nothing to apologise for, Gertrude,' said Marcus, 'But, please don't look for the Tocketts Tunnel again. You won't be able to enter.'

'I hadn't considered it,' Bell said, but she looked

disappointed. 'But perhaps I shall return to Arabia.' She rallied, smiling at Connie and Cook. 'Do take care, both of you.'

Connie nodded at her. 'You too, out in the desert.'

Bell walked along the time strand toward the portal. She paused on the threshold and called back, 'Just remember, Connie –'

'I know. An English woman is never afraid.' Connie called back.

Bell beamed. 'Quite.'

Connie watched the purple mist close around Bell, blotting out the serene image of the well-stocked Red Barns garden, so different from the closed-up house and overgrown grounds she knew.

'What happens to Miss Gertrude?' asked Cook.

Connie glanced over toward him. She knew of course, but to James Cook, Gertrude Bell was an unknown. She opened her mouth to reply, but stopped as Marcus raised his hand, his index finger aloft. He shook his head and Connie bit her lip.

Cook looked at both of them in turn, his lips pursing, an edge of indignation and childhood petulance crossing his features. 'Why won't you tell me?' he asked Connie, evidently deciding she would be the more likely to concede.

'I'm not supposed to.' Connie shuffled uncomfortably and gestured to Marcus. Cook turned.

Marcus had shrugged out of the thick black Raven's jacket and was hanging it on a nodule by the console. Connie was surprised she'd not noticed it before. He dusted it off, deliberately avoiding eye contact with Cook. Connie looked at Imara, who shook her head. She sighed. 'Why can't you tell him a bit, Marcus?' she asked, 'Bell saved his life, and who's going to believe him if he says anything?'

Marcus remained silent. He placed the control elements onto the TQC and began gliding them over its surface, reconfiguring the Chamber to open another time point, the time strand extending and widening to it, glowing just as Bell's had. Connie stared at his back, James Cook copied her. Marcus was humming as he worked, studiously ignoring them. Behind her, Connie heard Imara chuckle.

'Marcus,' Connie said firmly, she still had trouble thinking of him as Dad.

Marcus winced at her use of his name, then sighed and turned to face her. 'You have no idea of the repercussions that can come from what you're asking, Conn,' he said.

'Really? I just had time fracture around me and fell from a house that hasn't existed since before I was born. I've spent the last four days running around with Gertrude Bell and James Cook. They can't erase me, or this place, from their memories and you just sent Bell home knowing that. Time's already changed.'

Marcus looked over Connie to Imara. 'Is she always like this?'

'Always,' laughed Imara. A silent look passed between the pair and Connie held her breath. 'And she's not wrong. Though you're not right, either, Connie.'

'What?' Connie and Cook said together.

Marcus shook his head and raised his eyebrows. He adjusted the control element and the mist began to swirl around the time point, dilating it. A scene materialised through the fog. Marcus turned back to Connie and Cook, his lips pursed. He considered for a moment and let out a long breath. 'Gertrude Bell, James, is, was and will be, an incredible and daring woman. She, of all of you, has seen an Infinity Chamber before entering this one, though it wasn't an active one. These rooms take huge energy supplies to power. Some simply cannot be managed, and they are left to dereliction.' He shrugged, 'So, when she was in it, she didn't know what it was. But, sometime soon, after she fails to enter the Tocketts Tunnel again –'

'You told her not to do that,' interrupted Cook.

'And she'll try anyway,' said Marcus. 'After she fails, she'll recall that cavern. She'll connect it with this one. She's going to spend the rest of her life searching for it again, but she's also dedicated. She'll map and excavate and learn about the desert in a way no Westerner has done before.'

'Which desert?'

'That isn't important for you to know. The search for the Infinity Chamber will drive her, but she'll shape the world while she searches.'

Cook stared at Marcus, wide-eyed. 'Will she find it again?'

'No, or if she does, it is long after I die.' Marcus turned back to the TQC, fine-tuning the landscape appearing through the mist.

'That doesn't sound right,' Connie said, her mind working overtime.

Marcus ignored her.

'I think that will make her sad,' Cook said, looking into the time point. 'Is that Roseberry?'

'Mmm,' Marcus glanced at him. Connie felt irritated, she hated being ignored. She tried again.

'Marcus,' she said. 'You said, after you die. You mean before you're born? How could Gertrude possibly find something after you die?

'Connie Rees, if you learned nothing else from this experience, you should understand by now that both of those things are true.' Connie whipped round and blinked at Imara, who was sitting on the floor cross-legged, rubbing her head. She was still unnaturally pale, but she had an unusually stern expression on her face.

'How?' Connie asked, splaying her arms wide. 'Gertrude lives her whole life before I'm born, and Marcus is born long after that.' She turned to Marcus. 'You must know whether she finds another Chamber or not.'

Marcus chuckled. 'But I'm your Dad, and as you just pointed out, I was born a long time after you've died.'

Connie rolled her eyes. She could hear Imara laughing too. 'Not you as well?' she said. 'How come you understand this?'

'Easy,' said Imara. 'Travel through time a bit and you stop thinking linearly. You're right, Gertrude Bell died before you were born, but she's also just lived some of her life with you. Her life's "timeline" if you like, includes life out of her own time. So don't oversimplify it. If Gertrude can live after she's died, then she can find something after your Dad has died too.'

'What?' Connie stared at Imara blankly.

'Stop being linear, Connie. Our experience of time – as humans – might be linear, but if there is one thing I learned travelling with your father, it is that time itself is much more complex.'

Connie looked at her mum, her mouth agape, then she shook her head and frowned at the dais. Light pulsed out from it in a regular, even beat. She couldn't find any fault in her mum's logic, but there was something else about what Imara was saying. Connie couldn't quite work it out, it was staying stubbornly in the grey edges of her mind. 'But…' she trailed off, huffing. The thought wouldn't crystallise. Behind her, she heard Marcus laugh.

'Trust the philosopher, Connie. She's right and she said it much better than I could have.' He beamed at Imara.

'You mean physicist,' Connie said, frowning at him. She caught the look her parents were sharing and shook herself. She wasn't used to seeing her mum look at anyone like that. 'Mum is a physicist,' she repeated slowly, staring at Marcus.

'Right,' Marcus said, turning back to Cook, who was staring at the three of them with a slack-jawed expression.

'So, in answer to your question, James. Gertrude could indeed find another Chamber, but if the time she enters through it is after my death, I cannot know she has done so. However, I doubt she'll find one. Desert Chambers are difficult to map even in my time, all that shifting sand. Does that make sense?'

Cook nodded mutely, then looked at Connie. 'You are right, Connie' he said. 'No one would believe me. They'd think me addled.'

'Home time, Mr Cook,' said Marcus, motioning to the time strand. Connie looked into the vortex. Through it she could make out the familiar shark tooth summit of Rosebery Topping. She frowned, that wasn't Cook's time, but as she watched, the summit began to morph into a sugar loaf.

Connie, Cook, Marcus and Imara stepped out onto the summit of Roseberry Topping. The sun blazed down and a warm breeze blew across the top. Connie stared in amazement. The Tees Valley was laid out below her, a sea of immaculate green farmland. 'It's so strange to see it like this,' she said, tucking a strand of hair behind her ear. Marcus crouched down, inspecting the rocky surface.

'I find it comforting,' Cook said, standing looking out to sea. 'It's back to normal.' He turned and looked at the rocky summit, crouching, his fingers skimming over the sandstone, emulating Marcus. He gulped and then stood, nodding his head.

'You don't need to worry about the land shifting again, James,' said Marcus pushing himself up. 'Bartholomew rent the plane to drag you out of history, imposing his construct after you fell. He can't do that anymore.'

'Sometimes, I prefer to be certain,' said Cook. 'Today seems very much like the day I left. We must have had a clear run of weather. I do not know what I shall say to my father.' He blinked, looking down at the farm nestled into the foot of the hill.

'You won't have to tell him anything, except perhaps why you climbed the hill instead of going straight home to assist after school,' Marcus said.

'I do not understand. I have been away for several days.'

'We have returned you to the point just after you fell into the time storm. This moment is only minutes after you fell.'

'No one has yet had time to miss me?' Cook asked, his eyes wide.

'No.'

Cook nodded. 'This is a little confusing, but I shall be glad to return to mathematics and more usual work.' He extended a hand to Marcus, suddenly stiffly formal. 'Thank you for bringing me home. I expect you cannot tell me what will become of me?'

Marcus shook his head.

'Perhaps it is as well. That way I can believe it is of my own making, rather than preordained. Though I think if I should adventure again, it will be upon the seas. I assume there are no more of these Chambers in the oceans?'

'Not to my knowledge.'

'But they could be discovered after you die?'

'Or before,' Marcus replied, his lips twitching.

Cook gulped away a bubble of apprehension and nodded, his eyes fixed wide. He turned to Connie, 'Thank you, Connie. I shall miss you.' He extended a hand to her.

Connie batted it away and wrapped him in a huge embrace. 'I'll miss you too, kiddo,' she said. She stepped back, biting her lip, before blurting out, 'And I think, if you do have another adventure, maybe you'll find the Whitby colliers will be useful in your *endeavours*.' From the corner of her eye, Connie saw Marcus frown at her.

'Connie,' he growled.

Imara stifled a laugh.

'You think I should have another adventure?' Cook asked.

'I think you're made for them,' Connie grinned.

The boy's eyes lit up and he returned Connie's grin. Marcus coughed. Cook looked at him. Marcus motioned to the farm at the bottom of the hill.

'I best get back to the farm,' Cook said, crouching down and jumping from the sandstone onto a lower part of the summit. He turned and raised a hand in farewell.

'Come on,' Marcus said, drawing Connie back into the portal. It was thickening around them, beginning to cloud the view and Cook from sight, but just as he turned from person to silhouette, Connie could swear she saw Cook mouth "Endeavour," although it could have been "Adventure."

'Let's get you two back. Before you,' Marcus said, looking at Connie pointedly, 'Cause any more trouble.' His tone was measured, but he was staring at Connie. Behind her, Connie could hear Imara still stifling giggles.

She bit her lip and shrugged her shoulders. 'What harm could that really do? I didn't actually tell him anything,' she said.

'Well,' Marcus said, fixing her with a stern look. 'You know that Cook's ship was never meant to be called the Endeavour.'

'It wasn't?' Connie blanched, suddenly feeling

sheepish. It had always been the Endeavour to her. 'What should it have been called?' she asked, her voice small.

'The Enterprise.'

'What? Really?' Connie frowned at Marcus. It took a while for her to realise he was laughing.

'Dad jokes? Really? I believed you!' she said, swiping at him. Imara gave up on stifling her laugh and peals of laughter filled the air, but Connie wasn't sure how to take this revelation. 'It wasn't really, was it?' she asked, suddenly and inexplicably worried despite the absurdity of the suggestion.

The mist drifted away, leaving Connie and her parents in the endless, glinting, purple depths of the Infinity Chamber. The TQC was pulsing with an ethereal glow. Marcus began manipulating the internal crystals, recalibrating them for the next time point. 'Well, you'll never know, will you?' he said, glancing over his shoulder to look at her, half a smile on his face. 'Your turn.' He spun the control element and the purple fog thickened once more, a new landscape materialising in its depths, one with the unmistakeable shape of a giant steel aviary.

36

Connie exited the mist and looked around, confused. It took several seconds for her to realise they'd emerged on the grass behind Preston Hall, on the river side. She looked over her shoulder to see Imara and Marcus emerge, arm in arm from the thinning mist. Soon, it was as though the mist had never been. Her parents paused, lost in some private joke. Connie turned away. She felt like she was intruding and it was uncomfortable to think of Marcus as her father. Over the treetops she could see the top of the old aviary, silent and dilapidated once more. She heaved out a breath.

'What's up, Conn?' asked Marcus, coming up beside her.

'I feel elated to have survived all of this, but sad that it's over and life is going back to normal. And weird, about you.' She gestured at him. 'Sorry.'

'I would've come, Connie. If I could have.'

'Yeah. It's just hard.'

'I get that.' He looked down to the river.

Imara walked up to join them, quietly entwining her hand in Marcus's.

Connie paused and glanced slyly at him, 'Could I

come with you? I'd get to know you better.'

Marcus laughed, 'Come where?'

'Your time.'

'No,' Marcus said. 'Against the rules.'

'Shame,' Connie said, 'Would have made me feel better after losing out on the DSE programme at the ESA.'

'Connie,' Imara said, giving her a stern sidelong glance.

'It's alright, Im,' Marcus said, squeezing her hand, 'I might not have learned much about parenting, but I'm not falling for that.'

Connie shrugged. 'Worth a try.'

A low sound of rustling from the trees along the river bank intermingled with the sounds of tents being taken down and festival goers making their way out of the park.

He opened his arms. 'Give your Dad a hug?' he asked.

Connie paused, somehow giving Marcus a hug felt more odd than embracing Cook. She caught a hurt expression fleetingly pass over his face and stepped forward, burying her face in his chest. He had saved her life at least twice. 'This was definitely a surreal way to meet my Dad,' she said into the linen of his coat, unexpectedly feeling at home. The smell of alcohol drifted into her nostrils and she realised it was from a spill on his jacket. The one that had made her think he was a drunk.

'How did you end up with alcohol on your

jacket?'

Marcus grimaced. 'Bartholomew did it when he spiked me, I think. Remember, that's why I had a cut on my hand when we first met and I was struggling to stand up? Although it's possible I knocked into someone, I can't really remember.'

She pushed back, laughing at the memory of her first impression of him. 'Are you staying?'

Marcus shook his head.

'Let me guess, against the rules?'

He nodded, 'Yep. I might get to pop by. Following the rules all the time gets a bit dull. And I miss your mother.' He fell silent, staring at Imara.

She smiled back at him and Connie moved out of the imaginary line that was being drawn between them. It felt magnetic even to her.

'Save it guys, I don't want to know,' she said, feeling awkward. They glanced at her and she rolled her eyes, 'God, I never thought having just one parent would be easier!'

Imara laughed, her teeth gleaming against her skin. Marcus grinned at Connie and scuffed her head playfully.

'We should really go, love,' Imara said to Marcus. Marcus nodded and Connie felt a wave of sadness roll off him.

'I'll give you two a minute,' Connie said, wandering off along the path. It suddenly occurred to her that he had the harder part of the bargain. She had Mum, and Mum had her. Her Dad was the one somehow left behind.

Connie ambled on until her parents caught up with her and then the three began walking around the house, heading toward the aviary. As they came closer Connie could see workers up in the high struts, taking down the art installation. She felt a wave of disappointment. She'd not made it to see the display. They headed down the path toward the river bank, the wide ribbon of the Tees scorched orange by the setting sun. It flowed on quietly, the only sound that of rushes shivering against the current. Connie leaned on the jetty railing, a simple wood and metal construction to enable passengers on the river cruise to embark and disembark at the park. She rubbed at the burned skin on her chest, where the stone had tugged at her. It had seared her flesh. The scar would be there for the rest of her life.

A thought gripped her, something Bell had said. She'd been convinced that the Raven's future had fallen away in their combined vision. So had Cook. Connie's eyes bulged. Marcus's punishment. 'What about the other future?'

'What about it, love?' Imara asked.

'I caused it, didn't I? I ruptured your future. You,' she turned to Marcus, 'You said I was a back-up, an anchor for memory, but I only knew about Cook and Bell. I didn't know enough to anchor you. That's how they punished you. When

I asked whether you were punished for helping Bartholomew, you said "yes and no."' She could feel her heart thumping against her rib cage. 'You saved everyone but yourself.' She looked away from Marcus and stared at the water, biting her bottom lip. 'They used me. I ruined it.' She choked out the words, her eyes big and round.

'That didn't have the impact you think it did, Conn,' Marcus said. He placed a hand on her elbow.

'Shouldn't you know, though?' Connie asked, feeling anguish clench at her throat, a lump blooming in it. She swallowed. She felt desperate.

Marcus shook his head and squeezed her elbow. Somehow it was comforting. 'It's not that simple, Connie, but I'm telling you that you have nothing to worry about. You did everything right. I've spent over two decades researching the Infinity Chambers, but they are way beyond my time.'

'What do you mean?' Connie asked, suddenly hopeful.

'I've lived these moments, not researched them. I'm coming to this time unknowing, just like you.' He shrugged. 'I guess we'll just have to see what comes.'

'That's it?' Connie stared at him. 'You just shrug and tell me not to worry?'

Marcus rocked on his heels, leaning out over the railing, considering. 'I'm not allowed to go into details, Connie,' he said, staring studiously at his hands. 'There are things that make a lot more sense to me now that I've lived through that storm, but that's because my past is far in your future. I can't tell you, the same way that you couldn't tell Cook or Bell. But nothing is lost, the Temporal Council would have already sent other Ravens if there was a problem.'

'What is the Temporal Council, actually?' Connie asked.

'It's the Board that maps time,' Marcus said. 'They catalogue the Lore and issue the law on the Infinity Chambers, recruit and train Ravens, predominantly from the future, but as you know, there are some outliers.'

'Friya, Morgana, Merlin and the rest.'

'Interesting that you remembered Friya,' Marcus said. 'The Council also monitor the temporal fabric and isolate changes, they ensure the Chambers are not misused and punish those who try. They are the wardens that identify the faults in the fabric. It's how we track criminals like Bartholomew,' Marcus said.

'Right, so not a massive brief then,' said Connie, astounded. She frowned. 'But what if there's a problem? What if I've ruined future history?'

Marcus caught her by the shoulders and looked down at her. 'Future history is not something you need to worry about, Connie,' he said. 'That's what Bartholomew didn't understand when he saw himself in the fabric. He saw his own notoriety and thought he'd discovered a destiny, that he had to shape it. Look where that got him. He got notoriety, briefly, and lost his future.'

Connie exhaled slowly. 'Because he failed? He had to erase his own time strand to take the others?'

Marcus nodded. 'Yes.'

Connie blinked. 'So there's no such thing as destiny?'

Marcus shook his head. 'No, Connie, there's no such thing as destiny. Only potential, and what you decide to do with it. And you've got some potential, Conn. I know we don't really know each other, and that makes you uncomfortable, but you should know not many teenagers could best John Bartholomew.'

'I barely managed it,' Connie said, embarrassed as she felt her cheeks flush.

'But you didn't give up. And however uncomfortable it makes you, you should know that you made me very proud in that storm, Conn. Very proud.'

Connie nodded. The heat in her cheeks was rising rapidly. 'Thanks,' she said, looking at the river.

Marcus patted her on the back awkwardly and took a deep, juddering breath. Connie got the feeling she wasn't the only one finding this tough. He blew out a long, low whistle through his teeth and looked at her. 'So the only thing

S.L. BISHOPSTONE

you need to worry about is what you're going to do about your own future.'

'Huh?'

'The ESA. You're really going to give up so easily?'

'Mum!' Connie glared at her mother.

Imara shrugged. 'You weren't listening to me, so I took the unprecedented opportunity to tag your Dad in.'

'I don't like this parenting tag team thing,' said Connie.

'Stop deflecting,' said Marcus. 'You missed your first shot, but if you want to achieve something like this, you need to keep at it. Like you did on that roof. Now I happen to know,' he tapped his Infinity Monitor. Connie still couldn't believe they'd made it look so mundane. Marcus continued, 'That there will be a reserve place opening up shortly, and it's not against the rules for me to tell you that. So, get working on your presentation, pick up on where they said you were weak. Have a little more faith in your own abilities.'

Connie squeezed her lips together and looked at her feet, her shoulders hunched.

'Connie, you just survived a time storm and saved the futures of two of the people you most admired. Were either of them perfect?'

'No,' she said, thinking about Bell's imperiousness and Cook's fear. Both had their flaws, but they'd still achieved great things. 'Guess we really shouldn't meet our heroes, huh?'

'Or maybe meeting them means you can cut yourself a break?' Marcus replied. 'Getting into the ESA, it's not about following in their footsteps. It's about leaving your own for others to follow. What do you have to give?'

Connie nodded, huffing out a laugh. She'd never really thought of it that way.

'Thanks,' she paused, 'Dad.'

Imara walked over and put an arm around Connie's shoulders. She squeezed Marcus's hand. 'You might not be keen on it, Connie, but I think I like the parenting tag team.' She swallowed. 'Shame we won't get to keep it going, M.'

Connie looked between the two of them. 'You aren't staying even for a little while?'

Marcus shook his head. 'I can't, Connie. I wish I could, but I'm bound to the Chamber. I'll visit, whenever I can, but I can't stay.'

A purple haze began to form behind Marcus, the vortex opening to allow him to leave. 'I'll miss you,' he said. 'I've always missed you.'

Connie felt as though she'd been punched in the gut. She watched Marcus step back into the vortex, his outline becoming indistinct. 'Wait,' she called, reaching forward.

A hand on her shoulder stopped her moving, Connie looked over her shoulder at her mum. Imara smiled sadly back at her. 'I wish he could stay too, but he can't. The Temporal Council won't allow it.'

Connie looked back to see a hand, raised in fare-well, disappearing into the mist.

37

'But why can't I just train to be a Raven?' Connie asked. She was frustrated, and aware that she was pouting, but it just seemed like a stupid rule. 'You and Dad both are.' She glowered at her mother from the sofa, head propped up on her hands.

Imara sighed and shook her head. She shifted on her chair, adjusting her legs. 'We've been through this. I'm not a Raven, Connie.'

'Yeah, and I don't believe you,' Connie said. In the background she was dimly aware of the weekend weather report being broadcast on the TV.

'Well, that's because I did lie,' said Imara, turning the page of her book. It was a physics periodical. 'And you are pretty good at telling when I'm lying.'

'I knew it,' said Connie.

Imara held up a hand. 'It's not what you're thinking. I wasn't lost the night I went down the Tocketts Tunnel. I was trespassing.'

Connie's jaw dropped. Her mother, the fastidious rule-keeper. 'You were trespassing?'

Imara nodded. 'There was a sign in the priory ruins. "Keep out." The usual rubbish. But the lab had picked up some interesting readings, so, I didn't.' Imara shrugged. 'I didn't think of it as trespassing though, I called it urban exploration.' She shrugged. 'I was young. Younger, anyway, and I was curious. And it turns out I am very good at bluffing.'

'Uh huh.' Connie wasn't sure what to make of it.

Imara smirked at her daughter's incredulous expression. 'Connie, I did have a life before you. It was part of my misspent youth.'

'That's the part I'm having trouble with. You having a misspent anything. You were trespassing? Or are you lying again?' She narrowed her eyes at her mother.

Imara burst out laughing. Tea spluttered out of her mouth. She wiped her chin with the heel of her hand. 'Anyway, the short of it is, you can't be a Raven. I don't think the Temporal Council would approve of my mishaps through time.'

In the hall there was a creak as letters flapped through the box. The postman raised a hand to them as he passed the front window.

Connie got up and headed for the hall on reflex. 'But you did it,' she said. 'So, why can't I?'

'Just get the post,' said Imara, mopping tea from her jumper.

Connie stood by the hall console flicking through the post. At the bottom of the pile there was one addressed to her with a smiling man in the moon logo and the letters "esa" in the upper right hand corner. She frowned at it and scratched the bridge of her nose.

'Anything interesting, love?' called Imara from the sitting room.

Connie pushed through the door, staring at the envelope in her hand.

Her mum was sitting in a plush wingback chair in the corner in front of a bookcase built into the inglenook beside the fireplace, her legs curled under her. 'What's that?' she asked over the remainder of her tea. She'd placed the periodical on top of one of the rows of books on the shelves in the inglenook.

Connie handed her the rest of the post and flopped down on the sofa, still staring at the logo.

Imara peered at the envelope. 'European Space Agency?' she said. 'I'd have thought you'd rip that one open in the hall. Especially after what your Dad told you.'

'Yeah,' Connie said, her brows creasing. She'd not given much thought to it after the park. She'd been badgering her mother about becoming a Raven. Slowly, she turned the envelope over and slid her thumb under the flap to open it. She felt heavy. She'd done no additional preparation in the month since she'd emerged from the time storm. Marcus had given her a lead-in and she'd been preoccupied with his life, not her own. She pulled the letter from the inside and hunched over it, elbows on her knees.

She fidgeted her feet, lifting up her heels so she was on tip toes. Her wiry hair dropped forward around her face.

'What does it say?' asked Imara. She had leaned back in the chair, giving Connie some space to read the letter.

Connie took a deep breath. 'It says they want me to,' she swallowed. 'They want me to go to Tirol and present for a place on NEP. The Near Earth Programme. A slot opened up.' She pressed her lips into a smile and looked up at her mum.

'That's wonderful news,' said Imara.

'Near Earth, Mum,' Connie said. 'I didn't even apply for that track.'

Imara took a deep breath and nodded. 'You never know what will happen. You're not really going to give up just because it's not exactly what you wanted are you? Would Gertrude have done that? Did you, on that roof?'

Connie was beginning to wish she hadn't told her mum about the fight with Bartholomew. She wasn't really sure she wanted to remember it at all. She wasn't daft. She knew she'd been lucky, not skilled, to survive it. She rolled her eyes and looked at the ceiling. 'No, but according to Marcus, Gertrude didn't think not being called to be a Raven meant she shouldn't search for another Infinity Chamber either. I'm not sure you want me following her example. Previous conversation case in point.'

In her peripheral vision, Connie saw her mother

wince.

She sighed. 'I still find it hard to think of him as anything except Marcus, Mum. I'm sorry,' she said.

'You know he'd have stayed if he could.'

'I know,' Connie said. 'You really miss him don't you?'

Imara nodded sadly, then forced her face into a smile. 'But, what I really want to know, Connie, is when are we going to Tirol?'

Connie looked back at the letter. 'I don't know, Mum.'

'What, they haven't given you a date?' Imara tried to reach for the letter. Connie pulled it away.

'It's in two weeks, I just meant I don't know if I want near Earth missions. That's not what attracted me to the programme.'

'Connie, you never know what'll happen once you're enrolled. Take the chance.' Imara said, looking at her pointedly 'Because despite your deflection, I wasn't talking about the tenacity of Gertrude Bell.'

Connie twirled her feet in front of her. She was hunched forward on the bench, thinking and re-thinking her paper. It was good, she knew that, but she'd put in some detail that was pertinent to the Deep Space programme. Edged it in, really. She hadn't been able to resist, but that was worrying her now. She'd already been rejected once because the Agency thought her attention was on the wrong area. She stared at the resin floor. Sunlight fell in a cube pattern, dissected by wooden window struts. Her shoes shone in the light, buffed to a high sheen that morning.

Connie hated to admit it, but she'd only buffed her shoes that much because she was so nervous. Now she was regretting it. She felt uncomfortable dressed in her blazer and chinos. She knew that her physical presentation was important but she'd been aiming for competent rather than preppy and she felt too uncomfortable to present competently. She huffed and swung her feet. She knew she could make the programme, after the time storm and the technology she had been exposed to, the kind of research and construction the Near Earth Programme was aiming for was nothing she couldn't handle. Near earth, deep space. It didn't matter. Confidence wasn't her problem. Comfort was. She shoved her finger inside the collar of her blouse. She should've gone for something less formal, she'd have been able to think better. *Really, this is what you're thinking about?* she admonished herself.

'Nervous?' asked Imara, sitting down beside her, her braids swinging over her shoulder, her hands wrapped around a reusable coffee cup. She took a sip.

'I think it would be more weird if I wasn't, but I wish I wasn't judging myself based on what I'm wearing. I'm distracted, Mum.'

Imara chuckled.

'Something funny?' asked Connie, pressing her face into her hands. She felt sick. Imara rubbed Connie's back. 'I just think that if you've got time to be worried about your appearance, you're probably all set, Connie.'

'But I should be thinking about vector calculations, physical resilience, unorthodox repair techniques. Stress loading.' Connie couldn't get anything sensible into her head. She was getting fractious.

Imara laughed. 'Connie, they aren't going to want to know about vector calculations. You already proved you had aptitude for the mathematics and mechanical requirements months ago. If you make the cut today you could be orbiting the earth for months, even years, at a time testing the deep space equipment. They want to make sure you'll fit into the team.' She waved her hand. 'The ESA will teach you vector calculations and solar repair work, and it'll be far more advanced than anything you've done up to now.'

Connie opened her mouth.

'Yes, even the projects you and I did together,' Imara said. 'It's the reason they've created this lovely training camp that's so far away from home.' She gazed down the sterile white hall. 'Could do with some colour though,' she said.

Connie rolled her eyes. 'Fashion and interior decoration. When did we become so shallow?'

she laughed. 'Anyway, I told you to apply for CERN.'

'Maybe,' Imara smiled.

Connie knew she wouldn't. Marcus was posted to the Gisborough Infinity Chamber, her mother would never see him if she moved to Switzerland.

A door opened down the hall and a man poked his head out. 'Miss Connie Rees, please,' he said in a thick German accent.

Connie pushed herself off the bench and smoothed down her jacket. The weight of facing the panel pushed everything except astrophysics from her head. She breathed a sigh of relief, closing her eyes. She was ready.

'Miss Connie Rees, please.'

Connie glanced down the hall toward the man and nodded. He disappeared inside. Connie flashed her mum a smile. 'How do I look?' she asked.

'Like an astronaut in waiting,' said Imara. 'You nervous?'

Connie pushed her chin up and gave her mother a level stare, 'An English woman, Mother, is never afraid.' She set off down the hall toward the committee room door.

Imara shook her head, 'That's not true though, is it?' she said.

Connie paused, her hand on the door. She glanced at Imara. 'We never tell them that, Mum,' she said, smiling. 'Never.'

***

End of book one of

Raven's Call

ACKNOWLEDGEMENTS

Writing this book has been a huge undertaking, and one that would not have been possible without the love, help and support of my family and friends. They have all contributed in their own way and I'm incredibly grateful for their support.

A few deserve particular mention; Marie, who listened one grey December day to a half-formed story and offered one very salient comment: 'Sarah, I think your protagonist needs to be a girl.' The story really took off when I took that on board. A special thank you to my ever-patient mother, who took long stints at Nanny duty when I needed to meet a deadline and then sat up late doing editing work for me. Thanks also to Catherine, Tom, Becks and Helen, who were the first to read the finished draft and gave me constructive (and sometimes picky, but all the better for it) feedback, and thank you to Chelsea, who created my lovely website, slbishopstone.com, in record time in the midst of an intercontinental move. At every turn, I felt the work got better and my determination to publish increased, so thank you to you all.

Thank you as well to all of those who listened

to me witter while I thought through problems and resolved plot holes, or just listened to me wax lyrical about actually writing a novel. Your patience and understanding in the midst of your own busy lives did not go unnoticed.

Finally, thank you to you, my readers, who have taken a chance on a new indie author and followed Connie's first story to the final page. I hope you will join us for Connie's next adventure.

Thank you for reading

Order of the Raven

If you enjoyed the book and want to know more about the people, places and legends in it, please subscribe to my author newsletter, where you'll also get first sight of upcoming releases and special offers.

slbishopstone.com

INSPIRATION FOR
ORDER OF THE RAVEN

The conversation below contains spoilers for the plot. If you have not read the book, I recommend you do not read this conversation until you have finished it.

How did you come up with the idea for *Order of the Raven?*

The *Order of the Raven* is a book that came in pieces, which all meshed together to form a story that entwined local history and legend into a fantastic adventure. It is a celebration of my childhood home and its history, a history that is often overlooked both locally and nationally.

In 2019, I returned to the North East with my children after spending some time living in Germany. I revisited places my grandparents and parents had taken me to with my own children and I was struck by how much had changed and how much was still the same. I went to old haunts and explored them again, seeing them with new eyes. A chance day out at steampunk festival at Preston Park – though it's not as big as in the book – got me pondering all these things together, and the *Nightfall* exhibition later in the year cemented the beginnings of a story in my head.

Connie and Marcus were clearest, though Connie was originally someone else. I built the story around them, drawing on real history from the area to cement it. I particularly loved retooling the legend of the Raven's Gold. That is a real, and somewhat timeless, legend in Guisborough and one that leant itself beautifully to my story. I found myself wanting to search for the Tockett's Tunnel. Who knows, maybe there really is an Infinity Chamber out there...

How did you come up with the idea of the Infinity Chamber?

Years ago, when I was travelling, I visited the Brisbane Art Museum and found a piece by Yayoi Kusama, titled "Infinity Room." It was a small, man-sized box, probably six-by-six- by-ten and you could sit inside it.

The interior was mirrored and lit so as to give the impression that you were floating in an infinite space and it was relatively soundproofed. I must have sat in there for about forty minutes, enjoying the vast peace inside this tiny space in the middle of a crowded city.

When I came to reframe the legend of the Raven's Gold, I remembered Kusama's art and realised that it was a perfect analogy for the Infinity Chamber, so I used her ability to generate 'infinite' space as a leaping off point.

How did you decide upon the constraints of the Infinity Chamber?

That was a tough one. These Chambers have vast power (a power we'll discover more about in subsequent books) but their power did need some constraints. The Chambers don't confer omnipotence on users and one of the ways I realised they could be limited was to make their impact and reach be identified as tied to place, and to make some moments inaccessible until there was a need. We see this in the reference to the Rann of Kutch earthquake and Allah Bund midway through the book, and in John Bartholomew's struggle to send Connie, Bell and Cook out to the Bolckow estate. The fallout from the misuse of the Kutch Chamber was limited to its locale. Similarly, any fallout that Bartholomew managed to wreak out of Gisborough would be limited to North Yorkshire and the people who lived, or became notable Persons, there.

Why doesn't Katherine Johnson appear in the novel?

As I mentioned, the influence on time that is exerted by the Infinity Chambers is limited to the place that they are constructed. There may well be an Infinity Chamber in Virginia, but that would no more pull Gertrude Bell to the US than the Gisborough Chamber would pull Katherine Johnson to the UK.

From a story telling perspective, this also

meant that Connie didn't need to constantly wonder why she couldn't meet her absolute hero, Katherine Johnson.

Gisborough or Guisborough? What's in the name?

For the grammatically inclined among you, the spellings of Gisborough Priory and Guisborough town probably caused some consternation in the novel, but in fact both are correct.

The town name of Guisborough first appears in the Domesday Book (noted in 1086) where it is referred to as "Ghigesburg." "Gigr" from which this name is derived, is linked to an Old Norse personal name. Old Norse is found in many place names in the North East, and particularly North Yorkshire, due to Viking settlers and settlements in the area. This is noted in the novel when Roseberry Topping is referred to as "Odinsberg" a name which has not been used for the hill for centuries.

Guisborough itself, as a town name, is a modern spelling derived from the Old Norse and it predates the spelling "Gisborough," which is used for two prominent buildings that are close to the town, Gisborough Hall and Gisborough Priory, as well as a baronial family title.

The name "Gisborough" is used by the Chaloner family, who had a family home (Gisborough Hall) built outside of the town in 1856. When this home was built by Admiral Thomas

Chaloner, it was named as Gisborough Hall. This was personal preference on the part of Chaloner to omit the "u" from the name. This variant of Gisborough eventually became the baronial name of the family, with the first Lord Gisborough, Richard Chaloner, using the title when he went to the House of Lords.

The spelling 'Gisborough' has also been adopted by the Priory, which was purchased by the Chaloner family in 1547 and excavated by Admiral Thomas Chaloner in the 1860s.

Gisborough Priory, which is near the centre of Guisborough town, is now in the care of English Heritage.

Connie Rees will return in

Future's Past

If you want to know what comes next for Connie, sign up to my author newsletter, and you'll get a first peek at Chapter One of *Future's Past.*

slbishopstone.com

DISCUSSION QUESTIONS

If you have read this book as part of a Book Club or Reading Group, here are a few questions you might want to consider. It's not a comprehensive list, but will hopefully open up conversation.

The questions on the next page contain spoilers for the plot.

If you have not read the book, I recommend you do not read the questions until you have finished it.

QUESTIONS

1. At the beginning of the book, Connie is faced with rejection from the ESA and constant, niggling belittlement by John Bartholomew. Despite her mental and physical aptitude, she struggles to assert herself in the early stages of the novel.
- How do you think she transforms throughout the book and learns to trust her instincts?
- What do you think catalyses her self-belief?

2. When Connie meets her heroes, she learns that they are fallible. Eventually, she also finds their fallibility reassuring. Why do you think this is?

3. The book deals with the complexities of time paradoxes, particularly the notion that in some cases, such as the Gisborough Time Storm, it is future events that define historical moments. This is something that Connie, even at the end of the book, finds difficult to comprehend.
- Do you agree with the suppositions being made, that there is no such thing as destiny, only potential and what you decide to do with it?
- Early in the novel, Gertrude Bell takes a posi-

tion that if she'd known she would only 'almost die' on the Finsteraahorn, she would certainly have still made the climb. Do you agree with the decision that Bell made? Why?

4. *Order of the Raven* is Connie's story and is told, with limited exceptions, from her perspective. If another character in the novel were to be given a fuller voice, whose perspective would you like to see and why?

5. Marcus Rees, Connie's father, has lived Connie's entire life without meeting her. He is so desperate to be part of her life that he has made a habit of acquainting himself with late twentieth century and early twenty-first century pop-culture to feel closer to her. As part of his bid for notoriety, John Bartholomew offers Marcus a chance to live the life he's missed out on, with his wife and daughter.

- If you were Marcus, would you have taken Bartholomew's offer? Why?

- How did you find seeing the vision of the future-not-seized in the glass house?

6. After discovering that Marcus is her father, Connie finds his clumsy attempts to parent her and joke with her unsettling, but by the end of the book is sympathetic to the predicament he is in, even reflecting that he has the harder part of the bargain.

- What did you think of Marcus's role in the

book?

- Do you think it was Marcus, Imara or Connie who had the hardest experience of discovering the extent of their family and the time that had been lost to them? Why?

7. The places involved in the story, Gisborough Priory, Marton Manor, Preston Hall and Roseberry Topping, are all real, and their description in the book is relatively accurate. Marton Manor did burn down after falling into dereliction and Roseberry Topping did sheer in a geological event in 1912.

- How do you think this impacts on the feeling of the story?

- Has it made you curious to visit the area, or investigate local places of interest close to you?

8. The legend of the Raven's Chest, as related by Gertrude Bell, is a real fable in North Yorkshire. Similarly, Muramasa was a legendary swordsmith in Muromachi Japan, whose swords gained a posthumous reputation for carrying curses. Marcus explains this in the book by telling Connie that the truth is often stranger than the fiction we create to explain it.

- How did you find the book's use of these legends to introduce the Infinity Chamber and Raven's Blade?

- What is your own opinion on how legends shape human understanding and experience?

Printed in Great Britain
by Amazon